PENGUIN BOOKS

THE ROYAL BENGAL MYSTERY

Satyajit Ray was born on 2 May 1921 in Calcutta. After graduating from Presidency College, Calcutta, in 1940, he studied art at Rabindranath Tagore's university, Shantiniketan. By 1943, Ray was back in Calcutta and had joined an advertising firm as a visualizer. He also started designing covers and illustrating books brought out by the Signet Press. A deep interest in films led to his establishing the Calcutta Film Society in 1947. During a six-month trip to Europe, in 1950, Ray became a member of the London Film Club and managed to see ninety-nine films in only four-and-a-half months.

In 1955, after overcoming innumerable difficulties, Satyajit Ray completed his first film, *Pather Panchali*, with financial assistance from the West Bengal Government. The film was an award-winner at the Cannes Film Festival and established Ray as a director of international stature. Together with *Aparajito* (The Unvanquished, 1956) and *Apur Sansar* (The World of Apu, 1959), it forms the *Apu* trilogy—perhaps Ray's finest work to date. Ray's other films include *Jalsaghar* (The Music Room, 1958), *Charulata* (1964), *Aranyer Din Ratri* (Days and Nights in the Forest, 1970), *Shatranj Ke Khilari* (The Chess Players, 1977), *Ghare Baire* (The Home and the World, 1984), *Ganashatru* (Enemy of the People, 1989), *Shakha Proshakha* (Branches of a Tree, 1990), and *Agantuk* (The Stranger, 1991). Ray also made several documentaries, including one on Tagore. In 1987, he made the documentary *Sukumar Ray*, to commemorate the birth centenary of his father, perhaps Bengal's most famous writer of nonsense verse and children's books. Satyajit Ray won numerous awards for his films. Both the British Federation of Film Societies and the Moscow Film Festival Committee named him one of the greatest directors of the second half of the twentieth century. In 1992, he was awarded the Oscar for Lifetime Achievement by the Academy of Motion Picture Arts and Science and, in the same year, was also honoured with the Bharat Ratna.

Apart from being a film-maker, Satyajit Ra␣␣␣␣␣␣␣␣␣␣ute. In 1961, he revived the children's magaz␣␣␣␣␣␣␣ his grandfather, Upendrakishore Ray, had s␣␣␣␣␣␣ his father used to contribute frequently. S␣␣␣␣␣␣␣␣ted numerous poems, stories and essays to S␣␣␣␣␣␣␣hed several novels in Bengali, most of whic␣␣␣␣␣␣. In

1978, Oxford University awarded him its D.Litt degree.

Satyajit Ray died in Calcutta in April 1992.

*

Gopa Majumdar was born in Delhi in 1956. She graduated in English Literature from Delhi University. Her first translations of Bengali short stories (including one by Ray) were published in the *Namaste* magazine. This was followed by more stories by Ray (*Twenty Stories*, *The Emperor's Ring*, *The Mystery of the Elephant God*, *Feluda's Last Case* and *The House of Death*), which were published by Penguin.

Among her other notable translations are Ashapurna Debi's novel *Subarnalata* and a collection of Bengali short stories called *In the Same Boat—Golden Tales from Bengal*. She is currently translating the remaining Feluda stories for Penguin.

In 1995, she was given the Katha award for translation. She lives in Britain at present.

Satyajit Ray

The Royal Bengal Mystery

AND OTHER FELUDA STORIES

Translated from the Bengali by
Gopa Majumdar

PENGUIN BOOKS

Penguin Books India (P) Ltd., 210 Chiranjiv Tower, 43 Nehru Place, New Delhi 110 019, India
Penguin Books Ltd., 27 Wrights Lane, London W8 5TZ, UK
Penguin Books USA Inc., 375 Hudson Street, New York, NY 10014, USA
Penguin Books Australia Ltd., Ringwood, Victoria, Australia
Penguin Books Canada Ltd., 10 Alcorn Avenue, Suite 300, Toronto, Ontario M4V 3B2, Canada
Penguin Books (NZ) Ltd., 182-190 Wairau Road, Auckland 10, New Zealand

First published in English by Penguin Books India (P) Ltd. 1997

Typeset in Palatino by Digital Technologies and Printing Solutions, New Delhi

The tiger illustration on the title page is by Satyajit Ray.

Contents

Contents

Translator's Note

Between 1965 and 1992, Satyajit Ray wrote thirty-four Feluda stories. Out of these, twenty-two have been published in translation so far, in five collections (*The Adventures of Feluda, The Emperor's Ring, The Mystery of the Elephant God, Feluda's Last Case* and *The House of Death*). There is no longer any need to introduce Feluda, Tapesh (Topshe) and Lalmohan Ganguli (Jatayu); nor is it necessary to provide an explanatory note to describe how this team works.

However, it is with considerable trepidation that I place this particular collection before the reader. To tell the truth, when I first began translating Feluda stories, I had marked four of these as Impossible to Translate. 'The Royal Bengal Mystery', 'The Curse of the Goddess', 'The Locked Chest' and 'The Mystery of the Walking Dead' were easily among the best stories that Ray ever wrote. I read them again and again and enjoyed them each time; yet, when it came to translating them, I cowered and put them off. The reason, simply, was this: each one of them contained what interested and intrigued Feluda's creator the most: plays on words, puns, puzzles and riddles. The main clues to the mysteries were hidden in these, and of course they were all Bengali words. They defied translation. Had Ray been alive, there would have been no problem. He was sure to have found a remedy, as he always did. But without his guiding hand, I could not see my way forward at all.

I was perfectly prepared to admit defeat, but had reckoned without the persuasive powers of David Davidar, the Editor and Publisher of Penguin India. 'You haven't even tried!' he growled, glaring through his glasses, and lighting a cigarette with the same aplomb with which Feluda lights his Charminar. Shamefaced, I retired once more to reread the stuff and see what could be done. Gradually, it dawned upon me that I could do it—or most of it, anyway—if I could make certain changes in the text.

Obviously, that meant taking enormous liberties. I could hardly do it without the author's permission. As I began biting my nails again, a short meeting with Mrs Bijoya Ray in Calcutta solved this problem. When I confessed my difficulties to her, she immediately told me to go ahead with the changes.

I could scarcely believe it, but got to work at once. The result is now before you. Those who have read the originals will, no doubt, notice the changes I have had to make, but I hope they will agree that these have not affected the main plot in any way.

I cannot thank Mrs Bijoya Ray enough for being so understanding and for her affection and trust. I only hope her trust has been well-placed. My thanks must also go to David Davidar, without whose encouragement and support I could not have completed this task.

Finally, I dedicate this translation to my young friends, Mallika and Partha, with the hope that Feluda in translation will bring as much joy as he did to hundreds of Bengali children when he first appeared thirty-two years ago.

London
September 1997   Gopa Majumdar

Kailash Chowdhury's Jewel

'See how you like my card.'

Feluda fished out a visiting card from his wallet and held it before me. It said: Pradosh C. Mitter, Private Investigator. Feluda was clearly trying to publicize what he did for a living. And why not? After his success over the missing diamond ring that had once belonged to Emperor Aurangzeb, he was fully entitled to tell everyone how clever he had been. But, of course, he didn't really have to worry about publicity. A lot of people had come to know about the case, anyway. In fact, Feluda had received a couple of offers already, but he didn't accept them as they were not challenging enough.

He put the card back in his wallet, and stretched his legs on the low table in front of him. 'It looks like I shall get the chance to exercise my brain during this Christmas break,' he said casually.

'Why? Have you found a new mystery?' I asked. Feluda's words had made me quite excited, but I didn't show it. He took out a small box from a side pocket and helped himself to some supari from it. 'You appear greatly excited,' he observed.

What? How did he guess? Feluda explained even before I could ask. 'Are you wondering how I knew? It isn't always possible to hide your feelings, you know, even if you try. Little things often give one away. When I made that remark about working during this Christmas break, you were about to yawn. My words made you close your mouth abruptly. If you were truly indifferent to what I said, you'd have finished your yawn in the usual way, without breaking it off.'

Once again I was startled by his powers of observation.

4 • *Satyajit Ray*

'Without being able to observe and take in even the minutest detail, no one can claim to be a detective,' Feluda had often said to me. 'Sherlock Holmes has shown us the way. All we need to do is follow him.'

'You didn't tell me why you will need to exercise your brain,' I reminded him.

'Have you heard of Kailash Chowdhury, of Shyampukur?'

'No. There are so many famous people in our city. I cannot have heard of all of them. I am only fifteen!'

Feluda lit a cigarette. 'His family owned a lot of land in Rajshahi. They were zamindars. But they also had property in Calcutta, so they moved here after Partition. Kailash Chowdhury is a lawyer. He used to go on shikar and, in fact, became quite well-known as a shikari. He even wrote two books on the subject. Sometime ago, an elephant went mad in the Jaldapara Reserve Forest and began creating such havoc that Kailash Babu was called in to kill it. His name was mentioned in almost every paper.'

'I see. What has all this to do with your brain? Is there a mystery regarding Kailash Chowdhury?'

Instead of giving me an answer, Feluda took out a letter from the front pocket of his jacket and passed it to me. 'Read it,' he said. I unfolded the letter and read what it said:

Dear Mr Mitter,
I decided to write to you after seeing your advertisement in the *Amrita Bazar Patrika*. I should be much obliged if you could come and meet me at the above address. I am sending this letter by express delivery. It should, therefore, reach you tomorrow. I shall expect you the day after, i.e. on Saturday, at 10 a.m.

Yours sincerely,
Kailash Chowdhury.

'But it's Saturday today!' I exclaimed, 'and nine o'clock already!'

'You're improving every day. I am very glad to note that you remember days and dates so well.'

A sudden doubt raised its head in my mind. 'This letter speaks only of meeting you. What if he objects to an extra person?'

Feluda took the letter back from me, and folded it carefully before replacing it in his pocket.

'He might not, as you're a young boy. He might not see you as sufficiently important to object to. But if he does, we'll pack you off to another room. You can wait there while we finish our talk.'

My heart began beating faster. I had been wondering what to do in the Christmas holidays. Now it seemed as if I was in for a very interesting time.

We got off a tram near Shyampukur Street at five minutes to ten. Feluda had stopped on the way to buy a book written by Kailash Chowdhury. It was called *The Passion of Shikar*. He leafed through it in the tram, and said, as we got down, 'God knows why a brave man like him needs to see a private detective!'

Kailash Chowdhury's house, 51 Shyampukur Street, turned out to be a huge old mansion. A long drive led to the main house. There were gardens on both sides, marble statues and a fountain. We passed these and made our way to the front door. There were footsteps on the other side within thirty seconds of pressing the bell. One look at the man who opened the door told me it was not Kailash Chowdhury. No brave shikari could have such a mouse-like appearance. He was a man of medium height, rather plump, possibly no more than thirty years old. His eyes held a look of childlike innocence. In his hand was a magnifying glass.

'Whom would you like to see?' he asked. His voice was as mild as his appearance.

Feluda took out one of his cards and handed it to the

gentleman. 'I have an appointment with Mr Chowdhury. He asked me to come here.'

The man cast a quick glance at the card, and said, 'Please come in.'

We followed him down the hall, up a flight of stairs and were ushered into what looked like a small office.

'Please have a seat. I'll go and inform my uncle,' he said and disappeared.

We took two old chairs with arms that faced an equally old table, painted black. Three sides of the room were lined with glass cases filled with books. On the table I noticed something interesting. Three fat stamp albums were stacked one on top of the other, and a fourth was lying open. Rows of stamps had been carefully pasted in it. A few loose stamps lay in a cellophane packet, together with the usual paraphernalia of stamp collectors: hinges, a pair of tweezers and a stamp catalogue. Now it was clear why the man who met us at the door was carrying a magnifying glass. He was obviously the collector of these stamps.

Feluda, too, was looking at these objects, but before either of us could make a remark, the same man returned and said, 'Uncle asked you to wait in the drawing room. He'll join you shortly.'

We were taken to the drawing room. It was a large room, with a chandelier, oil paintings, marble statues and a great number of vases that were strewn all over. Everything in it bore the mark of life during the Raj, at least life in an affluent household. On the floor was the skin of a Royal Bengal tiger, and from the walls stared four heads of deer, two cheetahs and a wild buffalo.

Nearly ten minutes later, a middle-aged man entered the room. He seemed pretty strong and agile for his age. His features were sharp, and he sported a thin moustache. He was wearing a red silk dressing gown over a pyjama-kurta.

We rose to our feet and said, 'Namaskar'. Mr Chowdhury returned our greeting, but raised his eyebrows slightly on seeing me.

'This is my cousin,' Feluda explained. Mr Chowdhury took the smaller sofa next to ours, and asked, 'Do you carry out your investigations together?'

Feluda laughed, 'No, not really. But Tapesh happened to be involved in all the cases I have handled so far. He's never caused any trouble.'

'Very well. Abanish, you may go now; and see if you can arrange a cup of tea for these people.'

The stamp-collector was standing near the door. At these words, he disappeared inside. Kailash Chowdhury looked at Feluda, and said, 'I hope you don't mind, but I'd like to see the letter I wrote to you. Did you bring it?'

Feluda smiled. 'Is this to make sure I am the right person? Here's your letter, sir.'

Mr Chowdhury glanced briefly at the letter, said 'Thank you', and returned it to Feluda.

'One has to be careful in these matters, I'm sure you understand. Anyway, I assume you know a little bit about my work. I am known as a shikari.'

'Yes, sir. I did know that.'

Mr Chowdhury pointed at the heads of various animals on the walls and said, 'I killed all those. I learnt to use a rifle at the age of seventeen. Before that, as a child, I had used airguns and killed small birds. I am not afraid to fight anyone—or anything—if I can face my opponent, if I can see him. But if the adversary is a secret one . . . if he doesn't come out in the open . . . what does one do?'

He paused. I could feel my heart thudding faster again. The details of a mystery were about to be revealed, but Mr Chowdhury was beating about the bush so much that the suspense was getting higher every minute. A few seconds later, he resumed speaking. 'I didn't expect you to be so young,' he said. 'How old are you?'

'Twenty-eight.'

'I see. Well, I could have gone to the police. But I don't really have a lot of faith in them. Instead of helping, they usually make a total nuisance of themselves. Besides, I respect the young. So you may well be the right person for the job. I think an old head on young shoulders can achieve a lot more than an entire police force.'

He paused again. Feluda seized this opportunity to ask quickly, 'If you could tell me what the problem is . . .?'

Silently, Mr Chowdhury took out a piece of paper from his pocket and passed it to Feluda. 'See what you can make of it,' he said. Feluda unfolded it. I leant across and read what was written on it:

Do not make things worse for yourself. You must return what does not belong to you. Go to Victoria Memorial on Monday, and leave it under the first plant of the first row of lilies that faces the south gate. This must be done by 4 p.m. Do not try to inform the police, or go to a detective. If you do, you will end up exactly like the animals you killed on your shikar.

'What do you think?' Mr Chowdhury asked gravely.

Feluda stared at the note for a few moments. Then he said, 'The writer tried to mask his handwriting, for the same letters have been written in different ways. And he wrote on the top sheet of a new pad.'

'How can you tell?'

'If you write on a pad, the leaves below the top one always carry a faint impression of what is written on the upper sheet. It may not be legible, but it is there. This sheet is absolutely smooth.'

'Very good. Can you tell anything else?'

'No, it's impossible to say anything more simply by looking at it. Did this arrive by post?'

'Yes. The postmark said Park Street Post Office. I got this note three days ago. Today is Saturday, the 20th.'

Feluda returned the note to Mr Chowdhury and said, 'I would now like to ask you a few questions, if I may. You see,

I know nothing about your life, except the tales of shikar that you wrote.'

'Very well. Go ahead with your questions. But please help yourself to the sweets before you begin.'

A bearer had come in a few minutes earlier and placed a silver plate before us, loaded with sweets. Feluda did not have to be told a second time. He picked up a rasgulla and popped it into his mouth. 'What,' he asked after a while, 'is this object that doesn't belong to you?'

'Frankly, Mr Mitter, I cannot think of anything like that at all. Everything I possess in this world, including things in this house, were either inherited or bought by me. Everything . . . except . . .' he stopped abruptly.

'Except what?'

'Well, there *is* something that's both valuable and tempting.'

'What is it?'

'A stone.'

'A precious stone?'

'Yes.'

'Did you buy it?'

'No.'

'Did it belong to your forefathers?'

'No, I found it in a jungle in Madhya Pradesh. There were four of us. We chased a tiger into the jungle and finally killed it. Then we found this ancient and abandoned temple. The stone was fixed on the forehead of the statue of the deity. I don't think anyone even knew of its existence.'

'Were you the first to see it?'

'Everyone else saw the temple, but yes, I was the first to notice the stone.'

'Who else was with you?'

'An American called Wright, a Punjabi called Kishorilal and my brother, Kedar.'

'Is your brother also a shikari?'

'He used to go on shikar with me sometimes, but now I don't know what he does. He went abroad four years ago.'

'Abroad?'

'Switzerland. Something to do with making watches.'

'When you found the stone, what happened? Didn't any of the others want to take it?'

'No, because none of us realized its value then. I came to know only when I had it assessed by a jeweller in Calcutta.'

'Who else got to know?'

'Not many people. I haven't got many relations. A couple of friends know about it, I told Kedar, and I think my nephew Abanish is aware of its value.'

'Do you keep the stone here in your house?'

'Yes, in my bedroom.'

'Why don't you keep it in a bank locker?'

'I did once. The very next day, I was almost run over by a car. Oh, I had a narrow escape, I can tell you. That made me think if I was separated from the stone it would bring me bad luck. Yes, I know it's superstition. Nevertheless, I brought it back from the bank.'

Feluda had finished eating. I could tell from the way he was frowning that he had started to think. He wiped his mouth, drank some water and said, 'Who else lives in this house?'

'My nephew, Abanish, and three old servants. Then there's my father, but he's very old and almost totally senile. One of the servants spends all his time looking after him.'

'What does your nephew do?'

'Nothing much, really. His passion is philately. He's talking of starting a shop to sell stamps.'

Feluda was quiet for a few moments, as if he was trying to come to a decision about something. Then he said slowly, 'Would you like me to find out who wrote that note?'

Mr Chowdhury seemed to force a smile. 'I am getting old, Mr Mitter. I can do without anxiety and tension. And it isn't just that note. Last night this man rang me. I couldn't recognize his voice. He said if I didn't place that object at the specified time and place, he'd come into my house and cause me bodily harm. But even so, I am not willing to part with that stone. Besides, this man cannot possibly have a legitimate claim on it. He's just hoping to frighten me by his threats. A crook like him ought to be punished. You must work out how.'

'There is only one thing that I can possibly do. I must go to Victoria Memorial on Monday and keep an eye on the lilies. This man has got to turn up.'

'He may not come himself.'

'That shouldn't matter. If we can catch whoever comes hoping to collect the stone, it won't be difficult to find out who is really behind the scene.'

'But the man might be dangerous. When he turns up at Victoria Memorial and discovers I have not placed the stone under that plant, God knows what he might do. Can't you do anything to find out who he is *before* Monday? I mean, there's that note and the phone call. Isn't that enough?'

Feluda got up and began pacing. 'Look, Mr Chowdhury,' he said, 'this man has said you'd get into trouble if you went to a private detective. Now, whether or not I take any action, you might be in trouble already. So really, *you* must decide whether you want me to go ahead.' Mr Chowdhury wiped his face with a handkerchief, although it was quite cold inside the room. 'You, and this young cousin of yours ... well, you don't appear to be investigators. This is an advantage. I mean, people may have heard your name, but how many know what you look like? No, I don't think there's much chance of you being recognized as the detective I have hired. If you are still prepared to take this job, I will certainly pay you your fee.'

'Thank you. But before I go, I would like to see that stone.'

'Sure.'

All of us got up. The stone was kept in the wardrobe in his bedroom, Mr Chowdhury said. We followed him upstairs. A marble staircase went up to the first floor, ending at one end of a long, dark corridor. There were rooms on either side of the corridor. I did not actually count them, but at a guess there were at least ten rooms. Some of them were locked. There was no one in sight. The slightest noise sounded unnaturally loud in the eerie silence. I began to feel uneasy.

Mr Chowdhury's bedroom was the last one on the right. When we were more or less half way down the corridor, I suddenly realized that the door to one of the rooms was ajar. Through a small gap, a very old man was peering out, craning his neck to look at us. His eyes were dimmed with age, but as we got closer, I was shocked to notice the expression in them. The old man was staring with murder in his eyes. But he said nothing. I now felt positively scared.

'That's my father,' Mr Chowdhury explained hurriedly, continuing to walk, 'I told you he was senile, didn't I? He keeps peeping out of doors and windows. And he thinks everyone neglects him. That's why he looks so cross most of the time. But I can assure you every effort is made to make sure he's all right.'

The bedroom had a huge, high bed, and the wardrobe was next to it. Mr Chowdhury opened it, pulled out a drawer and took out a small, blue velvet box from it. 'I bought this box from a jeweller just to keep the stone in it,' he informed us, and opened it. A glittering stone lay inside, about the size of a litchi, radiating a greenish-blue light.

'This is a blue beryl. It's usually found in Brazil. There cannot be many of these in India, and certainly none of this size. I know that for a fact.'

Feluda picked up the stone, held it between his forefinger and thumb and looked closely at it for a few moments before returning it to its owner. Mr Chowdhury put it back in the drawer, then took out his wallet from his pocket. 'This is an advance payment,' he said, offering five crisp ten-rupee notes, 'I'll pay you the rest when this business is cleared up. All right?'

'Thank you,' said Feluda, accepting the money. This was the first time I saw him actually being paid for his services.

'I will need that note you were sent, and I'd like to speak to your nephew, please,' Feluda said, as we climbed down the stairs. The phone in the drawing room started ringing just as we reached the last step. Mr Chowdhury went quickly to answer it, leaving us behind. 'Hello!' we heard him say. This was followed by silence.

When we entered the drawing room a few seconds later, Mr Chowdhury replaced the receiver and sat down quickly, looking pale and frightened. 'It . . . it was that same voice!' he whispered.

'What did it say?'

'It simply repeated the same threat, but this time it was more specific. He actually said he wanted what I had found in an abandoned temple.'

'Did he say anything else?'

'No.'

'And you didn't recognize the voice?'

'No, all I can say is that it was a most unpleasant voice. Maybe you'd like to think again about taking on this case?'

Feluda smiled. 'I have finished thinking,' he replied.

We left the drawing room soon after this and made our way to the room of Mr Chowdhury's nephew, Abanish Babu. We found him closely examining something on a table with a magnifying glass. As we entered the room, he swiftly covered the object with one hand and got to his feet.

'Come in, come in!' he invited.

'I can see that you are very interested in stamps,' Feluda remarked. Abanish Babu's eyes lit up. 'Yes, sir. That's my only interest in life, my only passion. All I ever think of are stamps!'

'Do you specialize in any one country, or do you collect stamps from all over the world?'

'I used to collect them from wherever they happened to be, but of late I've started to concentrate on India. I had to sift through hundreds of old letters to get them.'

'Did you find anything good?'

'Good? Good?' Abanish Babu began to look ecstatic, 'Are

you interested in this subject? Will you understand if I explain?'

'Try me,' Feluda smiled, 'I don't claim to be an expert, but like most other people, I was once keen on collecting stamps, and dreamt of acquiring the famous ones. You know, the one-penny stamp from the Cape of Good Hope, the two-penny from Mauritius and the 1856 ones from British Guiana. Ten years ago their price was in the region of a hundred thousand rupees. Now they must be worth a lot more.'

Abanish Babu grew even more excited. 'Well then,' he said with gleaming eyes, 'Well then, I'm sure you'd understand. I'd like to show you something. Here it is.' He took his hand off the table and revealed the object he had been hiding. It turned out to be very old stamp, detached from an envelope. Its original colour must have been green, but it had faded almost completely. Abanish Babu passed it to Feluda.

'What? What can you see?' he asked eagerly.

'An Indian stamp, about a hundred years old. It has a picture of Queen Victoria. I've seen such stamps before.'

'Have you? Yes, I'm sure you have. Now then, take another look through this magnifying glass.'

Feluda peered through the proffered glass.

'Now what do you see, eh?' Abanish Babu asked anxiously.

'There is a printing error.'

'Exactly!'

'The word is obviously POSTAGE, but instead of a "G", they printed a "C".'

Abanish Babu took the stamp back. 'Do you know how much that stamp is worth because of that error?'

'How much?'

'Twenty thousand.'

'What!'

'Yes, sir. I've checked with the authorities in UK. The catalogue does not mention the error. I was the first person to find it.'

'Congratulations! But . . . er . . . I wanted to discuss

something else with you, Abanish Babu. I mean, something other than stamps.'

'Yes?'

'Your uncle—Kailash Chowdhury—has a valuable jewel. Are you aware of that?'

Abanish Babu had to think for a few moments before replying, 'Oh yes, yes. I did hear about it. I know nothing about its value, but it's supposed to be "lucky", or so my uncle said. Please forgive me, Mr Mitter, but of late I have been able to pay no attention to anything except my stamps.'

'How long have you lived in this house?'

'For the last five years. I moved here soon after my father died.'

'Do you get on with your uncle?'

'Which one do you mean? I have two uncles. One of them lives abroad.'

'Oh? I was speaking of Kailash Babu.'

'I see. Well, he is a very nice man, but . . . '

'But what?'

Abanish Babu frowned. 'For the last few days . . . he's been sort of . . . different.'

'How do you mean? When did you first notice this?'

'Two or three days ago. I told him about this stamp, but he paid no attention at all. Normally, he takes a great deal of interest. Besides, some of his old habits seem to be changing.'

'How?'

'He used to take a walk in the garden every morning before breakfast. He hasn't done that for the last couple of days. In fact, he gets up quite late. Maybe he hasn't been sleeping well.'

'Do you have any particular reason to say this?'

'Yes. My bedroom is on the ground floor. The room directly above mine is my uncle's. I have heard him pacing in the middle of the night. I've even heard his voice. I think he was having an argument.'

'An argument? With whom?'

'Probably grandfather. Who else could it be? I've even heard footsteps going up and coming down the stairs. One night, I got up and went to the bottom of the stairs to see what was going on. I saw my uncle coming down from the roof, with a gun in his hand.'

'What time would that have been?'

'Around two o'clock in the morning, I should think.'

'What's there on the roof?'

'Nothing except a small attic. It was full of old papers and letters, but I took those away a month ago.'

Feluda rose. I could see he had no further questions to ask.

Abanish Babu said, 'Why did you ask me all this?'

Feluda smiled. 'You uncle has a lot on his mind at this moment. But you don't have to worry about it. Once things get sorted out, I'll come and have a look at your stamps. All right?'

We returned to the drawing room to say goodbye to Mr Chowdhury.

'I cannot guarantee anything, obviously, but I would like to say one thing,' Feluda told him, 'Please stop worrying and leave everything to me. Try to sleep at night. Take a sleeping pill, if necessary; and please do not go up to the roof. The houses in your lane are so close to one another that, for all we know, your enemy might be hiding on the roof of the house next door to keep an eye on you. If that is the case, he may well jump across and attack you.'

'You think so? I did go up to the roof one night, but I took my gun with me. I'd heard a strange noise, you see. But I couldn't see anyone.'

'I hope you always keep your gun handy?'

'Oh yes. But mental tension and anxiety can often affect one's aim. If this business isn't cleared up soon, God knows what's going to happen to mine.'

*

The next day was Sunday. Feluda spent most of his time

pacing in his room. At around four, I saw him change from his comfortable kurta-pyjama into trousers and a shirt.

'Are you going out?' I asked.

'Yes. I thought it might be a good idea to take a look at the lilies in the Victoria Memorial. You can come with me, if you like.'

We took a tram and got off at the crossing of Lower Circular Road. Then we walked slowly to the south gate of the memorial. Not many people came here. In the evening, particularly, most people went to the front of the building, to the north gate.

We slipped in through the gate. Twenty yards to the left, there stood rows of lilies. The blue beryl was supposed to be kept the next day under the first row of these. The sight of these flowers—beautiful though it was—suddenly gave me the creeps.

'Didn't your father have a pair of binoculars, which he'd taken to Darjeeling?' Feluda asked.

'Yes, he's still got them.'

'Good.'

We spent about fifteen minutes walking in the open ground surrounding the building. Then we took a taxi to the Lighthouse cinema. I got out with Feluda, feeling quite puzzled. Why did he suddenly want to see a film? But no, he was actually interested in a bookshop opposite the cinema. After leafing through a couple of other books, he picked up a fat stamp catalogue and began thumbing through its pages. I peered over his shoulder and whispered, 'Are you suspecting Abanish Babu?'

'Well, if he's so passionately fond of stamps, I'm sure he wouldn't mind laying his hands on some ready cash.'

'But . . . remember that phone call that came when we were still at Mr Chowdhury's? Abanish Babu could not have made it, surely?'

'No. That was made by Akbar Badshah. Or it may have been Queen Victoria.'

This made me realize Feluda was no longer in the right mood to give straight answers to my questions, so I shut up.

It was eight o'clock by the time we got back home. Feluda took off his jacket and threw it on his bed. 'Look up Kailash Chowdhury's telephone number in the directory while I have a quick shower,' he said.

I sat down with the directory in my lap, but the phone started ringing before I could turn a single page. Considerably startled, I picked it up.

'Hello.'

'Who is speaking?'

What a strange voice! I had certainly never heard it before.

'Who would you like to speak to?' I asked. The answer came in the same harsh voice: 'Why does a young boy like you go around with a detective? Don't you fear for your life?'

I tried calling out to Feluda, but could not speak. My hands had started to tremble. Before I could replace the receiver, the man finished what he had to say, 'I am warning you—both of you. Lay off. Or the consequences will be . . . unhappy.'

I sat still in my chair, quite unable to move. Feluda walked into the room a few minutes later, and said, 'Hey, what's the matter? Why are you sitting in that corner so quietly? Who rang just now?'

I swallowed hard and told him what had happened. His face grew grave. Then he slapped my shoulder and said, 'Don't worry. The police have been informed. A few men in plain clothes will be there. We *must* be at Victoria Memorial tomorrow.'

I didn't find it easy to sleep that night. It wasn't just the telephone call that kept me awake. I kept thinking of Mr Chowdhury's house and all that I had seen in it: the staircase with the iron railing that went right up to the roof; the long, dark veranda with the marble floor on the first floor, and the old Mr Chowdhury peering out of a half-open door. Why was he staring at his son like that? And why had Kailash Babu gone to the roof carrying his gun? What kind of noise had he heard?

Feluda said only one thing before switching off his light, 'Did you know, Topshe, that people who send anonymous notes and threaten others on the telephone are basically cowards?' It was perhaps because of this remark that I finally fell asleep.

*

Feluda rang Kailash Chowdhury the following morning and told him to relax and stay at home. Feluda himself would take care of everything.

'When will you go to Victoria Memorial?' I asked him.

'The same time as yesterday. By the way, do you have a sketch pad and pens and other drawing material?'

I felt totally taken aback. 'Why? What do I need those for?'

'Never mind. Have you got them or not?'

'Yes, of course. I have my school drawing book.'

'Good. Take it with you. I'd want you to stand at a little distance from the lilies, and draw something—the trees, the building, the flowers, anything. I shall be your drawing teacher.'

Feluda could draw very well. In fact, I knew he could draw a reasonable portrait of a man after seeing him only once. The role of a drawing teacher would suit him perfectly.

Since the days were short in winter, we reached the Victoria Memorial a few minutes before four o'clock. There were even fewer people around today. Three Nepali ayahs were roaming idly with their charges in perambulators. An Indian family—possibly Marwaris—and a couple of old men were strolling about, but there was no one else in sight. At some distance away from the gate, closer to the compound wall, stood two men under a tree. Feluda glanced at them, and then nudged me quietly. That meant those two were his friends from the police. They were in plain clothes, but were probably armed. Feluda knew quite a lot of people in the police.

I parked myself opposite the rows of lilies and began sketching, although I could hardly concentrate on what I was doing. Feluda moved around with a pair of binoculars in his hands, occasionally grabbing my pad to make corrections and scolding me for making mistakes. Then he would move away again, and peer through the binoculars.

The sun was about to set. The clock in a church nearby struck five. It would soon get cold. The Marwaris left in a big car. The ayahs, too, began to push their perambulators towards the gate. The traffic on Lower Circular Road had intensified. I could hear frequent horns from cars and buses, caught in the evening rush. Feluda returned to me and was about to sit down on the grass, when something near the gate seemed to attract his attention. I followed his gaze quickly, but could see no one except a man wrapped in a brown shawl, who was standing by the road outside, quite a long way away from the gate. Feluda placed the binoculars to his eyes, had a quick look, then passed them to me. 'Take a look,' he whispered.

'You mean that man over there? The one wearing a shawl?'

'Hm.'

One glance through the binoculars brought the man clearly into view, as if he was standing only a few feet away. I gave an involuntary gasp. 'Why . . . this is Kailash Chowdhury himself!'

'Right. Perhaps he's come to look for us. Let's go.'

But the man began walking away just as we started to move. He was gone by the time we came out of the gate. 'Let's go to his house,' Feluda suggested, 'I don't think he saw us. He must have gone back feeling worried.'

There was no chance of finding a taxi at this hour, so we began walking towards Chowringhee in the hope of catching a tram. The road was heavily lined with cars. Soon, we found ourselves outside the Calcutta Club. What happened here was so unexpected and frightening that even as I write about it, I can feel myself break into a cold sweat. I was walking by Feluda's side when, without the slightest warning, he pulled me sharply away from the road. Then he leapt aside himself, as a speeding car missed him by inches.

'What the devil—!' Feluda exclaimed, 'I missed the number of that car.'

It was too late to do anything about that. Heaven knew where the car had come from, or what had possessed its driver to drive so fast in this traffic. But it had disappeared totally from sight. I had fallen on the pavement, my sketch pad and pencils had scattered in different directions. I picked myself up, without bothering to look for them. If Feluda hadn't seen that car coming and acted promptly, there was no doubt that both of us would have been crushed under its wheels.

Feluda did not utter a single word in the tram. He just sat looking grim. The first thing he said on reaching Mr Chowdhury's house was: 'Didn't you see us?'

Mr Chowdhury was sitting in a sofa in the drawing room. He seemed quite taken aback by our sudden arrival. 'See you?' he faltered, 'Where? What are you talking about?'

'You mean to say you didn't go to Victoria Memorial?'

'Who, me? Good heavens, no! I didn't leave the house at all. In fact, I spent all afternoon in my bedroom upstairs, feeling sick with worry. I've only just come down.'

'Well then, Mr Chowdhury, do you have an identical twin?'

Mr Chowdhury's jaw fell open. 'Oh God, didn't I tell you the other day?'

'Tell me what?'

'About Kedar? He's my twin.'

Feluda sat down quickly. Mr Chowdhury's face seemed to have lost all colour.

'Why, did you . . . did you see Kedar? Was he there?' he asked anxiously.

'Yes. It couldn't possibly have been anyone else.'

'My God!'

'Why do you say that? Does your twin have a claim on that stone?'

Mr Chowdhury suddenly went limp, as though all the energy in his body had been drained out. He leant against the arm of his sofa, and sighed. 'Yes,' he said slowly, 'Yes, he does. You see, it was Kedar who found the stone first. I saw the temple, but Kedar was the one who noticed the stone fixed on the statue.'

'What happened next?'

'Well, I took it from him. I mean, I pestered and badgered him until he got fed up and gave it to me. In a way, it was the right thing to do, for Kedar would simply have sold it and wasted the money. When I learnt just how valuable the stone was, I did not tell Kedar. To be honest, when he left the country, I felt quite relieved. But now . . . perhaps he's come back because he couldn't find work abroad. Maybe he wants to sell the stone and start a business of his own.'

Feluda was silent for a few moments. Then he said, 'Do you have any idea what he might do next?'

'No. But I do know this: he will come and meet me here. I have stopped going out of the house, and I did not keep the stone where I was told to. There is no other way left for him now. If he wants the stone, he has to come here.'

'Would you like me to stay here? I might be able to help.'

'No, thank you. That will not be necessary. I have now made up my mind, Mr Mitter. If Kedar wants the stone, he can have it. I will simply hand it over to him. It's simply a matter of waiting until he turns up. You have already done so much, putting your life at risk. I am most grateful to you. If you send me your bill, I will let you have a cheque.'

'Thank you. You're right about the risk. We nearly got run over by a car.'

I had realized a while ago that one of my elbows was rather badly grazed, but had been trying to keep it out of sight. As we rose to take our leave, Feluda's eyes fell on it. 'Hey, you're hurt, aren't you?' he exclaimed, 'Your elbow is bleeding! If you don't mind, Mr Chowdhury, I think Tapesh should put some Dettol on the wound, or it might get septic. Do you—?'

'Yes, yes,' Mr Chowdhury got up quickly, 'You are quite right. The streets are filthy, aren't they? Wait, let me ask Abanish.'

We followed Mr Chowdhury to Abanish Babu's room. 'Do we have any Dettol in the house, Abanish?' Mr Chowdhury asked. Abanish Babu gave him a startled glance.

'Why, I saw you bring a new bottle only a week ago!' he said, 'Don't tell me it's finished already?'

Mr Chowdhury gave an embarrassed laugh. 'Yes, of course. I totally forgot. I *am* going mad.'

Five minutes later, my elbow duly dabbed with Dettol, we came out of the house. Instead of going towards the main road where we might have caught a tram to go home, Feluda began walking in the opposite direction. Before I could ask him anything, he said, 'My friend Ganapati lives nearby. He promised to get me a ticket for the Test match. I'd like to see him.'

Ganapati Chatterjee's house turned out to be only two houses away. I had heard of him, but had never met him before. He opened the door when Feluda knocked: a rather plump man, wearing a pullover and trousers.

'Felu! What brings you here, my friend?'

'Surely you can guess?'

'Oh, I see. You needn't have come personally to remind me. I hadn't forgotten. I did promise, didn't I?'

'Yes, I know. But that's not the only reason why I am here. I believe there's a wonderful view of north Calcutta from your roof. I'd like to see it, if you don't mind. Someone I know in a film company told me to look around. They're making a film on Calcutta.'

'OK, no problem. That staircase over there goes right up to the roof. I'll see about getting us a cup of tea.'

The house had four storeys. We got to the top and

discovered that there was a very good view of Mr Chowdhury's house on the right. The whole house—from the garden to the roof—was visible. A light was on in one of the rooms on the first floor, and a man was moving about in it. It was Kailash Chowdhury's father. I could also see the attic on the roof. At least, I could see its window; its door was probably on the other side, hidden from view.

Another light on the second floor was switched on. It was the light on the staircase. Feluda took out the binoculars again and placed them before his eyes. A man was climbing the stairs. Who was it? Kailash Chowdhury. I could recognize his red silk dressing gown even from this distance. He disappeared from view for a few seconds, then suddenly appeared on the roof of his house. Feluda and I ducked promptly, and hid behind the wall that surrounded Ganapati Chatterjee's roof, peering cautiously over its edge.

Mr Chowdhury glanced around a couple of times, then went to the other side of the attic, presumably to go into it through the door we could not see. A second later, the light in the attic came on. Mr Chowdhury was now standing near its window with his back to us. My heart began beating faster. Mr Chowdhury stood still for a few moments, then bent down, possibly sitting on the ground. A little later, he stood up, switched the light off and went down the stairs once more.

Feluda put the binoculars away and said only one thing: 'Fishy. Very fishy.'

*

He didn't speak to me on our way back. When he gets into one of these moods, I don't like to disturb him. Normally, if he is agitated about something, he starts pacing in his room. Today, however, I saw him throw himself down on his bed and stare at the ceiling. At half past nine, he got up and started to scribble in his blue notebook. I knew he was writing in English, using Greek letters. So there was no way I could read and understand what he'd written. The only thing that was obvious was that he was still working on Mr Chowdhury's case, although his client had dispensed with his services.

I lay awake for a long time, which was probably why I didn't wake the following morning until Feluda shook me. 'Topshe! Get up quickly, we must to go Shyampukur at once.'

'Why?' I sat up.

'I rang the house, but no one answered. Something is obviously wrong.'

In ten minutes, we were in a taxi, speeding up to Shyampukur Street. Feluda refused to tell me anything more, except, 'What a cunning man he is! If only I'd guessed it a little sooner, this would not have happened!'

When we reached Mr Chowdhury's house, Feluda saw that the front door was open and walked right in, without bothering to ring the bell. We crossed the landing and arrived at Abanish Babu's room. The sight that met my eyes made me gasp in horrified amazement. A chair lay overturned before a table, and next to it, lay Abanish Babu. His hands were tied behind his back, a large handkerchief covered his mouth. Feluda bent over him quickly and untied him.

'Oh, oh, thank God! Thank you!' he exclaimed, breathing heavily.

'Who did this to you?'

'Who do you think?' he sat up, still panting, 'My uncle—Kailash Mama did this. I told you he was going crazy, didn't I? I got up quite early this morning, and decided to get some work done. It was still dark outside, so I switched the light on. My uncle walked in soon after that. The first thing he did was switch the light off. Then he struck my head, and I fell immediately. Everything went dark. I regained consciousness a few minutes before you arrived, but could neither move nor speak. Oh God!' he winced.

'And Kailash Babu? Where is he?' Feluda shouted.

'No idea.'

Feluda turned and leapt out of the room. I followed a second later.

There was no one in the drawing room. We lost no time in going upstairs, taking three steps at a time. Kailash Chowdhury's bedroom was empty, although the bed looked as though it had been slept in. The wardrobe had been left open. Feluda pulled a drawer out and found the small blue velvet box. When he opened it, I was somewhat surprised to see that the blue beryl was still in it, quite intact.

By this time, Abanish Babu had arrived at the door, still looking pathetic. 'Who has the key to the attic?' Feluda demanded. He seemed taken aback by the question.

'Th-that's with my uncle!' he said.

'OK, let's go up there,' Feluda announced, grabbing Abanish Babu by his shoulders and dragging him up the dark staircase.

We reached the roof, only to find that the attic was locked. A padlock hung at the door. Anyone else would have been daunted by the sight. But Feluda stepped back, then ran forward and struck the door with his shoulder, using all his strength. On his third attempt, the door gave in noisily. A few old rusted nails also came off the wall. Even I was surprised by Feluda's physical strength.

The room inside was dark. We stepped in cautiously. A few seconds later, when my eyes got used to the dark, I noticed another figure lying in one corner, bound and gagged exactly like Abanish Babu. Who was this? Kailash Chowdhury? Or was it Kedar?

Without a word, Feluda released him from his bondage and then carried him down to the bedroom. The man spoke only when he had been placed comfortably in his bed.

'Are you . . . . the? . . .' he asked feebly, staring at Feluda.

'Yes, sir. I am Pradosh Mitter, the detective. I suppose it was you who had written me that letter, but of course I never got the chance to meet you. Abanish Babu, could you get him some warm milk, please?'

I stared at the man in amazement. So *this* was the real

Kailash Chowdhury! He propped himself up on a pillow and said, 'I was physically strong, so I managed to survive somehow. Otherwise . . . in these four days . . . '

Feluda interrupted him, 'Sh-sh. You mustn't strain yourself.'

'No, but I have to tell you a few things. Or you'll never get the whole picture. There was no way I could meet you personally, you see, for he captured me the day I wrote to you. He dropped something in my tea, which made me virtually unconscious. He could never have overpowered me in any other way.'

'And he began to pass himself off as Kailash Chowdhury from that day?'

Kailash Babu nodded his head sadly. 'It is my own fault, Mr Mitter. I cannot blame anyone else. Our entire family suffers from one big weakness. We are all given to exaggerating the simplest things, and telling tall stories for no reason at all. I had bought that stone in Jabalpore for fifty rupees. I have no idea what possessed me to tell Kedar a strange story about a temple in a jungle, and a statue with that stone fixed on its forehead. He swallowed the whole thing, and began to eye that stone from that day. He envied me for many reasons. Perhaps he could not see why I should be so lucky, so successful in life, when he appeared to fail in everything he did. After all, we were identical twins, our fortunes should not have been so very different. Kedar had always been the black sheep—reckless and unscrupulous. Once he got mixed up with a gang that made counterfeit money. He would have gone to jail, but I managed to save him.

'Then he went abroad, after borrowing a great deal of money from me. I was glad. Good riddance, I thought. But only about a week ago, I came back home one day and found the stone missing. I never imagined for a moment that Kedar had come back and stolen it from my room. I rounded up all the servants and shouted at them, but nothing happened. Two days later, I wrote to you. Kedar turned up the same evening, and returned the stone to me. He was absolutely livid, for by this time, he had learnt that it had no value at all. He had been dreaming of getting at least a hundred thousand for it. He said he needed money desperately, would I give him twenty thousand? I refused. So he waited till I ordered a cup of tea, then managed to drug me and carry me up to the attic. When I woke, he told me he'd keep me there until I agreed to do as told. In the meantime, he'd pretend to be me, and he'd tell my office I was on sick leave.'

'He obviously did not know you had written to me,' Feluda added, 'So when we turned up, he took ten minutes to write a fake anonymous note and then gave us a cock-and-bull story about an imaginary enemy. If he didn't, he knew I'd get suspicious. At the same time, my presence in this house or in his life was highly undesirable. So he tried a threat on the telephone, then got in a car and tried to run us over.'

Kailash Chowdhury frowned. 'That makes perfect sense,' he said, 'What doesn't, is why he left so suddenly. I did not agree to give him a single paisa. So why did he leave? Surely he didn't leave empty-handed?'

'No, no, no!' Shouted a voice at the door. None of us had seen Abanish Babu return with a glass of milk. 'Why should he leave empty-handed?' he screamed, 'He took my stamp! That precious, rare Victorian stamp has gone.'

Feluda stared at him, wide-eyed. 'What! He took your stamp?'

'Yes, yes. Kedar Mama has ruined me!'

'How much did you say it was worth?'

'Twenty thousand.'

'But—' Feluda turned to Abanish Babu and lowered his voice, 'according to the catalogue, Abanish Babu, it cannot possibly fetch more than fifty rupees.'

Abanish Babu went visibly pale.

'The Chowdhurys are prone to exaggerate everything to make an impression,' Feluda continued, 'and you are their nephew. So presumably, you inherited the same trait. Am I right?'

Abanish Babu began to look like a child who had lost his

favourite toy. 'What was I supposed to do?' he said with a tragic air, 'I spent three years going through four thousand stamped envelopes. Not one of them was any good, except that one. Oh, all right, it wasn't much, but people believed my story. I got them interested!'

Feluda started laughing. 'Never mind, Abanish Babu,' he said, thumping his back, 'I think your uncle is going to be suitably punished, and that should give you some comfort. Let me ring the airport. You see, I had guessed he might try to escape this morning. So I rang Indian Airlines, and they told me he had a booking on their morning flight to Bombay. I began to suspect your uncle only when he said he couldn't remember having bought a new bottle of Dettol just a few days ago.'

*

The police had no problem in arresting Kedar Chowdhury; and Abanish Babu's stamp was duly returned to him. Feluda was paid so handsomely by Kailash Babu that, even after eating out three times, and seeing a couple of films with me, he still had a substantial amount left in his wallet.

Today, as we sat having tea at home, I said to him, 'Feluda, I have been thinking this through, and have reached a conclusion. Will you please tell me if I am right?'

'OK. What have you been thinking?'

'It's about Kailash Chowdhury's father. I think he knew what Kedar had done. I mean, maybe a father can tell the difference between identical twins. Perhaps that's the reason why he was throwing such murderous glances at his son.'

'That may or may not be the case. But since your thoughts appear to be the same as mine on this subject, I am hereby rewarding you for your intelligence.'

So saying, Feluda coolly helped himself to a jalebi from my plate.

seventh live. When was I supposed to do? Be and within
began all," I spent three years going through that through and
I almost collapse. Now neither am was surprised the capital
one. Oh, all right, it wasn't much, but he also relieved by
she, 'so often there, he?'

Feluda leaned back thoughtfully, yet mind. Al much behind he
said, murmuring Lalmohan. "I think your uncle was going to be
suitable, animated and husband should give you someconfort, eat
nursing the injured. You? so I had guessed he event try to
expect this morning. So I rang Inspector An hee, and they told
me he first a rocking on their morning flight to Bombay. I
begun to see for your uncle, only when he said he couldn't
remember having forgotten. What, oh LD? Feluda relaxed a
dot.

The police had no problem in arresting Kesav Chowdhury,
and Ahmad Babu's stamp was duly returned to him. Feluda
was paid so handsomely by Kailash Babu, that even after
eating out three times, and seeing a couple of things with me
he still had a substantial amount left in his wallet.

'I dare say sitting tea at home, said Feluda, 'Feluda
I have been thinking this through, and I have reached a
conclusion. Will you please tell me all I am right?'

'OK. What have you been thinking?'

'It's about Kailash Chowdhury's father. Kailash he know
what Kedar had done. I mean, maybe a father even tell the
difference between identical twins. I can, but there's the reason
why he was throwing such numerous glances at his son.'

'That may or may not be the case, but since our thoughts
appear to be the same as in much this as there', another joy
few airing you for your malignalance.'

So saying, Feluda coolly helped himself in a plate from
my plate.

A Killer in Kailash

It was the middle of June. I had finished my school final exams and was waiting for the results to come out. Feluda and I were supposed to have gone to a film today, but ten minutes before we were to leave, it began raining so heavily that we had to drop the idea. I was now sitting in our living room, immersed in a Tintin comic *(Tintin in Tibet)*. Feluda and I were both very fond of these comics which had mystery, adventure and humour, all in full measure. I already had three of these. This one was new. I had promised to pass it on to Feluda when I finished with it. Feluda was stretched out on the divan, reading a book called *Chariots of the Gods?*. He had nearly finished it.

After a while, he shut the book, placed it on his chest and lay still, staring at the whirring ceiling fan. Then he said, 'Do you know how many stone blocks there are in the pyramid of Giza? Two hundred thousand.'

Why was he suddenly interested in pyramids? He went on, 'Each block weighs nearly fifteen tonnes. From what is known of ancient engineering, the Egyptians could not have polished to perfection and placed together more than ten blocks every day. Besides, the stone it's made of had to be brought from the other side of the Nile. A rough calculation shows that it must have taken them at least six hundred years to build that one single pyramid.'

'Is that what your book says?'

'Yes, but that isn't all. This book mentions many other wonders that cannot be explained by archaeologists and historians. Take our own country, for instance. There is an iron pillar at the Qutab Minar in Delhi. It is two thousand years old, but it hasn't rusted. No one knows why. Have you heard of Easter Island? It's a small island in the South Pacific Ocean. There are huge rocks facing the sea, on which human faces were carved thousands of years ago. These rocks were dragged from the middle of the island, taken to its edge and arranged in such a way that they were visible from the sea. Each weighs almost fifty tonnes. Who did this? How did the ancient tribal people get hold of adequate technology to do this? They didn't have things like lorries, tractors, cranes or bulldozers.'

Feluda stopped, then sat up and lit a Charminar. The book had clearly stirred him in a big way. 'In Peru,' he went on, 'there is an area which has geometric patterns drawn on the ground. Everyone knows about these patterns, they are visible from the air, but no one can tell when and how they came to be there. It is such a big mystery that scientists do not often talk about it.'

'Has the author of your book talked about it?'

'Oh yes, and he's come up with a very interesting theory. According to him, creatures from a different planet came to earth more than twenty-five thousand years ago. Their technological expertise was much higher than man's. They shared their knowledge with humans, and built structures like the pyramids—which, one must admit, modern man has not been able to match despite all his technical know-how. It is only a theory, mind you, and of course it need not necessarily be true. But it makes you think, doesn't it? The weapons described in our *Mahabharata* bear resemblances to atomic weapons. So maybe . . . '

' . . . the battle of Kurukshetra was fought by creatures from another planet?'

Feluda opened his mouth to reply, but was interrupted. Someone had braved the rain and arrived at our door, pressing the bell three times in a row. I ran and opened it. Uncle Sidhu rushed in, together with sprays of water. Then he shook his umbrella and shut it, sending more droplets flying everywhere.

Uncle Sidhu was not really a relation. He and my father used to be neighbours many years ago. Since my father treated him like an elder brother, we called him uncle.

'What a miserable day get me a cup of tea quick the best you've got,' he said in one breath. I ran back inside, woke Srinath and told him to make three cups of tea. When I returned to the living room, Uncle Sidhu was seated on a sofa, frowning darkly and staring at a porcelain ashtray.

'Why didn't you take a rickshaw? In this weather, really, you shouldn't have—' Feluda began.

'People get murdered every day. Do you know there's a different type of murder that's much worse?' Uncle Sidhu asked, as if Feluda hadn't spoken at all. We remained silent, knowing that he was going to answer his own question.

'I think most people would agree that our present downfall notwithstanding, we have a past of which every Indian can be justly proud,' Uncle Sidhu went on, 'And, today, what do we see of this glorious past? Isn't it our art, chiefly paintings and sculptures? Tell me, Felu, isn't that right?'

'Of course,' Feluda nodded.

'The best examples of these—particularly sculptures— are to be found on the walls of old temples, right?'

'Right.'

Uncle Sidhu appeared to know about most things in life, but his knowledge of art was probably the deepest, for two out of his three bookcases were full of books on Indian art. But what was all this about a murder?

He stopped for a minute to light a cheroot. Then he coughed twice, filling the whole room with smoke, and continued, 'Several rulers in the past destroyed many of our temples. Kalapahar alone was responsible for the destruction of dozens of temples in Bengal. You knew that, didn't you? But did you know that a new Kalapahar has emerged today? I mean, now, in 1973?'

'Are you talking of people stealing statues from temples to sell them abroad?' Feluda asked.

'Exactly!' Uncle Sidhu almost shouted in excitement, 'Can you imagine what a huge crime it is? And it's not even done in the name of religion, it's just plain commerce. Our own art, our own heritage is making its way to wealthy Americans, but it's being done so cleverly that it's impossible to catch anyone. Do you know what I saw today? The head of a yakshi from the Raja-Rani temple in Bhubaneshwar. It was with an American tourist in the Grand Hotel.'

'You don't say!'

I had been to Bhubaneshwar when I was a child. My father had shown me the Raja-Rani temple. It was made of terracotta and its walls were covered by beautiful statues and carvings.

Uncle Sidhu continued with his story, 'I had a few old Rajput paintings which I'd bought in Varanasi in 1934. I took those to Nagarmal to sell. I have known him for years. He has a shop in the Grand Hotel arcade. Just as I was placing my paintings on the counter, this American arrived. It seemed he'd bought a few things from Nagarmal before. In his hand was something wrapped in a newspaper. It seemed heavy. Then he unwrapped it, and—oh God!—my heart jumped into my mouth. It was the head of a yakshi, made of red stone. I had seen it before, more than once. But I had seen the whole body. Now the head had been severed.

'Nagarmal didn't know where it had come from, but could tell that it was genuine, not a fake. The American said he had paid two thousand dollars for it. If you added two more zeros after it, I said to myself, even then you couldn't say it was the right value. Anyway, that man went up to his room. I was so amazed that I didn't even ask him who had sold it to him. I rushed back home and consulted a few of my books just to make sure. Now I am absolutely positive it was from a statue on the wall of Raja-Rani. I don't know how it was done—possibly by bribing the chowkidar at night. Anything is possible these days. I have written to the Bhubaneshwar

Archaeological Department and sent it by express delivery, but what good is that going to do? The damage is already done!'

Srinath came in with the tea. Uncle Sidhu picked up a cup, took a sip, and said, 'This has to be stopped, Felu. I am now too old to do anything myself, but you are an investigator, it is your job to find criminals. What could be worse than destroying and disfiguring our ancient art, tell me? Shouldn't these criminals be caught? I could, of course, write to newspapers and try attract the attention of the police, but do you know what the problem is? Not everyone understands the true value of art. I mean, an old statue on a temple wall isn't the same as gold or diamonds, is it? You cannot put a market price on it.'

Feluda was quiet all this while. Now he said, 'Did you manage to learn the name of that American?'

'Yes. I did speak to him very briefly. He gave me his card. Here it is.' Uncle Sidhu took out a small white card from his pocket and gave it to Feluda. Saul Silverstein, it said. His address was printed below his name.

'A Jew,' Uncle Sidhu remarked, 'Most undoubtedly very wealthy. The watch he was wearing was probably worth a thousand dollars. I had never seen such an expensive watch before.'

'Did he tell you how long he's going to stay here?'

'He's going to Kathmandu tomorrow morning. But if you ring him now, you might get him.' Feluda got up and began dialling. The telephone number of the Grand Hotel was one of the many important numbers he had memorized.

The receptionist said Mr Silverstein was not in his room. No one knew when he might be back. Feluda replaced the receiver, looking disappointed. 'If we could get even a description of the man who sold that statue to him, we might do something about it.'

'I know. That's what *I* should have asked him,' Uncle Sidhu sighed, 'but I simply couldn't think straight. He was looking at my paintings. He said he was interested in Tantric art, so if I had anything to sell I should contact him. Then he gave me that card. But I honestly don't see how you'll proceed in this matter.'

'Well, let's just wait and see. The press may report the theft. After all, Raja-Rani is a very famous temple in Bhubaneshwar.'

Uncle Sidhu finished his tea and rose. 'This has been going on for years,' he said, collecting his umbrella, 'So far, the target seems to have been smaller and lesser known temples. But now, whoever's involved has become much bolder. Perhaps a group of reckless and very powerful people are behind this. Felu, if you can do something about it, the entire nation is going to appreciate it. I am positive about that.'

Uncle Sidhu left. Feluda then spent all day trying to get hold of Saul Silverstein, but he did not return to his room. At 11 p.m., Feluda gave up. 'If what Uncle Sidhu said is true,' he said, frowning, 'whoever is responsible is a criminal of the first order. What is most frustrating is that there's no way I can track him down. No way at all.'

A way opened the very next day, in such a totally unexpected manner that, even now, my head reels when I think about it.

What happened was a terrible accident. But, before I speak about it, there's something else I must mention. There was a small report in the newspaper the next day, which confirmed Uncle Sidhu's suspicions:

The Headless Yakshi

The head from the statue of a yakshi has been stolen from the wall of the Raja-Rani temple in Bhubaneshwar. This temple serves as one of the best examples of old Indian architecture. The chowkidar of the temple is said to be missing. The Archaeological Department of Orissa has asked for a police investigation.

I read this report aloud, and asked, 'Would that mean the chowkidar is the thief?'

Feluda finished squeezing out toothpaste from a tube of Forhans and placed it carefully on his toothbrush. Then he said, 'No, I don't think stealing the head was just the chowkidar's idea. A poor man like him would not have the nerve. Someone else is responsible, someone big enough and strong enough to think he is never going to be caught. Presumably, he—or they—simply paid the chowkidar to get him out of the way for a few days.'

Uncle Sidhu must have seen the report too. He would probably turn up at our house again to tell us proudly that he was right.

He did arrive, but not before half past ten. Today being

Thursday, our area had been hit by its regular power cut since nine o'clock. Feluda and I were sitting in our living room, staring occasionally at the overcast sky, when someone knocked loudly at the door and Uncle Sidhu rushed in a minute later, demanding a cup of tea once more. Feluda began talking of the headless yakshi, but was told to shut up.

'That's stale news, young man,' Uncle Sidhu barked, 'Did you hear the last news bulletin?'

'No, I'm afraid not. Our radio is not working. Today is . . .'

'I know, it's Thursday, and you've got a long power cut. That is why, Felu, I keep asking you to buy a transistor. Anyway, I came as soon as I heard. You'll never believe this. That flight to Kathmandu crashed, not far from Calcutta. It took off at seven-thirty, but crashed only fifteen minutes later. There was a storm, so perhaps it was trying to come back. There were fifty-eight passengers. All of them died, including Saul Silverstein. Yes, his name was mentioned on the radio.'

For a few moments, neither of us could speak. Then Feluda said, 'Where did it crash? Did they mention the place?'

'Yes, near a village called Sidikpur, on the way to Hasnabad. Felu, I had been praying very hard for that statue not to leave the country. Who knew my prayer would be answered through such a terrible tragedy?'

Feluda glanced at his watch. Was he thinking of going to Sidikpur?

Uncle Sidhu looked at him sharply. 'I know what you're thinking. There must have been an explosion and everything the plane contained must have been scattered over miles. Suppose, among the belongings of the passengers, there is—?'

Feluda decided in two minutes that he'd take a taxi and go to Sidikpur to look for the head of the yakshi. The crash had occurred three hours ago. It would take us an hour and a half to get there. By this time, the police and the fire brigade would have got there and started their investigation. No one could tell whether we'd succeed in our mission, but we could not miss this chance to retrieve what was lost.

'Those paintings I sold to Nagarmal fetched me a tidy little sum,' Uncle Sidhu told Feluda, 'I would like to give you some of it. After all, you are going to get involved only because of me, aren't you?'

'No,' Feluda replied firmly, 'it is true that you gave me all the details. But, believe me, I wouldn't have taken any action if I didn't feel strongly about it myself. I have thought a great deal about this, and—like you—I have come to the conclusion that those who think they can sell our ancient heritage to fill their own pockets should be caught and punished severely.'

'Bravo!' Uncle Sidhu beamed, 'Please remember one thing, Felu. Even if you don't need any money, you may need information on art and sculpture. I can always help you with that.'

'Yes, I know. Thank you.'

We decided that if we could find what we were looking for, we would take it straight to the office of the Archaeological Survey of India. The thief might still be at large, but at least the stolen object would go back to the authorities.

We quickly got ready, and got into a yellow taxi. It was 10.55 when we set off. 'I've no idea how long this is going to take,' Feluda said, 'We can stop for lunch at a dhaba on Jessore Road on our way back.'

This pleased me no end. The food in dhabas—which were usually frequented by lorry drivers—was always delicious. Roti, daal, meat curry . . . my mouth began to water. Feluda could eat anything anywhere. I tried to follow his example.

*

There was a shower as soon as we left the main city and reached VIP Road. But the sun came out as we got close to Barasat. Hasnabad was forty miles from Calcutta. 'If the road wasn't wet and slippery, I could have got there in an hour,' said our driver. 'There's been a plane crash there, sir, did you know? I heard about it on the radio.'

On being told that that was where we were going, he became very excited. 'Why, sir, was any of your relatives in that plane?' he asked.

'No, no.'

Feluda could hardly tell him the whole story, but his curiosity was aroused and he went on asking questions.

'I believe everything's been reduced to ashes. What will you get to see, anyway?'

'I don't know.'

'Are you a reporter?'

'I . . . well, I write stories.'

'Oh, I see. You'll get all the details and then use it in a story? Very good, very good.'

We had left Barasat behind us. Now we had to stop every now and then to ask people if they knew where Sidikpur was. Finally, a group of young men standing near a cycle repair shop gave us the right directions. 'Two miles from here, you'll see an unpaved road on your left,' said one of them, 'This road will take you to Sidikpur. It's only a mile from there.' From the way he spoke, it seemed obvious that he and his friends had already given the same directions to many others.

The unpaved road turned out to be little more than a dirt track. It was muddy after the recent rain and bore several sets of tyre marks. Thank goodness it was only June. A month later, this road would become impossible to drive through. Three other Ambassadors passed us. Several people were going on foot, and some others were returning from the site of the crash.

A number of people were gathered under a banyan tree. Three cars and a jeep were parked near it. Our taxi pulled up behind these. There was no sign of the crash anywhere, but it became clear that we couldn't drive any further. To our right was an open area, full of large trees. Beyond these, in the distance, a few small houses could be seen.

'Yes, that's Sidikpur,' one of the men told us, 'There's a little wood where the village ends. That's where the plane crashed.'

By this time, our driver had introduced himself to us. His name was Balaram Ghosh. He locked his car and came with us. As it turned out, the wood wasn't large. There were more banana trees than anything else. Only half a dozen mango and jackfruit trees stood amongst them. Each of them was badly charred. There were virtually no leaves left on their branches, and some of the branches looked as if they had been deliberately chopped off. The whole area was now teeming with men in uniform, and some others who were probably from the airline. There was a very strong pungent smell, which made me cover my face with a handkerchief. The ground was littered with endless pieces of broken, burnt and half-burnt objects, some damaged beyond recognition, others more or less usable. Feluda clicked his tongue in annoyance and said, 'If only we could have got here an hour ago!'

The main site had been cordoned off. There was no way we could get any closer. So we started walking around the cordon. Some of the policemen were picking up objects from the ground and inspecting them: a portion of a stethoscope, a briefcase, a flask, a small mirror that glinted brightly in the sun. The site was on our right. We were slowly moving in that direction, when suddenly Feluda saw something on a mango tree on our left and stopped.

A little boy was sitting on a low branch, clutching a half-burnt leather shoe. He must have found it among the debris. Feluda glanced up and asked, 'You found a lot of things, didn't you?' The boy did not reply, but stared solemnly at Feluda. 'What's the matter? Can't you speak?' Feluda asked again. Still he got no reply. 'Hopeless!' he exclaimed and walked on, away from the debris and towards the village. Balaram Ghosh became curious once more.

'Are you looking for something special, sir?' he asked.

'Yes. The head of a statue, made of red stone.'

'I see. Just the head? OK.' He started searching in the grass.

There was a peepal tree about a hundred yards away,

under which a group of old men were sitting, smoking hookahs. The oldest among them asked Feluda, 'Where are you from?'

'Calcutta. Your village hasn't come to any harm, has it?'

'No, Babu. Allah saved us. There was a fire as soon as the plane came down—it made such a big noise that we all thought a bomb had gone off—and then the whole village was filled with smoke. We could see the fire in the wood, but none of us knew what to do . . . but soon it started to rain, and then the fire brigade arrived.'

'Did any of you go near the plane when the fire went out?'

'No, Babu. We're old men, we were simply glad to have been spared.'

'What about the young boys? Didn't they go and collect things before the police got here?'

The old men fell silent. By this time, several other people had gathered to listen to this exchange. Feluda spotted a boy and beckoned him. 'What's your name?' he asked as the boy came closer. His tone was gentle and friendly.

'Ali.'

Feluda placed a hand on his shoulder and lowered his voice, 'A lot of things scattered everywhere when the plane crashed. You've seen that for yourself, haven't you? Now, there should have been the head of a statue among those things. Just the head of a statue of a woman. Do you know if anyone saw it?'

'Ask him!' Ali replied, pointing at another boy. Feluda had to repeat the whole process once more.

'What's your name?'

'Panu.'

'Did you see the head of a statue? Did you take it?'

Silence. 'Look, Panu,' Feluda said even more gently, 'it's all right. No one's going to get angry with you. But if you can give me that head, I'll pay you for it. Have you got it with you?'

More silence. This time, one of the old men shouted at

him, 'Go on, Panu, answer the gentleman. He hasn't got all day.'

Panu finally opened his mouth. 'I haven't got it with me now.'

'What do you mean?'

'I found it, Babu. I swear I did. But I gave it to someone else, only a few minutes ago.'

What! Could this really be true? My heart started hammering in my chest.

'Who was it?' Feluda asked sharply.

'I don't know. He was a man from the city, like you. He came in a car, a blue car.'

'What did he look like? Was he tall? Short? Thin? Fat? Did he wear glasses?'

This prompted many of Panu's friends to join the conversation. From the description they gave, it seemed that a man of medium height, who was neither thin nor fat, neither fair nor dark, and whose age was between thirty and fifty, had arrived half an hour before us and had made similar enquiries. Panu had shown him the yakshi's head, and he had bought it from him for a nominal sum. Then he had driven off in a blue car.

When we were driving to Sidikpur, a blue Ambassador had come from the opposite direction, passed us and gone towards the main road. All of us remembered having seen it.

'OK. Come on, Topshe. Let's go, Mr Ghosh.'

If Feluda was disappointed by what we had just learnt, he did not show it. On the contrary, he seemed to have found new energy. He ran all the way back to the taxi, with the driver and me in tow.

God knew what lay in store.

THREE

We were now going back the same way we had come. It was past one-thirty, but neither of us was thinking of lunch. Balaram Ghosh did suggest stopping for a cup of tea when we reached Jessore Road, but Feluda paid no attention. Perhaps our driver smelt an adventure in all this, so he, too, did not raise the subject of food again.

Our car was now going at 75 kmph. I was aware of only one thought that kept going over and over in my mind: how close we had got to retrieving the yakshi's head! If we hadn't had a power cut this morning, we would have heard the news on the radio, and then we would have reached Sidikpur sooner and most certainly we would have got hold of Panu. If that had happened, by now we would have been making our way to the office of the Archaeological Survey of India. Who knows, Feluda might have been given a Padma Shri for recovering the country's lost heritage!

The sun had already dried the road. I was beginning to wonder why we couldn't go a little faster, when my eyes caught sight of something by the roadside that caused a sharp rise in my pulse rate.

A blue Ambassador was standing outside a small garage.

'Should I stop here, sir?' Balaram Ghosh asked, reducing his speed. He had obviously paid great attention to what those boys had told us.

'Yes, at that tea stall over there,' Feluda replied. Mr Ghosh swept up to the stall and pulled up by its side with a screech. We got out and Feluda ordered three cups of tea. I noticed that tea was being served in small glasses, there were no cups.

'What else have you got?' Feluda asked.

'Biscuits. Would you like some? They're fresh, sir, and very tasty.'

Two glass jars stood on a counter, filled with large, round biscuits. Feluda asked for half-a-dozen of those.

My eyes kept darting back to the blue car. A mechanic was in the process of replacing a punctured tyre. A man—medium height, age around forty, thick bushy eyebrows, hair brushed back—was pacing up and down, inhaling every now and then from a half-finished cigarette.

Our tea was almost ready. Feluda took out a Charminar, then pretended he had lost his lighter. He patted his pocket twice, then shrugged and moved over to join the other man. The driver and I stayed near our taxi, but we could hear what was said.

'Excuse me,' Feluda began, 'do you . . . ?'

The man took out a lighter and lit Feluda's cigarette for him.

'Thanks,' Feluda inhaled, 'A terrible business, wasn't it?'

The man glanced at Feluda, then looked away without replying. Feluda tried once more.

'Weren't you at the site where that plane crashed? I thought I saw your car there!'

This time, the man spoke. 'What plane crash?'

'Good heavens, haven't you heard? A plane bound for Kathmandu crashed near Sidikpur.'

'I am coming from Taki. No, I hadn't heard of the crash.'

Taki was a town near Hasnabad. Could the man be telling the truth? If only we'd noted the number of his car when he passed us!

'How much longer will it take?' he asked the mechanic impatiently.

'A couple of minutes, sir, no more.'

Our tea had been served by this time. Feluda came back to pick up a glass. The three of us sat down on a bench in front of the stall. 'He denied everything . . . the man's a liar,' Feluda muttered.

'How can you be so sure, Feluda? There are millions of blue Ambassadors.'

'His shoes are covered by ash. Have you looked at your own sandals?'

I glanced down quickly and realized the colour of my sandals had changed completely. The other man's brown shoes were similarly covered with dark patches.

Feluda took his time to finish his tea. We waited until the blue car got a new tyre—this took another fifteen minutes instead of two—and went towards Jessore Road. Our own taxi left a minute later. There was quite a big gap between the two cars which, Feluda said, was no bad thing. 'He mustn't see that we're following him,' he told Mr Ghosh.

It began raining again as we reached Dum Dum. Everything went hazy for a few minutes and it became difficult to keep the blue car in view. Balaram Ghosh was therefore obliged to get a bit closer, which helped us in getting the number of the car. It was WMA 5349.

'This is like a Hindi film sir!' Mr Ghosh enthused, 'I saw a film only the other day—it had Shatrughan Sinha in it—which had a chase scene, exactly like this. But the second car went and crashed into a hill.'

'We've already had a crash today, thank you.'

'Oh, don't worry, sir. I've been driving for thirteen years. I haven't had a single accident. I mean, not yet.'

'Good. Keep it that way.'

Balaram Ghosh was a good driver, I had to admit. We were now back in Calcutta, but he was weaving his way through the busy roads without once losing sight of the blue car. I wondered where it was going.

'What do you think the man's going to do with the statue?' I asked Feluda after a while.

'Well, he's certainly not going to take it back to Bhubaneshwar.' Feluda replied, 'What he might do is find another buyer. After all, it isn't often that one gets the chance to sell the same thing twice!'

The blue car finally brought us to Park Street. We drove past the old cemetery, Lowdon Street, Camac Street, and then suddenly, it turned left and drove into a building called Queen's Mansion.

'Should I go in, sir?'

'Of course.'

Our taxi passed through the front gates. A huge open square faced us, surrounded by tall blocks of flats. A number of cars and a couple of scooters were parked before these. The blue car went to the far end and stopped. We waited in our taxi to see what happened next.

The man got out with a black bag, wound up the windows of his car, locked it and slipped into Queen's Mansion through a large door. Feluda waited for another minute, then followed him.

By the time we reached the door, the old-fashioned lift in the lobby had already gone up, making a great deal of noise. It came back a few seconds later. An old liftman emerged from behind its collapsible gate. Feluda went up to him.

'Did I just miss Mr Sengupta?' he asked anxiously.

'Mr Sengupta?'

'The man who just went up?'

'That man was Mr Mallik of number five. There's no Sengupta in this building.'

'Oh. I must have made a mistake. Sorry.'

We came away. Mr Mallik, flat number five. I must remember these details.

Feluda paid Balaram Ghosh and said he was no longer needed. Before driving off, he gave us a piece of paper with a phone number scribbled on it. 'That's my neighbour's number,' he said, 'If you ever need me, ring that number. My neighbour will call me. I'd love to be able to help, sir. You see, life's usually so boring that something like this comes as a tremendous . . . I mean, it makes a *change*, doesn't it?'

We made our way to the Park Street police station. Feluda knew its OC, Mr Haren Mutsuddi. Two years ago, they had worked together to trace the culprit who had poisoned a race horse called Happy-go-lucky. It turned out that Mr Mutsuddi was aware of the theft in Bhubaneshwar. Feluda told him briefly about our encounter with Mr Mallik and said, 'Even if Mallik is not the real thief, he has clearly taken it upon himself to recover the stolen object and pass it on to someone else. I have come to make two requests, Mr Mutsuddi. Someone must keep an eye on his movements, and I need to know who he really is and where he works. He lives in flat number five, Queen's Mansion, drives a blue Ambassador, WMA 5349.'

Mr Mutsuddi heard Feluda in silence. Then he removed a pencil that was tucked behind his ear and said, 'Very well, Mr Mitter. If you want these things done, they will be done. A special constable will follow your man everywhere, and I'll see if we have anything in our files on him. There's no guarantee, mind you, that I'll get anything, particularly if he hasn't actually broken the law.'

'Thank you. But please treat this matter as urgent. If that statue gets passed on to someone else, we'll be in big trouble.

'Why?' Mr Mutsuddi smiled, 'Why should you be in big trouble, Mr Mitter? You'll have me and the entire police force to help you. Doesn't that count for anything? We're not totally useless, you know. But there's just one thing I'd like to tell you. The people who are behind such rackets are usually quite powerful. I'm not talking of physical strength. I mean they often manage to do things far worse and much more vile than ordinary petty criminals. I am telling you all this, Mr Mitter, because you are young and talented, and I took upon you as a friend.'

'Thank you, Mr Mutsuddi. I appreciate your concern.'

We left the police station and went to the Chinese restaurant, Waldorf, to have lunch. Feluda went to the manager's room to make a call after we had placed our order.

'I rang Mallik,' he said when he came back, 'He was still

in his room and he answered the phone himself. I rang off without saying anything.' He sounded a little relieved.

We returned home at three o'clock. Mr Mutsuddi called us a little after four. Feluda spoke for nearly five minutes, noting things down in his notebook. Then he put the phone down and told me everything even before I could ask.

'The man's called Jayant Mallik. He moved into that flat about two weeks ago. It actually belongs to a Mr Adhikari, who is away in Darjeeling at the moment. Perhaps he's a friend, and he's allowed Mallik to use his flat in his absence. That blue Ambassador is Adhikari's. Mallik took it to the Grand Hotel at three o'clock today. He went in for five minutes, then came out and was seen waiting in his car for twenty minutes. After that, he went in once more and emerged in ten minutes. Then he went to Dalhousie Square. Mutsuddi's man lost him for a while after this, but then found him in the railway booking office in Fairly Place. He bought a ticket to Aurangabad, second class reserved. Mutsuddi's man will ring him again if there's more news.'

'Aurangabad?'

'Yes, that's where Mallik is going. And we are going immediately to Sardar Shankar Road, to visit Uncle Sidhu. I need to consult him urgently.'

'Aurangabad!' Uncle Sidhu's eyes nearly popped out, 'Do you realize what this means? Aurangabad is only twenty miles from Ellora, which is a sort of depot for the best specimens of Indian art. There is the Kailash temple, carved out of a mountain. Then there are thirty-three caves—Hindu, Buddhist, Jain—that stretch for a mile and a half. Each is packed with beautiful statues, wonderful carvings . . . oh God, I can hardly think! But why is this man going by train when he can fly to Aurangabad?'

'I think he wants to keep the yakshi's head with him at all times. If he went by air, his baggage might be searched by security men. No one would bother to do that on a train, would they?'

Feluda stood up suddenly.

'What did you decide?' Uncle Sidhu asked anxiously.

'We must go by air,' Feluda replied.

The look Uncle Sidhu gave him at this was filled with pride and joy. But he said nothing. All he did was get up and select a slim book from one of his bookcases. 'This may help you,' he said. I glanced at its title. *A Guide to the Caves of Ellora*, it said.

*

Feluda rang his travel agent, Mr Bakshi, as soon as we got back home.

'I need three tickets on the flight to Bombay tomorrow,' I heard him say. This surprised me very much. Why did he need three tickets? Was Uncle Sidhu going to join us? When I asked him, however, Feluda only said, 'The more the merrier. We may need an extra pair of hands.'

Mr Bakshi came back on the line. 'I'll have to put you on the waiting list,' he said, 'but it doesn't look too bad, I think it'll be OK.'

He also agreed to make our hotel bookings in Aurangabad and Ellora. The flight to Bombay would get us there by nine o'clock. Then we'd have to catch the flight to Aurangabad at half past twelve, reaching there an hour later. This meant we would arrive in Aurangabad on Saturday, and Mr Mallik would get there on Sunday.

Feluda rang off and began dialling another number. The doorbell rang before he could finish dialling. I opened it to find Lalmohan Babu. Feluda stared, as though he had seen a ghost, and exclaimed, 'My word, what a coincidence! I was just dialling your number.'

'Really? Now, that must mean I have got a telepathetic link with you, after all,' Lalmohan Babu laughed, looking pleased. Neither of us had the heart to tell him the correct word was 'telepathic'.

'It's so hot and stuffy . . . could you please ask your servant to make a lemon drink, with some ice from the fridge, if you don't mind?'

Feluda passed on his request to Srinath, then came straight to the point.

'Are you very busy these days? Have you started writing anything new?'

'No, no. I couldn't have come here for a chat if I'd already started writing. All I've got is a plot. I think it would make a good Hindi film. There are five fights. My hero, Prakhar Rudra, goes to Baluchistan this time. Tell me, how do you think Arjun Mehrotra would handle the role of Prakhar Rudra? I think he'd fit the part very well—unless, of course, *you* agreed to do it, Felu Babu?'

'I cannot speak Hindi. Anyway, I suggest you come with

us to Kailash for a few days. You can start thinking of Baluchistan when you get back.'

'Kailash? All the way to Tibet? Isn't that under the Chinese?'

'No. This Kailash has nothing to do with Tibet. Have you heard of Ellora?'

'Oh, I see, I see. You mean the temple? But isn't that full of statues and rocks and mountains? What have you to do with those, Felu Babu? Your business is human beings, isn't it?'

'Correct. A group of human beings has started a hideous racket involving those rocks and statues. I intend to put a stop to it.'

Lalmohan Babu stared. Feluda filled him in quickly, which made him grow even more round-eyed.

'What are you saying, Felu Babu? I had no idea stone statues could be so valuable. The only valuable stones I can think of are precious stones like rubies and emeralds and diamonds. But this—!'

'This is far more precious. You can get diamonds and rubies elsewhere in the world. But there is only one Kailash, one Sanchi and one Elephanta. If these are destroyed, there would be no evidence left of the amazing heights our ancient art had risen to. Modern artists do not—they cannot—get anywhere near the skill and perfection these specimens show. Anyone who tries to disfigure any of them is a dangerous criminal. In my view, the man who took that head from the statue of the yakshi is no less than a murderer. He has got to be punished.'

This was enough to convince Lalmohan Babu. He was fond of travelling, in any case. He agreed to accompany us at once, and began asking a lot of questions, including whether or not he should carry a mosquito net, and was there any danger of being bitten by snakes? Then he left, with a promise to meet us at the airport.

Neither of us knew how long we might have to stay in Aurangabad, but decided to pack enough clothes for a week. Since Feluda was often required to travel, he always had a suitcase packed with essentials such as a fifty-foot steel tape, an all-purpose knife, rail and air timetables, road maps, a long nylon rope, a pair of hunting boots, and several pieces of wire which came in handy to unlock doors and table-drawers if he didn't have a key. None of this took up a lot of space, so he could pack his clothes in the same suitcase.

He also had guide books and tourist pamphlets on various parts of the country. I leafed through the ones I thought might be relevant for this visit. Feluda set the alarm clock at 4 a.m. before going to bed at ten o'clock, then rang 173 and asked for a wake-up call, in case the alarm did not go off for some reason.

Ten minutes later, Mr Mutsuddi rang again. 'Mallik received a trunk call from Bombay,' he said, 'The words Mallik spoke were these: "The daughter has returned to her father from her in-laws. The father is taking her with him twenty-seventy-five." The caller from Bombay said: "Carry on, best of luck." That was all.'

Feluda thanked him and rang off. Mallik's words made no sense to me. When I mentioned this to Feluda, he simply said, 'Even the few grey cells you had seem to be disappearing, my boy. Stop worrying and go to sleep.'

*

The flight to Bombay was delayed by an hour. It finally left at half past seven. There were quite a few cancellations, so we got three seats pretty easily.

Lalmohan Babu had flown with us for the first time when we had gone to Delhi and Simla in connection with Mr Dhameeja's case. This was possibly the second time he was travelling by air. I noticed that this time he did not pull faces and grip the arms of his chair when we took off; but, a little later, when we ran into some rough weather, he leant across and said, 'Felu Babu, this is no different from travelling in a rickety old bus down Chitpur Road. How can I be sure the whole plane isn't coming apart?'

'It isn't, rest assured.'

After breakfast, he seemed to have recovered a little, for I saw him press a button and call the air hostess. 'Excuse please Miss, a toothpick,' he said smartly. Then he began reading a guide book on Bombay. None of us had been to Bombay before. Feluda had decided to spend a few days there with a friend on our way back—provided, of course, that our business in Ellora could be concluded satisfactorily.

When the 'fasten seat-belt' sign came on just before landing, there was something I felt I had to ask Feluda. 'Will you please explain what Mr Mallik's words meant?'

Feluda looked amazed. 'What, you mean you really didn't understand it?'

'No.'

'The daughter has returned to her father from her in-laws. "The daughter" is the yakshi's head, the "in-laws" refers to Silverstein who had bought it, and the "father" is Mallik himself.'

'I see . . . What about "twenty-seventy-five"?'

'That refers to the latitude. If you look at a map, you'll see that's where Aurangabad is shown.'

We landed at Santa Cruz airport at ten. Since our flight to Aurangabad was at half past twelve, we saw no point in going into the town, although an aerial view of the city had impressed me very much. We remained in the airport, had chicken curry and rice for lunch at the airport restaurant, and boarded the plane to Aurangabad at quarter to one. There were only eleven passengers, since it was not the tourist season.

This time, Lalmohan Babu and I sat together. Feluda sat on the other side of the aisle, next to a middle-aged man with a parrot-like nose, thick wavy salt-and-pepper hair brushed back and wearing glasses with a heavy black frame. We got to know him after landing at the small airport at Aurangabad. He was expecting to be met, he said, but no one had turned up. So he decided to join us to go to town in the bus provided by the airline.

'Where will you be staying?' he asked Feluda.

'Hotel Aurangabad.'

'Oh, that's where I shall be staying as well. What brings you here? Holiday?'

'Yes, you might call it that. And you?'

'I am writing a book on Ellora. This is my second visit. I teach the history of Indian art in Michigan.'

'I see. Are your students enthusiastic about this subject?'

'Yes, much more now than they used to be. India seems to inspire young people more than anything else.'

'I believe the Vaishnavas have got a strong hold over there?' Feluda asked lightly. The other gentleman laughed. 'Are you talking of the Hare Krishna people?' he asked, 'Yes, their presence cannot be ignored. They are, in fact, very serious about what they do and how they dress. Have you heard their keertan? Sometimes it is impossible to tell they are foreigners.'

It took us only fifteen minutes to reach our hotel. It was small, but neat and tidy. We checked in and were shown into room number 11. Lalmohan Babu went to room 14. Feluda had bought a newspaper at Bombay airport. I had seen him read it in the plane. Now he sat down on a chair in the middle of our room, spread it once more and said, 'Do you know what "vandalism" means?'

I did, but only vaguely. Feluda explained, 'The barbarian invaders who sacked Rome in the fifth century were called Vandals. Any act related to disfiguring, damaging or destroying a beautiful object has come to be known as vandalism.' Then he passed the newspaper to me and said, 'Read it.'

I saw a short report with the heading, 'More Vandalism'.

According to it, a statue of a woman had been broken and its head lifted from one of the walls of the temple of Kandaria Mahadev in Khajuraho. A group of art students from Baroda who were visiting the complex were the first to notice what had happened. This was the third case reported in the last four weeks. There could be no doubt that these statues and other pieces of sculpture were being sold abroad.

As I sat trying to grasp the full implications of the report, Feluda spoke. His tone was grim.

'As far as I can make out,' he said, 'there is only one octopus. It has spread its tentacles to various temples in different parts of the country. If even one tentacle can be caught and chopped off, it will make the whole body of the animal squirm and wriggle. It should be our aim here to spot that one tentacle and seize it.'

Aurangabad was a historical city. An Abyssinian slave called Malik Ambar had been brought to India. In time, he became the Prime Minister of the King of Ahmednagar and built a city called Khadke. During the time of Aurangzeb, Khadke changed its name and came to be known as Aurangabad. In addition to Mughal buildings and structures, there were about ten Buddhist caves—thirteen hundred years old—that contained statues worth seeing.

The gentleman we had met at the airport—whose name was Shubhankar Bose—came to our room later in the evening for a chat. 'You must see the caves here before going to Ellora,' he told us, 'If you do, you'll be able to see that the two are similar in some ways.'

Since it was drizzling outside, we decided not to go out immediately. Tomorrow, if the day was fine, we would see the caves and the mausoleum built in the memory of Aurangzeb's wife, called Bibi ka Makbara. We would have to remain in Aurangabad until the next afternoon, anyway, since Jayant Mallik was supposed to get here at eleven o'clock. He would probably go to Ellora the same day, and we would then follow him.

After dinner, Feluda sat down with his guide book on Ellora. I was wondering what to do, when Lalmohan Babu turned up.

'Have you looked out of the window, Tapesh?' he asked, 'The moon has come out now. Would you like to go for a walk?'

'Sure.'

We came out of the hotel to find everything bathed in moonlight. In the distance was a range of hills. Perhaps that was where the Buddhist caves were located. A paan shop close by had a transistor on, playing a Hindi song. Two men were sitting on a bench, having a loud argument. They were probably speaking in Marathi, for I couldn't understand a word. The road outside had been full of people and traffic during the day, but was now very quiet. A train blew its whistle somewhere far away, and a man wearing a turban went past, riding a cycle. I felt a little strange in this new place—there seemed to be a hint of mystery in whatever I saw, some excitement and even a little fear. At this moment, Lalmohan Babu suddenly brought his face close to my ear and whispered, 'Doesn't Shubhankar Bose strike you as a bit suspicious?'

'Why?' I asked, considerably startled.

'What do you think his suitcase contains? Why does it weigh 35 kgs?'

'Thirty-five?' I was very surprised.

'Yes. He was before me in the queue in Bombay, when we were told to check in. I saw how much his suitcase weighed. His was 35, your cousin's was 22, yours was 14 and mine was 16 kgs. Bose had to pay for excess baggage.'

This was news to me. I had seen Mr Bose's suitcase. It wasn't very large. What could have made it so heavy?

Lalmohan Babu provided the answer.

'Rocks,' he said, still whispering, 'or tools to break something made of stone. Didn't your cousin tell us there was a large gang working behind this whole business? I believe Bose is one of them. Did you see his nose? It's exactly like Ghanashyam Karkat's.'

'Who is Ghanashyam Karkat?'

'Oh ho, didn't I tell you? He is the villain in my next book. Do you know how I'm going to describe his nose? "It was like a shark's fin, rising above the water."'

I paid no attention to this last bit, but couldn't ignore his

remarks about Mr Bose. I would not have suspected him at all.
How could a man who knew so much about art be a criminal?
But then, those who go about stealing art must know
something about the subject. Besides, there really was
something sharp about his appearance.

'I only wanted to warn you,' Lalmohan Babu went on
speaking, 'Just keep an eye on him. He offered me a toffee, but
I didn't take it. What if it was poisoned? Tell your cousin not
to let on that he is a detective. If he does, his life may be at risk.'

*

The next day, we left in a taxi at half past six in the morning
and went to see Bibi ka Makbara (also known as the 'second
Taj Mahal'). Then we went to the Buddhist caves. The taxi
dropped us at the bottom of a hill. A series of steps led to the
caves. Mr Bose had accompanied us, and was talking
constantly about ancient art, most of which went over my
head. I still couldn't think of him as a criminal, but caught
Lalmohan Babu giving him sidelong glances. This often made
him stumble, but he did not stop.

Two other men had already gone into the caves. I had seen
them climbing the steps before us. One of them was a bald
American tourist, dressed in a colourful bush shirt and shorts;
the other was a guide from the tourist department.

Feluda took out his Pentax camera from his shoulder bag
and began taking photos of the hills, the view and,
occasionally, of us. Each time he peered at us through the
camera, Lalmohan Babu stopped and smiled, looking
somewhat self-conscious. After a while, I was obliged to tell
him that he didn't necessarily have to stop walking and, in fact,
photos often came out quite well even if one didn't smile.

When we reached the caves, Feluda suddenly said, 'You
two carry on, I'll join you in a minute. I must take a few photos
from the other side.'

'Don't miss the second and the seventh cave,' Mr Bose

called out to us, 'The first five are all in this area, but numbers six to nine are half a mile away, on the eastern side. A road runs round the edge of the hill.'

The bright sun outside was making me feel uncomfortably hot, but once I stepped into the first cave, I realized it was refreshingly cool inside. But there wasn't much to see. It was obvious that it had been left incomplete, and what little work had been done had started to crumble. Even so, Mr Bose began inspecting the ceiling and the pillars with great interest, jotting things down in his notebook. Lalmohan Babu and I went into the second cave. Feluda had given us a torch. We now had to switch it on. We were in a large hall, at the end of which was a huge statue of the Buddha. I shone the torch on the walls, to find that beautiful figures had been carved on these. Lalmohan Babu was silent for a few moments, taking it all in. Then he remarked, 'Did you realize, Tapesh, how physically strong these ancient artists must have been? I mean, a knowledge of art and a creative imagination alone wasn't enough, was it? They had to pick up hammers and chisels and knock through such hard rock . . . makes the mind boggle, doesn't it?'

*

The third cave was even larger, but the guide was speaking so loudly and rapidly that we couldn't stay in it for more than a few seconds. 'Where did your cousin go?' Lalmohan Babu asked as we emerged, 'I can't see him anywhere.'

This was true. I had assumed Feluda would catch up with us, but he was nowhere to be seen. Nor was Mr Bose. 'Let's check the other caves,' Lalmohan Babu suggested.

The fourth and the fifth caves were not far, but something told me Feluda had not gone there. I began to feel faintly uneasy. We started walking towards cave number six, which was half a mile away. This side of the hill was barren and rocky, there were few plants apart from the occasional small bush. I glanced at my watch. It was only a quarter past eight, but we could not afford to stay here beyond ten o'clock, for Mr Mallik was going to arrive at eleven.

Fifteen minutes later, we looked up and saw another cave. It was probably cave number six. There was no way of telling whether Feluda had come this way. Lalmohan Babu kept peering at the ground in the hope of finding footprints. It was a futile exercise, really, since the ground was absolutely dry.

Was there any point in going any further? Might it help if we called his name?

'Feluda! Feluda!' I started shouting.

'Pradosh Babu! Felu Babu! Mr Mit-te-er!' Lalmohan Babu joined me.

There was no answer. I began to get a sinking feeling in the pit of my stomach.

Had he climbed up the hill and gone to the other side? Had he seen or heard something that made him forget all about us?

After a while, Lalmohan Babu gave up. 'He's obviously nowhere here,' he said, shaking his head, 'or he'd have heard us. Let's go back. I'm sure we'll find him this time. He couldn't have left us without a word. He would not do an irresponsible thing like that, would he?'

We turned back and retraced our steps. In a few minutes, we saw the foreigner and his guide making their way to the sixth cave. I could see that the American was finding it difficult to cope with the guide and his endless patter. 'Look, here's Mr Bose!' Lalmohan Babu cried. Mr Bose was walking towards us with a preoccupied air. He raised his eyes as he heard his name. I went to him quickly and asked, 'Have you seen my cousin?'

'No. Didn't he say he was going off to take pictures?'

'Yes, but that was a long time ago. Maybe he's in one of these caves?'

'No. I have been to each one of them. If he was there, I would certainly have seen him.'

Perhaps my face registered my anxiety, for his tone

softened. 'He may have climbed a little higher. There is, in fact, a fantastic view of the whole city of Aurangabad if you can get to the top of the hill. Why don't you walk on and keep calling his name? He's bound to hear you sooner or later,' Mr Bose said reassuringly, and went off in the direction of cave number six.

Lalmohan Babu lowered his voice. 'I don't like this, Tapesh,' he said, 'I never thought there would be cause for anxiety even before we got to Ellora.'

I pulled myself together and kept walking. My speed had automatically become faster. All I could think of was that we were running out of time, we had to get back to the hotel by eleven to find out if Mr Mallik had arrived, but what were we to do if we couldn't find Feluda?

Without him . . .

'Charminar!' Lalmohan Babu cried suddenly, making me jump.

We were standing near the pillars of the fifth cave. A yellow packet of Charminar was lying under a bush a few feet away from the pillars. It had either not been there when we were here earlier, or we had somehow missed it. Had it dropped out of Feluda's pocket? I picked it up quickly and opened its top. It was empty. Just as I was about to throw it away, Lalmohan Babu said, 'Let me see, let me see!' and took it from me. Then he opened it fully, and a small piece of paper slipped out. There was a brief message scribbled on it in Feluda's handwriting.

'Go back to the hotel', it said.

Considerably relieved, we debated on what to do next. I couldn't think very clearly as Feluda's message said nothing about where he was or why he was asking us to go back. The empty feeling in my stomach continued to linger.

'How can we go back?' Lalmohan Babu said, 'Mr Bose is with us, and he has four more caves to see.'

'Why don't we return to the hotel,' I said slowly, forcing myself to think, 'and send the taxi back to fetch him?'

'Ye-es, we could do that, but shouldn't we stay here to watch his movements?'

'No. I don't think so, Lalmohan Babu. Feluda said nothing about Mr Bose. He just wanted us to go back, and that's what we ought to do.'

'Very well. So be it,' Lalmohan Babu replied, sounding a little disappointed.

Since he wrote mystery stories, Lalmohan Babu occasionally took it into his head to act like a professional sleuth. I could see that he wanted to follow Mr Bose, but I felt obliged to stop him. Our taxi dropped us at the hotel, then went back to the caves. It was nine o'clock. God knew how long we'd have to wait for Feluda.

Neither of us could remain in our room, so we came out of the hotel and began strolling on the road outside. The sky had started to cloud over. If it rained, it might cool down a bit, I thought.

Mr Bose returned at nine forty-five and looked rather puzzled when we told him Feluda had not returned. Naturally, we could not tell him the real reason why we were worried. After all, we did not know him well and Lalmohan Babu was still convinced he was one of the criminals involved. In order to stop him from asking further questions, I said quickly, 'I'm afraid my cousin often does things without telling others. He's done this before—I mean, he's gone off like this, but has returned later. I'm sure he'll be back soon.'

We stayed out for nearly an hour, then I went back to my room and began reading *Tintin in Tibet*. Just after eleven, I thought I heard a train whistle, and at quarter to twelve, a car drew up outside in the porch. Unable to contain myself, I went out to have a look.

Two men got out of the taxi. One of them was of medium height and pretty stout. His broad shoulders seemed to start just below his jaws; his neck was almost non-existent. For some reason, he seemed as if he might easily fly into a temper. The other man was just the opposite: tall, lanky, wearing bell-bottoms and a loose, cotton embroidered shirt. His face was covered by an unkempt beard and his hair rippled down to his shoulders. He looked like a hippie. The stout man had an old leather suitcase; the hippie had a new canvas bag. Both walked into the hotel. Another taxi arrived as soon as these men had gone in.

Jayant Mallik got out of it.

A sudden surge of relief swept over me. At least, this meant that we were on the right track. Our journey from Calcutta had not simply been a wild goose chase.

But where on earth was Feluda?

SIX

I waited for another ten minutes to see if Feluda turned up. When he didn't, I went in and knocked on Lalmohan Babu's door. He opened it at once and said with large, round eyes, 'I've seen it all from the lobby! Don't both those characters look highly suspicious? I wonder if they'll go to Ellora? One of them—you know, the bearded one—might well be into ganja and other drugs.'

I nodded. 'Jayant Mallik has also arrived and checked in,' I told him.

'Really? I didn't see him. I came back to my room as soon as that hippie walked in. What does Mallik look like?'

When I described him, Lalmohan Babu grew even more excited. 'Oh, I think he's been given the room next to mine. I saw him arrive and something struck me as very odd. A bearer was carrying his suitcase, but it was obviously extremely heavy. The poor man could hardly move. And no wonder. Isn't the yakshi's head supposed to be in it?'

I could think of nothing except Feluda's disappearance, so I said, 'What is much more important now is finding Feluda. Never mind about Mallik's suitcase. We've made no arrangements to go to Ellora. Mallik, I am sure, hasn't come here simply to see the sights of Aurangabad. If he reaches Ellora before us, he might damage more—'

'What's that?' Lalmohan Babu interrupted me, staring at the door. I had shut it after coming into the room. Someone had slipped a piece of paper under it. I leapt and grabbed it quickly. It was another note, written by Feluda:

'Collect all our luggage and wait outside the hotel at

one-thirty. Look out for a black Ambassador taxi, number 530. Have your lunch before you leave. All hotel bills have been paid in advance.'

I ran my eyes over these few lines and opened the door. There was no one in sight. A second later, however, Jayant Mallik came out of his room and went busily towards the reception desk. He caught my eye briefly, but did not seem to recognize me.

'He didn't lock his room,' Lalmohan Babu whispered, 'There's no one about. Shall I go in and have a look? Think of the stolen statue—!'

'No! We mustn't do anything like that without telling Feluda. It's nearly one o'clock now. I think we should both be getting ready to leave.'

Sometimes, Lalmohan Babu's enthusiasm caused serious problems. Luckily, he agreed to restrain himself.

We had a quick lunch and came out with our luggage—including Feluda's—at one twenty-five. An empty taxi arrived in a few minutes, but it was green and had a different number. Its driver stopped it a few feet away from us. I saw him raise his arms and stretch lazily.

Three minutes later, another taxi drove up to us. A black Ambassador, number 530. Its driver peered out of the window and said, 'Mr Mitter's party?'

'Yes, yes.' Lalmohan Babu replied with an important air. The driver got out and opened the boot for us. I put the three suitcases in it.

Two men came out of the hotel: Shubhankar Bose and Jayant Mallik. I had seen them having lunch together. They got into the green taxi. It roared to life and shot off down Adalat Road, which headed west. Ellora lay in the same direction.

All this suspense is going to kill me, I thought. Where were *we* going to go? Why wasn't Feluda with us? I couldn't help feeling annoyed with him for having vanished, although I knew very well he never did anything without a good reason.

Another man emerged from the hotel. It was the tall hippie, carrying his canvas bag. He came straight to us, stopped and said, 'Get in, Topshe. Quick, Lalmohan Babu!'

Before I knew it, I was sitting in the back of the taxi. The hippie opened the front door, pushed the bemused Lalmohan Babu in, then got in beside me. '*Chaliye*, Deendayalji,' he said to the driver.

I knew Feluda was good at putting on make-up and disguises, but had no idea he could change his voice, his walk, even the look in his eyes so completely. Lalmohan Babu appeared to be speechless, but he did turn around and shake Feluda's hand. My heart was still speeding like a race horse, and I was dying to know why Feluda was in disguise.

Feluda opened his mouth only when we had left the main town and reached the open country. 'The disguise was necessary,' he explained, 'because Mallik might have recognized me, although we had exchanged only a few words in that garage in Barasat. Naturally, his suspicions would have been aroused if he saw that the same man who had asked him awkward questions was also going to Ellora. I didn't tell you about my plan, for I wanted to see if my make-up was good enough. When neither of you recognized me, I knew I didn't have to worry about Mallik . . . I had these clothes and everything else in my shoulder bag this morning. When I said I was going off to take photos, I actually walked ahead and disappeared into cave number six. Not many people go in there, since it's far from the others and one has to climb higher to get there. When I finished, I climbed down and walked back to town. First I arranged this taxi, then went to the station to see if Mallik got off the train. When he did, I followed his taxi, having collected another passenger who also wanted to go to our hotel. This helped me as I could then share the taxi fare with him. Now, if Shubhankar Bose asks you anything about me, tell him I've sent you a message saying I had to go to Bombay on some urgent business. I cannot remove my disguise until I go to bed. In fact, we shouldn't even let Mallik see that you and I know each other. You and Lalmohan Babu will share a room. I will be in a separate room wherever we stay.'

'But who *are* you?'

'You don't have to bother with a name. I am a photographer. I'm here to take photos for the *Asia* magazine of Hong Kong.'

'OK. What about Lalmohan Babu and myself?'

'You are his nephew. He teaches history in the City College. You are a student in the City School. You are interested in painting, but you want to join your uncle's college next year to study history. Your name is Tapesh Mukherjee. Lalmohan Babu need not change his name, but please read up on Ellora. Basically, all you need to remember is that the Kailash temple was built during the reign of Raja Krishna of the Rashtrakut dynasty, in the eighth century.'

Lalmohan Babu repeated these words to himself, then took out his little red notebook and noted them down, although writing wasn't easy in the moving car. Now I could see why Feluda had asked him to come with us. He must have known he'd have to be in disguise and pretend he didn't know me. Lalmohan Babu's presence ensured that there was an extra pair of eyes to check on Mallik's movements, and I had an adult to accompany me. I didn't mind having to call Lalmohan Babu 'uncle', but pretending Feluda was a total stranger was going to be most difficult. But I had no choice.

I looked out of the window. There were hills in the distance, and the land on either side of the road was dry and barren. Cactus grew here and there, but it was a different kind of cactus, not the familiar prickly pear I had seen elsewhere. These bushes were larger and taller by several feet.

Another car behind us had been honking for sometime. Our driver slowed down slightly to let it pass. It had the bald American we had seen this morning, and the stout man who had travelled with Feluda in the same taxi.

Half an hour later, we found ourselves getting closer to

the distant hills. To our left stretched a small town, called Khuldabad. We were going to stay in the dak bungalow here. At any other time, it would have been impossible to find rooms at such short notice. Thank goodness it was not the regular tourist season. However, the absence of tourists also meant that the thieves and vandals could have a field day.

A little later, to our right, the first of the many caves of Ellora came into view.

'To the dak bungalow?' our driver asked, 'Or would you like to see the caves first?'

'No, let's go straight to the dak bungalow,' Feluda replied.

Our car made a left turn where the road curved towards Khuldabad. I was still staring at the rows of caves in the hills. Which one of them was Kailash?

There were two major places to stay in Khuldabad. One was the dak bungalow where we were booked, and the other was the more expensive and posh Tourist Guest House. The two stood side by side, separated by a strong fence. I spotted the green taxi standing outside the guest house, which meant that was where Jayant Mallik had checked in. Our bungalow was smaller, but neat and compact. Feluda paid the driver, then asked him to wait for fifteen minutes. We would leave our things in our rooms, and go to Kailash. The driver could drop us there, and return to Aurangabad.

There were four rooms in the bungalow. Each had three beds. Feluda could have remained with us, but decided to take a separate room. 'Remember,' he whispered before he left us, 'your surname is Mukherjee. Lalmohan Babu is your uncle . . . Rashtrakut dynasty . . . eighth century . . . Raja Krishna . . . I'll join you in ten minutes.' Then he went into his own room and shouted, 'Chowkidar!' in a voice that was entirely different from his own.

Lalmohan Babu and I had a quick wash and went into the dining hall, where we were supposed to wait for Feluda. We found another gentleman in it, the same man we had just seen travelling with the American. Clearly, he was going to stay in the bungalow with us. At first, he had struck me as a boxer or a wrestler. Now I noticed his eyes: they were bright and intelligent, which suggested he was educated and, in fact, might well be a writer or an artist, for all I knew. His eyes twinkled as they caught mine.

'Off to Kailash, are you?' he asked with a smile.

'Yes, yes,' Lalmohan Babu replied eagerly, 'We are from Calcutta. I am a . . . what d'you call it . . . professor of history in the City College; and this is my nephew, you see.'

There was no need to tell him anything else. But, possibly because he was nervous about playing a new role, Lalmohan Babu went on speaking, 'I thought . . . you know . . . that we must see this amazing creation of the Rashtraput—I mean kut—dynasty. My nephew is . . . you know . . . very interested in art. He wants to get into an art college. He paints quite well, you know. Bhuto, don't forget to take your drawing book.'

I said nothing in reply, for I had not brought my drawing book.

Thankfully, Feluda came out at this moment and glanced casually at us.

'If any of you want to go to the caves, you may come with me. I've still got my taxi,' he said in his new voice.

'Oh, thank you, that's very kind,' Lalmohan Babu turned to him, looking relieved. Then courtesy made him turn back to the other gentleman. 'Would you like to come with us?' he asked.

'No, thank you. I'll go later. I must have a bath first.'

We went out of the bungalow.

'Tell me a bit more about the history of this place, Felu Babu,' Lalmohan Babu pleaded in a low voice, 'I can't manage unless I have a few more details.'

'Do you know the names of different periods in Indian history?'

'Such as?'

'Such as Maurya, Sunga, Gupta, Kushan, Chola . . . things like that?'

Lalmohan Babu turned pale. Then, getting into the taxi, he said, 'Tell you what, why don't I pretend to be deaf? Then, if anyone asks me anything about the history of the caves, or anything else I might find difficult to answer, I can simply ignore them. Isn't that a good idea?'

'All right. I have no objection to that, but remember your acting must be consistent at all times.'

'No problem with that. Anything would be better than trying to remember historical facts. Didn't you see how I messed things up just now? I mean, saying "put" instead of "kut" was hardly the right thing to do, was it?'

We were passing the guest house. Jayant Mallik was standing outside, his hands in his pockets, staring at our bungalow. The green Ambassador was still parked by the road. On seeing Mr Mallik, Feluda took out a small comb from his bag and passed it to me. 'Change your parting,' he said, 'Make a right parting.' I looked at myself in the rear view mirror and quickly changed the parting in my hair as Feluda suggested. Who knew a little thing like that would make such a lot of difference? Even to my own eyes, my face looked different.

We reached the main road. Another road rose up the hill from here, curved around and finally brought us to the famous Kailash temple. We got out here, and the taxi returned to Aurangabad.

At first, I didn't realize what the temple was like. However, as soon as I'd passed through its huge entrance, my head began reeling. For a few moments, I forgot all about the yakshi's head, the gang of crooks, Mr Mallik, Shubhankar Bose, everything. All I was aware of was a feeling of complete bewilderment. I closed my eyes and tried to imagine a group of men, carving the whole temple out of the hill twelve hundred years ago, using no other tools but hammers and chisels. But I could not. It seemed as if the temple had always been there. It couldn't be man-made at all. Or maybe it had been created by magic; or perhaps—as Feluda's book had suggested—creatures from a different planet had come and built it.

The temple had hills rising on three sides. A narrow passage went around it. On both sides of the temple were a number of caves—that looked like cells—which had more statues in them. We started walking down the passage to go around the temple. Feluda kept up a running commentary, 'This place is three hundred feet in length, one hundred and fifty feet in width and the height of the temple is a hundred feet. Two hundred thousand tonnes of rock must have been excavated to build it . . . they built the top first, then worked their way down to the base . . . the statues include gods and goddesses, men and women, animals, events from the *Ramayana* and the *Mahabharata*, the lot. Just think of their skill, the precision of their calculations, their knowledge of engineering, quite apart from the aesthetics . . . ' he stopped. There were footsteps coming towards us. Feluda fell behind deliberately and began inspecting the statue of Ravana shaking Kailash.

Shubhankar Bose emerged from behind the temple. In his hand was a notebook, and a bag hung from his shoulder. He seemed engrossed in looking at the carvings. Then his eyes fell on us. He smiled, then seemed to remember something and asked anxiously, 'Any news of your cousin?'

'Yes,' I replied, trying to sound casual, 'he sent a message. He had to go to Bombay on some urgent work. He'll be back soon.'

'Oh, good.' Mr Bose went back to gazing at the statues. A faint click behind us told me Feluda had taken a picture. His camera was hanging from his neck. If he was to pass himself off as a photographer, the camera naturally had to stay with him whenever he went out.

I turned my head slightly and saw that Feluda was following us. We finished walking around the temple, and had almost reached the main entrance again when we saw someone else. Blue shirt, white trousers. Mr Jayant Mallik. He had probably just arrived. He was standing quietly, but moved towards the statue of an elephant as soon as he saw us. In his hand was the same bag I had seen him carrying before. He had travelled from Barasat to Calcutta with it. I had seen him walk into Queen's Mansion, clutching it. Feluda had now almost caught up with us. I was dying to know what that bag contained. Why didn't Feluda go up to the man, grab him by his collar and challenge him straightaway? Why didn't he say, 'Where's that broken head? Take it out it at once!'

But no, I knew Feluda would not do that. He could not, without sufficient evidence. It was true that Mallik had gone to Sidikpur where that plane had crashed; it was true that he had travelled all the way to Ellora, and had been heard speaking to someone in Bombay, talking about a daughter having returned to her father. But that was not really enough. Feluda would have to wait a bit longer before speaking to him.

There was, however, one way of finding out if Mallik's bag contained anything heavy. I saw Feluda walk past us, go up to Mallik and give him a push. 'Oh, sorry!' he said quickly, and began focusing his camera on a statue. I saw the bag swing from side to side with the push. Its contents did not appear to be very heavy.

We left the temple. On our way out, we saw two other men. One of them was the stout gentleman Lalmohan Babu had recently tried to impress, and the other was the bald American.

The former was explaining something with elaborate gestures; the latter was nodding in agreement.

For some strange reason, I suddenly began to think everyone around us was a suspicious character. Each one of them should be watched closely.

Was Feluda thinking the same thing?

Feluda wanted to stop at the guest house on our way back. 'I want to see what newspapers they get,' he said by way of an explanation.

Lalmohan Babu and I returned to the bungalow. We were both feeling hungry, so Lalmohan Babu called out to the chowkidar and asked him to bring us tea and biscuits. The dining room faced the small lobby. The room to its right—number one—was ours. Number two was empty. Opposite these two were rooms three and four. The stout gentleman was in one of them, and Feluda had the other.

Lalmohan Babu was still in a mood to snoop. 'Listen, Tapesh,' he said, sipping his tea, 'I think we can leave the American out of this, at least for the moment. That leaves us with three other people: Bose, Mallik and that man who's staying here. We know something about Bose and Mallik—true or false, God only knows—but we know absolutely nothing about the third man, not even his name. We could peep into his room now, it doesn't appear to be locked.'

I did not like the idea, so I said, 'What if the chowkidar sees us?'

'He cannot see us if I go in, and you stay here to look out for him. If you see the chowkidar coming this way, start coughing. I will get out of that room at once. I think your cousin will appreciate a helping hand. This man's suitcase also struck me as quite heavy.'

The whole world was suddenly full of heavy suitcases. But I could not stop him. To be honest, although I had never done anything like this before for anyone except Feluda, there was a scent of adventure in the suggestion, so I found myself agreeing.

I went to the back veranda. There was a small courtyard facing the veranda, across which was the kitchen and, next to it, the chowkidar's room. A cycle stood outside this room. A boy of about twelve—presumably his son—was cleaning it with great concentration. I turned my head as I heard a faint creaking noise and saw Lalmohan Babu sneak into room number three. A couple of minutes later, it was he who coughed loudly to indicate that he had finished his job. I returned to our room.

'There was nothing much in there,' Lalmohan Babu said, 'His suitcase seemed pretty old, but it was locked and it did not open even when I pulled the handle. On the table was an empty spectacle-case with "Stephens Company, Calcutta" stamped on it, a bottle of indigestion pills and a tube of Odomos. Apart from these things, there was nothing that I . . .'

'Whose possessions are you talking about?' asked Feluda. We looked up with a start. He had walked into our room silently, almost like a ghost.

This called for an honest confession. Much to my surprise, he did not get cross with either of us. All he said was, 'Was there any particular reason for doing this?'

'No, it's just that we don't know anything about the man, do we?' Lalmohan Babu tried to explain, 'I mean, he hasn't even told us his name. And he looks kind of hefty, doesn't he? Didn't you say there was a whole gang involved in this? So I thought . . . '

'So you thought he must be one of them? There was no need to search his room just to get his name. He's called R N Raxit. His name's written on one side of his suitcase. I don't think we need to know any more about him at this moment. Please don't go into his room again. It simply means taking unnecessary risks. After all, we haven't got any concrete reason to suspect him.'

'Very well. That just leaves the American.'

'He's called Lewison, Sam Lewison. Another Jew, and also very wealthy. He owns an art gallery in New York.'

'How do you know all this?' I asked, surprised.

'The manager of the guest house told me. We got talking. He's a very nice man, passionately fond of detective novels. In fact, he's been waiting for thieves and crooks to arrive here ever since he read about the thefts in other temples.'

'Did you tell him why you were here?'

'Yes. He can help us a great deal. Don't forget Mallik is staying in his guest house. Apparently, Mallik has already tried to ring someone in Bombay, but the call didn't come through.'

That night, all four guests in the bungalow sat down to dinner together. Feluda did not speak a word. Mr Raxit turned to Lalmohan Babu and tried to make conversation by asking him if he specialized in any particular period of history. In answer to that, Lalmohan Babu said he didn't know very much about pyramids, except that they were in Egypt. Then he went back to dunking pieces of chapati into his bowl of daal. Mr Raxit cast me a puzzled glance. I placed a hand on my ear and shook my head to indicate that my 'uncle' was hard of hearing. Mr Raxit nodded vigorously and refrained from asking further questions.

After dinner, Feluda went straight to his room and Lalmohan Babu and I went out for a walk. It was quite windy outside. A pale moon shone between patches of dark clouds. From somewhere came the fragrance of hasnahana. Lalmohan Babu, inspired by all this, decided to start singing a classical raga. I suddenly felt quite lighthearted. Just at that moment, we saw a man walking towards us from the guest house. Lalmohan Babu stopped singing (which was a relief since he was singing perfectly out of tune) and stood still. As the man got closer, I recognized him. It was Shubhankar Bose. 'I wish your cousin was here!' Lalmohan Babu whispered.

'Out for a walk, eh?' Mr Bose asked. Then he cleared his

throat, looked around a couple of times, lowered his voice and said, 'Er . . . do you happen to know that man in the blue shirt?'

This time, Lalmohan Babu couldn't pretend to be deaf. Mr Bose had spoken with him before.

'Why, did *he* say he knew us?' Lalmohan Babu asked.

Mr Bose looked over his shoulder again. 'That man is most peculiar,' he told us, 'He says he is interested in Indian art and this is his first visit to Ellora. Yet, when I met him at the temple, he didn't seem moved by any of it. I mean, not at all. *I* felt just as thrilled by everything, even though this is my second visit. Now, if the man does not care for art and sculpture, why is he here? Why is he pretending to be something he clearly isn't?'

We remained silent. What could we say?

'Have you read the papers recently?' Mr Bose went on.

'Why do you ask?'

'Pieces of our ancient art are being sold off. Statues from temples are disappearing overnight.'

'Really? No, I didn't know that. What a shame! It's a regular crime, isn't it?' Lalmohan Babu declared. His acting was not very convincing, but luckily Mr Bose did not seem to notice. He came closer and added, 'The man left the guest house a while ago.'

'Which man?'

'Mr Mallik.'

'What!' We both spoke together. Lalmohan Babu was right. Feluda ought to have been here.

'Why don't we go, too?' Mr Bose asked, his voice trembling with excitement.

'N-now? Wh-where to?' Lalmohan Babu stammered.

'To the caves.'

'But they must be closed now. Surely there are chowkidars?'

'Yes, but there are only two guards for thirty-four caves. So *that* shouldn't be a problem. I saw Mallik leave with a bag. He and that hippie in your bungalow keep going about with bags. In fact, that hippie also strikes me as suspicious. Do you know who he is?'

Lalmohan Babu nearly choked. 'He . . . he is a photographer. A very good one. He showed us some of his photos. He's here on an assignment.'

Someone came out of the bungalow. It was Mr Raxit, carrying a stout walking stick in one hand, a torch in the other. He was wearing a dark, heavy raincoat. He stopped for a minute to shout into Lalmohan Babu's ear: 'After dinner, walk a mile!' Then he smiled and disappeared in the direction of the guest house. Mr Bose said, 'Good night!' and followed him. Lalmohan Babu frowned and said, 'Why did that man tell me to walk a mile?'

'That should help your digestion. Come on now, let's go and find Feluda. He must be told what we just heard. Everyone seems to have gone off to the caves. I don't like it. Let's see what Feluda thinks.'

It was dark inside the bungalow, except for a lantern in the chowkidar's room. This surprised us. Mr Raxit had naturally switched off his light before going out, and so had we. But why was Feluda's door closed? Why couldn't I see any light under it? Had he already gone to sleep? It was only ten-thirty.

His room had a window that opened out on the veranda. At this moment, however, it was firmly shut and the curtains drawn. I walked up to it and softly called out Feluda's name. There was no reply. He must have gone out. But if he had used the main exit, we would certainly have seen him. Perhaps he had gone out of the little back door behind the chowkidar's room?

Rather foolishly, we went back to our own room and switched the light on. At once, our eyes fell on a piece of paper that was lying on the floor. 'Stay in your room,' it said in Feluda's handwriting.

'Tapesh, my boy,' Lalmohan Babu said with a sigh, 'do you know what is worrying me the most? It's your cousin's behaviour. That is what is most mystifying. Otherwise, frankly, I cannot see too many mysteries in this case.'

Feluda had told us to stay in, but had said nothing about when he might return. There was no question of going to bed. So I spent the next thirty minutes playing noughts-and-crosses with Lalmohan Babu. Then he said he'd tell me the plot of his next novel. 'This time,' he announced, 'I've introduced a new type of fight. My hero's hands and feet are going to be tied, but he'll still manage to defeat the villain, simply by using his head.'

I was about to ask whether by this he meant Prakhar Rudra's brain power, or was his hero simply going to butt his way to victory, when Feluda returned. We looked up expectantly, but he said nothing. By this time, we had both learnt that if Feluda did not wish to part with information, even a thousand questions couldn't make him open his mouth. On the other hand, he'd tell us everything, if *he* so wished.

What he finally said took us by surprise. 'Lalmohan Babu,' he asked solemnly, 'did you bring a weapon this time?'

Lalmohan Babu had a passion for collecting weapons. When we had gone to Rajasthan, he had taken a Nepali dagger with him. Then, when he went to Shimla, he had a boomerang. At Feluda's question, his eyes started glinting. 'Yes, sir,' he said, 'This time, I've got a bomb.'

'A *bomb*?'

I could hardly believe him. Lalmohan Babu opened his suitcase and took out a heavy brown object, shaped a little like a torch. He passed it to Feluda, saying, 'My neighbour Mr Samaddar's son, Utpal, is in the army. He came to my house last March and gave it to me. "Look, Uncle, see what I brought for you!" he said, "This is a bomb. It is used in serious warfare." Utpal loves reading my novels.'

Feluda inspected it briefly before saying, 'Let me keep this. It's too dangerous to remain anywhere else.'

'Very well. How many metaguns do you think it weighs?'

What he meant obviously was 'megaton', but Feluda

ignored this last remark completely. He put the 'bomb' in his shoulder bag and said, 'Let's go out. Everyone else has gone, so why should we stay in?'

When we left the dak bungalow, it was half past eleven. The moon was now almost totally obliterated by clouds. It was still windy. One of the rooms in the guest house had a light on. It was the American's room, Feluda said. It was impossible to tell whether Bose and Mallik had returned.

By the time we reached the main road, the eastern sky was heavily overcast. A loud rumble in the sky made Lalmohan Babu exclaim, 'Good heavens, what if we get caught in the rain?'

'If we can get to the caves before it starts raining, we'll have plenty of places to seek shelter,' Feluda reassured us.

Fortunately, it remained dry for quite sometime after this. We reached Kailash, but Feluda did not go in through the main entrance. He turned left instead. A little later, he left the path and began climbing up the hill. I was familiar enough with his techniques to realize that he was trying to see if there was another way to get into the temple, without using the main passage. There were bushes and loose stones everywhere, but the moonlight—fleeting though it was—helped us find our way.

Feluda turned right. We were now going back the way we came, but were walking several feet above the path that visitors normally used. A few minutes later, Feluda suddenly stopped. He was looking at something on his right. I followed his gaze.

In the distance, it seemed as if a long silk ribbon was spread on the ground. It was the road that led to the main town. A man was quickly walking down this road, either to the guest house or to the bungalow.

'Not Raxit,' Lalmohan Babu whispered.

'How do you know?'

'Raxit was wearing a raincoat.' He was right.

The man turned a corner and vanished from sight. We

resumed walking. Only a few moments later, however, we had to stop again. There was a strange noise—something like a cross between a scrape and a rustle. Where was it coming from?

Feluda sat down. So did we. A large cactus bush hid us from view. The noise continued for sometime, then stopped abruptly.

We emerged cautiously. Huge, dark clouds had now spread all over the sky. We could hardly see our way. Nevertheless, Feluda kept going. Soon, we could vaguely see the temple again. Its spire was before us. Several feet below the spire, on the roof, stood four lions, facing the east, west, north and the south. Far below them were the two elephants that stood at the entrance.

We kept walking. The noise had come from this direction, but I couldn't see anything suspicious. Feluda had a torch, but I knew he wouldn't switch it on, in case it was seen by whoever happened to be in the vicinity.

We passed the temple and came to a cave. It was cave number fifteen. We moved on to the next. Feluda stopped again. I could see that his whole body was tense. 'Torch,' he whispered, 'Someone in number fifteen has switched on a torch. Look at the courtyard in front of it. Doesn't it seem brighter than the others?'

It was true. Neither Lalmohan Babu nor I had noticed it. Only Feluda's sharp eyes had picked it up. We stood holding our breath for a couple of minutes. Then Feluda did something entirely unexpected. He picked up a small pebble and threw it in the direction of the courtyard. I heard it fall with a soft thud. A second later, the faint light coming from the cave went out. The torch was switched off. Then a man came out and slipped away, moving stealthily like a thief. 'Could that be Raxit?' Lalmohan Babu said softly. I couldn't recognize the man, but could see that he was not wearing a raincoat.

What followed next took my breath away. Without a word of warning, Feluda began climbing down. He leapt, crawled, scraped himself on the ground, then swinging from a branch like a monkey, disappeared from sight. I stared speechlessly. Lalmohan Babu said, after a moment's silence, 'He'll do very well in a circus!'

Cave number fifteen was at a lower level. That was where Feluda had gone. Three minutes later (it felt like three hours), he climbed up again, more or less in a similar fashion. How he could do it with a torch in one hand, a bag hanging from his shoulder and a revolver tucked into his waist, I do not know.

'That one's the Das Avatar cave,' he told us, panting, 'It has two storeys, and some exquisite statues.'

'Did you . . . did you see who it was?' I asked breathlessly.

Feluda did not reply immediately. Then he said, 'It's not as simple as I'd thought. It'll take me a while to unravel this tangled mess.'

We found the main path again and climbed down to the bottom of the temple. But Feluda had not finished. He found one of the chowkidars and asked him if he had seen anyone going up.

'No, sir,' the chowkidar replied.

'Did you hear any noise? Anything suspicious at all?'

'No, sir. There's been a lot of thunder. I didn't hear anything else.'

'Can we go into the temple?'

I knew the man would refuse, and he did.

'No, sir. I have orders not to let anyone in at this time of night.'

We made our way back to the bungalow. As we got closer, we saw something extremely strange. Two windows on the eastern side of the building overlooked the street. We could see these from outside. One of them was Feluda's, the other was Mr Raxit's. Feluda's room was in darkness. But a light flashed in Mr Raxit's room. It was the light from a torch, but it did not stay still. In fact, whoever was holding it seemed to have gone mad. The light danced all over the room, then came to the window, shone once in the direction of the guest house, fell and moved on the bushes by the road before going back to the room. We could not see who it was. 'Highly interesting!' Feluda muttered.

We returned to the bungalow. By now, it had started to drizzle, and was pitch dark outside.

EIGHT

I had noticed in the past that our adventures often took totally unexpected turns. When this happened, Feluda seldom lost his equanimity. In fact, I had always marvelled at his ability to keep calm while dealing with unforeseen complications. This time, however, what happened made him very cross.

Before going to bed at night, we had decided to leave early in the morning to go back to the spot where we had heard that funny noise. It required investigation, Feluda said. So we rose at five o'clock and left the bungalow half an hour later after having a cup of tea. Feluda was up before us to replace his make-up. I remembered to maintain a right parting in my hair. Lalmohan Babu expressed the desire to make some change in his appearance as well, but Feluda said 'No!' so firmly that he had to desist.

The caves were going to open for visitors as soon as the sun rose. We wanted to be the first, so we got there at 6 a.m. To our complete astonishment, we found the place crawling with people. A large number of cars and vans were parked outside. It was the sight of a reflector that told me what was going on. This was a film unit. They had arrived from Bombay to shoot a Hindi film, we learnt. The actors hadn't yet arrived, but the rest of the crew were getting things ready. 'Oh no!' Feluda cried in dismay, 'Why couldn't they find some other place?'

A young man was bustling about, clutching a film magazine. Lalmohan Babu called him aside.

'What is the name of this film, do you know?' he asked.

'Oh yes. *Krorpati.*'

'Who's acting in it?'

'Three of the top stars. Today's shots will include Rupa, Arjun Mehrotra and Balwant Chopra. The heroine, hero and the villain.'

The mention of Arjun Mehrotra made Lalmohan Babu grow round-eyed. 'Will there be songs?' he asked.

'No, no. We've come to shoot fights. Stuntmen, doubles and the fight director are all here. The hero will chase the villain from a cave into the main temple.'

'And the heroine?'

'She'll stay in the cave. The villain has imprisoned her in there, you see. But now the hero's here, so the villain has to run for his life. The climax takes place on the spire.'

'The *spire*?'

'Yes.'

'Who's the director?'

'Mohan Sharma. But these shots today will be taken by the fight director, Appa Rao.'

'How long do you think the whole thing will take?'

'Well . . . that's difficult to say. We *hope* to start by ten o'clock. Then we should finish by one.'

That meant they would occupy the whole complex virtually the whole day.

'I don't believe this!' Feluda said through clenched teeth, 'How did they get permission to take the whole place over?'

Since we couldn't get into the temple, we decided to climb over it, just as we'd done the previous night. But even the hills around the temple had men from the film unit setting up equipment. We learnt here that although the film crew were not letting ordinary visitors into the temple, they could not go in themselves, as the official letter giving them the necessary permission to shoot had not yet arrived. It was being brought in a different car. The chowkidar on duty had flatly refused to unlock the main door unless the letter was produced.

Feluda clicked his tongue in annoyance and said, 'Let's not waste any more time. Let's see if we can get into cave number fifteen. At least we can look at those beautiful statues, away from all this noise.'

We climbed down from the other side and were walking towards the cave when we saw a huge yellow American car making its way to the temple. The three major stars and the fight director had arrived.

Feluda had already told us the fifteenth cave was the Das Avatar cave. We ran into two modern *avatars* on our way. They were Lewison and Raxit. We had spotted them from a distance, standing near the entrance and speaking rather animatedly. As we got closer, we heard the American say angrily, 'I see no point in my staying here any longer.' Then he strode off in a huff. Mr Raxit walked up to us, shrugged and smiled somewhat bitterly. 'He was complaining about the arrangements here. I mean, in the guest house. He said to me, "How can you expect me to spend my dollars here, when you don't even know how to fry an egg?" Just because he's rich, he thinks he owns the whole world.'

'That's strange!' Feluda remarked, 'Isn't he supposed to be a connoisseur of art? How can he talk of fried eggs, standing in a place like this, surrounded by the best specimens of Indian art?'

'How,' Lalmohan Babu wanted to know, 'do they fry eggs in America, anyway?'

Mr Raxit opened his mouth to speak, but had to shut it immediately. A loud scream from the temple made us all start violently. Lalmohan Babu was the first to recover. 'That must be the villain!' he exclaimed, 'They've started shooting. The villain's shouting and making his escape.'

But no. A babel had broken out. There were many other voices, also screaming and yelling. There was something wrong, obviously. Feluda had already begun walking in that direction. We followed him quickly. As we returned to the temple's entrance, we saw a man in a purple bush shirt being carried out. He appeared to be unconscious. He was taken to the yellow car. Then came the three stars. Rupa was walking slowly, leaning heavily on Arjun Mehrotra. Balwant was holding her hand, and murmuring into her ear, as if she was a frightened child, in need of comforting.

A second later, we saw the same young man we had spoken to earlier.

'What happened? What's wrong?' Lalmohan Babu asked him.

'There's a ... there's a dead body lying behind the temple. It's horrible!'

'Oh my God! Who was that man they carried out to the car?'

'Appa Rao. He was the first to discover the body. One look, and he fainted.'

Feluda and Mr Raxit had gone into the temple. The film crew were all coming out. There was now no question of shooting a film here today.

Lalmohan Babu and I walked along the passage to our left. To our right, below us, were several statues of elephants and lions. They looked as though they were carrying the whole temple on their shoulders. We stopped as the passage turned right. There was a group of men, peering down into a gorge. Perhaps that was where the body was lying. Mr Raxit emerged from the crowd and stopped us. 'Don't go any further,' he said, 'It's not a pretty sight.' Quite frankly, I had no wish to see the body, but I did feel curious about the dead man. Who was he? Feluda came out and answered this question even before I could ask it.

'Shubhankar Bose,' he said, 'I think he fell off the edge of the cliff straight onto the rocks below.'

'Strange, how strange!' Lalmohan Babu muttered under his breath, 'This is exactly how my own villain, Ghanashyam Karkat, is supposed to die!'

Feluda started walking away, so Lalmohan Babu and I had to move on. Mr Raxit was ahead of us, but he turned and stopped. 'I saw him last night,' he said, shaking his head, 'I told him not to try climbing in the dark. But he paid no attention to me. How was I to know that he was planning to commit suicide?'

Mr Raxit left, having given us something to ponder on. The idea of a suicide had not occurred to me. I looked at Feluda, but he had started to climb the hill on the left of the temple. Mr Bose must have climbed the same hill.

The people gathered near the cliff had gone. Mr Bose's death had, in a way, made things easier for our investigation. Feluda went close to the edge of the cliff and examined the area carefully.

There was a small hole in the ground, only a few feet away from the edge. People had walked over it and around it, making it almost disappear. But when Feluda took out a steel tape from his bag and pushed it in, we realized it was a fairly deep hole. Now Feluda peered closely at the ground again. Lalmohan Babu and I both saw what had claimed his attention.

There was a deep crease on the ground, running from the edge of the cliff to the hole.

'Do you know what this is?' Feluda asked me. I couldn't answer. Feluda went on, 'This mark was left by a rope. Someone had tied a rope to a crowbar, dug the crowbar deep into the ground, and gone down—or tried to go down—the cliff, using that rope. Remember the noise we heard yesterday? It was the noise of the rope being pulled back. Since there was no way to get into the cave below from the front, someone found this way to reach it from the rear.'

'But . . . what sort of a rope could it have been?' Lalmohan Babu asked, 'I mean . . . if you had to climb down a hundred feet, you'd need a remarkably strong rope, wouldn't you?'

'Yes. A nylon rope would to the trick. It would be light, but very, very strong.'

'That means there was a second person here,' I said slowly, 'I mean, apart from Mr Bose.'

'Right. This second person removed the rope, and the crowbar. We don't yet know whether he was Bose's friend or foe, but there is something that indicates he might have been the latter.'

I looked quickly at Feluda. What did he mean? In reply, he took out a small object from his pocket and placed it on his palm. It was a piece of blue cloth, torn presumably from a shirt. Who was wearing a blue shirt yesterday?

Mr Jayant Mallik!

'Where did you find it?' I asked. My voice shook.

'Bose was lying on his stomach. His arms were spread wide. His right hand was closed around this piece of cloth, but a small bit was sticking out between two fingers. He and this other man must have struggled with each other by the cliff. Bose clutched at the shirt the other man was wearing. But then he fell, taking this little piece with him.'

'You mean he was deliberately pushed off the cliff?' Lalmohan Babu gasped, 'You m-mean it was m-m-murder?'

Feluda did not give a direct answer. After a few seconds of silence, he simply said, 'If the statues in the temple are still intact, we must thank Mr Bose for it. It was because of his presence here last night that the thief couldn't get away with it.'

When we climbed down eventually and went back to the main entrance to the temple, the members of the film unit had all disappeared. There were knots of local people, curious and excited. The big American car had been replaced by a jeep. An intelligent and smart looking man—possibly in his mid-thirties—saw Feluda and came forward to greet him. It turned out to be Mr Kulkarni, the manager of the Tourist Guest House.

'We realized only this morning that Mr Bose had not returned last night,' he said, shaking his head regretfully, 'I sent a bearer to look for him, but of course he couldn't find him anywhere.'

'What is going to happen now?' Feluda asked.

'The police in Aurangabad have been informed. They're sending a van to collect the body. Mr Bose had a brother in Delhi. He'll have to be informed, naturally. . . It is really very sad. The man was a true scholar. He came once before, in 1968. I believe he was writing a book on Ellora.'

'Isn't there a police station here?'

'Yes, but it's only a small outpost. An assistant sub-inspector is in charge, a man called Ghote. He's inspecting the body at the moment.'

'Could I meet him?'

'Certainly. Oh, by the way—' Mr Kulkarni stopped, looking doubtfully at Lalmohan Babu and me.

'They are friends, you may speak freely before them,' Feluda said quickly.

'Oh. Oh, I see,' Mr Kulkarni sounded relieved, 'Well, someone rang Bombay this morning.'

'Mallik?'

'Yes.'

'What did he say?'

Mr Kulkarni took out a piece of paper from his pocket and read from it: 'The daughter's fine. Leaving today.'

'Today? Did he tell *you* anything about leaving today?'

'He did. He wanted to leave this morning. But I thought of you, Mr Mitter, and had a word with his driver. Mallik has been told there's something wrong with his car, it'll take a while to repair it. So he cannot leave immediately.'

'Bravo! Thank you, Mr Kulkarni, you've been a great help.'

Mr Kulkarni looked pleased. Feluda lit a Charminar and asked, 'Tell me, what kind of a man is this Ghote?'

'A very good man, I should say. But he doesn't like it here. He longs for a promotion and a posting in Aurangabad. Come with me, I will introduce you to him.'

Mr Ghote had emerged from the cave. Mr Kulkarni brought him over and introduced Feluda as 'a very famous private detective'. Mr Ghote's height was about five feet five inches. His width matched his height and, to top it all, he had a moustache like Charlie Chaplin. But his movements were surprisingly brisk and agile.

'Why don't you go back to the bungalow?' Feluda said to me, 'I'll have a word with Mr Ghote, and then join you there.'

Neither of us had the slightest wish to return without Feluda, but there was no point in arguing. So we went back. On reaching the bungalow, we realized we were both quite hungry; so I stopped to tell the chowkidar to send us toast and eggs. Then I walked into our room, to find Lalmohan Babu sitting on his bed, looking a little foolish.

'Tell me, Tapesh,' he said on seeing me, 'did we lock our room before going out this morning?'

'Why, no! There was no need to. We have nothing worth

stealing. Besides, the cleaners usually come in the morning, so I thought . . . why, has anything been taken?'

'No. But someone has been through my things. Whoever did it sat on my bed and opened my suitcase. In fact, when I came in, the bed was still warm. See if he touched your suitcase as well?'

He had, I realized this the minute I opened the case. Nothing was in place. Not only that, one of my pillows was lying on the floor. Judging by the way my chappals had been thrown in two different directions, the intruder had even looked under the bed.

'I was most worried about my notebook,' Lalmohan Babu confided, 'But he didn't take it, thank God.'

'Did he take anything else?'

'No, I don't think so. What about you?'

'The same. Whoever came in was looking for something specific, I think. He didn't find it here.'

'Let's ask the chowkidar if he saw anything.'

But the chowkidar could not help. He had gone out shopping for a while, so if anyone stole in while he was out, he couldn't have seen him. Normally, theft was a rare occurrence in these parts. The chowkidar seemed most puzzled by the thought that anyone's room should be broken into and their belongings searched.

Had Feluda's room been similarly ransacked? I went to have a look, but saw that his room was locked. He had to be extra careful because of his disguise. 'Should we try asking Raxit?' Lalmohan Babu asked.

Having seen the flashing light in his room the night before, I was feeling rather curious about the man. So I agreed and we both went up to his room. I knocked softly. The door opened almost at once.

'What is it? Come in.'

Mr Raxit did not seem very pleased to see us; but we went into his room, anyway.

'Did anyone break into your room as well?' Lalmohan Babu asked as soon as he'd stepped in.

From the way Mr Raxit looked at Lalmohan Babu, it was obvious that he was not in a good mood. He spoke in a low voice, but his tone was sharp. 'What's the use of speaking to you?' he said, 'You can't hear a word, can you? Let me speak to your nephew. Not only did someone get into my room, but he actually removed something valuable.'

'What . . . what was it?' I asked timidly.

'My raincoat. I had bought it in England, and had been using it for the last twenty-five years.' Lalmohan Babu looked at me silently. He wasn't supposed to have heard anything. I repeated the words to him, speaking loudly, trying not to laugh.

'Could it have been stolen last night?' Lalmohan Babu suggested, 'We saw you looking for something. I mean, we saw your torch . . . '

'No. A small bat had somehow got into my room last night. I switched the main lights off and used my torch to get rid of it. Nothing was stolen yesterday. It happened this morning. I believe the culprit is that young boy of the chowkidar's.'

I had to shout once more and repeat the whole thing to Lalmohan Babu.

'I am very sorry to hear this,' Lalmohan Babu said gravely, 'We must keep an eye on the boy.'

There didn't seem to be anything else to say. We apologized for disturbing him and came away.

The chowkidar had served us breakfast in the dining hall. We began eating. I had no idea what American fried eggs tasted like, but what I had been given here was quite tasty. I kept wondering who might have broken into our room, but decided in the end that it must have been the chowkidar's son. I had seen him walking in the backyard and throwing curious glances in the direction of our rooms.

Feluda had told us to go back to the bungalow, but hadn't

said that we had to stay in. So after breakfast, we locked our room, and went out in the street.

The guest house was not clearly visible from the main gate of our bungalow, the view being partially obstructed by a large tree. The sudden noise of a car starting made us go forward quickly. Now the guest house was fully visible. The taxi that had brought Mr Raxit and Lewison from Aurangabad was now ready to leave. The luggage-rack on its roof was loaded. Mr Sam Lewison, the American millionaire, was giving a tip to one of the bearers.

But who was that?

Another man had come out of the guest house and was speaking to Lewison. Lewison nodded twice, which clearly meant that he had agreed to do something for the other man. The latter went back to the guest house and reappeared with a suitcase. The driver opened the boot of the car, and placed the suitcase in it. My heart began beating faster. Lalmohan Babu clutched my sleeve. There could be no doubt about the implication of what we had just seen. Mr Jayant Mallik was not going to wait for his own car to be repaired. He was trying to escape with Sam Lewison.

The driver took his seat.

'The cycle!' I cried, 'The chowkidar's cycle!'

The car started. I ran back to the bungalow and managed to drag the cycle out. Luckily, no one saw me.

'Come on!' I said to Lalmohan Babu. He stood there looking as though he had never ridden on the crossbar of a cycle before. But there was no time to argue, our culprit was running away. He jumped up a second later, and I began pedalling as fast as I could. Feluda had taught me to cycle when I was seven. Now I could put it to good use.

If we had walked, it would have taken us twenty minutes to get back to the temple. I covered that distance in five. There was Feluda, and Ghote, and Kulkarni!

'Feluda!' I panted, 'Mr Mallik ran off . . . in that American's car . . . five minutes ago!'

Just that one remark from me set so many things in motion that the whole thing now seems almost like a blur. Mr Ghote jumped into his jeep, with Feluda beside him, and Lalmohan Babu and myself at the back. I had no idea even a jeep could travel at 60 mph. Very soon, we saw Lewison's taxi, overtook it and made it stop. Lewison got out, looking furious and giving vent to his anger by uttering a range of specially chosen American swear words. These had no effect on Mr Ghote. He ignored Lewison completely and approached Mallik, who turned visibly pale. Mr Ghote then opened his suitcase, quelling an abortive attempt by Mallik to stop him, and took out an object wrapped heavily in a large Turkish towel. With one swift movement, he removed the towel and revealed the yakshi's head. Sam Lewison shut up immediately, gaped in horror and stammered, 'B-b-but . . . b-but I . . . I . . . !' Lalmohan Babu heaved a sigh of relief and proclaimed, 'End's well that all's well!' Finally Lewison was allowed to travel back to Aurangabad. We returned to Khuldabad with the culprit, caught red-handed.

Mr Ghote took Mallik away, to keep him somewhere in the police outpost. He went quietly, too dazed to say anything.

We were dropped at the guest house, for Mr Kulkarni was waiting anxiously for our return. He appeared very pleased on being told that our mission had been entirely successful. However, Feluda seemed to pour cold water over his enthusiasm by saying, 'We haven't yet finished our job, Mr Kulkarni. There's plenty more to be done. Don't forget to make enquiries about that number in Bombay, and let me know as soon as you hear anything.'

I didn't understand what this last instruction meant, but thought no more about it.

Mr Kulkarni had ordered coffee for all of us. When it arrived, I suddenly remembered we had not told Feluda about our room being searched. He sipped his coffee quietly as I quickly explained what had happened. Then he frowned and asked Mr Kulkarni, 'What sort of a man is that chowkidar?'

'Who, Mohanlal? A very good man, most trustworthy. He's been doing that job for the last seventeen years. I have never heard anyone complain against him.'

Feluda thought for a second, then turned to me. 'Are you sure nothing was stolen?'

'Yes. We are both absolutely sure. Mr Raxit thinks it was the chowkidar's boy who did it.'

'Very well. Let's go and have a look, especially since Lalmohan Babu says the intruder actually sat on his bed and kept it warm for him. See you soon, Mr Kulkarni, perhaps you had better keep this with you.' He passed the yakshi's head—still wrapped in the towel—to Mr Kulkarni, who put it in a safe in his office and locked it.

We returned to the bungalow. Feluda came into our room with us, bolted the door and then went through our belongings with meticulous care. Apart from his clothes, Lalmohan Babu's suitcase contained a small box of homoeopathic pills, two books on criminology, one on Baluchistan and his own notebook. For some reason, Feluda spent a long time going through this notebook, but did not tell us what was so intriguing about it. Finally, he put everything away and said, 'If my guesses turn out to be correct, this whole business is going to be settled tonight, one way or the other. If that happens, you will both have to play an important role. Please remember, at all times, that I am with you, keeping an eye on you, even if you cannot see me. Don't tell anyone about Mallik's arrest. And don't leave your room. In any case, I don't think you can, for it looks like it's going to rain.'

Feluda peered out of the window as he spoke, then got up silently and went and stood by it. I followed him. We were looking out of the western side. There was a lawn, across which stood a number of tall trees. I could recognize eucalyptus amongst them. A man came out of the trees, crossed the lawn and went to the front of the bungalow. A minute later, he entered the dining hall. This was followed by the sound of a room being unlocked, and then locked again from inside.

Feluda nodded and muttered 'Yes, yes!' almost to himself.

The man who had come in was Mr Raxit.

'Wait until you hear from me,' Feluda said, 'and then simply do as you're told. Don't be afraid.'

He opened the door and went out.

We remained in our room. Thunder rumbled outside. The sky was overcast.

Staring at the walls, thinking things over, it suddenly occurred to me that the man who was probably the most mysterious was Mr Raxit. We did not know anything about him.

And Mallik? How much had we learnt about Jayant Mallik?

Not much. Not enough. Suddenly, it seemed to me that we had made no progress at all.

TEN

It began pouring soon after twelve o'clock. The rain was accompanied by frequent thunder. Lalmohan Babu and I sat in our room trying—in vain—to work out what possible role we might have to play later in the day. Mallik had been arrested, the yakshi's head was safely locked away. As far as we were concerned, that was the end of the story. What else could Feluda be thinking of?

The chowkidar told us at one o'clock that lunch was ready. We went into the dining hall without Feluda. He was probably having lunch with Mr Kulkarni in the guest house.

Mr Raxit joined us. He had seemed extremely cross this morning when we had spoken to him, but now he appeared cheerful once more. 'On a day like this,' he said, 'a Bengali ought to have khichuri, pakoras and fried hilsa. I have lived out of Bengal for many years, but haven't forgotten Bengali habits.'

The meal we were served here was different, but no less tasty. I finished my bowl of daal, and had just helped myself to the meat curry, when a car drew up outside the front door and a thin, squeaky voice cried: 'Chowkidar!' The chowkidar rushed out, clutching an umbrella. Mr Raxit soaked a piece of his chapati in the curry, put it in his mouth and said, 'A tourist? In this weather?'

A tall man walked in, taking off his raincoat. Most of his hair was grey. He had a short moustache and goatee, and he wore glasses. 'I've already had my lunch,' he told the chowkidar, who was carrying his aged leather suitcase. Then he turned to us and asked, 'Who has been arrested?'

Feluda had told us not to say anything about Mallik's arrest, so we simply stared foolishly. Mr Raxit gave a start and said, 'Arrested?'

'Yes. Some vandal. He was apparently trying to steal a statue from one of the caves, and was caught. At least, that's what I've just heard. I only hope they won't decide to close the caves because of this. I've travelled quite far simply to see the statues here. Why, haven't you heard anything?'

'No.

'Anyway, I'm glad the fellow was caught. I must say the police here are quite efficient.'

The man was given the third empty room. He disappeared into it, but we could hear him talking to himself. Perhaps he was slightly mad.

The rain stopped at around two-thirty. Half an hour later, I saw the new arrival walking towards the eucalyptus trees. He came back in five minutes.

The chowkidar brought us our tea at four-thirty. I noticed a small piece of paper on the floor as he left. It turned out to be another message from Feluda: 'Go to cave number fifteen at seven o'clock. Wait in the south-eastern corner on the first floor'.

He was still running a campaign, totally unseen. This had never happened before.

Fortunately, it did not rain again. When we left the bungalow at six-thirty, both Mr Raxit and the man with the goatee appeared to be in their rooms, for their lights were on. Lalmohan Babu muttered a short prayer as we set out. My own feelings were so confused that I am not even going to try to describe them. My hands felt cold. I thrust them into my pockets.

We reached Kailash ten minutes before seven. The western sky was still quite bright since the sun did not set here at this time of year until after six-thirty. The caves and hills seemed darker, but the sky had cleared.

We turned right after reaching Kailash. The next cave was

number fifteen, the Das Avatar cave. It was at this one that Feluda had thrown a pebble last night.

There was no one around. We walked on. The courtyard before the cave was large. There was a small shrine in the middle of it. We crossed it quickly and climbed a few steps to go through the main entrance that took us into the cave. We had been told to find the first floor. I could dimly see a flight of steps going up. God knew if there was anyone already hiding in the dark. We went up the steps, trying not to make any noise at all.

The stairs led us to a huge hall. Rows of carved pillars stood supporting the roof, as though they were carrying it on their heads. There were scenes from Indian mythology, beautifully carved on the northern and the southern walls.

We found the south-eastern corner. It was too dark inside to see clearly. I had taken off my sandals before climbing the stairs, but now the rocky floor felt so cold that I had to put them on again. As neither of us knew how long we might have to wait, we sat down, leaning against the wall. Who knew what was going to happen next in this cave, built twelve hundred years ago, and filled with amazing specimens of ancient art?

Something happened almost immediately. As soon as we had sat down, my eyes fell on something that made me give an involuntary gasp. Only a few feet away from where we were sitting, barely visible in the dark, was a solid round object lying on the floor. Sticking out from under it was a white square object. Neither was a part of the temple decorations. Someone had placed them there deliberately. What could they be? Who had kept them there, and for whom?

'P-paper?' Lalmohan Babu whispered, pointing at the white object.

We rose and went closer. What we saw made us stare in utter disbelief. It was indeed a piece of paper, but what had been used as a paperweight was the yakshi's head! There could be no mistake. We had seen it only this morning—first in Mr Ghote's hand, and then in Mr Kulkarni's, who had locked it away in his safe.

I shone the torch on the piece of paper. It was another message from Feluda, this time addressed to Lalmohan Babu. 'Keep the head with you,' it said, 'If anyone demands it, hand it over to him.'

What could this mean? But there was no time to think. Lalmohan Babu said, 'Jai Guru!' and picked up the head. I put Feluda's message into my pocket, and we returned to our positions.

Our eyes were now getting used to the dark. There appeared to be a faint moonlight outside. We could see a portion of the western sky through the pillars. It had turned a deep purple. Gradually, it changed its hue. Perhaps the moon had risen higher. It didn't seem as dark inside the cave as before.

'Eight o'clock!' Lalmohan Babu muttered, letting go of a long sigh.

Suddenly, a faint noise reached my ears. Someone was coming up the stairs, placing each foot with extreme caution. Then the noise stopped. A second later, the footsteps continued. The man was now walking on flat ground, among the pillars. There, now he was visible through a couple of pillars. He stopped, and looked around. Then, with a click, he lit a lighter. The small flame went out almost as soon as it had appeared, but it was enough to illuminate his face. We recognized him instantly.

Jayant Mallik!

How could he be here? He was supposed to be in police custody. My head began reeling. After this, I thought, if the dead Shubhankar Bose turned up in person, I should not be surprised.

Mr Mallik resumed walking, but did not come toward us. He made his way to the north-eastern corner. That part of the hall was in total darkness. He disappeared from sight.

My throat felt dry. I could hardly think clearly. Only one

thing kept going round and round in my head. Where was
Feluda? Where was Feluda? Where was Feluda? Lalmohan
Babu had once declared he would give up writing crime
stories because his real-life experiences were so much
stranger. What would he say after today?

The moonlight grew stronger as we waited. A dog barked
somewhere in the distance. Then it was quiet once more.

But not for long. A second man was climbing up the steps.
Like Mr Mallik, he stopped for a moment on reaching the flat
surface where the stairs ended. Then we could see him
walking, but could not tell who he was. He did not stop to use
a lighter.

He was coming towards us, getting closer and closer,
walking with slow, measured steps. Then without the slightest
warning, our eyes were dazzled by a powerful light. The man
was shining a torch directly into our eyes. The footsteps came
even closer, and a voice spoke, softly, but with biting sarcasm.

'Dreaming of the moon, weren't you, you puny little
dwarf? Who taught you to write threatening letters? "Come to
the Das Avatar cave at 8 p.m. . . then you'll get back what
you've lost, or else . . ." where did you learn all this, Professor?
A professor of history, didn't you say? Can you hear me now?
Or are you still pretending to be deaf? How did you get
involved in this, anyway? You had noted everything down in
your notebook, hadn't you? I saw it myself—a Fokker
Friendship crashes, a yakshi from Bhubaneshwar gets stolen,
the Kailash temple in Ellora, even plane timings . . . ! Why have
you got a child with you? Is he your bodyguard? Can you see
what I've got in my right hand?'

I had recognized the voice as soon as it had started to
speak. It was Mr Raxit. In his left hand was a torch. In his right
was a pistol.

'I . . . I . . . ' Lalmohan Babu stammered.

'Stop whimpering!' Mr Raxit's voice boomed out,
'Where's the real thing?'

'Here it is. I kept it for you,' Lalmohan Babu offered him the yakshi's head.

Mr Raxit took it with his left hand, making sure his right hand did not waver. 'Not everyone can play this game, do you understand?' he went on, still sounding furious, 'It's not for the likes of you, you stupid little—' he broke off.

A strange thing had started to happen. Great clouds of smoke were coming into the cave, spiralling up and slowly enveloping everything—the pillars, the carvings, the statues. As we stood gaping in absolute amazement at this thick sheet of haze, another voice rang out, almost like a bullet. It was Feluda.

'Mr Raxit!' he called, his voice as cold and hard as the stony floor we were standing on, 'There isn't one, but two revolvers pointing at you at this very moment. Put your gun down. Go on, throw it down.'

'What . . . what's the meaning of this?' Mr Raxit cried, his voice suddenly uncertain.

'Let me explain,' Feluda replied, 'We are here to punish you for your crime, and it isn't just one crime, either. First, you destroyed and damaged a part of India's history. Second, you sold bits of your—and our—own heritage to foreigners. Third, you killed Shubhankar Bose.'

'No! Lies, these are all lies!' Mr Raxit shrieked, 'Bose slipped and fell into the gorge. It was an accident.'

'If anyone is lying, it is you. The crowbar you had used has been found behind a cactus bush fifty yards from where Bose's body was found. It is heavily stained with blood. Had Mr Bose slipped and fallen by accident, he would certainly have screamed for help. None of the guards here heard a scream. Besides, you had hidden a blue shirt among the plants behind the bungalow where we were all staying. A portion of this shirt is torn. I found it. The piece of blue fabric Bose was found clutching is the same—'

Mr Raxit did not stop to hear any more. He leapt up and tried to dash out of the smoky curtain, only to find himself being embraced by three different men. To our right, Jayant Mallik lit his torch. Now I could see Feluda, who had taken off his make-up. Next to him was Mr Ghote and a constable. At a nod from him, the constable put handcuffs on Mr Raxit.

Feluda turned to Mr Mallik. 'I must ask you to do something for me,' he said, 'See that other cave over there? You'll find Mr Raxit's raincoat in it, tucked away in the left-hand corner. Could you get it for me, please? Well, we mustn't stay in this smoke any longer. Come along, Topshe. Are you all right, Lalmohan Babu? This way, please.'

*

Feluda explained everything to us over dinner that night. We had dinner at the guest house. With us were Mr Kulkarni, Mr Ghote and Mr Mallik.

'The first thing I should tell you,' Feluda began, 'is that Raxit isn't his real name. His real name is Chattoraj. He is a member of a gang of criminals, who operate from Delhi. Their main aim is to steal valuable statues, or even parts of statues, from old temples, and sell them to foreign buyers, thereby filling their own pockets with tidy little sums. There must be many other gangs like this one, but at least we have managed to get hold of one. Chattoraj was made to come clean, and he gave us all the details we needed. It was he who had stolen that head, brought it to Calcutta and sold it to Silverstein. Then, when he heard of the plane crash, he rushed to the spot, bought it back from that boy called Panu for just ten rupees, and then chased Lewison all the way to Ellora. He wanted to kill two birds with one stone. The yakshi's head could be sold to Lewison, and Chattoraj could steal another statue from Kailash. Sadly for him, he couldn't do either of those things. Lewison agreed to buy the stolen statue, but Chattoraj lost it before he could pass it on to Lewison. As a result, Lewison got very cross with him and left. He might have succeeded in removing a statue from Kailash, but two things stopped him.

One was the sudden appearance of Shubhankar Bose. The other was a small pebble, thrown on the courtyard before cave number fifteen.'

Feluda stopped for breath. I started feeling most confused. 'What about Mr Mallik?' I blurted out.

Feluda smiled. 'The presence of Jayant Mallik can be very easily explained. In fact, it was so simple that even I could not figure it out at first. Mr Mallik was simply following Chattoraj.'

'Why?'

'For the same reason that I was chasing him! He wanted to retrieve the statue, like me. But that isn't all. He and I do the same job. Yes, he's a private detective, just like me.'

I cast a startled glance at Mr Mallik. He said nothing, but I saw that he was grinning, looking at Feluda and waiting for him to explain further.

'When I made enquiries about him,' Feluda went on, 'I discovered that he worked for an agency in Bombay. They sent him to Calcutta recently, in connection with a case. He stayed in a friend's flat in Queen's Mansion, and used his car while the friend was away on holiday. Normally, the kind of cases these agencies handle are all ordinary and pretty insignificant. Mr Mallik was getting bored with his job. He wanted to do something exciting, much more worthwhile and become famous. Is that right?'

'Yes.' Mr Mallik admitted, 'I got the chance to work on such a case, most unexpectedly. My old job took me to the Grand Hotel last Thursday, and I happened to be in Nagarmal's shop when an American visitor showed that yakshi's head to him. At that time, I paid no attention. All that I grasped was that the man was immensely wealthy, and his name was Silverstein. But, when I heard about the plane crash the next morning and they said he had been on that flight, it suddenly struck me that it might be possible to retrieve that statue. I have a little knowledge of ancient art, and I knew that what I'd seen Silverstein carrying was extremely valuable. So

I thought if I could get it back, it might be reported in the press, which would be a good thing for the agency as well. So I rang my boss in Bombay and told him what I wanted to do. He agreed, and asked me to keep him posted. I left for Sidikpur immediately, but it was too late. I missed Chattoraj by just five minutes. He got there first and bought the head back. There didn't seem to be anything I could do, but—'

'Do you remember the colour of his car?' Feluda interrupted him.

'Oh yes. It was a blue Fiat. I decided to follow Chattoraj. But I ran into some more problems. A burst tyre meant an unnecessary delay . . . so I lost him for the moment. However, by then I was absolutely determined not to give up. I knew he'd want to sell the statue again. So I went back to the Grand Hotel. It meant waiting for a while, but eventually I found him and followed him to the Railway Booking Office. He bought a ticket to Aurangabad. So did I. He was still carrying a heavy bag, so it was clear that he had not been able to get rid of the statue. I came back to my flat, rang my office in Bombay and told them what had happened.'

'Yes, we know about that. You had said, "The daughter has returned to her father". What we did not know was that by "father" you meant Chattoraj, not yourself.'

Mr Mallik smiled, then continued, 'I kept waiting for a suitable opportunity to remove the stolen object. I knew if I could catch the thief at the same time, it would be even better. But that proved much too difficult. Anyway, last night I went and hid near Kailash. When I saw that everyone from the bungalow had gone out in the direction of the caves, I returned quickly, slipped into the bungalow through the side door that only the cleaners use, and removed the statue from Chattoraj's room.'

'I see. Did you have any idea *you* were being watched by a detective?'

'Oh no. That's why I couldn't speak a word when you arrested me! I must have looked very foolish.'

Mr Ghote burst out laughing. Feluda took up the tale, 'When I saw that you had travelled with Lewison in the same car for many miles, but had done nothing to sell him the statue, I realized you were innocent. Until then, although I'd come to know you were a detective, I could not drop you from my list of suspects.'

'But Chattoraj was also on this list, wasn't he?'

'Yes. Mind you, initially it was no more then a slight doubt. When I saw that this his name had been freshly painted on an old suitcase, I began to wonder if the name wasn't fake. Then, Lalmohan Babu told us yesterday that he had gone out wearing a raincoat. When we were passing cave number fifteen, I noticed someone was in it, and threw a pebble in the courtyard. That made the man run away. I then went into the cave and began searching the surrounding area. In a smaller cave behind the big one, I found the raincoat. It had a specially large pocket, in which was a hammer, a chisel and a nylon rope. I left everything there. It became obvious that Raxit—or Chattoraj—was the real culprit. As we returned to the bungalow, we saw him desperately searching for something in his room. In fact, he seemed to have gone mad, which is understandable since he had come back to his room to find that his precious statue had gone. This morning, Mr Kulkarni told me you had called Bombay and said, "The daughter is fine". That meant you had the stolen statue with you. So you had to be arrested.'

Feluda stopped. No one said anything. After a short pause, he went on, 'While we were worrying about statues and thieves, Shubhankar Bose got killed. On examining his dead body, we found a piece of blue cloth in one of his hands. You were wearing a blue shirt yesterday. But I didn't think of you, since my suspicions had already fallen on Chattoraj. What really happened was that he reached Bose's body before me and, pretending that he was trying to feel his pulse, pushed in that torn piece into the dead man's hand. It had become essential for Chattoraj to throw suspicion on someone else for

Bose's death. The torn piece had, of course, come from Chattoraj's own shirt. He had cut out a piece and hidden the shirt amongst the plants and bushes behind the bungalow. I found it myself.

'However, although I had gathered some evidence against Chattoraj, it was not enough to actually accuse him of murder and theft. As I was wondering what to do, Tapesh and Lalmohan Babu told me that someone had been through their belongings. This had to be Chattoraj, for he had lost something valuable and was naturally looking for it everywhere. In Lalmohan Babu's suitcase was his notebook, which mentioned the theft of the statue from Bhubaneshwar, Silverstein and the plane crash. I knew at once that Chattoraj had read every detail and was feeling threatened, thinking it was Lalmohan Babu who had stumbled on the truth. So I sent him a little note, pretending it had been written by Lalmohan Babu, asking Chattoraj to meet him in the Das Avatar cave at 8 p.m. Before that, however, I told Chattoraj that whoever had tried to steal a statue from Kailash the night before had been arrested. I knew this would set his mind at rest, and he would stop being on his guard.'

'That man with the goatee!' Lalmohan Babu and I cried together, 'Was that *you*?'

'Yes,' Feluda laughed, 'That was my disguise number two. I felt I had to stay close to you, since we were dealing with a dangerous man. Anyway, he swallowed my bait at once. He thought a few sharp words from him would really make Lalmohan Babu return the head to him, and he could get away with it once again. Well, we all know what happened next.

'There is only one thing left for me to say: Mr Mallik and his agency will get full credit for their share in catching this gang. And I will pray for a promotion for Mr Ghote. I must also thank Mr Kulkarni for the important role he played, but if a medal for courage and bravery could be given to anyone, it should go jointly to Tapesh Ranjan Mitter and Lalmohan Ganguli.'

'Hear, hear!' said Mr Mallik and the others clapped enthusiastically.

When the applause died down, Lalmohan Babu turned to Feluda and said a little hesitantly, 'Does that mean . . . this time my weapon didn't come into any use at all?'

Feluda looked perfectly amazed. 'Not come into use? What are you talking about? Where do you think all that smoke came from? It was no ordinary bomb, sir. Do you know what it was? A 356 megaton special military smoke bomb!'

The Royal Bengal Mystery

ONE

Old Man hollow,
pace to follow,
people's tree.
Half ten, half again
century.
Rising sun,
whence it's done,
can't you see?
Between hands,
below them stands,
yours, it be.

Feluda said to me, 'When you write about our adventure in the forest, you must start with this puzzle.'

'Why? We didn't get to know of the puzzle until we actually got there!'

'I know. But this is just a technique, to tickle the fancy of the reader.'

I wasn't happy with this answer. Feluda realized it, so a couple of minutes later, he added, 'Anyone who reads that puzzle at the outset will get the chance to use his own intelligence, you see.'

So I agreed to start my story with it. I should, however, point out at once that it's no use trying to work out what it means. It's not easy at all. In fact, it took even Feluda quite a long time to discover its meaning, although when he eventually explained it to me, it seemed simple enough.

In talking about our past experiences, I have so far used

real names and real places. This time, I have been specifically asked not to do so. I had to turn to Feluda for advice on fictitious names I might use. 'You can mention the place was near the border of Bhutan, there's no harm in that,' Feluda said, 'but you can change its name to Laxmanbari. The chief character might be called Mr Sinha-Roy. Many old zamindar families used to have that name. In fact, some of them originally came from Rajputana. They came to Bengal and joined the army of Todar Mal to fight the Pathans. Then they simply stayed on, and their descendants became Bengalis.'

I am doing what Feluda told me to do. The names of places and people are fictitious, but not the events. I shall try to relate everything exactly as I saw or heard it.

The story began in Calcutta. It was Sunday, the 27th of May. The time was 9.30 a.m. My summer holidays had started. Of late, the maximum temperature had hit 100° F, so I was keeping myself indoors, pasting stamps from Bhutan into my stamp album. Feluda had recently finished solving a murder case (catching the culprit by using a common pin as a clue), which had made him quite famous. He had also been paid a fat fee. At this moment he was resting at home, stretched out on a divan, reading Thor Heyerdahl's *Aku-Aku*. A minute later, Jatayu turned up.

Lalmohan Ganguli—alias Jatayu—the writer of immensely popular crime thrillers, had started visiting us at least twice a month. The popularity of his novels meant that he was pretty well off. As a matter of fact, he was once rather proud of his writing prowess. But when Feluda pointed out dozens of factual errors in his books, Lalmohan Babu began to look upon him with a mixture of respect and admiration. Now, he got his manuscripts corrected by Feluda before passing them on to his publisher.

Today, however, he was not carrying a sheaf of papers under his arm, which clearly meant that there was a different reason for his visit. He sat down on a sofa, took out a green face towel from his pocket, wiped his face with it, and said without looking at Feluda, 'Would you like to see a forest, Felu Babu?'

Feluda raised himself a little, leaning on his elbow. 'What is your definition of a forest?'

'The same as yours, Felu Babu. Cluster of trees. Dense foliage. That sort of thing.'

'In West Bengal?'

'Yes, sir.'

'Where? I can't think of any place other than the Sunderbans, or Terai. Everything else has been wiped clean.'

'Have you heard of Mahitosh Sinha-Roy?'

The question was accompanied by a rather smug smile. I had heard of him, too. He was a well-known shikari and a writer. Feluda had one of his books. I hadn't read it, but Feluda had told me it was most interesting.

'Doesn't he live in Orissa, or is it Assam?' Feluda asked.

'No, sir,' Lalmohan Babu replied, taking out an envelope from his pocket with a flourish, 'He lives in the Dooars Forest, near the border of Bhutan. I dedicated my latest book to him. We have exchanged letters.'

'Oh? You mean you dedicate your books even to the living?'

Perhaps I should explain here the business of Lalmohan Babu's dedications. Nearly all of them are made to famous people who are now dead. *The Antarctic Anthropophagi* was dedicated to the memory of Robert Scott; *The Gorilla's Grasp* said, 'In the memory of David Livingstone', and *The Atomic Demon* (which Feluda said was the most nonsensical stuff he'd ever read) had been dedicated to Einstein. Then, when he wrote *The Himalayan Hemlock*, he dedicated it to the memory of Sir Edmund Hilary. Feluda was furious at this.

'Why, Lalmohan Babu, why did you have to kill a man who is very much alive?'

'What! Hilary is alive?' Lalmohan Babu asked, looking both apologetic and embarrassed, 'I didn't know. I mean . . . he hasn't been in the news for a long time, and he does go about climbing mountains, doesn't he? So I thought perhaps he'd slipped and . . . well, you know . . . ' his voice trailed away.

The mistake was rectified when the second edition of the book came out.

Mahitosh Sinha-Roy might be a well-known shikari, but was he really as famous as all these other people? Why was the last book dedicated to him?

'Well, you see,' Lalmohan Babu explained, 'I had to consult his book *The Tiger and the Gun* quite a few times when I was writing my own. In fact,' he added with a smile, 'I used a whole episode. So I felt I had to please him in some way.'

'Did you succeed?'

Lalmohan Babu took out the letter from its envelope. 'Yes. He wouldn't send an invitation otherwise, would he?'

'Well, he may have invited you, but surely he didn't include me?'

Lalmohan Babu looked faintly annoyed. 'Look, Felu Babu,' he said, frowning, 'I know you would never go anywhere unless you were invited. You are well known yourself, and you have your prestige. I am well aware of that. What happened was that I told him that the book had seen four editions in four months. And I also told him—only a hint, that is—that I knew you. So he sent me this letter. Read it yourself. We've both been invited.'

The last few lines of Mahitosh Sinha-Roy's letter said, 'I believe your friend Pradosh Mitter is a very clever detective. If you can bring him with you, he might be able to help me out in a certain matter. Please let me know if he agrees to come.'

Feluda stared at the letter for a few moments. Then he said, 'Is he an old man?'

'What do you mean by old?' Lalmohan Babu asked, his eyes half-closed.

'Say, around seventy?'

'No, sir. Mr Sinha-Roy is much younger than that.'

'His writing is like an old man's.'

'How can you say that? This writing is absolutely beautiful.'

'I agree. But look at the signature. I think the letter was written by his secretary.'

It was decided that we would leave for Laxmanbari the following Wednesday. We could go up to New Jalpaiguri by train. After that we'd have to go by car to Laxmanbari, which was 46 miles away. Mahitosh Babu had already offered to send his own car to collect us at the New Jalpaiguri station.

*

It came as no surprise to me that Feluda agreed to visit a forest so readily. My own heart was jumping with joy. The fact was that one of our uncles was a shikari as well. Our ancestral home was in the village of Shonadeeghi, near Dhaka. My father was the youngest of three brothers. The oldest worked as the manager of an estate in Mymansinh. He was renowned in the area for having killed wild deer, boars and even tigers in the Madhupur forest to the north of Mymansinh. The second brother—Feluda's father—used to teach mathematics and Sanskrit in a school. However, that did not stop him from being terrific at sports, including swimming, wrestling and shooting. Unfortunately, he died very young after only a brief spell of illness. Feluda was nine years old at the time. Naturally, his father's death came as an enormous shock to everyone. Feluda was brought to our house and raised by my parents. My own father has never shown any interest in anything that calls for great physical strength, but I do know that his will-power and mental strength is much stronger than most people's.

Feluda himself has always been fascinated by tales of shikar. He has read every book written by Corbett and Kenneth Anderson. Although he's never been on a shikar, he did learn to shoot and is now a crack shot. There is no doubt in my mind that he could easily kill a tiger, should he be required to do so. He has often told me that the mind of an animal is a lot less complex than that of humans. Even the simplest of men would have a more complex mind than a ferocious tiger. Catching a criminal was, therefore, no less difficult than killing a tiger.

Feluda was trying to explain this to Lalmohan Babu in the train. Lalmohan Babu was carrying the first book Mahitosh Sinha-Roy had written. The front page had a photograph of the writer, which showed him standing with one foot on a dead Royal Bengal tiger, a rifle in his hand. His face wasn't clear, but it was easy to spot the set of his jaws, his broad shoulders and an impressive moustache under a sharp, long nose.

Lalmohan Babu stared at the photo for a few seconds and said, 'Thank goodness you are going with me, Felu Babu. In front of such a personality, I'd have looked like a . . . a worm!' His height was five foot four inches, and at first glance his appearance suggested that he might be a comedian on the stage or in films. Anyone even slightly taller and better built than him made him look like a worm. Certainly, when he stood next to Feluda, the description seemed apt enough.

'What is strange,' he continued, 'is that although this is his first book—and he began writing at the age of fifty—it reads as though it's been written by an experienced writer. He has a wonderful style.'

'He probably turned to writing when hunting as a sport was banned by the Indian government,' Feluda remarked, 'Many other shikaris have proved to be skilful writers. Corbett's language is wonderful. Perhaps it's something to do with being close to nature. Think of the sages who wrote the scriptures. Didn't they live in jungles?'

I had noticed lightning ripping the sky soon after we left Calcutta. By the time we reached the New Farakka station, it was past midnight. I woke when the train stopped to find that it was pouring outside, and there was frequent thunder.

However, when we alighted at New Jalpaiguri in the morning, there was no evidence of rain, although the sky was overcast.

The man who had been sent to meet us turned out to be Mahitosh Babu's secretary, Torit Sengupta. He was under thirty, thin, fair, wore glasses with thick black frames, and his hair was dishevelled. He greeted us politely, but without any excessive show of warmth. I told myself hurriedly that it might not necessarily mean he was displeased to see us. Feluda had warned me often enough not to jump to conclusions or judge people simply by their outward behaviour. But Mr Sengupta was clearly an intelligent man, for he didn't have to be told who amongst us was Lalmohan Ganguli, and who was Pradosh Mitter.

We stopped for ten minutes to have toast and omelettes. Then we climbed into the jeep waiting outside. Our luggage consisted only of two suitcases and a shoulder-bag. There was plenty of room in the jeep to sit comfortably. 'Mr Sinha-Roy sent his apologies for not being able to receive you himself,' Mr Sengupta said before we started, 'His brother has not been keeping well. So he had to stay home because the doctor was expected.'

This was news to us. None of us knew Mahitosh Babu had a brother.

'I hope it's nothing serious?' Feluda asked. I could tell he wasn't happy about staying in a house where someone was ill. Our visit might well turn into an imposition on our host.

'No, no,' Mr Sengupta replied, 'Devtosh Babu—that's his brother—doesn't have a physical problem. His problems are mental, and he's been . . . well, not quite normal . . . for many years. But don't get me wrong. He isn't mad. In fact, he seems fine most of the time. But occasionally he gets very restless. So the doctor has to put him on sedatives.'

'How old is he?'

'Sixty-four. He's older by five years. He was once a very learned man. He had . . . has . . . an extensive knowledge of history.'

I looked out of the jeep. To the north were the Himalayas. Somewhere in that direction lay Darjeeling. I had been there three times, but never to Laxmanbari. It wasn't very warm as there was no sun. The scenery changed as soon as we left the town. We passed a few tea estates. Now I could see mountains even to the east.

'Bhutan,' Mr Sengupta said briefly, pointing at these. The tea estates gave way to forests soon after we crossed the river Teesta. At one point, we saw a herd of goats emerging from a wood. Lalmohan Babu got very excited, and shouted, 'Look, deer, deer!'

'At least he didn't say tigers. Thank heaven for that!' Feluda muttered under his breath.

'There is a forest called Kalbuni within a mile of where we live,' Mr Sengupta informed us, 'It was once full of tigers, many of which were killed by the Sinha-Roys. Now, I'm not sure if any Royal Bengals are left, but about three months ago there were rumours of a man-eater in Kalbuni.'

'Rumours? How do you mean?'

'Well, the body of an adivasi boy was found in the jungle. There were scratches on it that suggested it had been attacked by a tiger.'

'Just scratches? Didn't the tiger eat the flesh?'

'Yes, the flesh was partially eaten. But a hyena or a jackal may have been responsible for that.'

'What did Mahitosh Babu have to say?'

'He wasn't here at the time. He had gone to visit his tea estate near Hasimara. The officers of the Forest Department thought it might be a tiger, but when Mr Sinha-Roy got back, he said that couldn't be. A lot has been done in these few months to find that tiger, without any success whatsoever.'

'I see. No one else was attacked after that one incident?'

'No.'

The very mention of a man-eater gave me goose pimples. But Mahitosh Babu must have been right. Lalmohan Babu said, 'Highly interesting!' and began staring at the trees, a frown across his brows.

We crossed a small river, went past a village and another forest, and turned left. The road was unpaved here, so our ride became noticeably bumpy. It did not last for very long, however. Only five minutes later, I saw the top of a building, towering over the trees. The rest of it came into view in a few moments. The trees thinned out to reveal a large mansion that stood behind tall iron gates. Once it must have been white, but now there were black marks all over its walls, making the whole house look as if it had been attacked and left badly bruised. Only the window panes glowed with colour. Not a single one from the colours of a rainbow was missing.

The gates were open. Our jeep passed through them and stopped at the portico. I noticed a marble slab on the gate that said: 'The Sinha-Roy Palace'.

TWO

Mahitosh Sinha-Roy turned out to be a little different from his photograph. The photo had not done justice to his complexion. He was remarkably fair. His height seemed nearly the same as Feluda's, and he had put on a little weight since the photo had been taken. His voice was deep and strong. Enough to frighten a tiger if he simply spoke to it, I thought.

He met us at the front door and ushered us into a huge drawing room.

'Please sit down,' he invited warmly. Feluda mentioned his writing as soon as we had all been introduced. 'The events you describe are amazing enough. But even apart from those, your language and style are so good that from the literary point of view as well, I think you have made a remarkable contribution.'

A bearer had come in and placed glasses of mango sherbet on a low table. Mahitosh Babu gestured at these and said, 'Please help yourselves.' Then he smiled and added, 'You are very kind, Mr Mitter. It may be that writing was in my blood, but I didn't know it until four years ago when I first started to write. My grandfather and father were both writers. Mind you, I don't think their forefathers had anything to do with literature. We were originally Kshatriyas from Rajputana. Oh, you knew that, did you? So, once we were in the business of fighting with other men. Then we left the men and turned to animals. Now I've been more or less forced to abandon my gun and pick up a pen.'

'Is that your grandfather?' Feluda asked, looking at an oil painting on the wall.

'Yes. That is Adityanarayan Sinha-Roy.'

It was an impressive figure. His eyes glinted, in his left hand was a rifle, and the right one was placed lightly on a table. He looked directly at us, holding himself erect, his head tilted proudly. His beard and moustache reminded me of King George V.

'My grandfather exchanged letters with Bankim Chandra Chatterjee. He was in college at the time *Devi Chowdhurani* was published. He wrote to Bankim after reading the book.'

'The novel was set in these parts, wasn't it?'

'Yes,' Mahitosh Babu replied with enthusiasm, 'The Teesta you crossed today was the Trisrota river described in the book. Devi's barge used to float on this river. But the jungles Bankim described have now become tea estates.'

'When did your grandfather become a shikari?' Lalmohan Babu asked suddenly. Mahitosh Babu smiled. 'Oh, that's quite a story,' he replied, 'My grandfather was very fond of dogs. He used to go and buy pups from all over this region. There was a time when there must have been at least fifty dogs in this house, of all possible lineages, shapes, sizes and temperament. Among these, his favourite was a Bhutanese dog. There is a Shiva temple near here called the temple of Jalpeshwar. The local people hold a big fair every year during Shivaratri. A lot of people from Bhutan come down for that fair, bringing dogs and pups for sale. My grandfather bought one of these—a large, hairy animal, very cuddly—and brought it home. When the dog was three and a half years old, he was attacked and killed by a cheetah. Grandfather was then a young man. He decided he would settle scores by killing all the cheetahs and any other big cat he could find. He got himself rifles and guns, learnt to shoot and then . . . that was it. He must have killed around one hundred and fifty tigers in twenty-two years. I couldn't tell you how many other animals he killed—they were endless.'

'And you?'

'I?' Mahitosh Babu grinned, then turned to his right, 'Go on, Shashank, tell them.'

I noticed with a start that while we were all listening to Mahitosh Babu's story, another gentleman had quietly entered the room and taken the chair to our left.

'Tigers? Why, you have written so many books, *you* tell them!' Shashank Babu replied with a smile.

Mahitosh Babu turned back to us. 'I haven't been able to reach three figures, I must admit. I killed seventy-one tigers and over fifty leopards. Meet my friend, Shashank Sanyal. We've known each other since we were small children. He looks after my timber business.'

There seemed to be a world of difference between Mahitosh Babu and his friend. The latter was barely five feet eight inches tall, his complexion was dark, his voice quiet, and he spoke very gently. Yet, there had to be some common interest to hold them together as friends.

'Mr Sengupta mentioned something about a man-eater. Has there been any further news?' Feluda asked.

Mahitosh Babu moved in his chair. 'A tiger doesn't become a man-eater just because a few people choose to call it so. I would have known, if I had been here and could have seen the body. However, the good news is that whatever animal attacked that poor boy has not yet shown further interest in human flesh.'

Feluda smiled. 'If indeed it was a man-eater, I am sure you would have dropped your pen and picked up your gun, at least temporarily,' he remarked.

'Oh yes. If a tiger went about eating men in my own area, most certainly I would consider it my duty to destroy it.'

We had finished our drinks. Mahitosh Babu said, 'You must be tired after your journey. Why don't you go to your room and have a little rest? I'll get someone in the evening to take you around in my jeep. A road goes through the forest. You may see deer, or even elephants, if you are lucky. Torit, please show them the trophy room and then take them to their own.'

The trophy room turned out to be a hall stashed with the heads of tigers, bears, wild buffalo and deer. Crocodile skins hung on a wall. There was hardly enough room for us all. I felt somewhat uncomfortable to find dozens of dead animals staring at me through their glassy eyes. But that wasn't all. The weapons that had been used to kill these animals were also displayed on a huge rack. None of us had ever seen so many guns: single-barrelled, double-barrelled, guns to kill birds with, guns for tigers, and even some for elephants. There seemed to be no end to them.

'Have you ever been on a shikar?' Feluda asked Torit Sengupta, looking at the various weapons. Mr Sengupta laughed and shook his head. 'No, no, not me. You are a detective. Can't you tell by looking at me I have nothing to do with killing animals?'

'One doesn't have to be physically very large and hefty to be a shikari. It's all to do with a steady nerve, isn't it? You do not strike me as someone who might lack it.'

'No, my nerve is steady enough. But I come from an ordinary middle-class family in Calcutta. Shikar is something I've never even thought of.'

We left the trophy room and began climbing a staircase. 'What is a man from a city doing in a place like this?' Feluda asked.

'He is simply doing a job, Mr Mitter. I couldn't find one in the city, when I finished college. Then I saw the advertisement Mr Sinha-Roy had put in for a secretary. I applied, came here for an interview and got it.'

'How long have you been here?'

'Five years.'

'You like walking in the forest, don't you? I mean, even if you're not a shikari?'

Mr Sengupta looked at Feluda in surprise. 'Why, what do you mean?'

'There are scratch marks on your right hand. Bramble?'

Mr Sengupta smiled again. 'Yes, you're right. You *are* remarkably observant, I must say. I got these marks only yesterday. Walking in the forest has become something like an addiction for me.'

'Even if you're unarmed?'

'Yes. Normally, there's nothing to be afraid of,' Mr Sengupta replied quietly, 'The only things I have to watch out for are snakes and mad elephants.'

'And man-eaters?' Lalmohan Babu whispered.

'If a man-eater's existence is proved one day, I suppose I shall have to give up my walks.'

There was a door at the top of the stairs, beyond which lay a long veranda. There were several rooms running down one side. The first of these was Mahitosh Babu's study. Mr Sengupta worked in it during the day. The veranda curved to the left a little later, taking us to the west wing of the building. Our rooms were among the ones that lined this section of the veranda.

'Are all these in use? Who stays in these rooms?' asked Feluda.

'No one. Most of these stay locked. Mr Sinha-Roy and his brother live in the eastern side. Shashank Sanyal and I are in the southern wing. Two rooms in our side of the house are always kept ready for Mr Sinha-Roy's sons. He has two sons. Both work in Calcutta. They come here occasionally.'

Now I noticed another figure standing on the opposite veranda: a man wearing a purple dressing gown, leaning against the railing and staring straight at us. 'Is that Mahitosh Babu's brother?' Feluda asked. Before Mr Sengupta could reply, the man spoke. His voice was as deep as his brother's.

'Have you seen Raju? Where is he?'

The question was clearly meant for us. He moved closer quickly. There were visible resemblances between the two brothers, specially around the jaw. Mr Sengupta answered on our behalf, 'No, they haven't seen him.'

'No? What about Hussain? Have they seen Hussain?'

His eyes were odd, unfocussed. His hair was much thinner than his brother's, and almost totally white. He might have been just as tall, but he stooped and so appeared shorter.

'No, they haven't seen Hussain, either,' said Mr Sengupta and motioned us to go inside our room. 'They know nothing,' he added firmly, 'They are only visiting for a few days.' Devtosh Babu looked openly disappointed. We slipped into our room quickly.

'Who are Raju and Hussain?' Feluda wanted to know. Mr Sengupta laughed.

'Raju is another name for Kalapahar. And Hussain is Hussain Khan, who used to be the Sultan of Gaur. Both of them destroyed several Hindu temples in Bengal. The head of the statue in the temple of Jalpeshwar here was broken by Hussain Khan.'

'Were you a student of history?'

'No, literature. But Mr Sinha-Roy is writing the history of his family. So, as his secretary, I am having to pick up a few details here and there about past events in this area.'

Mr Sengupta left. For the first time since our arrival, we were left by ourselves. I could now relax completely. The room was large and comfortable. There were two deer heads fixed over the door. Spread on the floor was a leopard skin, including the head. Perhaps it had not been possible to accommodate it anywhere else. There were two proper beds, and a smaller wooden cot, which had clearly been added because there were three of us. All three beds had been carefully made, with thick mattresses, embroidered bedsheets and pillowcases. Mosquito nets hung around each bed. Feluda looked at the cot and said, 'This one was probably once used as a machaan. Look, there are marks where it must have been tied with ropes. Topshe, you can sleep on it.'

Lalmohan Babu seemed quite satisfied with what he saw. He sat down on his bed and said, 'I think we are going to enjoy the next three days. But I hope Devtosh Babu won't come back to ask about his friend Raju. Frankly speaking, I feel very uncomfortable in the presence of anyone mentally disturbed.'

The same thought had occurred to me. But Feluda did not appear concerned at all. He began unpacking, stopping only for a moment to frown and say, 'We still don't know what kind of help Mahitosh Babu is expecting from me.'

THREE

Mr Sengupta could not go with us in the evening as he had some important work to see to. Mahitosh Babu's friend, Shashank Sanyal, came with us instead. Having lived in these parts for many years, he, too, seemed to have learnt a lot of about the local flora and fauna. He kept pointing out trees and plants to us, although it was quickly getting dark and not very easy to see from the back of the jeep. He had lived here for thirty years, he said. Before that, he was in Calcutta. Mahitosh Babu and he had attended the same school and college.

Our jeep stopped by the side of a small river. The sun was just about to set.

'Let's get down for a while,' Mr Sanyal said, 'You'll never get the feel, the real atmosphere in a forest from a moving jeep.'

I realized the minute we stepped out how dense and quiet the forest was. There was no noise except the gently rippling river and the birds going back to roost. Had there not been a man carrying a rifle, I would certainly have felt uneasy. This man was called Madhavlal. He was a professional shikari. When shikaris from abroad used to come here, it was always Madhavlal who used to act as their guide. Apparently, he knew everything about where a machaan should be set up, where a tiger was likely to be spotted, what might it mean if an animal cried out. He was about fifty, tall and well-built without even a trace of fat on his body. I was very glad he had been sent with us.

We walked slowly over to the sandy bank and stood on the pebbles that were spread on the ground like a carpet. After chatting with Mr Sanyal for a few minutes, Feluda suddenly asked, 'What is the matter with Devtosh Babu? How did he happen to . . .?'

'Heredity. There is a history of madness in their family. Mahitosh's grandfather went mad in his old age.'

'Really? Did he have to stop hunting?'

'Oh yes. Every firearm was removed out of sight. But, one day, he found an old sword hanging on the wall in the drawing room. He grabbed it and went into the jungle to kill yet another tiger. Rumour has it that he wanted to do what Sher Shah had done. You must have been told in your history lessons in school how Sher Shah got his title: "In his later years, he is said to have beheaded a tiger with one stroke of his sword, which earned him the title of Sher Shah". In a fit of madness, Adityanarayan wanted to do the same.'

'And then?' Lalmohan Babu asked, his eyes round and his voice hushed.

'He never returned. This time, the tiger won. There was virtually nothing left, except his sword.'

An animal called loudly from behind a bush. Lalmohan Babu nearly jumped out of his skin. Mr Sanyal laughed. 'Mr Ganguli, you are a writer of adventure stories. You shouldn't get frightened so easily. That was only a fox.'

Lalmohan Babu pulled himself together. 'Er . . . you see, it is because I am a writer that my imagination is livelier than others. We were talking about tigers, weren't we, and then I heard that animal. So I thought I could actually see a flash of yellow behind that bush.'

'Well . . . something yellow and striped may well start moving behind bushes if we hang around,' Mr Sanyal remarked, suddenly lowering his voice.

'What!'

'Was that a barking deer?' Feluda whispered.

A different animal had started to call. It sounded like the barking of a dog. Feluda had told me once that if a tiger was spotted close by, barking deer often called out to warn other animals. Mr Sanyal nodded in silence and motioned us to get back into the jeep. We crept back and took our places in absolute silence. It was now appreciably darker. My heart started thumping loudly. Madhavlal, too, had moved closer to the jeep, clutching his rifle tightly. Lalmohan Babu touched my hand briefly. His palm felt icy.

We waited in breathless anticipation until six o'clock; but no animal came into view. We had to return disappointed.

It was totally dark by the time we reached our room. To our surprise, we realized that in this short time, large thick clouds had gathered in the western sky. Thunder rumbled in the distance, and lightning spread its roots everywhere in the sky, dazzling our eyes. We were all staring out of the window, watching this spectacle, when someone knocked at the door. It had been left open. We turned around to find Mahitosh Sinha-Roy standing there.

'How was your trip to the forest?' he asked in his deep voice.

'We almost saw a tiger!' Lalmohan Babu shouted, excited like a child.

'If you had come here even ten years ago, you would certainly have seen one,' said our host, 'If you failed to see one today, I must admit I—and other shikaris like me—are to blame, for shikar was considered to be a sport. Even in ancient times, kings used to go on hunting expeditions which they called mrigaya. So did Mughal badshahs, and in modern times, our British masters. It became a tradition, which we followed blindly. Can you imagine how many animals have been killed in these two thousand years? But that isn't all, is it? Just think of the number of animals that are caught every year for zoos and circuses!'

None of us knew what to say. Was a famous shikari now sorry for what he'd done? Feluda offered him a chair, but he declined. 'No, thank you,' he said, 'I didn't come here to stay. I came only to show you something. Let's go to my grandfather's room. I think you'll find it interesting.'

Adityanarayan's room was in the northern wing. 'We

heard how he'd lost his mind in his old age,' Feluda said as we began moving in that direction.

Mahitosh Babu smiled. 'Yes, but until that happened, till he was about sixty, there were few men with his intelligence and sharpness.'

'Do you still have the sword he'd taken to kill a tiger?'

'Yes, it's kept in his room. Come, I'll show you.'

Bookshelves occupied three sides of Adityanarayan's room. Each of them was packed with books, papers, manuscripts and stacks of old newspapers. The fourth side had two chests and a glass case. It is impossible to make a list of its contents that ranged from tigers' nails and a rhino's horn to metal statues and jewellery from Bhutan. The collar that his favourite dog had worn was also there. It was studded with stones, like all the Bhutanese jewellery. Apart from these, there was a silver pen and ink-well, binoculars from Mughal times and two human skulls. All these things occupied the top two shelves. The bottom two contained only weapons: a three hundred year old carved pistol, eight daggers and kukris, and the famous sword. Only a mad man could think it would be enough to kill a tiger, for it was neither very big nor heavy. The swords I had seen in Bikaner Fort that had once belonged to Rajput rulers were much more impressive.

While we were examining these objects, Mahitosh Babu had opened one of the chests and brought out a small ivory box. Now he took out a folded piece of paper from it and said, 'Detectives, I believe, have a special gift to unravel puzzles and riddles. See what you make of this one, Mr Mitter.'

'A riddle? I *was* once interested in things of that sort, but . . . '

Mahitosh Babu passed the piece of paper to Feluda. 'You said you wanted to spend three days here. If you cannot figure it out in that time, I am prepared to give you another three days; but no more than that.'

His tone changed as he spoke the last few words, as did the look in his eyes. I realized with a shock that our genial host had a streak of cold sternness—perhaps even ruthlessness—in him. Obviously, there were times when this side to his character was exposed. Feluda asked quickly, even before Mahitosh Babu's eyes could lose their cold, remote look: 'And what if I succeed?' His own tone was light, and there was a hint of a smile around his lips. But it was clear that Feluda didn't lack the ability to deal with Mahitosh Babu, no matter how stern he might be.

Mahitosh Sinha-Roy laughed, his good humour restored. 'If you succeed, Mr Mitter, I will give you a whole tiger skin, taken from one of the biggest tigers I have killed.'

This was quite generous, I had to admit. The value of a whole tiger skin today was not to be laughed at.

Feluda now looked at the piece of paper and read aloud the riddle:

Old man hollow,
pace to follow,
people's tree.
Half ten, half again,
century.
Rising sun,
whence it's done,
can't you see?
Between hands,
below them stands,
yours, it be.

'Hidden treasure,' Feluda murmured.

'You think so?'

'Yes, that's what the last line seems to indicate. I mean, "yours, it be" could only mean finding something after solving that riddle and being rewarded for it. It has to be money. But what we must consider is whether your grandfather was the kind of man who'd hide his wealth and then leave a coded message for its recovery. Not many people would think of doing such a thing.'

'My grandfather would. He was very different from ordinary men, I have told you that. He loved practical jokes, and having a laugh at the expense of others. When he was a child, I believe one day, he was cross with all the grown ups for some reason. So he stole their shoes in the middle of the night and hung them in bundles from the highest branches of a tree. Yes, I can well believe—what is it, Torit?'

None of us had noticed Torit Sengupta come into the room. He was standing near the door. 'I came to return a dictionary I had taken from that shelf,' he replied quietly.

'Very well, put it back. And . . . have you finished with those proofs?'

'Yes, sir.'

'Then you must take them with you tomorrow. And ask them why there were so many errors even in the second proof. Don't let them get away with it!'

Mr Sengupta slipped the book he was carrying into an empty space on a shelf, and left.

'Torit is going to Calcutta tomorrow for a week. His mother is ill,' Mahitosh Babu explained. Feluda was still staring at the rhyme.

'Who else knows about this riddle?' he asked.

Mahitosh Babu switched the light off and began moving towards the door. 'We found it only ten days ago. I was going through old papers and correspondence as I want to start writing the history of our family. Many of my grandfather's personal papers were found in an old steel trunk. That ivory box was hidden under a pile of letters. Only three people know about it: Shashank, Torit and myself. But none of us have the required skill to decipher the message. One needs to know about words—one single word can have different meanings, can't it? Do you think you can crack it, Mr Mitter?'

Feluda returned the piece of paper of Mahitosh Babu.

'What! Are you giving up already?' he cried in dismay.

'No, no,' Feluda smiled, 'I can remember all the words. I'll go and write them down in my notebook. That paper belongs to you and your family. It should stay with you.'

'You will get a tiger skin, Felu Babu, but what about me?' Lalmohan Babu asked, sounding disappointed.

We had finished dinner an hour ago. Our host had regaled us after dinner with exciting stories about his experiences in the wild. We had only just wished him a good night and returned from the drawing room.

'Why do you say that, Lalmohan Babu? Whoever solves this code will get that skin. At least, he should. So why don't you give it a go yourself, eh? You are a writer, you have a good command over your language, and you have imagination. So come on!'

'Pooh! My command over language would never get me through all that hollow-follow and hands-stands and what have you. You're the one who is going to get the reward. Do you think he might give you this one?' He looked at the skin that lay sprawling on the floor.

'No, I don't think so. Didn't he mention a big tiger? I have no interest in leopards.'

Feluda had already written down the few lines that made up the puzzle and was now staring at his notebook.

'Is it making any sense at all?' Lalmohan Babu persisted.

'No, not really, except that I am positive it involves hidden treasure,' Feluda replied without looking up.

'How can you tell? What's all that about following a hollow old man?'

'I don't know yet, but I think the word "follow" is important, and so is "pace". Perhaps it's simply telling you where you should go—take paces *to* something, or *from* something. Nothing else is clear. So we must—' Feluda couldn't finish speaking. Someone had walked in through the open door. It was Devtosh Babu.

He was still wearing the purple dressing gown. His eyes held the same wild look, as though he suspected everyone he met of having committed a crime. He looked straight at Lalmohan Babu and said, 'Did the Bhot Raja send you?'

'Bh-bhot?' Lalmohan Babu gulped, 'Do you mean vote? El-elections?'

'No, I think he is talking of the Raja of Bhutan,' Feluda said softly. Devtosh Babu turned his eyes immediately on Feluda, thereby releasing Lalmohan Babu from an extremely awkward situation.

'Are the Bhots coming back?' he wanted to know.

'No, I don't think so,' Feluda replied, his voice absolutely normal, 'But it is possible now to travel to Bhutan quite easily.'

'Really?' Devtosh Babu sounded as though this was the first time he'd heard the news. 'Good,' he said, 'That's good. They had once been very helpful. It was only because of them that the soldiers of the Nawab couldn't do anything. They know how to fight. But not everyone knows that, do they?' He sighed deeply, then added, 'Not everyone can handle weapons. No, not everyone can be like Adityanarayan.'

He turned abruptly and began walking to the door. Then he stopped, turned back, looked at the leopard skin on the floor and said something perfectly weird.

'Do you know about the wheels of Yudhisthir's chariot? They never touched the ground. Yet . . . in the end, they did. They had to.' Then he quickly left the room.

We sat in silence after he'd gone. After a few minutes, I heard Feluda mutter: 'He was wearing clogs. The soles were lined with rubber to muffle the noise.'

*

Our first night turned out to be quite eventful. I shall try to describe what happened in the right order. A grandfather clock on the top of the stairs helped me to keep track of time.

The first thing we realized within ten minutes of going to bed was that although we had been given thick mattresses and beautiful linen, no one had thought of checking the mosquito nets. There were holes in all three, which simply meant an open invitation to all the mosquitoes in the region. Thank goodness Feluda always carried a tube of Odomos with him. Each of us had to use it before going back to bed. When I did, suitably embalmed, I could hear the clock outside strike eleven. The clouds had dispersed to make way for the moon. I could see a patch of moonlight on the floor and was looking at it when, suddenly, someone spoke on the veranda.

'I am warning you for the last time. This is not going to do you any good!'

It was Mahitosh Sinha-Roy. He sounded furious. There was no reply from the other person. On my right, Lalmohan Babu had started to snore. I turned to my left and whispered, 'Feluda, did you hear that?'

'Yes,' Feluda whispered back, 'Go to sleep.'

I said nothing more. I must have fallen asleep almost immediately, but woke again a little later. The moon was still there, but the thunder was back, rolling in the distance. I lay quietly listening to it, but as the last rumble died away, it was replaced by another noise: *khut-khut, khut-khut, khut-khut!* It did not continue at a regular pace, but stopped abruptly. Then it started again. Now it became clear that it was coming from inside our room. It got drowned occasionally by the thunder outside, but it did not stay silent for long. I could hear Feluda breathing deeply and regularly. He was obviously fast asleep.

But why had Lalmohan Babu stopped snoring? I glanced at his bed, but could see nothing through the nets. Then I became aware of another noise, a faint, chattering noise which I recognized instantly. A few years ago, during a visit to Shimla, Lalmohan Babu had slipped and fallen on the snow as a bullet came and hit the ground near his feet. He had made the same noise then. It was simply the sound of his teeth chattering uncontrollably.

Khut-khut, khut-khut, khut!

There it was again. I raised my head to look at the floor. The mosquito net rustled with this slight movement, which told Lalmohan Babu that I was awake.

'T-t-t-tapesh!' he cried in a strange, hoarse voice, 'The l-l-l-eopard!'

I sat up to look properly at the leopard skin. What I saw froze my blood. Moonlight was still streaming in through a window to shine directly on the head of the leopard. It was rising and turning every now and then, first to the left and then to the right, making that strange noise. 'Feluda!' I called, unable to stop myself. I knew Feluda would wake instantly and be totally alert, no matter how deeply he had been sleeping.

'What is it? Why are you shouting?' he asked. I tried to tell him, but discovered that, like Lalmohan Babu, my throat had gone completely dry. All I could manage was, 'Look . . . floor!'

Feluda climbed out of his bed and stood staring at the moving head of the leopard. Then he stepped forward coolly and placed a finger under its chin, tilting it up. A large beetle crawled out. With unruffled calm, he picked it up and threw it out of the window. 'Didn't you know about the demonic strength of a beetle? If you place a heavy brass bowl over it, it will drag it about all over the house!' Feluda said.

I could feel myself go limp with relief. From the way Lalmohan Babu sighed, I could tell he was feeling the same. But why was Feluda still standing at the window? What was there to see in the dead of night?

'Topshe, come and have a look,' he invited. Lalmohan Babu and I joined him. Our room, which was in the rear portion of the house, overlooked the Kalbuni forest. In the last couple of minutes, thick clouds had once again obliterated the moon. There was lightning and the sound of thunder appeared closer. But what surprised me was that, in addition to the lightning, another light flashed in the distance. It kept moving about among the trees in the forest. Someone with a torch was out there. There was no doubt about that.

'Highly suspicious!' Lalmohan Babu muttered.

Then the torch was switched off. In the same instant, there was a blinding flash, followed by an earsplitting noise. Almost immediately, it began to pour in great torrents. We had to pull the shutters down quickly.

'It's past one o'clock,' Feluda said, 'Let's try and get some sleep. We're supposed to go to the temple of Jalpeshwar in the morning, remember?'

The three of us got back into bed, behind the mosquito nets. I stared at the windows. Although they were shut, their multicoloured panes shone brightly each time there was a flash of lightning, flooding the room with all the hues of a rainbow.

I couldn't tell when this colourful display stopped, and I fell asleep.

FIVE

The next morning, I woke at seven o'clock. Feluda was already up, and had finished doing his yoga, bathing and shaving. Mr Sengupta was supposed to collect us at eight, and take us to the temple. One of the three bearers, called Kanai, brought us our morning tea at half past seven. Feluda picked up his cup, then went back to staring at the notebook lying open in his lap. 'Bravo, Adityanarayan!' I heard him murmur, 'What a brain you had!'

Lalmohan Babu slurped his tea noisily, and said, 'Very good tea, I must say. Why, Felu Babu, have you made any progress?'

Feluda continued to mutter, "Half ten". That's five. "Half again, century". Century would mean a hundred, so half of that is fifty. Five and fifty, that's fifty-five. OK, he probably means fifty-five paces. But what does it relate to? The tree? What is a people's tree? I must think . . . '

My heart lifted suddenly. He had started to solve the riddle. I felt sure he'd be able to get the entire meaning before we left—with the tiger skin, of course.

The clock outside struck eight. Mr Sengupta should be here soon, I thought. A few minutes passed, but there was no sign of him. Feluda didn't seem to be aware of the delay. He was still engrossed in the puzzle.

'Rising sun?' I heard him say, 'Could it mean the east? Yes. Fifty-five paces to the east of something. What can it mean? The tree . . . the tree . . .'

Someone knocked on the door. It was Shashank Sanyal, not Mr Sengupta.

'Er . . . haven't you finished your tea? Oh, I'm sorry,' he said. Feluda put his notebook away and got to his feet. Mr Sanyal was looking visibly upset.

'What is it? What is the matter?' Feluda asked quickly. Mr Sanyal cleared his throat, then spoke somewhat absently, 'There's some bad news, Mr Mitter. Torit Sengupta . . . Mahitosh's secretary . . . died last night.'

'Wha-at! How?' Feluda asked. Lalmohan Babu and I simply stared speechlessly.

'It seems he went into the forest last night. No one knows why. His body was found only a little while ago, by a woodcutter.'

'But how did he die? What happened?'

'Apparently, his body has been partially eaten by some animal. Quite possibly, a tiger.'

The man-eater! My hands suddenly felt cold and clammy. Lalmohan Babu had been standing in the middle of the room. He now took three steps backwards to grab the corner of a table and lean against it. Feluda stood still, looking extremely grim.

'I am sorry,' Mr Sanyal said again, 'You only came yesterday for a holiday and now this has happened. I'm afraid we are going to be rather busy . . . I mean, we have to go and see the body for ourselves, naturally.'

'Can we go with you?'

At this question, Mr Sanyal glanced swiftly at us and said, 'You may be used to gory deaths, Mr Mitter, but the others . . . ?'

'They will stay in the jeep. I will not let them see anything unpleasant.'

Mr Sanyal agreed. 'Very well. We have two jeeps. You three can travel in one.'

'Are we going to carry a gun?'

This question came from Lalmohan Babu. At any other time, Mr Sanyal would have laughed at the idea. But now he said seriously, 'Yes. There's nothing to be afraid of during the day, but we *are* going to be armed.'

*

None of us spoke in the jeep. I hadn't yet got over the shock. Only last evening, he was alive. He had spoken with us. And now he was dead . . . killed by a man-eater. What was he doing in the forest in the middle of the night? The light we saw moving among the trees . . . was it coming from Mr Sengupta's torch?

There was another jeep in front of ours. In it were Mahitosh Babu, Mr Sanyal, a man called Mr Datta from the Forest Department, the shikari Madhavlal, and the woodcutter who had found the body and come running to the house. Mahitosh Babu, who had told us so many exciting stories only the previous night, seemed to have aged considerably in the last couple of hours. What I couldn't figure out was whether it was because of the tragic death of his secretary, or because of the implications of having a man-eater running loose in the area.

We did not have to go very far into the forest. Only five minutes after taking the road that ran through the forest, the jeep in front of us slowed down, and then stopped. The road was lined with large trees. I recognized teak, silk-cotton and neem. There was a huge jackfruit tree and a number of bamboo groves. Evidence of last night's rain lay everywhere. Every little hole and hollow in the ground was full of water.

'Look!' Feluda said as our jeep stopped. I looked in the direction he pointed and noticed, after a few seconds, a light green object on a bush. It was a torn piece of the shirt Mr Sengupta had worn the night before. I had no problem in recognizing it.

Our jeep stood at least fifty yards away from where Mr Sengupta's body lay—hidden out of sight, thankfully. Everyone from the other jeep climbed out. The woodcutter began walking. Feluda, too, got out and said, 'You two wait here. It must be a horrible sight.'

The others disappeared behind a bamboo grove. Although we were at some distance from them, I could hear what they said, possibly because the forest was totally silent. The first person to speak was Mahitosh Babu. 'My God!' he exclaimed, slapping his forehead with his palm.

'It's useless now to look for pug marks—the rain would have washed them away—but it does look like an attack by a tiger, doesn't it?' asked Mr Datta.

'Yes, undoubtedly,' Mahitosh Babu replied.

'It stopped raining after two o'clock last night. From the way the blood's been washed away, it seems he was killed before it started to rain.'

Feluda spoke next: 'But does a man-eater always start eating its prey on the same spot where it kills it? Doesn't it often carry its dead prey from one place to another?'

'Yes, that's true,' Mahitosh Babu replied, 'but don't think we can find traces of the body being dragged on the ground. No mark would have stayed for very long in all that rain. In any case, a tiger is quite capable of carrying the body of a man in such a way that it wouldn't touch the ground at all. So I don't think we'll ever find out where exactly Torit was attacked.'

'If we could find his glasses, maybe that would . . .' Feluda's voice trailed away.

This was followed by a few minutes' silence. Through the leaves, I saw Mr Sanyal move. Perhaps he was trying to look for pug marks.

'Madhavlal!' called Mahitosh Babu, but could get no further, for Feluda interrupted him.

'Can a tiger use just one single nail to leave a deep wound?' he asked.

'Why? What makes you say that?'

'Perhaps you didn't notice—there's a wound on his chest. Something narrow and very sharp pierced through his clothes and went into his body. If you come this way, sir, I'll show you what I mean.'

Everyone gathered round the body once more. Then I heard Mahitosh Babu cry, 'Oh God! Dear God in heaven, this is murder! That kind of injury couldn't possibly have been caused by an animal. Someone killed him *before* the tiger found him. Oh, what a terrible disaster!'

'Murder . . . or it may be attempted murder,' Feluda spoke slowly, 'He was stabbed, that much is clear. But may be his assassin left him injured and ran away. When the tiger came along, an injured prey must have made his job that much easier. If only we could find the weapon!'

'Shashank, please inform the police at once,' Mahitosh Babu said.

Everyone then returned to the jeep, leaving only Madhavlal with his gun to guard the body. When Feluda joined us, I was shocked to see how grim he looked. He didn't speak another word on the way back; neither were we in the mood to talk. We passed a herd of deer a few moments later, but even that did not bring me any joy. We had faced danger many times in the past, and had had to deal with unforeseen complexities, but this seemed utterly bizarre. Not only was there a mysterious death, a possible murderer to be found and arrested, but—to top it all—a man-eater!

I stole a glance at Lalmohan Babu. Never before had I seen him look so ashen.

SIX

We were back in our room. It was now 5 p.m. Shashank Sanyal had informed the police, who had started their investigation. At this moment, there was really nothing for us to do. We had just had tea. Despite all my mental turmoil, I couldn't help noticing just how good the tea was. It was from Mahitosh Babu's own estate, we were told. Feluda was pacing, frowning and cracking his knuckles, stopping occasionally to light a Charminar, then stubbing it into a brass ashtray after just a couple of puffs. I sat staring out of the window. The sky today was quite clear. Lalmohan Babu kept lifting up the head of the leopard on our floor and inspecting its teeth. I saw him do this at least three times.

'If only I'd had the chance to get to know him better!' Feluda muttered. This was truly unfortunate. Mr Sengupta had died before we could learn anything about him. How could Feluda get anywhere unless he knew what kind of a man he had been, who would want to kill him, whether he had had any enemies?

A few minutes after the clock on the veranda struck five, a servant came up to inform us that Mahitosh Babu wanted to see us. We rose at once and went to the drawing room. Besides our host and Mr Sanyal, there was a third man in the room, wearing a police uniform.

'This is Inspector Biswas,' Mahitosh Babu said, 'When I told him you were the first one to suspect murder, he said he'd like to meet you.'

'Namaskar,' said Feluda and took a chair opposite the inspector. We found a settee for ourselves.

Mr Biswas was very dark and quite bald, although he could not have been more than forty. He sported a thin moustache, one side of which was longer than the other. Perhaps he hadn't been paying attention while trimming it. He cast a sharp glance at Feluda and said, 'I believe you are an amateur detective?'

Feluda smiled and nodded.

'Do you know the difference between your lot and mine? There's usually a murder when you visit a place; we visit a place *after* there's been a murder.' Mr Biswas laughed loudly at his own joke.

Feluda went straight to the point. 'Has the murder weapon been found?'

Mr Biswas stopped laughing and shook his head. 'No, but we're still looking for it. You can imagine how difficult it is to find something in a forest, especially when there's a man-eater lurking in it. Even the police are men, aren't they? I mean, which man wants to get eaten? Ha ha ha ha!'

Feluda forced a smile since the inspector was laughing so much, but grew serious immediately.

'Is it true that he died because he was stabbed?' he asked.

'That's impossible to tell, from what's left of the body. The tiger finished nearly half of it. There will be a post-mortem, naturally, but I don't think that's going to be of any use. There is no doubt that he was stabbed. We have to catch whoever did it. Now, whether he died as a result of stabbing, or whether it was because of the tiger's attack, we do not know. In any case, what the tiger did is not our concern. That's for Mr Sinha-Roy to sort out.'

Mahitosh Babu was staring at the carpet. 'Already,' he said grimly, 'there is pretty widespread panic among the villagers. Some of my own men who work as woodcutters come from local villages. They have to work for another couple of months, after which the monsoon will start, so their work will have to stop. But they're not willing to risk their lives right now. I . . . I simply do not know what to do. Before I do

anything at all, I *must* learn who killed Torit, why did he have
to die? If I cannot hunt the tiger down, the Forest Department
must find someone. After all, I am not the only shikari in this
area.'

Mr Biswas cleared this throat. 'There is only one question
in my mind,' he told us, 'why did your secretary go to the forest
in the middle of the night? The motive for killing, I think, is
relatively simple. We didn't find a wallet or any money or any
other valuables on his person. So whoever killed him simply
wanted those, I think. Plain robbery, there's your motive.'

'If that was the case,' Feluda said quietly, lighting a
cigarette, 'he could simply have been knocked unconscious
with a rod, or even a heavy walking stick. He did not have to
be killed.' Mr Biswas laughed again, a little dryly this time.
'No,' he said, 'but if you rule out robbery, can *you* think of a
suitable motive, Mr Mitter? Torit Sengupta worked for Mr
Sinha-Roy, his world consisted of books and papers, he
arrived here five years ago, didn't go out much and didn't
know anyone except those in this house. Who would wish to
kill a man like that, unless he—or they—came upon him by
chance and decided to rob him of what possessions he had?'

Feluda frowned in silence.

'Yes, I know an amateur detective wouldn't appreciate
the idea of a simple robbery,' Mr Biswas mocked, 'You like
complications, don't you? You like mysteries? Well then,
here's a first class mystery for you, Mr Mitter: why did Mr
Sengupta go into the forest in the first place? What was he
doing there? Try and solve that one!'

No one made a reply. Mr Sanyal was sitting next to his
friend in absolute silence. Mahitosh Babu was still looking pale
and exhausted. He kept shaking his head and muttering under
his breath, 'I don't understand . . . nothing makes sense . . .!'

There didn't seem to be anything else to say. We rose a
minute later. To my surprise, Mr Biswas spoke quite kindly
before we left. 'You may carry on with your own investigation,

Mr Mitter,' he said, 'We don't mind that in the least. After all, you were the first person to notice the stab wound.'

We left the drawing room, but did not return to our own. Feluda went out of the front door, through the portico and turned right to go behind the house, past the old stables, and possibly where elephants used to be kept.

I glanced up once we were at the back of the house, and saw a row of windows on the first floor. Some were shut, others open. Through one of the open windows, I could see Lalmohan Babu's towel hanging on his bedpost. Had it not been there, it would have been impossible to identify our own room. There was a door on the ground floor, directly below our window. Perhaps this acted as the back door. Mr Sengupta might have slipped out of it to go to the forest last night.

About fifty yards away, there was a tiny hut with a thatched roof. A group of men were huddled before it. I recognized one of them. It was Mahitosh Babu's chowkidar. Perhaps the hut belonged to him. Feluda strode forward in that direction, closely followed by Lalmohan Babu and me. The forest Kalbuni stretched in the background, behind which lay a range of bluish-grey mountains.

The chowkidar gave us a salute as we got closer.

'What is your name?' Feluda asked him.

'Chandan Mishir, huzoor.' He was an old man, with close-cropped hair and wrinkles around his eyes. From the way he spoke, it was obvious that he chewed tobacco. Feluda started chatting with him. From what he told us, it appeared that the local people were far more worried about the man-eater than about Mr Sengupta's death. Chandan—who had spent fifty years working for the Sinha-Roys—had seen or heard of mad elephants in the jungle which came out at times, but there hadn't been a man-eater for at least thirty years.

It was Chandan's belief that the tiger had been injured by a poacher, which now hampered its ability to find prey in the forest. This could well be true. Or maybe the tiger was old.

Sometimes tigers became man-eaters when their teeth became worn and weak. I had even read that trying to eat a porcupine might injure a tiger to such an extent that it would then be forced to kill humans, which is easier than hunting other animals in the wild.

'Do the locals want Mahitosh Babu to kill this tiger?' Feluda asked.

Chandan scratched his head. 'Yes, of course. But our babu has never been on a shikar in these parts. He's been to the jungles in Assam and Orissa, but not here,' he said.

This came as a big surprise to us all.

'Why? Why hasn't he ever hunted here?'

'Babu's grandfather and father were both killed by tigers, you see. So Mahitosh Babu went away from here.'

We had no idea his father had also been killed by a tiger. Chandan told us what had happened. Apparently, Mahitosh Babu's father had shot a tiger from a machaan. The tiger fell and lay so still that everyone thought it had died. Ten minutes later, when he climbed down from the machaan and went closer to the tiger, it sprang up and attacked him viciously. Although he was taken to a hospital, his wounds turned septic and he died in a few days.

Feluda stood frowning when Chandan finished his tale. Then he pointed at the hut and said, 'Is that where you live?'

'Ji, huzoor.'

'When do you go to sleep?'

Chandan looked profoundly startled by this question. Feluda stopped beating about the bush.

'The man who was killed last night—'

'Torit Babu?'

'Yes. He left the house quite late at night and went into the forest. Did you see him go?'

'No, not last night. But I saw him go in there the day before yesterday, and a few days before that. He went there more than once, often in the evening. Last night . . .'

'Yes?'

'I saw not Torit Babu, but someone else.'

The expression on Feluda's face changed instantly. 'Who did you see?' he asked urgently.

'I don't know, huzoor. The torch Torit Babu used to carry was a large one—an old one with three cells. This man had a smaller torch, but its light was just as strong.'

'Is that all you saw? Just the light from a torch? Nothing else?'

'No, huzoor. I didn't see who it was.'

Feluda started to ask something else, but had to stop. One of the servants from the house was running towards us.

'Please come back to the house, sir!' he called, 'Babu wants to see you at once.'

We quickly went back to the front of the house. Mahitosh Babu was waiting for us near the portico.

'You were right,' he said as soon as he saw Feluda, 'Torit was not killed by a passing hooligan in the forest.'

'How can you be so sure?'

'The murder weapon was taken from our house. Remember the sword I showed you yesterday? It is missing from my grandfather's room!'

It was the servant called Kanai who had first noticed that the sword was missing when he went in to dust the room. He informed his master immediately. The room was not locked, since it contained several books and papers which Mahitosh Babu frequently needed to refer to. All the servants were old and trusted. Nothing had been stolen from the house for so many years that people had stopped worrying about theft altogether. What it meant was that anyone in the house could have taken the sword.

Feluda examined the glass case carefully, but did not find a clue. It was just the sword that was missing. Everything else was in place. 'I'd like to see Mr Sengupta's bedroom, and the study where he worked,' Feluda said when he'd finished, 'But before I do that, I need to know if you suspect anyone.'

Mahitosh Babu shook his head. 'No, I simply cannot imagine why anyone should want to kill him. He hardly ever saw anyone outside this house. All he did was go on long walks. If that sword was used to kill him, then it has to be someone from this house who did it. No, Mr Mitter, I cannot help you at all.'

We made our way to Mr Sengupta's bedroom. It was as large as ours. Among his personal effects were his clothes, a blue suitcase, a shoulder bag and a shaving kit. On a table were a few magazines and books, a writing pad and a couple of pencils. A smaller bedside table had a flask, a glass, a transistor radio and a packet of cigarettes. The suitcase wasn't locked. Feluda opened it, to find that it was very neatly packed. 'He was obviously all set to leave for Calcutta,' he remarked, closing it again.

Five minutes later, we came out of the bedroom and went into his study.

'What exactly did his duties involve?' Feluda asked Mahitosh Babu.

'Well, he handled all my correspondence. Then he made copies of my manuscripts, since my own handwriting is really quite bad. He used to go to Calcutta and speak to my publishers on my behalf, and correct the proofs. Of late, he had been helping me gather information about my ancestors to write a history of my family. This meant having to go through heaps of old letters and documents, and making a note of relevant details.'

'Did he use these notebooks to record all the information?' Feluda asked, pointing at the thick, bound notebooks neatly arranged on a desk. Mahitosh Babu nodded.

'And are these the proofs for your new book he was correcting?'

Stacks of printed sheets were kept on the desk, next to the notebooks. Feluda picked up a few sheets and began leafing through them.

'Tell me, was Mr Sengupta a very reliable proof-reader?'

Mahitosh Babu looked quite taken aback by the question. 'Yes, I think so. Why do you ask?'

'Look, there's a mistake in the first paragraph of the first page, which he overlooked. The "a" in the word "roar" is missing; and . . . again, look, the second "e" in "deer" hasn't been printed. But he didn't spot it.'

'How strange!' Mahitosh Babu glanced absently at the mistakes Feluda pointed out.

'Had he seemed worried about something recently? Did he have anything on his mind?'

'Why, no, I hadn't noticed anything!'

Feluda bent over the desk, and peered at a writing pad on which Mr Sengupta had doodled and drawn little pictures.

'Did you know he could draw?'

'No. No, he had never told me.'

There was nothing else to see. We stepped out of the room and reached the veranda outside. A deep, familiar voice reached our ears, speaking in a somewhat theatrical fashion: 'Doomed . . . Doomed! Destruction and calamity! The very foundation of truth is being rocked . . . the end is nigh!'

We only heard his voice. Devtosh Babu remained out of sight. His brother sighed and said, 'Every summer, he gets a little worse. He'll be all right once the rains start, and it cools down.'

We had reached our room. Feluda said, 'I was thinking of going back to the forest tomorrow. I need to search . . . find things for myself. What do you say?'

Mahitosh Babu thought for a moment. Then he said, 'Well, I don't think the tiger will return to the spot where Torit's body was found, at least not during the day. That's what my experience with tigers tells me, anyway. So if you stay relatively close to that area, you're going to be safe. To tell you the truth, what I find most surprising is that a large tiger is still left in Kalbuni!'

'May we take Madhavlal with us, and a jeep?'

'Certainly.'

Mahitosh Babu left. The police had to be informed about the missing sword.

It was now quite dark outside, although the sky was absolutely clear. Lalmohan Babu switched the fan on and sat down on his bed.

'Did you think you'd get a murder mystery on a short holiday? It's a bonus, isn't it, Felu Babu? You have to thank me for it,' he laughed.

'Sure, Lalmohan Babu, I am most thankful,' Feluda replied, sounding a little preoccupied. He had picked up two things from Torit Sengupta's room and brought them back with him. One was a book on the history of Coochbehar, and the other was the writing pad. I saw him staring at the little pictures, frowning deeply.

'These are not just funny doodles,' he said, almost to himself, 'I am sure it has a meaning. What could it be? Why do I feel there's something familiar about these pictures?'

Lalmohan Babu and I went and stood next to him. Mr Sengupta had drawn a tree on the pad. A tree with a solid trunk and several leafy branches. A few leaves were lying loose at the bottom of the tree. Their base was broad, but they tapered off to end on a thin narrow point. I had no problem in recognizing them. They were peepal leaves.

But that was not all. He had drawn footprints, going away from the tree, towards what looked like a couple of hands. I peered more closely. Yes, they were two hands—or, rather, two open palms. He had even drawn tiny lines on them, just as they appear on human hands. Behind these was a sun. Not a full round one, but one that had only half-risen. Between the two hands was a tiny cross. Something began stirring in my own mind. This picture was meant to convey a message. Was it a message that perhaps I had heard before? Where? I began to feel quite confused.

Feluda cleared all confusion in less than a minute. 'Yes, yes, yes!' he exclaimed softly, '*Of course*! Well done, Mr Sengupta, well done!' Then he caught me looking expectantly at him. 'Do you see what this is Topshe? It's a picture of the puzzle. Torit Sengupta had cracked it, possibly quite soon after they found it among Adityanarayan's papers. Let's have a look.' He opened his notebook. "Old man hollow". Now, that's the only bit that's not clear. But "pace to follow" means fifty-five paces—those are the footprints—going from the "people's tree", which is simply a peepal tree. Adityanarayan called it a people's tree either because it sounded similar to "peepal", or because it was for some reason important to people. That rising sun, as I'd guessed myself, means the east. So, fifty-five paces to the east of a peepal tree are . . .'

' . . . Two hands?' Lalmohan Babu asked hopefully.

'Yes and no. Look at the picture. They are palms. So there must be two palms—palm trees—near the peepal. And if you dig the ground between these palms, you'll probably find the treasure.'

'It makes no sense to me,' Lalmohan Babu complained, 'Tell me what the whole message is.'

'But I just did! In the forest somewhere, there is a peepal tree. Fifty-five paces—that would be about fifty-five yards—to the east of this tree are two palms. And . . .'

'OK, between those palms—"below them stands"—so you mean below the ground is the buried treasure, whatever that might be. I get it now. But, Felu Babu, there may be dozens of peepal trees in that forest and scores of palms, all within fifty yards of one another. How many will you look for?'

Feluda was silent, still frowning, 'Yes,' he said at last, 'The first line—"old man hollow"—is probably an indicator. I mean, that's what actually identifies the tree, and tells you which particular peepal tree to look for. But what can it mean? Even this picture doesn't tell us anything, does it? The old man—' he had to stop.

'Who is talking of old men?' asked Devtosh Babu, lifting the curtain and walking into the room. He was still wearing the same purple dressing gown. Didn't he have anything else to wear?

'Oh, please do come in, sir, have a seat,' Feluda invited. Devtosh Babu paid no attention to him. 'Do you know why Yudhisthir's chariot got stuck to the ground?' he asked. He had said this before. Why was he obsessed with Yudhisthir's chariot?

'No. Why?' Feluda answered calmly.

'Because he had told a lie. He had to be punished. One single lie . . . and it can finish you.'

'Devtosh Babu,' Feluda said conversationally, 'may I ask you something?'

He looked perfectly amazed. 'Ask *me* something? Why? No one ever asks me anything.'

'I'd like to, because I know about your knowledge of local history. Can you tell me if there's a tree associated with an old man? I mean, here in the forest? Did an old man sit under a tree?'

It was a shot in the dark. But it made Devtosh Babu's sad and intense face suddenly break into a smile. It transformed his whole appearance.

'No, no. No old man actually sat under the tree. It was in the tree itself.'

What! Was he talking nonsense again? But his eyes and his voice seemed perfectly normal.

'There was a hollow in the tree trunk,' he explained quickly, 'that looked like the face of an old man. You think I'm mad, don't you? But I swear, that hollow looked exactly as though an old man was gaping with his mouth open. We loved that tree. Grandfather used to call it the tree of the toothless fakir. He used to take us there for picnics.'

'What kind of a tree was it?'

'A peepal. Have you seen the temple of the Chopped Goddess? That was Raju's doing. This tree was behind the temple. In fact, it was from this same tree that Mahi—!'

'Dada! Come back here at once!' shouted a voice outside the door.

Devtosh Babu broke off, for his brother had appeared at the door, looking and sounding extremely cross. Mahitosh Babu stepped into the room. His face was set, his eyes cold.

'Did you take your pills?' he asked sternly.

'What pills? I am fine, there's nothing wrong with me. Why should I have to take pills?'

Without another word, Mahitosh Babu dragged his brother out of our room. We could hear him scolding him as they moved away, 'Let the doctor decide how you are. You will kindly continue to take the pills you have been prescribed. Is that understood?'

Their footsteps died away.

'Pity!' Lalmohan Babu remarked, 'He seemed quite normal today, didn't he?'

Feluda did not appear to have heard him. He was looking preoccupied again.

'The tree of the toothless fakir,' he said under his breath, 'Well, that takes care of both the old man and the hollow. All we need to do now, friends, is find the temple of the Chopped Goddess!'

Feluda did not go to bed until late that night. Lalmohan Babu and I stayed up with him until eleven, talking about Torit Sengupta's death. None of us could figure out why a young and obviously intelligent man like him had to die such an awful and mysterious death. Even Feluda could not find answers to a lot of questions. He made a list of these:

1. Who, apart from Mr Sengupta, had gone to the forest that night? Was it the murderer? Was it the person who had stolen the sword? Or was it a third person? Who could have a small but powerful torch?
2. We had all heard Mahitosh Sinha-Roy having an argument with someone the same night. Who was he speaking to?
3. Devtosh Babu was about to tell us something concerning the peepal tree and his brother, when the latter interrupted him. What was he going to say?
4. Why did Devtosh Babu mention Yudhisthir's chariot, more than once? Was it simply the raving of a mad man, or did it have any significance?
5. Why does Shashank Sanyal speak so little? Is he quiet and reserved by nature, or is there a specific reason behind his silence?

Lalmohan Babu heard him read out this list, then said, 'Look, Felu Babu, there's one man who continues to make me feel uneasy. Yes, I am talking of Devtosh Babu. He spoke quite normally a few hours ago, but at other times he isn't normal, is he? What if he came upon someone accidentally in the forest, and decided it was Kalapahar, or Raju as he calls him? He might attack this person, mightn't he?'

Feluda stared at Lalmohan Babu for a few seconds before speaking. 'Working with me has clearly improved both your imagination and powers of observation,' he remarked, 'Yes, I agree Devtosh Babu is certainly physically capable of striking someone with a sword. But consider this: whoever took that sword knew Mr Sengupta had gone to the forest. So he deliberately took the weapon, followed him—don't forget it was a stormy night—found him, and then killed him. Could a madman have thought all this out and acted upon it, especially when it meant finding his way in the dark in inclement weather, then holding the torch in one hand and using the sword with the other? No, I don't think so. What is essential now is a return visit to the forest, and seeing if we can pick up a clue. There's no point in speculating here. The only thing I am sure of is that Mr Sengupta had gone into the forest to look for the hidden treasure. Perhaps he wanted to collect it and take it back to Calcutta. But what still doesn't make sense is why he was so sorely tempted in the first place. He was living here very comfortably, and was clearly very well paid. Did you see his clothes and toiletries? Everything was expensive and of good quality. Even the cigarettes he smoked were imported.'

Lalmohan Babu shook his head, and declared he was now ready for bed. I fell asleep soon after this, but Feluda stayed awake for a long time.

I woke to find the sky overcast once again, and Feluda dressed and ready. Then we heard the sound of a jeep arriving, and a servant came up to say we were wanted in the drawing room.

Inspector Biswas was waiting for us.

'Are you happy now?' he asked Feluda.

'Why should I be happy?'

'You found a mystery, didn't you? The murderer took the

weapon from this house and finished his victim with it. Isn't that great news?'

'It is true that a sword is missing. But surely you are not assuming that the same sword was used to kill Mr Sengupta, just because it is no longer here?'

'No, I am not assuming anything at all. But what about you? Didn't the thought cross your mind?'

Both men were speaking politely, but it was obvious that a silent undercurrent of rivalry was flowing between them. This was quite unnecessary. I felt cross with the inspector. It was he who had started it. Feluda lit a cigarette and spoke quietly, 'I haven't yet reached any conclusion. And if you think I am happy about any aspect of this case, you are quite wrong. Murder never makes me happy, particularly when it is the murder of a young and clever man.'

'A clever man?' Mr Biswas jeered openly, 'Why should a clever man leave the comforts of his room and go walking in a dark forest in the middle of the night? What's so clever about that? Can you find a satisfactory answer to this question, Mr Mitter?'

'Yes, I can.'

All the three men present in the room, apart from ourselves, seemed to stiffen at Feluda's words. 'There was a very good reason for Mr Sengupta's visit to the forest that night,' Feluda said clearly, looking at Mahitosh Babu, 'I have worked out the meaning of the puzzle you showed me. But Torit Sengupta had done the same, long before me. That tiger skin should really have gone to him. It is my belief that he was in the forest looking for the treasure.'

Mahitosh Babu opened his mouth to speak, but could not find any words. His eyes nearly popped out. Feluda hurriedly explained about the puzzle and how he had discovered its meaning. But Mahitosh Babu continued to look perplexed.

'The tree of the toothless fakir?' he said, surprised, 'Why, I have never heard of it!'

'Really? But your brother told us you used to go for

picnics with your grandfather when you were both small. He said you sat under that tree? . . .'

'My brother?' Mahitosh Babu said a little scornfully, 'Do you realize how much fact there is in what my brother says, and how much of it is fiction? Don't forget he isn't normal.'

Feluda could not say anything in reply. How could he possibly comment on Mahitosh Babu's brother's illness? After all, he was only an outsider.

Mahitosh Babu, however, had now started to look openly distressed. 'This means . . . this means Torit was planning to run away to Calcutta with the treasure! And I had no idea.' Mr Biswas stood up, curling his right hand into a fist. Then he struck his left palm with it and said, 'Well, at least we know why he was in the forest. That's one problem solved. Now we must find his assassin.'

'It has to be someone from this house. I hope you realize that, Mr Biswas?' Feluda blew out a smoke ring.

Mr Biswas gave a twisted smile. 'Sure,' he replied, narrowing his eyes, 'but that would have to include you. You had seen the sword, you knew where it was kept. You had every opportunity to remove it, just like the others in this house. We don't know whether you knew Torit Sengupta before you came here, or whether there was any enmity between the two of you, do we?'

Feluda sent another smoke ring floating in the air. 'You're right,' he said, 'No one knows anything about that. However, everyone is aware of two things. One, I was invited here. I did not come on my own. Two, I was the one who pointed out that Mr Sengupta had been attacked by a sharp instrument. If I didn't, people would have assumed a wild animal had killed him, and no further questions would have been asked.'

Mr Biswas laughed unexpectedly. 'Relax, Mr Mitter,' he said, 'Why are you taking me so seriously? Don't worry, we are not interested in you. Someone else concerns us far more.' I noticed that when he said this, he exchanged a glance with Mahitosh Babu, just for a fleeting second.

'You told me something yesterday, Mr Biswas. Does that still stand?' Feluda asked.

'What did I tell you?'

'Can I continue with my own investigation?'

'Of course. But we must not clash with each other, you know.'

'We won't. I wish to confine myself to working in the forest. You're not interested in that, are you?'

The inspector shrugged. 'As you wish,' he said carelessly.

Feluda turned to Mahitosh Babu. 'You mean to say there is absolutely no point in talking to your brother?'

Mahitosh Sinha-Roy seemed to clench his jaw at this question. Was he perhaps beginning to lose his patience? However, when he spoke, he sounded perfectly friendly. 'My brother seems to have taken a turn for the worse,' he explained quietly, 'I really don't think he should be disturbed.'

Feluda stubbed his cigarette out in an ashtray and stood up. 'Well, I can hardly remain here indefinitely as your guest. Tomorrow will be the last day of our visit. May we go to the forest today? If you could please tell Madhavlal, and get us a jeep—'

Mahitosh Babu nodded. It was now eight-thirty. We decided to leave by ten o'clock. Feluda and I had brought hunting boots to walk in the forest. We put these on, although I had a feeling I wouldn't be allowed to climb out of the jeep at all. I had expected Lalmohan Babu to say he had no wish to leave the jeep but, to my surprise, he disappeared into the bathroom and changed into khaki trousers. Then he took out a pair of rather impressive sturdy boots from his suitcase and began to slip them on. Feluda gave him a sidelong glance, but made no comment.

'Felu Babu,' Lalmohan Babu began, marching up and down in his new boots in military style, 'is it true what they say about a tiger's eyes? I mean, the look in its eyes is supposed to be absolutely terrifying, or so I've heard. Could it be true?'

Feluda was staring out of the window, waiting to be told

that Madhavlal and the jeep had arrived. We were all ready to leave.

'Yes, I've heard the same,' he replied, 'But do you know what some famous shikaris have said? Tigers are just as afraid of men. If a man can manage to return a tiger's stare and just stand with a steady eye contact, the tiger would make an about turn and go away. And if simply a stare doesn't help, then screaming and shouting and waving may produce the same result.'

'But . . . what about a man-eater?'

'That's different.'

'I see. So why are you? . . .'

'Why am I going? I am going because the chances of the tiger coming out during the day are virtually nil. Even if it does appear, we will have a rifle to deal with it. Besides, we'll have the jeep; so we can always make a quick escape, if need be.'

Lalmohan Babu did not say another word until the jeep arrived. When it did, he simply said, 'I can't understand anything about this murder. Nothing makes sense, I am in total darkness.'

'Efforts are being made to make sure we do not see the light, Lalmohan Babu. It should be our job to foil every attempt.'

We reached the spot where Mr Sengupta's body had been found. The clouds having dispersed, it was much brighter today. Sunlight streamed through the leaves to form little patterns on the ground here and there. There also appeared to be many more birds chirping in the trees. Lalmohan Babu gave a start each time he heard a bird call, thinking it was an alarm call for an approaching tiger.

The body had been removed the same day. Torit Babu's family in Calcutta had been informed, and his brother had arrived to take care of the funeral. There was no sign left of that hideous incident near the bamboo grove. Even so, Feluda began inspecting the ground closely, assisted by Madhavlal. The more I saw Madhavlal, the more I liked him. He seemed a cheerful fellow. He smiled often, which made deep creases appear on both sides of his mouth. Even when he didn't smile, his eyes twinkled. He told us on the way that the news of the man-eater had spread through people in the Forest Department. Apparently, a number of shikaris had offered to kill it. Among them was a Mr Sapru, who had killed many tigers and other animals in the Terai. He was expected to arrive the next day.

Now he stopped to chat with us and began telling us stories of the many expeditions he had been on. At this moment, Feluda called him from the bamboo grove. Madhavlal stopped his tale and went forward quickly, closely followed by Lalmohan Babu and myself. Feluda had raised no objection today to our getting out of the jeep.

We found him kneeling on the ground, bending over a bamboo stem.

'Take a look at this!' he said to Madhavlal.

Madhavlal glanced at it briefly and declared, 'It was hit by a bullet, sir.'

There was a mark on the stem which I now saw. All of us—including Feluda—felt astounded.

'Can you tell me how old that mark might be?' Feluda asked, a little impatiently.

'Not older than a couple of days,' Madhavlal replied.

'What can it mean?' Feluda muttered, half to himself, 'A sword . . . a gun . . . I'm getting all confused. Torit Sengupta was struck by the sword, then someone shot at the tiger but missed, by the looks of things. Or else . . .' he broke off. Madhavlal had found something under the bamboo. I saw what it was only when I got closer. He was clutching what looked like fluff, about two inches in length.

'Hair from the tiger's body?' Feluda asked.

'Yes, sir. The bullet must have scraped one side.'

'Is that why the tiger ran away without finishing its meal?'

'Looks like it.'

Feluda began moving forward without another word. Madhavlal followed him, rifle in hand, his eyes alert. Lalmohan Babu and I placed ourselves between these two men, which struck us as the safest thing to do. Feluda was carrying a loaded revolver, but that wasn't enough to deal with a man-eater. The sound of an engine starting told me the driver of our jeep was following us. It meant that he would get closer, although he couldn't actually be by our side for we had left the road and were now amidst the trees and bushes.

Three minutes later, Feluda appeared to notice something on a thorny bush, and quickly made his way to it, walking diagonally to the right. There was a piece of green cloth stuck to it, which had undoubtedly come from Mr Sengupta's shirt. The tiger had obviously come this way carrying his body, and the shirt had got stuck on that bush.

When we started walking again, Madhavlal took the lead. He could probably guess which way the man-eater had come from. He moved with extreme caution, partly because we were behind him and partly because the area abounded with briar and other prickly plants. He stopped abruptly under a large tamarind tree, looking closely at the ground. We gathered around him and saw what had caught his attention. I had never seen such a thing before, but knew instantly I was looking at a pug mark. There were several others that seemed to have come from the same direction we were now going in.

Lalmohan Babu whispered, 'Is th-this a t-two legged tiger?'

Madhavlal laughed. 'No,' Feluda explained, 'That is how a tiger walks. It puts its hind legs exactly where it puts its forelegs. So it seems as if it's a two-legged animal.'

Madhavlal continued walking. I could no longer hear the jeep. A faint gurgling noise told me there was a nullah somewhere in the vicinity. Lalmohan Babu's new boots, which had been squeaking rather loudly at first ('Ideal for arousing the man-eater's curiosity,' Feluda had remarked) were now silent, being heavily streaked with mud.

We passed a silk-cotton tree, and then Madhavlal stopped again.

'You have a revolver, sir, don't you?' he asked Feluda. His voice was low.

A few yards ahead of us, something was emerging from the long grass, parting it to make its way. 'Krait,' Madhavlal said softly. I had read about kraits. They were extremely poisonous snakes. A second later, it came into view and stopped. It was black, striped with yellow. It had no hood.

I did not see Feluda take out his revolver, but heard the earsplitting noise as he fired it. The head of the snake disappeared, and it was all over. A number of birds cried out, and a group of monkeys grew rather agitated, but the body of the snake lay still. '*Shabaash!*' said Madhavlal. Lalmohan Babu made a noise that appeared to be a mixture of laughter, a sneeze and a cough.

We resumed walking. The forest was not thick everywhere. The trees thinned to our left. 'That's where the nullah is,' Madhavlal said, 'and the area is rocky. Tigers often rest there during the day behind rocks and boulders. I suggest we walk straight on.'

We took his advice. Feluda was still looking around everywhere, hoping for more clues. This time, Lalmohan Babu helped him find one, purely by accident. He stumbled against something and kicked it, making it spring up in the air and land a few feet away.

It was a dark brown leather wallet. Feluda picked it up and opened it. There were two hundred-rupee notes, and a few smaller ones. Besides these, in the smaller compartments, were two folded old stamps, cash memos and a prescription. The wallet was wet and dirty, but the money inside it could be used quite easily. Feluda put everything back in the wallet, then put it in his pocket.

We began walking again. The trees had suddenly grown very thick. Almost unconsciously, I began to look for a peepal tree. I knew Feluda was doing the same. I did see a couple of peepals, but there were no palms near them. Madhavlal had stopped for a minute to cut two small branches from a tree, which he then passed on to Lalmohan Babu and me. We were now using these as walking sticks.

'A pug mark can tell you a lot about the size of the tiger, can't it?' Feluda asked.

'Yes, sir,' Madhavlal replied, 'Our man-eater appears to be a big fellow.'

Feluda asked another question: 'Mahitosh Babu has never killed anything in this forest, has he?'

'No, sir. Many shikaris have superstitions. Mahitosh Babu is no exception. My own father did. Once, he happened to brush against a stinging nettle just as he set off from home. He killed a ten-foot tiger that day. From then on, every time he went on shikar, he used to rub his hands on stinging nettle, no matter how much it hurt.'

'Jim Corbett was superstitious, too. If he could see a snake before going off to look for a tiger, that used to make him happy.'

If his grandfather and father had both been killed here, it was entirely understandable why Mahitosh Babu had taken himself off to Assam and Orissa.

Twenty minutes later, Feluda finally found what he was really looking for. Telling Madhavlal to stop, he began peering behind a thick bush, which was laden with small purple flowers. We joined him and saw it. The stone-studded handle of Adityanarayan's sword was visible just outside the bush. The blade was hidden behind it.

Feluda picked it up in one swooping movement. The blade was stained with blood, although the stains had faded to some degree. Feluda turned it over and inspected the handle closely. 'Madhavlalji,' he said, 'the actual spot where the murder took place cannot be far from here. Can we walk on?'

'Sure. But a hundred yards from here, you'll find a temple.'

'A temple?' Feluda asked sharply.

'Yes, sir. The locals call it the temple of the Chopped Goddess. There's nothing left in it. Only the basic structure is still standing somehow.'

None of us said anything. Behind this temple was the tree of the toothless fakir. And fifty-five yards to the east! . . . Without a word, Feluda strode ahead, the sword in his hand, as though *he* was Sher Shah, out to destroy a tiger.

Madhavlal was right about the temple. It was certainly an ancient building, its walls broken and cracked. Plants had grown out of the cracks. Roots from a banyan tree hung down from all sides, as if they wanted to crush what was left of the roof. What must have been the inner sanctum was still there, but it was so dark inside that I didn't think there was any question of going in.

Feluda, however, was not looking at the temple at all. He was staring behind it. About twenty yards away, just as Devtosh Babu had said, stood a large, old peepal tree. Its branches were dry, shrivelled and bare. There were virtually no leaves left. But what the tree did have, visible even from a distance, was a big hollow, at least five feet up from the ground.

We followed Feluda in breathless anticipation. As we got closer, wĕ saw to our amazement that funny marks and patches on the tree trunk near the hollow, together with its uneven surface, had truly helped create the appearance of an old, toothless man with a gaping mouth. 'Is that the east?' Feluda asked, turning his eyes to the right.

'Yes, sir,' Madhavlal replied.

'Look, the two palms! And I don't think I need even bother with measuring the distance. It's got to be fifty-five paces.'

The two palms were clearly visible, fifty-five yards away. We moved towards them, and spotted it almost immediately: the ground between the palms had been dug quite recently. There was a fairly large hole, now filled with water. Any treasure that might have been there had gone.

'What! Hidden treasure vanished?' Lalmohan Babu was the first to find his tongue. He forgot to whisper.

Feluda was looking grim again, although what we had just seen could hardly be regarded as a new mystery. Whoever killed Mr Sengupta had obviously removed the treasure. Feluda stared at the hole in the ground for a few seconds, then said, 'Why don't you rest for a while? I'd like to make a quick survey.'

My legs were aching after walking stealthily for such a long time. I was quite thankful for this chance to rest, and so was Lalmohan Babu. We found a dry area under the peepal tree, and sat down. Madhavlal put his rifle down, placing it against the tree trunk and began to tell us a story of how he had been attacked by a bear when he was thirteen, and how he had managed to escape. But I couldn't give him my full attention, for my eyes kept following Feluda. He lit a cigarette, placed it between his lips and began examining the ground around the ancient temple. I saw him pick something up—possibly a cigarette stub—and then drop it again. Then he knelt, and bent low to look closely at the ground, his face almost touching it.

After ten minutes of close scrutiny outside, Feluda went into the dark hall. I could only marvel at his courage, the temple was probably crawling with snakes and other reptiles. When the temple was in use, it was supposed to have had a statue of Durga. Kalapahar chopped off its head and four of its ten arms. Hence its current name.

Feluda emerged a minute later, and made a rather cryptic remark. 'This is amazing!' he exclaimed, 'Who knew one would have to step into darkness in order to see the light?'

'What, Felu Babu, do you mean the darkness has gone?' Lalmohan Babu shouted.

'Partly, yes. You might call it the first night after a moonless one.'

'Oh. That would mean waiting for a whole fortnight to get a full moon!'

'No, Lalmohan Babu. You are only thinking of the moon. There is such a thing as the sun, remember? It comes out at the end of each dark night, doesn't it?'

'You mean to say tomorrow . . . tomorrow we might see the climax of this story? The end?'

'I am saying nothing of the kind, Lalmohan Babu. All I am prepared to tell you is that, after hours of darkness, I think I am beginning to see a glimmer of light. Come on, Topshe, let's go home.'

We had left the house at ten o'clock. By the time we got back, it was half past twelve. Feluda wanted to return the sword to Mahitosh Babu, but we discovered on our return that he had gone with Mr Sanyal to visit the Head of the Forest Department in the Forest Bungalow in Kalbuni. So we went to our room, taking the sword with us.

Before we did this, however, we spent some time on the ground floor. Feluda went to the trophy room. I could not tell what he was thinking, but he began to examine all the guns that were displayed there. He picked up each one, and inspected its barrel, its butt, trigger and safety catch. Lalmohan Babu began to ask him something, but Feluda told him to be quiet.

'This is a time to think, Lalmohan Babu,' he said, 'not to chat.' By this time, Lalmohan Babu had become quite familiar with Feluda's moods, so he promptly shut up.

Feluda finished inspecting the trophy room and turned to go upstairs. We followed silently. He spoke again on reaching the veranda on the first floor. 'What's this?' he asked, stopping suddenly and staring at Devtosh Babu's room, 'Why is the elder brother's room locked?'

There was a padlock on the door. Where could he have gone? Why had he left the room locked? Feluda said nothing more. We reached our room.

Feluda spent the next few minutes sitting quietly, frowning; then he got up and paced restlessly, stopped short and sat down again. Two minutes later, he was back on his feet. I knew this mood well. He always acted like this as he got closer to unravelling a complex mystery.

'Since there is no one about, and Devtosh Babu's room is locked,' he said suddenly, 'it might not be a bad idea to do a bit of snooping.'

He left the room. I stuck my head out of the door and saw him go into Mahitosh Babu's study. I came back into our room to find Lalmohan Babu stretched on the leopard skin on the floor. He was using its head as a pillow. Clearly, seeing a tiger's pug mark in the forest had gone a long way to boost his courage. After a few seconds of silence, he remarked, 'Thank goodness I thought of dedicating my book to Mahitosh Sinha-Roy! Could we ever have had such a thrilling experience if I hadn't? Just take this morning: a bullet in a bamboo grove, a snake in the grass, pug marks of a Royal Bengal, a ruined old temple, a famous peepal tree . . . what more could anyone want? All that's left to make the experience complete is an encounter with the man-eater.'

'Do you really want that?' I asked.

'I am not scared any more,' he replied, yawning noisily. 'If you have Madhavlal on one side, and Felu Mitter on the other, no man-eater can do anything to you!'

He closed his eyes, and seemed to go to sleep. I picked up Mahitosh Babu's book and had read a few pages, when Feluda returned. His footsteps made Lalmohan Babu open his eyes and sit up.

'Did you find anything?'

'No. I did not find what I was looking for, but that is what is significant.' After a brief pause, Feluda asked, 'Do you remember why Yudhisthir's chariot got stuck to the ground?'

'Because he told a lie?'

'Exactly. But these days, a liar doesn't always get punished by God. Other men have to catch and punish him.'

I could not ask him what he meant, for a jeep arrived as he finished speaking. Only a few minutes later, a servant turned up to say Mahitosh Babu had returned, and lunch had been served.

Despite all that had happened, we had all enjoyed our meals every day. Mahitosh Babu obviously had a very good cook. Today, the food looked inviting enough, but our host began a conversation on a rather sombre note. 'Mr Mitter,' he said solemnly, 'since you have discovered the meaning of Adityanarayan's message, I don't think I have the right to keep you here any longer. If you like, I can make arrangements for your return. One of my men is going to Jalpaiguri. He can book your tickets for you.'

Feluda did not reply immediately. Then he said slowly, 'I was thinking of going back myself. You have been an excellent host, but naturally we cannot stay here indefinitely. But, if you don't mind, I'd like to stay here tonight and leave tomorrow morning. You see, I am a detective, and there's been a murder. I'm sure you'll appreciate why I want to stay a bit longer to see if any light can be thrown on the case. It is immaterial whether I can discover the truth, or the police do their job. I only want to know what happened, and how it happened.'

Mahitosh Babu stopped eating and looked straight at Feluda. 'There is no one in this house who would plan a murder in cold blood, Mr Mitter,' he said firmly.

Feluda paid no attention. 'Where is your brother?' he asked casually, 'Has he been taken somewhere else? His room was locked.'

Mahitosh Babu replied in the same grave tone, 'My brother is in his room. But since last night, his . . . ailment has become worse. He has to be restrained, or he might cause serious damage to whoever came his way, yourself included. Sometimes, he starts imagining he's seen people who died hundreds of years ago—you know, characters out of a history book. Then he attacks them if he thinks they did anything wrong in the past. Once he mistook Torit for Kalapahar and nearly throttled him to death. One of the servants saw him, luckily, and managed to take him away.'

Feluda continued to eat. 'Did you know,' he said conversationally, 'the death of Mr Sengupta is not the only mystery we are dealing with? Someone ran off with your treasure, possibly the same night.'

'*What!*' Mahitosh Babu turned into a statue, holding his food a few inches from his mouth, 'You mean you went and checked?'

'Yes, the treasure's gone, but we found the sword, with bloodstains on it.'

Mahitosh Babu opened his mouth to speak, but could only gulp in silence. Feluda dropped the third bombshell. 'When the tiger attacked Mr Sengupta, someone shot at the tiger. The bullet hit a bamboo stem, but it is likely that it grazed the tiger's body, for we found a few strands of hair. So it seems Torit Sengupta was not the only one who had gone to the forest that night. Different people with different purposes in mind . . .'

'Poacher!' Mr Sanyal spoke unexpectedly, 'It must have been a poacher who entered the forest *after* Torit was killed. It was this poacher who shot at the tiger.'

Feluda nodded slowly. 'That possibility cannot be ruled out. So, for the moment, we need not worry about where the bullet came from. However, we still have the bloodstained sword and the missing treasure to explain.'

'Never mind the sword. The treasure is far more important,' Mahitosh Babu declared, 'Mr Mitter, we've *got* to find it. The history of the family of Sinha-Roys will remain incomplete unless it is found.'

'Very well,' Feluda suggested, 'If that is the case, why don't we all return to the spot later today? It is very close to the temple of the Chopped Goddess.'

*

Mahitosh Babu agreed to accompany us back to the forest. However, torrential rain—which began at half past three and continued well after six—forced us to abandon our plan. Feluda had been looking withdrawn; now he looked positively depressed. It was obvious that Mahitosh Babu wanted us to leave. If the weather did not improve the next day, we might well have to go back without solving the mystery surrounding Mr Sengupta's death. How another visit to the temple could make a difference, I could not tell, but I knew Feluda was definitely on to something. The occasional glint in his eyes told me that very clearly.

Unable to sit in our room doing nothing, we came out and stood on the veranda when the grandfather clock struck five. The door to Devtosh Babu's room was still locked.

'There's no one around,' Lalmohan Babu whispered, 'Why don't we try looking through the shutters? What can the man be doing?'

Like many of Lalmohan Babu's other suggestions, Feluda ignored this one.

The sky cleared after seven. When the stars came out, they looked as if someone had polished them before pasting them on an inky-black sky. Feluda sat on his bed, holding the sword. Lalmohan Babu and I were standing at the window, admiring the stars, when suddenly he clutched at my sleeve and said in a low voice, 'A small torch!'

The chowkidar's hut was visible from our window. There was a large tree near it. A man was standing under it. Another man—carrying a torch—was approaching him. His torch was of the kind that can be plugged into an electric socket and recharged. It had a small bulb, and an equally small point, but the light it gave out was very bright.

Feluda switched the light off in our room and joined us at the window.

'Madhavlal!' he murmured. I, too, had recognized the man who had been waiting under the tree as Madhavlal, for I could vaguely see his yellow shirt even in the dark. But it was impossible to see the other man. It could have been Mahitosh Babu, his brother, Mr Sanyal, or someone else.

The torch was switched off, but the two men were still standing close, talking. After a while, the yellow shirt moved away. The torch light came back on and returned to the house. Feluda waited for a few seconds before switching on our own light.

Lalmohan Babu was probably carrying out an investigation on his own. I saw him slip out to the veranda and return a moment later.

'What did you see? Is that door still locked?' Feluda asked. Lalmohan Babu gave an embarrassed laugh. 'Yes,' he replied.

'Did you really think it was Devtosh Babu who was speaking with Madhavlal?'

'Yes. I told you I did not trust him. A madman must not be trusted. We used to have one where I live. He was often seen standing in the middle of the road, throwing stones at passing trams and buses. Just think how dangerous that was?'

'What did the locked door prove?'

'That he didn't go down just now.'

'How can you be so sure? Have you heard any noises from that room today? How do you know that room isn't empty?'

Lalmohan Babu began to look rather crestfallen.

'Felu Babu, I try so hard to follow your methods and work on the same lines as you, but somehow . . . I get it all wrong!'

'That is only because you work in reverse gear. You pick your criminal first, then try to dump the crime on him. I try to understand the nature of the crime before looking for the person who might have committed it.'

'Are you doing the same in this case?'

'Of course. There is no other way.'

'But where did you start from?'

'Kurukshetra.'

After this, Lalmohan Babu did not dare ask another question.

When I went to bed that night, I had no problem in falling asleep, for the mosquito nets had been changed. But, in the middle of the night, a sudden shout woke me. I sat up, startled, to find Feluda standing in the middle of the room, clutching Adityanarayan's sword. Moonlight poured in through an open window, making the weapon shine brightly. Feluda looked steadily at the metal blade, and repeated the word he had just spoken very loudly. Only, this time he lowered his voice.

'Eureka! Eureka!' he said.

Thousands of years ago, Archimedes had said the same thing when he had found what he was looking for. There was no way of telling what Feluda had discovered.

ELEVEN

Mr Sanyal arrived in our room the following morning, just as we finished our bed-tea. What did he want so early in the morning? I looked at him in surprise, but Feluda greeted him warmly. 'We haven't really had the chance to get to know each other, have we?' he said, offering our visitor a seat, 'As Mahitosh Babu's friend, you must have had a lot of interesting experiences yourself.'

Mr Sanyal took a chair opposite the table. 'Yes. I have known Mahitosh for fifty years, since our school days.'

'May I ask you something?'

'About Mahitosh?'

'No, about Torit Sengupta.'

'Yes?'

'What sort of a man was he? I mean, what was your impression?'

'He was a very good man. I found him intelligent, diligent and very patient.'

'How was he at his work?'

'Brilliant. Absolutely brilliant.'

'Yes, I got that impression myself.'

Mr Sanyal gave Feluda a level look. 'I have come to make a request, Mr Mitter,' he said simply.

'A request?' Feluda asked, offering him a cigarette. Mr Sanyal accepted it and waited until it had been lit for him. I saw him smoking for the first time. He inhaled deeply before replying. 'Yes. You have seen a lot in the last three days,' he said. 'You are far more clever than ordinary men, so obviously you have drawn your own conclusions from what you've seen.

Today is probably the last day of your stay. No one knows what the day has in store. No matter what happens today, Mr Mitter, I'd be very grateful if you could keep it to yourself. I am sure Mahitosh would want the same thing. If you look at the history of any old family in Bengal—particularly the zamindars—I'm sure you'll find a lot of skeletons in their cupboards. The Sinha-Roys are no exception. However, I see no reason why the facts that come to light should be made public. I am making the same appeal to your friend, and to your cousin.'

'Mr Sanyal,' Feluda replied, 'I have enjoyed Mahitosh Babu's hospitality for three days. I am very grateful to him for his generosity. I can never go back to Calcutta and start maligning him. None of us could do that. I give you my word.'

Mr Sanyal nodded silently. Then Feluda asked another question, possibly because he couldn't help himself. 'Devtosh Babu's room is still locked. Can you explain why?'

Mr Sanyal looked a little oddly at Feluda. 'By the end of this day, Mr Mitter, the reason will become clear to you.'

'I take it that the police are still working on this case?'

'No.'

'What! Why not?'

'Well, suspicion has fallen on someone . . . but Mahitosh does not want the police to harass this person at all.'

'You mean Devtosh Babu?'

'Yes, who else could I mean?'

'But even if that's true, even if he did kill, he's not going to be charged or punished in the usual way, is he? I mean, considering his medical condition?'

'Yes, you are probably right. Nevertheless, the news would spread, wouldn't it? Mahitosh doesn't want that to happen.'

'Simply to save the good name of his family?'

'Yes. Yes, that's the reason Mr Mitter. Let's just leave it at that, shall we?'

Mr Sanyal rose, and left.

*

We left at half past eight. There were two jeeps once again, like the first day. Feluda, Lalmohan Babu and I were in one; in the other were Mahitosh Babu, Mr Sanyal, Madhavlal and a bearer called Parvat Singh. There were three rifles with us today. Madhavlal had his, Mahitosh Babu had another, and the third was with Feluda. He himself had asked for a rifle. Having heard from Madhavlal how he had killed the snake with his revolver, Mahitosh Babu had raised no objection. 'You can choose whatever you like,' he had said. 'The .375 would be suitable for a tiger.'

I did not understand what the number signified, but could see that the rifle was most impressive in size, and probably also in weight.

As a matter of fact, I was the only one who was not armed. Feluda had handed the sword to Lalmohan Babu this morning, saying, 'Hang on to it. This sword has an important role to play today. You'll soon get to see what I mean.' Lalmohan Babu was therefore clutching it tightly, wearing an air of suppressed excitement.

When we woke this morning, the sky was clear. But now it had started to cloud over again. The road being muddy and slippery, we took longer to reach the forest. Each driver took his jeep half a mile further into the forest than the last time, but then could go no further. 'Never mind,' Madhavlal said, 'I know the way. We have to cross a nullah and walk for fifteen minutes to get to the temple.'

We began our journey amidst the rustle of leaves, a cool breeze and the occasional rumble in the sky. Feluda loaded his gun before getting out of the jeep. Mahitosh Babu's gun was being carried by Parvat Singh. Apparently, he had always accompanied his master on hunting expeditions. A short but well-built man, he clearly did not lack physical strength.

I saw a herd of deer in a few minutes. A sudden surge of

joy filled my heart, but then it leapt in fear. Somewhere in this forest—perhaps not very far away—was a man-eater. Normally, a tiger could easily walk more than twenty miles and travel from one forest to another to look for a prey. But if it was injured, it might not be able to walk very far. In any case, the forest here was not all that big. Large areas of woodland had been cleared to make tea estates, and farms. Besides, although tigers didn't usually come out of hiding during the day, they were likely to do so if the day was dark and cloudy. This was something I had learnt from Feluda only this morning.

Soon, we came to the nullah. It had probably been quite dry even a day ago, but was now gurgling merrily. A lot of animals had left their footprints on the wet sand by its sides. Madhavlal pointed out the marks left by deer, wild boars and a hyena; but there was no sign of a tiger. We crossed it and continued to walk. I could hear a hoopoe in the distance, a peacock cried out once, and there were crickets in the bushes we passed. The faint rustling noise in the grass told me lizards and other smaller reptiles were quickly moving out of our way to avoid being crushed to death under our feet.

The route we took today was a different one, but it did not take us very long to reach the spot we had visited yesterday. There was the bush with the purple flowers. That was where we had found the sword. Madhavlal moved silently, and each one of us tried to do the same. Actually, it was not all that difficult to muffle the noise our feet made, for the ground was wet and there were no dry leaves.

Piles of broken bricks came into view. We had reached the temple of the Chopped Goddess. No one spoke. Madhavlal stopped in front of the temple. We joined him noiselessly. Since my attention had been wholly taken up the day before by the peepal tree and the two palms, I hadn't noticed the other big trees in the area. A cool breeze now wafted through their leaves, and the nullah still rippled faintly in the background.

Feluda walked over to the palms. Mahitosh Babu

followed him swiftly. The hole in the ground was even more full of water today. After a while, Feluda broke the silence.

'This is where Adityanarayan had hidden his treasure,' he said.

'But . . . where did it go?' Mahitosh Babu asked hoarsely.

'It has not gone far, unless someone removed it yesterday after we left.'

Mahitosh Babu's eyes began gleaming with hope.

'Do you really think so? Are you sure?' he asked eagerly.

Feluda turned to face him squarely. 'Mahitosh Babu, can you tell us what that treasure consists of? What exactly was buried under the ground?'

Mahitosh Babu's face had gone red with excitement. A couple of veins stood out on his forehead.

'I don't know, Mr Mitter, but I can guess,' he spoke with an effort, 'One of my ancestors—called Yashwant Sinha-Roy—was the chief of the army in the princely state of Coochbehar. The money he had been paid by the Maharaja was kept in our house. There were more than a thousand silver coins, four hundred years old. When Adityanarayan decided to hide these, he had crossed sixty and was beginning to lose his mind. He had started to indulge in childish pranks. No one could find those coins after he died. Now, after all these years, his coded message has told us where they were hidden. I can't afford to lose them again, Mr Mitter. *I have got to find them!*'

Feluda turned from Mahitosh Babu and began walking towards the temple. He stopped for a second as he passed me, and said, 'Here, Topshe, hold my rifle for me. I don't think I'll need it inside that hall. A revolver should be good enough.'

My hands started to tremble, but I pulled myself together and took the rifle from him. Then I realized just how heavy it was.

Feluda walked on and entered the dark hall once more. I saw him put his hand into his pocket before he disappeared through its broken door.

In less than five seconds, we heard him fire twice. No one

said anything, but I could feel a shiver go down my spine. Then Feluda's voice spoke from inside the temple: 'Mahitosh Babu, could you please send your bearer here?'

Parvat Singh handed the rifle to his master, and went into the temple. A couple of seconds later, he emerged with a dirty, muddy brass pitcher in his hands. Feluda followed him. Mahitosh Babu rushed forward towards his bearer.

'Who knew a cobra would be attracted to silver coins?' Feluda said with a smile, 'I had heard its hiss yesterday. Today, I found it wound around that pitcher, as if it was giving it a tight embrace!'

Mahitosh Babu had thrown aside his rifle. I saw him pounce upon the pitcher and put his hand into it. Just as he brought it out, clutching a handful of coins, an animal cried out nearby. It was a barking deer. Monkeys joined it immediately, jumping from branch to branch, making an incessant noise.

A lot of things happened at once. Even now, as I write about it, I feel shaken and confused. To start with, a remarkable change came over Mahitosh Babu. Only a moment ago, he had seemed overjoyed at the sight of his treasure. Now, he dropped the coins, jumped up and took three steps backwards, as if he had received an electric shock. Each one of us turned into a statue. Feluda was the first to speak, but his voice was low. 'Topshe!' he whispered, 'Climb that tree. You, too, Lalmohan Babu. Go on, be quick!'

We were standing near the famous peepal tree. I returned the rifle to Feluda, placed a foot in the big hollow and grasped a branch. In about ten seconds, I was a good ten feet from the ground. Lalmohan Babu followed suit, with surprising agility, having passed me the sword. Soon, he was sitting on a branch higher than mine. He told us afterwards that he'd had a lot of practice in climbing trees as a child, but I had no idea he could do it even at the age of forty.

I saw what followed from the treetop. Lalmohan Babu saw some of it, then fainted quietly. But his arms and legs were so securely wrapped around a big branch that he did not fall down.

It was obvious to everyone that there was a tiger in the vicinity. That was why Feluda had told us to get out of the way. Mahitosh Babu's reaction was the most surprising. I could never have imagined he would behave like that. He turned to Feluda and spoke fiercely through clenched teeth, 'Mr Mitter, if you value your own life, go away at once!'

'Go away? Where could I go, Mahitosh Babu?'

Both men were holding their rifles. Mahitosh Babu raised his, pointing it at Feluda.

'Go!' he said again, 'The jeep is still waiting, over there. Get out of here. I *command* you—' he couldn't finish. His voice was drowned by the roar of a tiger. It sounded as if not one, but fifty wild animals had cried out together.

Then I saw a flash of yellow—like a moving flame—through the leaves of the trees that stood behind the temple. It moved swiftly through the tall grass and all the undergrowth, and slowly took the shape of a huge, striped animal: a Royal Bengal tiger. It began making its way to the open area where the others were still standing.

Mahitosh Babu lowered his gun. His hands were trembling uncontrollably.

Feluda raised his own rifle. There were three other men—Shashank Sanyal, Madhavlal and Parvat Singh. Parvat Singh gave a sudden leap and vanished from sight. I could not see what the other two were doing, for my eyes kept moving between Feluda and the tiger. It was now standing beside the temple. It bared its fangs and growled. Never before had it had such a wide choice of prey. I felt positive about that.

Then I saw it stop, and crouch. It would spring up and attack perhaps in less than a second. I had read about this. Sometimes a tiger could—

Bang! Bang!

Shots rang out almost simultaneously from two different rifles. My ears started ringing. Just for a moment, even my vision seemed to blur. But I did not miss seeing what happened to the tiger. It shot up in the air, then seemed to strike against an invisible barrier, which made it take a somersault and drop to the ground. It crashed where the brass pitcher stood, its tail lashing at it, making it turn over noisily, spilling its contents. Then the tiger lay still, surrounded by four hundred year old silver coins.

Feluda slowly put his rifle down.

'It's dead, sir,' Madhavlal announced, sounding pleased.

'Who killed it? Which of the two bullets did the trick, I wonder?' Feluda asked.

Mahitosh Babu was in no condition to reply. He was sitting on the ground, clutching his head between his hands. His rifle had been snatched away by his friend, Shashank Sanyal. It was he who had fired the second shot.

Mr Sanyal walked over to the dead tiger.

'Come and have a look, Mr Mitter,' he invited, 'One of the bullets caught him under the jaw and went through the head; the other hit him near an ear. Either of those could have killed him.'

The sound of double shots had brought the local villagers running to the spot. Thrilled to see their enemy killed, they were now making arrangements to tie the tiger to bamboo poles and carry it to their village. There was no doubt that this was the man-eater, for two other bullet marks had been found on its body: one on a hind leg, the other near the jaw. These had clearly made the tiger lose its natural ability to hunt for prey in the wild. Besides, the heavy growth of hair on its jowls indicated it was an old tiger, anyway. Perhaps that was another reason why it had become a man-eater.

Parvat Singh had returned and helped his master to get up and sit on one of the broken steps of the temple. Mahitosh Babu was still looking shaken and was wiping his face frequently. Lalmohan Babu had regained consciousness and climbed down from the tree, with a little assistance from me. Then he had calmly taken the sword back, as though carrying a sword and climbing trees was something he did every day.

After a few minutes' silence, Feluda spoke. 'Mahitōsh Babu,' he said, 'you are worrying unnecessarily. I had already promised Mr Sanyal I would not disclose any of your secrets. No one will ever find out that you are not a shikari, and that you cannot even hold a gun steadily. I had my suspicions right from the start. Your signature on Lalmohan Babu's letter made me think you were old. So I began to wonder how you could shoot, if you could not even write with a steady hand. Then I thought perhaps your hands had been affected only recently and all those tales in your books were indeed true. I started to believe this, but something your brother said raised fresh doubts in my mind. Yes, I know most of what he said was irrelevant, but I didn't think he would actually make up a story. On the contrary, what he said often made perfect sense, if one thought about it. He obviously knew you had written books on shikar, and that the whole thing was based on lies. This distressed him very much, which is why he kept talking about Yudhisthir's punishment for telling a lie. He also told me not everyone could be like your grandfather. Not everyone could handle weapons . . .'

'Yes, they could!' Mahitosh Babu interrupted, breathing hard and speaking very fast, 'I killed mynahs and sparrows with my airgun when I was seven, from a distance of fifty yards. But . . . ' he glanced at the peepal tree, 'one day, we came here for a picnic, and I climbed that tree. In fact, I was sitting on the same branch where your cousin was sitting a while ago, when my brother suddenly said he could see a tiger coming. I jumped down to see the tiger, and—'

'—you broke your arm?'

'Compound fracture,' Mr Sanyal stepped forward, 'It never really healed properly.'

'I see. And yet you wanted to be known as a shikari, just because that was your family tradition? So you moved from here and went to Assam and Orissa where no one knew you? It was Mr Sanyal who killed all those animals, but everyone was convinced you were a worthy successor of your forefathers. Is that right, Mahitosh Babu?'

'Yes,' Mahitosh Babu sighed deeply, 'that's right. What Shashank did for his friend is unbelievable. He is a much better shikari than anyone in my family.'

'But recently . . . were you two drifting apart?'

Both men were silent. Feluda continued, 'I hadn't heard of Mahitosh Sinha-Roy before his books began to be published. Nor, I am sure, had thousands of others. But when these books came out, Sinha-Roy became a famous name, didn't it? He was praised, admired, even revered. And what was his fame based on? Nothing but lies. No one knew the name of Shashank

Sanyal. No one ever would. You had begun to resent this, Mr Sanyal, hadn't you? You had done a lot for your friend, but perhaps the time had come to draw a line? We heard Mahitosh Babu speak very sternly to someone on our first night. I assume he was speaking to you. You two had started to disagree on most things, hadn't you?'

Neither man made a reply. Feluda stared steadily at Mahitosh Babu for a few moments.

'Very well,' he said, 'I shall take silence for assent. But there is another thing. I suppose silence is the only answer to that, as well.'

Mahitosh Babu cast a nervous glance at Feluda.

'I am now talking of Torit Sengupta,' Feluda went on, 'You never wrote a single line yourself, just as you never killed a single animal. You said something about your manuscript, which made me go and look for it in your study. But I didn't find anything with your handwriting on it. All you ever did was just relate your stories to Mr Sengupta. It was he who wrote them out beautifully. They were his words, his language, his style; yet, everyone thought they were yours, and you earned more praise, also as a gifted writer. Yes, it is true that you paid him well and he lived here in great comfort. But how long could he go on seeing someone else take the credit for his talent, his own hard work? Anyone with creative abilities wants to see his efforts appreciated. If he continued to work for you, there was no way his own name could ever become well known. Disappointed and frustrated, he was probably thinking of leaving, but suddenly you chanced upon that puzzle left by Adityanarayan, and Mr Sengupta saw it. It could be that he had already found references to those coins among your grandfather's papers; so he knew what the treasure consisted of. He solved the puzzle, and decided to leave with the treasure. He even found it . . . but then things went horribly wrong.'

Mahitosh Babu struggled to his feet, not without difficulty. 'Yes, Mr Mitter, you are quite right in all that you've said,' he remarked, 'It is very painful for me to hear these things, but do tell me this: who killed Torit? He might have resented—even hated—me for what I was doing, but who could have disliked *him* so intensely? I certainly know of no one. Nor can I imagine who else might have come to the forest that night.'

'Perhaps I can help you there.'

Mahitosh Babu had started to pace. He stopped abruptly at Feluda's words and asked, 'Can you?'

Feluda turned to Mr Sanyal. 'Didn't you pick up a Winchester rifle from the trophy room that night and come here, Mr Sanyal? I noticed traces of mud on its butt.'

Perhaps being a shikari had given him nerves of steel. Mr Sanyal's face remained expressionless. 'What if I did, Mr Mitter?' he asked coolly, 'What exactly are you trying to say?'

Feluda remained just as calm. 'I am not suggesting for a moment that you came looking for the hidden treasure,' he said, 'You were and still are loyal to your friend. You would never have cheated him. But is it not true that you knew Mr Sengupta had solved the puzzle?'

'Yes,' Mr Sanyal replied levelly, 'I did. As a matter of fact, Torit had offered me half of the treasure since he felt we were both being deprived in the same way. But I refused. Moreover, I told him more than once not to go into the forest, because of the man-eater. But that night, when I saw the light from his torch, I had to follow him in here. Yes, I took that rifle from the trophy room. When I got here, I found that he had dug the ground and found that pitcher, but there was no sign of him. Then I looked around closely, and saw blood on the grass, and pug marks. So I quickly put the pitcher away inside the temple, and followed the marks up to the bamboo grove. Then . . . there was a flash of lightning, and I saw the tiger crouched over Torit's body. It was too dark to see clearly, but I shot at it, and made it run away. I knew I couldn't do anything to help Torit. It was too late. However . . .' he broke off.

'However, that isn't all, is it? Please allow me to finish

your story. Correct me if what I say is wrong. I can only guess the details.'

'Very well.'

'You were talking to Madhavlal last night, weren't you?'

Mr Sanyal did not deny this. Feluda asked another question: 'Were you asking him to place a bait for the tiger? See those vultures over that tree? I think they are there because a dead animal is lying under it.'

'A calf,' Mr Sanyal muttered.

'That means you wanted the tiger to come out today, while we were here, so that you could show at least a few people *you* were the real shikari, not your friend. Is that right?'

Mr Sanyal nodded silently. Before Feluda could say anything else, Mahitosh Babu came forward and placed a hand on Feluda's shoulder.

'Mr Mitter,' he pleaded, 'I'd like to give you something. Please do not refuse.'

'What are you talking about?'

'These coins. This treasure. You are entitled to at least some of it. Please let me—'

Feluda smiled, looking at Mahitosh Babu. 'No, I don't want your silver coins,' he said, 'but there *is* something I'd like to take back with me.'

'What is it?'

'Adityanarayan's sword.'

Lalmohan Babu walked over to Feluda immediately and handed him the sword.

'What!' Mahitosh Babu sounded amazed, 'You would like that old sword instead of these priceless coins?'

'Yes. In a way, this sword is priceless, too. It is not an ordinary sword, Mahitosh Babu. No, I don't mean just the history attached to it. There is something else.'

'You mean something to do with Torit's murder?'

'No. Mr Sengupta was not murdered.'

'What! You mean he killed himself?'

'No, it was not suicide, either.'

'Then what was it, for heaven's sake? Why are you talking in riddles?' Mahitosh Babu said impatiently, sounding stern once more.

'No, no, I am not talking in riddles. Let me explain what happened. We were so busy looking for a murderer that the obvious answer did not occur to anyone. Mr Sengupta had removed the sword himself.'

'Really? Why?'

'Because he needed something to dig the ground with. He didn't have time to look for a spade. That sword was handy, so he took it.'

'And then?'

'I am coming to that. But before I do, I'd like to show you what's so special about it.'

Feluda stopped and began moving towards Mr Sanyal with the open sword in his hand. Brave though he was, Mr Sanyal moved restlessly as Feluda got closer. But Feluda did not hurt him. He merely stretched his arm, so that the iron blade could get closer to the point of the gun in Mr Sanyal's hand. A second later, the two pieces of metal clicked together with a faint noise.

'Good heavens, what is this? A magnet?' Mr Sanyal cried.

'Yes, it is now a magnet. I mean the sword, not your gun. Let me point out that when I saw this sword the first time, it was no different from other swords. There were various pieces of metal lying near it, but they were not sticking to the blade. It was magnetized the same night when Mr Sengupta died.'

'How did that happen?' Mahitosh Babu asked. We were all waiting with bated breath to hear Feluda's explanation.

'If a person happens to be carrying a piece of metal in his hand when lightning strikes, that piece of metal gets magnetized,' Feluda went on, 'Not only that, it may actually attract the lightning. What happened that night, I think, was this: it started raining as soon as Mr Sengupta finished digging the ground. He got the pitcher, but had to leave it there. I think he then ran towards that peepal tree to avoid getting wet. He was still carrying the sword, perhaps without even realizing it. Lightning struck the tree only a few seconds later. Mr Sengupta was lifted off the ground and flung aside under its impact . . . As he fell, the point of the sword pierced his clothes and left a deep wound in his body, purely by accident. No one killed him. It is my belief that he was already dead when he fell. Then the tiger found him.'

Mahitosh Babu was shaking violently. He looked up and stared at the peepal tree.

'That's why . . . that explains it!' he said, his voice sounding choked, 'I was wondering all this while why that tree had suddenly grown so old!'

*

We were going back to Calcutta today. The sun was shining brightly, but because of the recent rains, it felt pleasantly cool. We had finished packing, and were sitting in our room. Devtosh Babu's room was now unlocked. I could hear his voice from time to time. Lalmohan Babu had grazed a knee while climbing down from the tree. He was placing a strip of sticking plaster on it, when a servant arrived, carrying a steel trunk on his head. He put it down on the ground and said Mahitosh Babu had sent it. Feluda opened it, and revealed a beautiful tiger skin, very carefully packed. There was a letter, too. It said, 'Dear Mr Mitter, I am giving you this tiger skin as a token of my gratitude. I should be honoured if you accept it. The tiger was killed by my friend, Shashank Sanyal, in a forest near Sambalpur, in 1957.'

Lalmohan Babu read the letter and said, 'Ah, so you get both the sword and this skin!'

'No, Lalmohan Babu. I am going to present the tiger skin to you.'

'To me? Why?'

'For your remarkable achievement. I have never known anyone who could lose consciousness on the top of a tree, and yet manage to stay put, without crashing to the ground. I would not have thought it possible at all. But you have proved it can be done!'

Lalmohan Babu waved a dismissive hand.

'Did I tell you why I fainted in the first place? It was only because of my very lively imagination, Felu Babu. When you mentioned a tiger, do you know what I saw? I saw a burning torch, its orange flame shooting up to the sky. An awful monster sat in the middle of it, pulling evil faces, and I could hear the roar of engines. An aircraft was about to take off . . . and I knew it was going to land on me! Hey, what else could I do after this, except close my eyes and pass into oblivion?'

The Locked Chest

Village: Ghurghutia
P.O.: Plassey
Distt: Nodia
3 November, 1974
To:
Mr Pradosh C Mitter
Dear Mr Mitter,
I am writing to invite you to my house. I have heard a lot about your work and wish to meet you in person. There is, of course, a special reason for asking you to come at this particular time. You will get to know the details on arrival. If you feel you are able to accept this invitation from a seventy-three year old man, please confirm your acceptance in writing immediately.

In order to reach Ghurghutia, you need to disembark at Plassey, and travel further south for another five and a half miles. There are several trains from Sealdah, out of which the Up Lalgola Passenger leaves at 1.58 p.m. and reaches Plassey at 6.11. I will arrange for you to be met at the station and brought here. You can spend the night at my house, and catch the same train at 10.30 a.m. the following morning to Calcutta.

I look forward to hearing from you.

With good wishes,
Yours sincerely,
Kalikinkar Majumdar

I handed the letter back to Feluda, and asked, 'Is it the same Plassey where that famous battle was fought?'

'Yes. There is no other Plassey in Bengal, dear boy. But if you think the place has got any evidence left of that historic battle, you are sadly mistaken. There is absolutely no sign left, not even the palash trees in the woods that stood in Siraj-ud-daula's time. The name "Plassey" came from these trees. Did you know that?'

I nodded. 'Will you go, Feluda?'

Feluda stared at the letter for a few seconds.

'I wonder why an old man wants to see me,' he said thoughtfully, 'It doesn't seem right to refuse. To be honest, I am quite curious. Besides, have you ever been to a village in the winter? Have you seen how the mist gathers in open fields at dawn and dusk? All that remains visible are tree trunks and a little area over one's head. Darkness falls suddenly, and it can get really cold . . . I haven't seen all this for years. Go on, get me a postcard, Topshe.'

Mr Majumdar was told to expect us on 12 November. Feluda chose this date, keeping in mind that a letter from Calcutta would take at least three days to reach him. We took the 365 Up Lalgola Passenger and reached Plassey at 6.30 p.m. I saw from the train what Feluda had meant by darkness falling quickly. The last lingering rays of the setting sun disappeared from the rice fields almost before I knew it. By the time we left the station after handing over our tickets to the collector at the gate, all lights had been switched on, although the sky still held a faint reddish glow. The car that was parked outside had to be Mr Majumdar's. I had never seen a car like that. Feluda said he might have seen one or two when he was a child. All he knew was that it was an American car. Its colour must have been dark red once, but now the paint had peeled off in many places. The hood, too, bore patches here and there and showed signs of age. In spite of all this, there was something rather impressive about the car. I couldn't help feeling a certain amount of awe.

A car like that ought to have had a chauffeur in uniform. The man who was leaning against it, smoking a cigarette, was dressed in a dhoti and a shirt. He threw away his cigarette as he saw us and straightened himself. 'To see Mr Majumdar?' he asked.

'Yes, to Ghurghutia.'

'Very well, sir. This way, please.'

The driver opened a door for us, and we climbed into the forty year old car. He then walked over to the front of the car to crank the handle, which made the engine come to life. He got behind the wheel, and began driving. We settled ourselves comfortably, but the road being full of potholes and the springs in the seat being old, our comfort did not last for very long. However, once we had passed through the main town of Plassey and were actually out in the country, the scenery became so beautiful that I ceased to feel any discomfort. It wasn't yet totally dark, and I could see tiny villages across large rice fields, surrounded by trees. In their midst, the mist rose from the ground and spread like a smoky blanket a few feet above the ground. 'Pretty as a picture' was the phrase that came to mind.

An old, sprawling mansion in a place like this came as a total surprise. Ten minutes after we started, I realized that we were passing through private land for the trees were now mango, jamun and jackfruit. The road then turned right. We passed a broken and abandoned temple, and suddenly found ourselves facing a huge white, moss-covered gate, on the top of which was a naubatkhana (a music room). The driver sounded his horn three times before passing through the gate. The mansion came into view immediately.

The last traces of red had disappeared from the sky, leaving a deep purple hue. The dark house stood against the sky, like a towering cliff. We got out and followed the driver. As we got closer, I realized the whole house could be kept in a museum. Its walls were all damp, plaster had peeled off in several places, and small plants had grown out of cracks in the exposed bricks. We stopped before the front door.

'No one in this area has electricity, I take it?' Feluda asked.

'No, sir. For nearly three years, all we've heard are promises. But nothing's happened yet,' the driver replied.

I glanced up. From where I was standing, a lot of windows on the first floor were visible. But each room was in darkness. On our right, through a couple of bushes, a light flickered in a tiny hut. Perhaps that was where a mali or chowkidar lived. I shivered silently. What sort of a place was this? Perhaps Feluda should have made more enquiries before agreeing to come.

Light from a lantern fell in the doorway. Then an old servant appeared at the door. The driver had gone, possibly to put the car away. The servant glanced at us with a slight frown, then said, 'Please come in.' We stepped in behind him.

There was no doubt that the house sprawled over a large area. But everything inside it seemed surprisingly small. The doors were not high, the windows were half the size of windows in any house in Calcutta, and it was almost possible to touch the ceiling if I raised my arm. 'This house clearly belonged to a zamindar,' Feluda remarked, 'All the houses built by zamindars in the villages in Bengal about two hundred years ago were built like this.'

We crossed a long passage, then turned right to go up a flight of stairs. A strange contraption met my eyes as we got to the first floor. 'This is called a "covered door". It's like a trapdoor, really,' Feluda told me, 'These were built to stop burglars and dacoits from getting in. If you shut it, it would cease standing upright. Then it would fold automatically and lie flat, stretching diagonally across, to form a kind of ceiling over our heads. So anyone trying to climb up would be shut out. See those holes in the door? Spears used to be slipped out of those holes to fight intruders.'

Luckily, the door was now standing wide open. We began

crossing another long corridor. An oil lamp burnt in a niche in the wall where it ended. The servant opened a door next to this niche, and ushered us in.

The room we stepped into was quite large. It might have seemed even larger had it not been stuffed with so much furniture. Nearly half of it had been taken up by a massive bed. To the left of this bed was a table and a chest. Besides these, there were three chairs, a wardrobe, and bookshelves that went right up to the ceiling. Each shelf was crammed with books. An old man was lying on the bed, a blanket drawn upto his chin. In the flickering light of a candle I saw that through a salt-and-pepper beard and moustache, he was smiling at us.

'Please sit down,' he invited.

'Thank you. This is my cousin, Tapesh. I wrote to you about him,' Feluda said. Mr Majumdar smiled again and nodded. I noticed that he did not fold his hands in reply to my 'namaskar'.

We took the chairs nearest to the bed.

'My letter must have made you curious,' Mr Majumdar observed lightly.

'Yes, it certainly did. Or I'd never have travelled this distance.'

'Good.' Mr Majumdar looked genuinely pleased, 'If you hadn't come, I would have felt very disappointed, and thought you to be arrogant; and you would have missed out on something. But perhaps you have read these books already?' Mr Majumdar's eyes turned towards the table. Four bound volumes were arranged in a pile next to a candle. Feluda got up and picked them up. 'Good heavens!' he exclaimed, 'These are all extremely rare, and they are all to do with my profession. Did you ever . . .?'

'No, no,' Mr Majumdar laughed, 'I never tried to become a detective myself. It has always been a hobby. You see, fifty-two years ago, someone in our family was murdered. An English investigator called Malcolm caught the killer. After speaking to Malcolm and learning something about his work,

I became interested in criminology. That was when I bought those books. I was also very fond of reading detective novels. Have you heard of Emile Gaboriau?'

'Yes, yes,' Feluda replied with enthusiasm, 'Wasn't he a French writer? He wrote the first detective novel, I think.'

'That's right,' Mr Majumdar nodded, 'I've got all his books. And, of course, books by writers like Edgar Allan Poe and Conan Doyle. I bought all these forty years ago. Of late, I believe, there has been a lot of progress, and now there are many scientific and technical ways to catch a criminal. But from what little I know of your work, you strike me as one who depends more on old-fashioned methods, and uses his brain more than anything else, very successfully. Am I right?'

'I do not know how successful I've been, but you're certainly right about my methods.'

'That is why I asked you to visit me.'

Mr Majumdar paused. Feluda returned to his chair. After a while, Mr Majumdar resumed speaking, staring straight at the flame of the candle, 'I am not only old—I crossed seventy some years ago—but also ailing. God knows what's going to happen to my books when I die. So I thought if I could give you a few, they'd be appreciated and looked after.'

Feluda looked at the books in the shelves in surprise. 'Are all of those your own?' he asked.

'Yes. I was the only one in my family with an interest in books. Criminology wasn't the only subject that held my interest, as you can see.'

'Yes, of course. I can see books on archaeology, painting, gardening, history, biographies, travelogues . . . even drama and the theatre! Some of them appear to be new. Do you still buy books?'

'Oh yes. I have a manager called Rajen. He goes to Calcutta two or three times every month. I make him a list of books, and he goes and gets them from College Street.'

Feluda looked once more at the books kept on the table. 'I don't know how to thank you.'

'You don't have to. It would have given me a lot of pleasure if I could actually hand them over to you myself, but both my hands are useless.'

Startled, we stared at him. His hands were hidden under the blanket, but I would never have thought that that had a special significance.

'Arthritis,' Mr Majumdar explained, 'has affected all my fingers. My son happens to be visiting me at the moment, so he's looking after me now. Usually, it is my servant Gokul who feeds me every day.'

'Did you get your son to write the letter to me?'

'No, Rajen wrote it. He takes care of everything. If I need to see a doctor, he fetches one from Behrampore. Plassey doesn't have good doctors.'

I had noticed Feluda casting frequent glances at the chest kept near the bed while he was talking to Mr Majumdar. 'That chest appears to be different from most,' he now said. 'I can't see any provision for a key. Does it have a combination lock?'

'Correct,' Mr Majumdar smiled. 'All it has is a knob, with numbers written around it. The chest opens only if you move the knob to rest against some specific numbers. These areas were once notorious for armed burglars. You knew that, didn't you? In fact, my ancestors became wealthy enough to buy masses of land chiefly by looting others. Years later, we ourselves were attacked by dacoits, more than once. So I thought a chest with a combination lock might be safer than any other.'

Mr Majumdar stopped speaking, and frowned for a second. Then he called, 'Gokul!'

The old servant appeared almost instantly. 'Bring that bird over here,' his master commanded. 'I'd like these people to see it.'

Gokul disappeared and came back a minute later with a parrot in a cage. Mr Majumdar turned to it and said softly, 'Go on, sweetie. Say it. Shut the door . . . say it!'

For a few seconds, nothing happened. Then, suddenly,

the parrot spoke in an amazingly clear voice. 'Shut the door!' it said. I gave a start. I had never heard a bird speak so distinctly. But that wasn't all. 'O big fat hen!' the bird added. This time, I saw Feluda turn his head sharply. Before anyone could say anything, the parrot said both things together, very rapidly: 'Shut the door, O big fat hen!'

'What does it mean?' Feluda asked after a moment's pause. Mr Majumdar burst out laughing. 'I am not going to tell you. All I can say is that what you just heard was a code, and it's to do with that locked chest over there. You have twelve hours to work it out.'

'I see. May I ask why the bird has been taught to say it?'

'You may indeed, and I am going to tell you why. Age does strange things to one's memory. About three years ago, one day, I suddenly discovered that I couldn't remember the combination that would open the chest. Can you believe that? After using the same numbers for years, almost every day, it had simply vanished from my mind, just like that. All day, I tried to remember the numbers. Then, finally, it came back in a flash, in the middle of the night. I could have written it down, but didn't want to, in case it fell into the wrong hands. It was far better to keep it in my head, but now I realized I could no longer depend on my memory. So the next morning, I made up that code and taught my parrot to say it. Now it says it every now and then, just as other parrots say, "Radhey Shyam", or "how are you?".'

Feluda was still staring at the chest. I saw him frown suddenly and get up to peer at it closely. Then he picked up the candle and began examining its lid.

'What is it?' Mr Majumdar asked anxiously. 'What have you found? Do your trained eyes tell you anything?'

'I think, Mr Majumdar, someone tried to force this chest open.'

'Are you sure?' Mr Majumdar had stopped smiling.

Feluda put the candle back on the table. 'There are some marks on it,' he said, 'Ordinary dusting and cleaning couldn't have left marks like those. But is there anyone who'd want to open it?'

Mr Majumdar thought for a moment. Then he said slowly, 'Not many people live here, Mr Mitter. Apart from myself, there's Gokul, Rajen, my driver Monilal, a cook and a mali. Vishwanath—that's my son—arrived five days ago. He lives in Calcutta, and visits me rarely. He's here now because of my illness. You see, last Monday I had been sitting in the garden. When I tried to get up, everything suddenly went dark and I fell down on the bench. Rajen rang Vishwanath from Plassey, and he came the next day with a doctor from Calcutta. It appears to have been a mild stroke. In any case, I know I haven't got long to live. But . . . don't tell me I have to spend my last few days in doubt and anxiety? Always afraid that a thief might get into my room and force open that chest?'

'No, no. There is no need to jump to conclusions. I may be quite wrong,' Feluda said reassuringly. 'Those marks may have appeared when the chest was first installed in that corner. I can't see very clearly in the light from one candle, so I cannot tell whether those marks are old or new. I'll have another look in the morning. Is your servant trustworthy?'

'Absolutely. He's been with me for thirty years.'

'And Rajen?'

'Rajen has also spent a good many years here. But then, where's the guarantee that someone who has honoured my trust until today won't betray it tomorrow?'

Feluda nodded in agreement. 'No, there's no guarantee at all, unfortunately. Anyway, tell Gokul to keep an eye on things. I don't really think there's any immediate danger.'

'Oh. Good.' Mr Majumdar appeared relieved. We rose.

'Gokul will show you your room,' he said. 'You'll find blankets and quilts and mosquito nets. Vishwanath has gone to Behrampore, he should be getting back soon. You must have your dinner as soon as he returns. Tomorrow morning, if you like, you can go for a ride in my car, though there isn't much to see in this area.'

Feluda picked up the books from the table and thanked him again. Before saying good night, Mr Majumdar reminded him about the code. 'If you can crack it, Mr Mitter, I will give you the whole set by Gaboriau.'

Gokul came back with a lantern and took us to our room. It was smaller than Mr Majumdar's but with less furniture, which made it easier to move about. Two beds had been made with considerable care. A lantern burnt in a corner. Feluda sat down on the spotless sheet that covered his bed, and said, 'Can you remember the code?'

'Yes.'

'Very well. Here's my notebook and a pen. Write it down. I would love to get those books by Gaboriau.'

I wrote the words down. None of it made any sense. How on earth was Feluda going to find its meaning?

'I simply cannot see how the numbers for a combination lock can be hidden in this strange message!' I complained, 'I mean, this is pure nonsense, isn't it? How can a hen shut a door?'

'That's where the challenge lies, don't you see? Nobody's actually asking a hen to shut a door. That much is obvious. Each word has a separate meaning. I have to figure it out somehow by tomorrow morning.'

Feluda got up and opened a window. The moon had risen by this time, and everything was bathed in moonlight. I went and stood by his side. Our room overlooked the rear portion of the house. 'There's probably a pond over there on the right,' Feluda remarked, pointing. Through a thick growth of plants and shrubs, I could see the shimmering surface of water. The only noise that could be heard was that of jackals calling in the distance, and crickets in the bushes. Never before had I visited a place so totally isolated and remote.

Feluda shut the window again to keep out the cold night air. In the same instant, we heard a car arrive. It was obviously a different car, not the American one we had travelled in.

'That's probably Vishwanath Majumdar,' Feluda remarked.

Good, I thought. This might mean we'd soon be called in to dinner. To tell the truth, I was feeling quite hungry. We had left after an early lunch, since our train was at two o'clock. We did get ourselves a cup of tea and some sweets at Ranaghat, but even that was a long time ago. Ordinarily, I would probably not be thinking of food at eight in the evening, but since there was nothing else to do in a place like this, I quite liked the idea of dinner and an early night.

Looking around in the room, my eyes suddenly fell upon something I hadn't noticed before. It was the portrait of a man that took up most of the opposite wall. There could be no doubt that he was one of Mr Majumdar's ancestors. He was sitting in a chair, looking rather grim. His torso was bare, which showed to perfection his very broad shoulders. His eyes were large, and his moustache thick, its edges turning upwards. His hair rippled down to his shoulders.

'I bet he used to wrestle, and use heavy clubs regularly,' Feluda whispered. 'Perhaps he was the first bandit who became a zamindar.'

There were footsteps outside. Both of us looked at the door. Gokul had left a lantern on the veranda. A shadow blocked out its light for a second, then fell on the threshold. It was followed by the figure of a man. Could this be Vishwanath Majumdar? Surely not? This man was wearing a short dhoti and a grey kurta, had a bushy moustache and glasses with thick lenses. He was peering into the room, trying to find us.

'What is it, Rajen Babu?' Feluda asked.

Rajen Babu finally found what he was looking for. His eyes came to rest upon Feluda.

'Chhoto Babu has just returned,' he said in a gruff voice that suggested he might have a cold, 'I have asked Gokul to serve dinner. He'll come and call you in a few minutes.'

He left. 'What is that smell, Feluda?' I asked as soon as he'd gone.

'Naphthalene. I think he just took that woollen kurta out of a suitcase and put it on.'

Silence fell once more as the sound of footsteps faded away. Had Feluda not been with me, I could never have spent even five minutes in such an eerie atmosphere. How did Mr Majumdar and the others manage to live here day after day? Suddenly, I remembered someone had been murdered in this house. God knew in which room it had taken place.

Feluda, in the meantime, had dragged the table with the lantern on it closer to his bed and opened his notebook to look at the code. I heard him mutter, 'Shut the door . . . shut the door . . .' a couple of times. Thoroughly bored, I decided to step out of the room and stand on the veranda outside.

Oh God, what was that? My heart nearly jumped into my mouth. Something was moving in the distance, where the faint light from the lantern gave way to complete darkness. I forced myself to stay silent and stared at the moving object. A couple of seconds later, I realized it was only a cat, not black or white, but one with stripes on its body like a tiger. It returned my stare sombrely, then gave a yawn before walking lazily back into the darkness. A few moments later, the parrot gave a raucous cry, and then all was silent once more. I wondered where Vishwanath Majumdar's room was. Was it on the ground floor? Where did Rajen Babu live? Why had we been given a room from which it was impossible to hear noises in other parts of the house?

I came back to the room. Feluda was sitting crosslegged on the bed, his notebook in his lap. 'Why are they taking so long?' I couldn't help sounding cross. Feluda looked at his watch. 'You're right, Topshe. Rajen Babu left at least fifteen minutes ago.' He then went back to staring at his notebook.

I began going through the books Feluda had been given. One was on analyzing fingerprints, one was simply called *Criminology*, and the third was called *Crime and its Detection*. I picked up the fourth, but could not understand what its name meant. It was full of pictures, chiefly of firearms. Had Feluda brought his revolver?

No, why should he? After all, he hadn't come here to solve a crime. There was no reason for him to have brought his revolver. I put the books in our suitcase and was about to sit down, when the sound of an unfamiliar voice startled me again. Another man was standing at the door. This time, there was no problem in recognizing him. He wasn't Gokul, or Rajen Babu, or the driver Monilal. He had to be Kalikinkar's son, Vishwanath.

'Sorry to have kept you waiting,' he said, folding his hands and looking at Feluda. 'My name is Vishwanath Majumdar.'

Now I could see that he resembled his father to a great degree. He had the same eyes and the same nose. He was probably in his mid-forties. His hair was still black, he was clean-shaven and had very thin lips. I took an instant dislike to him, though I couldn't find a proper reason for it. It was perhaps simply because he had made us wait a long time, and I was tired. Or it could be that—but this could just be my imagination—when he smiled, his eyes remained cold and aloof. He seemed as though he wasn't really pleased to see us. Perhaps it was only our departure that would make him happy.

Feluda and I went with him down to the ground floor to the dining room. I had half expected to be asked to sit down on the floor for a traditional meal, but found to my surprise that there was a dining table. Silver plates and bowls and glasses were placed on it.

When we were all seated, Vishwanath Majumdar said, 'I like having a bath twice a day, be it summer or winter. That's what took so long, I'm afraid.'

He was still reeking of perfumed soap and, possibly, an expensive cologne. Clad in grey trousers, a white silk shirt and a dark green sleeveless pullover, he was clearly a man fond of the good things in life.

We began eating. Several little bowls were placed in a semicircle around our plates, each containing a different dish. There were three different vegetables, daal and fish curry.

'Have you spoken to my father?' Vishwanath Majumdar asked.

'Yes. I am rather embarrassed by what he did.'

'You mean the books he gave you?'

'Yes. Even if those books were still available, they would have cost at least a thousand rupees.'

Vishwanath Majumdar laughed. 'When he told me he'd asked you to come here, I was at first quite annoyed with him,' he told us. 'I didn't think it was fair to invite people from the city to a place like this.'

'Why not?' Feluda protested, 'Why should you have objected to that? I have lost nothing by coming here. On the contrary, I have gained such a lot!'

Vishwanath Majumdar did not pay much attention to these words. 'Speaking for myself,' he declared, 'I'd be perfectly happy to go back tomorrow. The last four days have been quite enough for me, thank you. I have no idea how my father can live here permanently.'

'Doesn't he go out at all?'

'No. He spends most of his time in that dark room. He used to go out and sit in the garden a couple of times every day. But now the doctor has forbidden all movement.'

'Did you say you were returning tomorrow?'

'Yes. Father is not in any immediate danger. Will you be catching the train at half past ten?'

'Yes.'

'I see. That means I shall leave soon after you get to the station.'

Feluda poured daal over his rice. 'Your father is interested in so many different subjects. Are you interested in anything other than your business?'

'No, sir. I simply don't have the time for anything else

once my day's work is done. I am entirely happy being a businessman, and no more.'

By the time we said good night to Vishwanath Majumdar and returned to our room, it was half past nine. It didn't really matter what time my watch showed, for time seemed to have very little significance here. Seven o'clock had seemed like midnight.

'Do you mind if I keep my pillow on the other side?' I asked Feluda.

'No, but why do you want to do that?'

'I have no wish to see that grim face on the wall the minute I open my eyes in the morning.'

Feluda laughed. 'All right. I think I'll do the same,' he said, 'I must say I don't like the look in his eyes, either.'

Just before going to bed, Feluda picked up the lantern and turned its light down. The room seemed to shrink in size. In just a few minutes, I could feel my eyes growing heavy with sleep. But, just as I was about to drop off, I heard Feluda muttering, which made me open them at once.

'Shut the door . . . and open the gate . . . no, that's wrong. Pick up sticks. Yes, that comes first.'

'Feluda!' I cried, slightly alarmed, 'Wake up Feluda! You are talking in your sleep. What's the matter with you?'

'No, no,' I heard him chuckle in the darkness, 'I am fully awake, and no, I haven't gone mad, I assure you. What has just happened, Topshe, is that I think I've won that set by Gaboriau.'

'What! You've cracked the code?'

'Yes, I think so. It was actually ridiculously simple. I should have spotted it at once.'

'It still makes no sense to me.'

'That's only because you aren't thinking. How were you taught to count when you were a child?'

'Very simply. One, two, three, four . . . that was all.'

'Was it? Think, dear boy, think. Did no one try to make it easier for you? Weren't you taught a rhyme?'

'A rhyme to go with numbers? You mean something that began with one, two . . . no, I don't think . . . hey, wait a minute! Feluda, Feluda, I know what you mean! Yes, I've got it.' I sat up in excitement. I could dimly see Feluda turn his head to look at me. He was grinning.

'Very well. Let's have it, then.'

Softly, I began to chant a rhyme I had been taught in nursery school:

'One, two
Buckle my shoe.
Three, four
Shut the door.
Five, six
Pick up sticks.
Seven, eight
Open the gate.
Nine, ten
A big fat hen.
Eleven, twelve
Dig and delve . . .'

'That'll do. Now what do you think the full message means?'

'Shut the door . . . that would mean 3 and 4. Big fat hen would mean 9 and 10. Right?'

'Right. But there's an "O" before "big fat hen". That means the whole number is 340910. Simple, isn't it? Now, go to sleep.'

I lay down again, marvelling at Feluda's cleverness. But just as I began to close my eyes once more, footsteps sounded on the veranda. It was Rajen Babu again. What did he want at this time of night?

'Yes, Rajen Babu?' Feluda called.

'Chhoto Babu told me to find out if you needed anything.'

'No, no. We're fine, thank you.'

Rajen Babu disappeared silently. This time, sleep came very quickly. All I was aware of as I closed my eyes was that the moonlight that had seeped through closed shutters had suddenly gone pale. I thought I heard distant thunder, and the cat meeaowed a couple of times. Then I fell asleep.

When I woke in the morning, Feluda was opening the windows. 'It rained last night,' he said. 'Did you hear it?'

I hadn't. But now I could see through the window that the clouds had gone. The sun shone brightly on the leaves I could see from my bed.

Gokul appeared with two cups of tea half an hour later. Looking at him in daylight, I was considerably surprised. Not only did he seem old, but his face held an expression of deep distress.

'Has Kalikinkar Babu woken up?' Feluda asked. Perhaps Gokul was hard of hearing. He did not answer Feluda's question at first. All he did was stare at him vacantly. Feluda had to raise his voice and ask again before he nodded and left the room quickly.

We made our way to old Mr Majumdar's room at around seven-thirty, and found him exactly as we'd left him the night before. He was still lying in his bed, a blanket covering most of his body including his arms. The window next to his bed was shut, possibly to avoid direct sunlight. The only light that came into the room was through the open door. I noticed a photograph on the wall over his bed. It must have been taken many years ago, for it showed a much younger Kalikinkar Majumdar. His hair and beard were both jet black.

He greeted us with a smile.

'I got Rajen to take out the books by Gaboriau. I knew you could do it,' he said.

'Well, it is for you to decide whether I've got the right number. 340910. Is that it?'

'Well done!' Mr Majumdar's voice held both pleasure and admiration, 'Go on, take those books and put them in your bag. And please take another look at those marks on the chest. I had a look myself. They didn't strike me as anything to worry about.'

'Well then, that settles it. If you're not worried about it, nothing else matters.'

Feluda thanked him once more before collecting the four books written by the first writer of detective fiction.

'Have you had tea?' Mr Majumdar asked.

'Yes, sir.'

'I told the driver to bring the car out. Vishwanath left very early this morning. He said he wanted to reach Calcutta by ten. Rajen has gone to the local market. Gokul will help you with your luggage. Would you like to go for a drive before you catch your train?'

'I was actually thinking of going by an earlier train. We don't really have to wait until ten-thirty. If we left immediately, perhaps we could catch the 372 Down.'

'Very well. I have no wish to keep anyone from the city in this small village any longer than is necessary. But I'm really pleased that you could come. I mean that.'

*

Soon, we were on our way to the railway station. The road went through rice fields, which glistened in the early morning sun after a rainy night. I was looking at these with admiration, when I heard Feluda ask a question. 'Is there any other way to get to the station?'

'No, sir, this is the only way,' Monilal replied.

Feluda was suddenly looking rather grave. I wanted to ask him if he had noticed anything suspicious, but didn't dare open my mouth.

The road being wet and muddy, it took us longer to reach the station. Feluda took the luggage out of the car and thanked the driver, who then drove off. But Feluda made no attempt to go to the ticket counter to buy tickets for our return journey. He found the stationmaster's room instead and left our luggage with him. Then he came out once more and approached one of the cycle-rickshaws that were waiting outside.

'Do you know where the local police station is?'

'Yes, sir.'

'Can you take us there? We're in a hurry.'

We climbed into the rickshaw quickly. The driver began pedalling fast, honking as loudly as he could, weaving his way through the milling crowds, narrowly avoiding collisions more than once. We reached the police station in five minutes. The officer left in charge was sub-inspector Sarkar. It turned out that he knew Feluda's name. 'We have heard a lot about you, sir,' he said, 'What brings you here?'

'What can you tell me about Kalikinkar Majumdar of Ghurghutia?'

'Kalikinkar Majumdar? As far as I know, he is a perfect gentleman, who keeps himself to himself. Why, I've never heard anything nasty said about him!'

'What about his son, Vishwanath? Does he live here?'

'No. I think he lives in Calcutta. Whatever's the matter, Mr Mitter?'

'Can you take your jeep and come with me? There's something seriously wrong.'

Mr Sarkar did not waste another minute. We began bumping our way back to Ghurghutia in a police jeep, splashing mud everywhere. Feluda's face held a look of suppressed excitement, but he opened his mouth only once. I was the only one who could hear his words:

'Arthritis, those marks on the chest, the late dinner, the hoarseness in Rajen Babu's voice, the naphthalene . . . every little piece has fallen into place, Topshe. I tend to forget sometimes that there are other people just as clever as Felu Mitter.'

The first thing that I noticed with considerable surprise on reaching the old mansion was a black Ambassador standing outside the main gate. It obviously belonged to Vishwanath Majumdar. 'Look at its wheels,' Feluda said as we got out of the jeep. 'There is no trace of mud anywhere. This car has only just come out of a garage.'

A man—possibly its driver, whom I hadn't seen before—was standing near the car. He turned visibly pale and frightened at the sight of our jeep.

'Are you the driver of this car?' Feluda asked him.

'Y-yes, s-sir.'

'Is Vishwanath Majumdar at home?'

The man hesitated. Feluda ignored him and walked straight into the house, followed closely by the inspector, me and a constable.

Together, we ran up the stairs, and down the long passage that led to Kalikinkar's room. It was empty. The blanket lay on the bed, all the furniture was in place, but its occupant had vanished.

'Oh no!' Feluda exclaimed. I found him staring at the chest. It was open. Judging by its gaping emptiness, nearly all of its contents had been removed.

Gokul came and stood outside the door. He was trembling violently. There were tears in his eyes. He looked as though he might collapse any minute. Feluda caught him by his shoulders.

'Gokul, where is Vishwanath Majumdar?'

'He . . . he ran out of the back door!'

'Mr Sarkar!'

The inspector left with the constable without a word.

'Listen,' Feluda shook Gokul gently, 'if you tell me a single lie, you will go to prison. Do you understand? Where is your master?'

Gokul's eyes widened in fear, looking as though they would soon pop out of their sockets.

'He . . . he has been murdered!' he gasped.

'Who killed him?'

'Chhoto Babu.'

'When?'

'The day he arrived, that same night. He had an argument

with his father, and asked for the numbers to open the chest. The master said, "I am not going to give it to you. Ask my parrot". Then . . . a while later . . . Chhoto Babu and his driver . . . they got together . . . ' Gokul choked. He uttered the next few words with great difficulty: 'The two of them dropped the dead body into the lake behind the house. They . . . they tied a stone round its neck. And Chhoto Babu said if I breathed a word to anyone, he'd k-kill me, too!'

'I see,' Feluda helped him sit down, 'Now tell me, am I right in thinking there is no one called Rajen Babu at all?'

'Yes, sir. We did once have a manager by that name, but he died two years ago.'

Feluda and I leapt out of the room, and began running down the stairs. There was a door to the left where the stairs ended, which led to the rear of the house. We heard Mr Sarkar's voice as we emerged through this door.

'It's no use trying to escape, Mr Majumdar. I have a gun in my hand!' he shouted.

This was followed immediately by a loud splash and the sound of a revolver going off.

We continued running, jumping over small bushes and crashing through thick foliage. Eventually, we found Mr Sarkar standing under a large tamarind tree, with a revolver in his hand. Behind the tree was the lake we had glimpsed last night through our window. Its surface was covered almost totally with weed and algae.

'He jumped before I could fire,' Mr Sarkar said, 'but he cannot swim. Girish, see if you can drag him out.'

Vishwanath Majumdar was fished out in a few minutes by the constable, and transferred behind bars, very much like his father's parrot. The money and the jewellery he had stolen from the chest were recovered by the police. It appeared that although he ran a successful business, he used to gamble rather heavily, and was up to his neck in debt.

Feluda explained how he'd arrived at the truth. 'Rajen Babu came to our room twenty minutes after we left

Kalikinkar; and we saw Vishwanath Majumdar half an hour after Rajen Babu's departure. Then Rajen Babu came back briefly after dinner. Not once did we see father and son and their manager together. This made me wonder whether there were indeed three different people, or whether one single person was playing different roles. Then I remembered the books on drama and acting. Perhaps those books belonged to Vishwanath Majumdar? Maybe he was interested in acting and was good at putting on make-up? If so, it wouldn't have been difficult for him to wear a false beard and different wigs and change his voice, to fool a couple of visitors in a dark house. He had to hide his hands, though, for presumably his knowledge of make-up wasn't adequate to turn his own hands into those of a seventy-three year old man. But my suspicions were confirmed when I noticed this morning that although he was supposed to have left quite early, there were no tyre marks on the ground.'

'But who had actually written to you, asking you to come here?' I put in.

'Oh, that letter was written by Kalikinkar himself, I am sure. His son knew about it. So he did nothing to stop our arrival, for he knew he could use me to find out the combination numbers.'

In the end we got so delayed that we couldn't catch a train before half past ten. Before we left, Feluda took out the eight books he had been given and handed them to me. 'I have no wish to accept gifts from a murderer,' he said. 'Topshe, go and put these back.'

I replaced the books, filling each gap in the shelves and came out quietly. The parrot's cage was still hanging outside in the veranda.

'Shut the door!' it said to me. 'Shut the door . . . O big fat hen!'

The Mystery of the
Walking Dead

ONE

'Didn't you once tell me you knew someone in Gosaipur?'
Feluda asked Lalmohan Babu.

We—the Three Musketeers—had just visited the Victoria
Memorial and come walking to the river. We were now sitting
under the domes near Princep Ghat, enjoying the fresh breeze
and munching daalmut. It was five o'clock in the evening.

'Yes,' Lalmohan Babu replied, 'Tulsi Babu. Tulsicharan
Dasgupta. He used to teach mathematics and geography in
my school. Now he's retired and lives in Gosaipur. He's asked
me to visit him more than once. He loves my books. In fact, he
writes for children himself. A couple of his stories were
published in *Sandesh*. But why are you suddenly interested in
Gosaipur?'

'Someone called Jeevanlal Mallik wrote to me from there.
His father's called Shyamlal Mallik. I believe the Malliks were
once the zamindars of Gosaipur.'

'What did Jeevanlal Mallik write?'

'He is worried about his father. He thinks someone is
planning to kill him. If I can go and throw some light on the
matter, he'll be very grateful and he'll pay me my fee.'

I knew the letter had arrived this morning, but had no idea
about its contents. Now I remembered seeing Feluda looking
thoughtful and smoking quietly after he'd finished reading it.

'Why don't we all go?' Lalmohan Babu sounded quite
enthusiastic, 'Look, we are both free at this moment, aren't we?
Besides, I think we'll enjoy a visit to a small village after all the
hectic travelling we have done in the past.'

'To be honest, I was thinking of going, too. Mr Mallik said

he could not have me stay in his house—there is some problem, apparently. He's spoken to a relative who lives three miles away. I could stay with him, but then I'd have to travel in a rickshaw every day. It struck me that it might be simpler to stay somewhere within walking distance. That's why I thought of your friend.'

'My friend will be delighted, especially if he hears you are going to join me. He's a great admirer of yours.'

*

Lalmohan Babu wrote to his friend the next day, and Feluda answered Jeevanlal's letter. Tulsi Babu was so pleased that he wrote back instantly, saying that the Gosaipur Literary Society wanted to give a joint reception to Lalmohan Babu and Feluda. Lalmohan Babu was thrilled by the idea, but Feluda put his foot down. 'Leave me out of receptions, please,' he said firmly, 'No one must know who I really am and why I'm visiting Gosaipur. Please tell your friend not to tell anyone.'

Rather reluctantly, Lalmohan Babu passed the message on, adding that *he* was perfectly happy about the reception. With this event in mind, he even packed a blue embroidered kurta.

We had to take a train to Katoa Junction, and then a bus to get to Gosaipur, which was seven miles from Katoa. Tulsi Babu was going to wait for us at a provision store near the bus stop. His house was just ten minutes away.

On our way there, I saw a palki from the bus. This surprised me very much for I didn't know palkis were still in use. Feluda and Lalmohan Babu were similarly taken aback.

'I wonder which century these people think they live in?' Lalmohan Babu exclaimed, 'I hope Gosaipur has electricity. I'd no idea the area was so remote.'

The conductor of the bus knew where we wanted to get off. He stopped the bus before the provision store, shouting,

'Gosaipur! Go-o-sai-pu-u-r!' We thanked him and got down quickly.

The elderly gentleman who came forward to greet us with a smile had the word 'ex-schoolmaster' written all over him. In his hand was an ancient patched-up black umbrella, on his feet were brown canvas shoes, on his nose were perched his glasses and under his arm was a very old copy of the *National Geographic* magazine. He was wearing a kurta and a short dhoti. On being introduced to Feluda, he winked and said, 'I did what you said. I mean, I didn't tell anyone about you. You are only a tourist, you've lived in Canada for years, now you want to see an Indian village. I thought of this because it occurred to me that you might have to ask questions, or visit places unseen. A tourist can claim to be both curious and ignorant. No one's going to be offended by what you say or where you go.'

'Good. I hope you have books on Canada I can read?' Feluda asked with a smile. 'Don't worry about that,' Tulsi Babu grinned. Then he turned to Jatayu, 'For you, my friend, I have arranged a function on Friday. It's going to be a small informal affair—a couple of songs and dances, then you'll be presented with a citation, and there'll be speeches. The barrister, Suresh Chakladar, will preside. The citation is being written out by a young boy, but its contents—I mean the actual words—are mine, heh heh.'

'There was no need . . . you didn't have to . . .' Lalmohan Babu tried to look modest.

'We wanted to. It isn't every day that a celebrity deigns to visit us!'

'We saw a palki on the way,' Feluda said. 'Is that still used here as a mode of transport?'

Tulsi Babu stopped to prod a young calf with his umbrella to get it out of the way. Then he looked at Feluda and replied, 'Oh yes. If you want a palki, you'll get it here. But that isn't all. We specialize in providing all sorts of things from the past. Do you want guards in uniform, carrying spears and shields?

You'll find them here. A man who spends his time getting hookahs ready? You'll find him here. A punkha-puller? Oil lamps? Yes, we've got those, too!'

'But you've got electric connections, haven't you?'

'Oh yes. Every house has electricity, except the one where it's most needed.'

'What do you mean?'

'The house where Mr Mallik lives.'

All of us stared at him in surprise.

'Shyamlal Mallik?' Feluda asked.

'Yes, sir. There's no other Mallik in Gosaipur. They used to be local zamindars. Shyamlal's father, Durlabh Singh, was an utterly ruthless man. People were terrified of him. Shyamlal himself did not stay a zamindar long, for by then the government had changed the laws regarding the zamindari system. However, he went to Calcutta, built a plastic factory and made a lot of money. Then, one day, he came home in the dark and tried to switch on the light. He did not know that there was a loose, exposed wire in the switchboard. He nearly got electrocuted! After spending a few weeks in a hospital, he handed over his business to his son, returned to Gosaipur and removed the electric connection to his house. If he had stopped there, it might have made some sense. But he decided to remove everything that was modern, or "western". He gave up smoking cheroots, and went back to hookahs. He stopped using fountain pens, his toothbrush was replaced by neem twigs, every book in his house that was written in English was thrown out, as were all the medicines. Now he relies purely on ayurvedic stuff. The only man to benefit from all this was the local ayurvedic doctor, called Tarak Kaviraj. And yes, Shyamlal's car has been sold as well. What he uses is a palki. There was an old palki in his house. He simply had it repaired and painted. He's appointed four bearers to carry it for him. There are many other things that he's started to do . . . you'll get to see everything for yourself, I am sure.'

'Yes, I probably shall. I am here because his son asked me to come.'

'I know his son is visiting him, but why did he want you here?'

'Are you aware that someone is planning to kill Shyamlal Mallik? Have you heard any rumours or gossip?'

Tulsi Babu appeared quite taken aback by this. 'Why, no! I've certainly heard nothing. But if someone wants to get rid of him, you shouldn't have to look very far to see who it is.'

'What do you mean?'

'The same man who wrote to you. He and his father don't get along at all. Mind you, I don't blame Jeevanlal. It can't be easy to deal with a father who has such perfectly weird ideas. After all, Jeevanlal has to stay in the same house when he visits. It's enough to drive one mad.'

We reached Tulsi Babu's house just before four o'clock. His wife had died a few years ago, and his sons worked in Calcutta. He had only one daughter, who was married. She lived in Azimganj. Tulsi Babu lived here alone, with a servant called Ganga. 'In a place like this,' he told us with a smile, 'one may live alone, but there's no chance of being lonely. My neighbours and other friends in the village drop in at all times. We look after one another very well.'

Ganga was told to make tea as soon as we arrived. Feluda had brought a packet of good quality tea. That was the only thing he was really fussy about. A few minutes later, Ganga served us tea on the front veranda, with plates of beaten-rice and coconut, a typical evening snack in rural Bengal.

There were two bedrooms on the ground floor, one of which was Tulsi Babu's. We were given a much bigger room on the first floor. Three beds had been placed in it. One of its doors opened on to a terrace.

'I told Jeevanlal I'd call on him at five-thirty,' Feluda said, sipping his tea, 'so I'll have to find his dark and dingy house.'

'I'll take you there myself, don't worry. Shyamlal's house is only five minutes from here. But I hope you'll come back soon? I am expecting a few people later in the evening. They want to talk to Lalmohan Babu, and then I'd like to take you to see Atmaram Babu.'

'Atmaram Babu? Who's he?'

'That's what some people call him. His real name is Mriganka Bhattacharya. He can speak to the dead, get souls and spirits to visit him in seances . . . you know, that kind of thing. He's one of our local attractions. But I think he's really got a certain power. I don't laugh the whole thing off.'

I wanted to ask what had made him think so, but couldn't, for at this moment we saw the palki again. Tulsi Babu's veranda overlooked the main road. The palki was making its way to the village. As it got closer, Tulsi Babu said, 'Why, Jeevanlal appears to be in it!'

A man was peering out of the window. The bearers were carrying the palki in exactly the same style that one reads about, making a strange rhythmic noise. The noise stopped as they put the palki down. The man inside got out with some difficulty. Clad in trousers and a shirt, he looked terribly incongruous as he emerged.

'Mr Mitter?' he asked, looking at Feluda with a smile.

'Yes.'

'I am Jeevanlal Mallik.'

'Namaskar. This is my friend, Lalmohan Ganguli, and that's my cousin, Tapesh. You know Tulsi Babu, don't you?'

'Yes. Namaskar. Er . . . do you think you could come to my house?'

Lalmohan Babu stayed back to wait for his visitors. Feluda and I went with Jeevanlal Mallik. He left the road and began walking through a bamboo grove, possibly to take a short cut.

'I had to go to the station to make a phone call,' he said.

'Is that why you had to take the palki?'

Jeevanlal gave Feluda a sidelong glance. 'Did Tulsi Babu tell you everything about my father?'

'Yes, we learnt what an electric shock did to him.'

'Things were not so bad in the beginning. He simply did not want to have anything to do with electricity. That was understandable. But now . . . he's become absolutely impossible. You'll soon see what I mean.'

'Do you come here often?'

'Once every two months, to talk about business matters.'

'You mean your father still takes an interest in his business?'

'Oh no. But I don't want to give up. I keep trying to bring him back to normal.'

'Have you had any luck?'

'No, not so far.'

Mr Mallik's house was clearly quite old, but had been well maintained. It was large enough to be called a mansion, if not a palace. As we passed through the front gate, I saw a pond to our right. A number of trees behind the house suggested a garden. Only the compound wall did not appear to have been repaired for some time. It was broken in many places, showing gaps. Seedlings had grown through large cracks in it.

A guard stood at the gate, clutching a shield and a spear, looking as if he was dressed for a part in a historical play. A bearer, wearing an old-fashioned uniform and looking just as peculiar, gave us a smart salute at the front door. It was all done seriously, and certainly the atmosphere inside the house was far from lighthearted, but both men looked so comical that I almost burst out laughing.

We were taken into the living room. It had no furniture. A mattress, covered with a spotless sheet, was spread on the floor. We went and sat on it. There were a few pictures on the wall, of Hindu gods and goddesses and scenes from the *Ramayana*. There were bookshelves on the wall, but apart from half-a-dozen books in Bengali, they were empty.

'Would you like the fan? If so, I can ask Dashu to pull it for you,' Jeevanlal said.

I had not noticed it at first, but now I glanced up and saw the fan—two mats edged with large frills—hanging from an iron rod. The rod hung from two hooks fixed to the ceiling. A rope tied to the rod went outside to the veranda, through the wall over the door to our left. I had only read about such fans.

The servant called Dashu presumably sat on the veranda and pulled the rope, so that the fan swung from side to side, creating a breeze. But it was an October evening. None of us needed a fan.

'Let me show you something. Can you tell me what this is?' said Jeevanlal, opening a cupboard and taking out a square piece of cloth. What made it special was that one corner was knotted around a small stone.

Feluda frowned, then swung the cloth a few times in the air.

'Topshe, stand up for a minute.'

I rose. Feluda stood a few feet away from me swinging the cloth once more. Then he threw it at me as though it was a fishing net. The end that was knotted around the stone wound itself round my neck instantly.

'Thugee!' I cried.

Feluda had told me about thugees. They were bandits who used to attack travellers in this fashion and then loot their possessions. One swift pull was usually enough to tighten the noose and kill their innocent victims.

Feluda nodded, took the cloth away and asked, 'Where did you get something like this?'

'Someone threw it into my father's room through an open window, in the middle of the night.'

'When?'

'A few days before I got here.'

'What were the guards doing?'

'Guards?' Jeevanlal laughed, 'They like dressing up to please their master, but that's as far as it goes. They are bone idle, each one of them. Besides, they know their master has become quite senile, and there's really no one to control them.'

'Who else lives here?'

'My grandmother. *She* is perfectly happy with these old-fashioned arrangements. Then there's Bholanath Babu. He is a sort of manager—in fact, he takes care of everything from shopping to running errands for my father, fetching the doctor if need be, going to the next town to get things we can't get in the village . . . everything. There is no one else except a cook, two guards and a bearer. They live here. The four bearers for the palki and the punkha-puller come from the village.'

'Where did Bholanath Babu originally come from?'

'He is from this village. His family were our tenants. His forefathers were farmers. But he went to school, and I believe was quite bright as a student. Now he's nearly sixty.'

'Is that your grandfather?' Feluda asked, pointing at a painting on the wall. It was the portrait of a man with an impressive moustache. I had not noticed it so far. He was sitting on a chair, holding a walking stick with a silver handle in one hand, the other resting on a marble table. The look in his eyes was cold and hard.

'Yes, that is Durlabh Singh Mallik.'

'The zamindar everyone was terrified of?'

'Yes, I am afraid so. He was devoid of compassion or mercy.'

A bearer brought two glasses and a cup on a saucer on a tray and placed the tray before us. Feluda glanced at the hot drink they contained and said, 'Does this mean your father still drinks tea?'

'No, no. That's coffee, and it's mine. I always bring a cup and a tin of Nescafé. He couldn't find other cups and saucers, so you've been given glasses. I hope you don't mind.'

'No, of course not. I have drunk coffee out of bronze glasses in south India.'

A loud tapping noise coming from upstairs made Feluda glance up. 'Does your father wear clogs?'

'Oh yes. Isn't that far more natural than wearing shoes?'

'Yes, I suppose so. Tell me, was it just this piece of cloth that made you think someone was planning to kill your father, or was there something else?'

In reply, Jeevanlal simply took out a piece of paper from his pocket and offered it to Feluda. Written on it in pencil with large, distinct letters, were the following words:

You have been given a death sentence to atone for
your ancestor's sins.
Be prepared to die.

'This came on 5 October, the day before I got here. It had
been posted in Katoa, which doesn't really tell us anything for
anyone from Gosaipur could have gone there and posted it.'

'If you don't mind, can you tell us what "ancestor's sins"
might mean?'

'Well, as I told you before, Mr Mitter, my grandfather
treated his tenants very badly. I have no idea which particular
crime has been referred to.'

'Why didn't you go to the police?'

'There were two reasons,' Jeevanlal said, 'One, people
here would not recognize you. So, hopefully, whoever wrote
that note would feel no need to be on his guard. Two, if I called
the police, I would have been their prime suspect.'

Feluda and I both looked at him in surprise. Jeevanlal
explained quickly, 'Everyone knows I have not been able to
get on with my father ever since this change came over him. I
still live in the city, I find it impossible to do without certain
modern amenities. I admit what happened to my father gave
him more than just a physical shock. It also caused him great
mental trauma. What really happened was that he and I
returned together one evening, and stepped into our living
room, which was dark. My father groped for the switchboard
and received a shock from a live wire. I ran out and switched
the mains off in five seconds. But, for some reason, he got the
impression that I did not act quickly enough. This happened
five years ago. But since that incident, he has stopped trusting
me. We have violent arguments sometimes. Once I lost my
temper and threw a burning kerosene lamp on a mattress,
which naturally caught fire . . . and then there was hell to pay.
The news spread, and everyone started to think I disliked my
father intensely. That's the reason why I did not call the police.

Besides, I knew of your reputation, and how well you had handled your previous cases. So I thought you were the best person to turn to.'

We finished our coffee. The same bearer brought an oil lamp and put it down in a corner. 'Would you like to meet my father?' Jeevanlal asked.

'Yes, I ought to.'

We rose and made our way upstairs. The few lamps and lanterns the servants had lit had done nothing to illuminate the staircase. In fact, most of the house was in darkness. Jeevanlal took out a small torch from his pocket and said, 'Even this had to be smuggled in secretly. He hates torches.'

We found Shyamlal Mallik seated on a mattress, clutching the pipe of his hookah and leaning against a bolster. His face bore a marked resemblance to that of his father. If he grew a thick moustache, he would probably look stern like Durlabh Singh. When he spoke, I could tell that if he ever got angry and raised his voice, one might do well to stay away from him.

'You may go now,' he said in his deep voice. The person he addressed was sitting on one corner of the mattress. Jeevanlal introduced him as Tarak Kaviraj, the ayurvedic doctor. He got to his feet and greeted us, but left immediately.

'What the hell is a detective going to do?' asked Shyamlal Mallik as soon as Feluda had been introduced. He sounded extremely annoyed. 'Durlabh Singh's soul has already told me my enemy is in my own house. I have that written on a piece of paper. A departed soul can see it all . . . no one can hide the truth from it. What more can a detective from the city do for me?'

Jeevanlal looked profoundly startled. He obviously did not know anything about Durlabh Singh's soul.

'Did you go to Mriganka Bhattacharya's house?' he asked.

'No, why should I have gone to him?' his father barked, 'He came to me. I called him. I had to know who was trying to cause me such distress. Now I do.'

'When did he visit you?'

'The day before you came.'

'You did not tell me.'

Shyamlal Mallik made no reply. He began smoking.

'May we see what Durlabh Singh told you?' Feluda asked politely. Shyamlal Mallik stopped smoking and glared at him.

'How old are you?' he asked abruptly. Feluda told him.

'I am amazed,' the old man announced, 'by your impertinence. Do you really think you'd understand the spiritual significance of a departed soul writing a message? Is that something to be shown to all and sundry?'

'Please forgive me,' Feluda said gently, 'All I want to know is whether your dead father told you how you might get out of your present difficulties.'

'I could tell you what he said. There's no need to look at the writing. He simply said there was only one thing to be done: get rid of the enemy.'

For a few minutes, none of us could speak. Then Jeevanlal said slowly, 'You are asking me to go away?'

'When did I ever ask you to come here?'

Jeevanlal refused to give up. 'Baba,' he said, 'you have begun to trust Bholanath Babu much more than you trust me. Have you forgotten his family history? Durlabh Singh's men had gone and set fire to his house because his father had failed to pay the rent on time. And—'

'Fool!' Shyamlal Mallik shouted. 'Bholanath was only a small child at the time. Are you suggesting that he has waited almost sixty years to plan his revenge? How absurd can you get?'

At this point, we decided to leave. 'Let me take you back,' Jeevanlal offered. 'I don't think you can manage the short cut in the dark.' As we came out of the house, he added, 'I had no idea he would insult you like that. I am terribly sorry.'

'Don't be,' Feluda replied. 'The first thing a detective learns to grow is a thick skin. I am used to handling slights and insults. It is *you* I am more concerned about. You must realize one thing, Jeevan Babu. Suspicion is more likely to fall on you *because* that anonymous letter points at Bholanath.'

'But when that cloth and the note arrived, I was in Calcutta, Mr Mitter.'

'So what? How do I know you haven't got an accomplice here in Gosaipur?'

'Even you are turning against me?' Jeevanlal sounded deeply distressed.

'No. Right now, Jeevan Babu, I am not flinging accusations at anyone; nor am I making assumptions about anyone's innocence. But I must ask you something. What kind of a man is Bholanath Babu?'

After a moment's silence, Jeevanlal replied, 'Very reliable and trustworthy. I have to admit that. But that's no reason to suspect *me*, surely?' He sounded a little desperate.

Feluda raised a hand. 'Jeevan Babu,' he said soothingly, 'you must appreciate my position. I have to assess the whole situation objectively and impartially. You will simply have to be patient. Neither you nor I have a choice in the matter. We must wait until I learn the truth. The only thing I can promise you is that I will definitely protect whoever is innocent.'

Jeevanlal did not reply. It was impossible to see his face in the dark and tell whether Feluda's words had reassured him. Feluda asked him something else as we emerged from the bamboo grove, 'Does your father ever walk barefoot outside the house?'

'Outside the house? Never. Why, he doesn't take off his clogs even inside the house. Why do you ask?'

'I thought I saw traces of mud on his feet. And . . . doesn't he use a mosquito net?'

'Of course. Everyone here uses mosquito nets. They have to.'

'Perhaps you have not noticed it, but his face, neck and arms were covered with mosquito bites.'

'Really? No, I hadn't noticed. It's strange, because he certainly uses a net.'

'Then perhaps the net is torn. Could you please check?'

Tulsi Babu and Lalmohan Babu were waiting for us. I felt immensely relieved to see electric lights again.

'Can you imagine,' said Lalmohan Babu, 'even in this tiny village, I found as many as twenty people who had read more than fifty per cent of my books? Of course, many of them got them from the school library, but those who had bought a few copies had them signed by me.'

'Very good. I am very pleased to hear that, Lalmohan Babu.'

Tulsi Babu turned to Feluda, 'Let's go and call on Atmaram. We can see the Bat-kali temple tomorrow.'

'Bat-kali temple? What on earth is that?'

'Yet another local attraction. There is an old and abandoned Kali temple in the bamboo grove you just came through. It's two hundred years old. It must have once had a statue of Kali, but it's gone now. Dozens of bats live in it, which is why people call it the Bat-kali temple. When it was in use, it must have seen a lot of activity.'

'I see. By the way, does your Atmaram come from this village?'

'No, but he has been living here for some time. Two years ago, his special power came to light. Besides, he knows astrology and palmistry as well. People from Calcutta often come here to consult him.'

'Does he charge a fee?'

'Yes, he probably does. But I've never heard of him charging any of the locals. He holds seances on Mondays and Fridays. Today, we'll just go and meet him.'

'All right, let's go.'

I could see that, somehow, Mriganka Bhattacharya had become a part of Feluda's investigation. We left the house once more.

Although lights were on in every house in the vicinity, it was very dark outside, possibly because of the large number of big trees. The moon had not yet risen. Crickets and owls and jackals in the distance had started a regular concert, which made me think that, in a place like this, it was Shyamlal Mallik's palki and the flickering light from his oil lamps that fitted the atmosphere far better. Lalmohan Babu whispered into my ear, declaring that he had never seen a place so full of mystery and excitement. 'You know, Tapesh,' he said, 'I had thought of Guatemala as the place of action for my next novel; but now I think I will change it to Gosaipur.'

'Really?' Feluda laughed, having overheard this remark. 'But you haven't even seen the thugee's noose. Can you think of anything more exciting?'

'What are you talking about, Felu Babu?'

Feluda explained quickly. He also mentioned the anonymous note.

'If Mr Bhattacharya got Durlabh Singh's spirit to come and reveal the truth, you need not look any further, Mr Mitter,' Tulsi Babu remarked. 'Shyamlal Mallik's enemy *must* be in his house.'

No one said anything after this, for we had reached Mr Bhattacharya's house. This house did not appear to have an electric connection, either. Perhaps souls found it easier to re-enter the earth if they could move in the faint and hazy light of lanterns.

Mriganka Bhattacharya turned out to be a man with an impressive appearance. It was impossible to guess his age. His hair had thinned, but not turned grey. His features were sharp, his skin smooth, except around his eyes and mouth. He was seated on a divan, facing three chairs and two benches. He clearly did not share Shyamlal Mallik's aversion to furniture.

A young man of about twenty-five was sitting on one of the benches, leafing through an astrological magazine. We learnt later that he was Mr Bhattacharya's nephew, Nityanand. He helped his uncle in hailing spirits.

Tulsi Babu touched Mr Bhattacharya's feet quickly and said, 'These are my friends from Calcutta. I brought them here so that they could meet the man Gosaipur is so proud of.'

Mr Bhattacharya raised his eyes and looked at us. Then he glanced at the chairs. The three of us sat down. Tulsi Babu remained standing.

Mr Bhattacharya closed his eyes, sat erect, his legs crossed in the lotus position. A few moments later, he suddenly opened his eyes and said, 'Sixteen, three, thirteen. Which one of you has those initials?'

We stared at him, perfectly taken aback. Feluda was the first to speak, after a short pause. 'I do,' he said. 'My full name is Pradosh Chandra Mitter, and you are quite right. P, C, M, are the sixteenth, third and thirteenth letters from the alphabet.'

I felt considerably surprised by this. Tulsi Babu had certainly not mentioned our names. How did Mr Bhattacharya guess Feluda's initials? I saw Tulsi Babu cast an admiring glance at Mr Bhattacharya. Then he asked, 'Can you guess his profession?'

By this time, another man—possibly a client—had entered the room. Feluda naturally did not want his profession disclosed before a stranger. So he said hurriedly, 'Oh, there's no need to do that.' Tulsi Babu realized his mistake and began to look embarrassed.

'I'll bring them back on Friday,' he said, changing the subject, 'We came today only to meet you.'

Mr Bhattacharya looked steadily at Feluda. 'You simply seek the truth, don't you? Stop worrying, sir, nobody will understand my meaning if I say that.'

We took our leave and left soon after this. 'He must have

a very strong sixth sense,' Lalmohan Babu remarked as we began walking, 'and he can speak in riddles. Remarkable!'

Someone was coming from the opposite direction, carrying a lantern in one hand. It swung as he moved, making his shadow sweep the ground. Tulsi Babu raised the torch in his hand, shone it on the man's face and said, 'Off to see Bhattacharya? You've started visiting him pretty frequently, haven't you?'

The man smiled, hesitated for a second, then went on his way without saying anything.

'That was Bholanath Babu,' Tulsi Babu informed us, 'Bhattacharya's latest devotee. I believe Bhattacharya went to his house once and spoke to a spirit. Whose, I couldn't say.'

*

Tulsi Babu's cook, Ganga, produced an excellent meal that night, including moong daal, three types of vegetables and egg curry. After dinner, our host regaled us with stories of his life as a schoolteacher. When we said good night to him and went to bed, it was only half past nine, though it seemed like midnight. We had brought our own bedding and mosquito nets. Feluda said he'd use Odomos and not bother with a net. I had noticed that he'd plunged into silence since our return from Mr Bhattacharya's house. In the last couple of hours, he had opened his mouth only to praise Ganga's cooking. What was he thinking?

Lalmohan Babu lit a lantern and placed it by his bed. He needed the light, he said, to work on his speech for his reception. He didn't want to disturb us by keeping the main light on.

I couldn't go to sleep without asking Feluda something that was puzzling me very much.

'How did that man guess your initials, Feluda? And he knew about your profession, too!'

'Yes, those are questions I have been asking myself. I

haven't got an answer yet, Topshe. Sometimes . . . some people do turn out to have extraordinary powers that cannot be rationally explained.'

FOUR

The next morning, we went for a long walk and explored the whole village. The local club, Jagarani, were rehearsing for a play. We were invited to watch their rehearsal. A lot of people were curious about life in Canada, so Feluda ended up giving a short lecture on the subject. Then we met the only mime artist of Gosaipur, called Benimadhav. He offered to visit us on Friday and show us what he could do. 'I can climb stairs without any props . . . I can show you what happens to a man caught in a storm . . . change the expression on my face— through six different steps—from sad to happy!'

In the evening, Tulsi Babu took us to a fair in the next village. By the time we returned, having enjoyed ourselves hugely, it was nearly six o'clock. The sun had set, but it wasn't yet dark. Feluda said he'd like to visit Jeevanlal Mallik. Tulsi Babu went home to wait for us.

Jeevanlal came out of his house even before we could reach the front door.

'I saw you coming from my bedroom window,' he explained.

'Has there been any new development?' Feluda asked.

'No.'

'May I look at your garden?'

'Of course.'

The 'garden' was not really a garden: that is to say, there were no flower beds or a lawn. It was simply a large, open area in which stood a number of tall trees. Feluda began inspecting it carefully. I had no idea what he was looking for. I saw him stop at one point and stare at the ground for a few minutes.

After a while, a voice cried out from a balcony on the first floor: 'Who's there? What are you doing among the trees?'

It was Jeevanlal's grandmother. 'It's all right, Grandma!' he shouted back, 'It's only me, and my friends.'

'Oh. I keep seeing people roaming about in the garden. God knows what they do.'

'Can she see well?' Feluda asked.

'No, not very well; nor can she hear unless one shouts.'

'I don't suppose anyone looks after the garden?'

'No, not really. Bholanath Babu does what he can, but obviously that's not enough.'

'Do the guards keep an eye on it at night?'

'At night? You've got to be joking. No guard here would dream of staying awake to do their duty.'

'The front door is locked, surely?'

'Oh yes. That's Bholanath Babu's job. But when I am here, I lock the front door and keep the key with me.'

'I haven't yet met Bholanath Babu. Could you call him, please?'

Jeevanlal asked one of his bearers to call Bholanath Babu, and bring us some lemonade. We were sitting outside by the pond. The recent monsoon rains had filled it to its brim. It was now covered with shaluk flowers.

Bholanath Babu arrived in a couple of minutes. He was wearing a dhoti and a shirt, but his appearance was really no different from an ordinary farmer. I could easily picture him working in a field, tilling the land.

Feluda began talking with him. There was no noise anywhere except the faint strains of music from a distant transistor. Had that not been there, it would have been quite easy to pretend we had travelled back in time by more than a hundred years.

'Has Mriganka Bhattacharya visited this house just once?' Feluda asked.

'Recently, yes. Just once.'

'You mean he has visited Mr Mallik before?'

'Yes, a few times. I think the master had asked him to draw up his horoscope.'

'And did he?'

'I don't know.'

'What made him pay a visit recently? Who asked him to come?'

'The master did. Er . . . the doctor and I had both told him it might help.'

'You visit Mr Bhattacharya regularly, don't you?'

'Yes, sir.'

'Do you believe in his powers?'

Bholanath Babu bent his head. 'What can I say, sir? I had a daughter—Lakshmi, she was called. Beautiful like the goddess, and she had manners to match. But . . . when she was only eleven, she got cholera and . . . she died. I was devastated. Then Mr Bhattacharya came to me and said, "Do you want to hear from her how she is?"'

Bholanath Babu stopped, and wiped his eyes with one corner of his dhoti. Then, with an effort, he pulled himself together and went on, 'He then spoke to her. She came and she said she had found peace and was very happy where she was, so I must stop feeling sad. I mean, she didn't actually say all this, but the words were written on paper. I . . . from that day . . . I . . .' he choked again.

Feluda did not press him any more. 'Were you present when Mr Bhattacharya contacted the dead Durlabh Singh?' he asked, changing the subject.

'Yes, but I was not in the room. The master did not want his mother to find out, so he told me to stand at the door and watch out for her. In the room were Mr Bhattacharya, his nephew Nityanand and the master.'

'Did you hear anything at all?'

'I heard very little, sir, They were totally silent for the first ten minutes. Then, a jackal called in the distance, and I remember hearing the master's voice the same instant. He said, "Are you there? Has anyone come?" But I heard nothing else after that. When it was over, I took Mr Bhattacharya home.'

Feluda finished his lemonade and lit a Charminar. 'Durlabh Singh Mallik's men had set fire to your house. Do you remember that?'

After a brief pause, Bholanath Babu uttered two words: 'I do.'

'Don't you wish to take revenge? Have you never thought of settling old scores?'

I had heard Feluda ask such hard-hitting questions before. A lot depended, he had told me once, on how a person reacted to such questions.

Bholanath Babu shook his head mutely. Then he said, 'Never. The master may have changed in the last few years, but certainly *I* don't know anyone more kind, or more generous.'

Feluda had no further questions for him.

'May I go now, sir?' Bholanath Babu asked after a few seconds. 'I'd like to go to Mr Bhattacharya's house again, sir, if you don't mind.'

'Oh no, please go ahead. Thank you for your help.'

Bholanath Babu left. Jeevanlal started fidgeting.

'What is it, Jeevan Babu?' Feluda asked.

'Nothing. It's just that I'm curious about whether you have made any progress.' He was obviously worried about himself.

'Bholanath Babu struck me as a very good man,' Feluda replied. This seemed to upset Jeevanlal even more.

'You mean that I . . . ?' he began.

'No, no. I liked Bholanath Babu. That does not automatically mean that I dislike you. Look, to be honest, I still haven't reached any conclusions. I have a few doubts about certain things, but those aren't enough to build a case, particularly when I can't see how they can be linked to the main problem. I have to wait until something happens, something that might—' he was interrupted.

'Who's there? Jeevan, is that you?' shouted Jeevanlal's grandmother again. We could hear her only because it was so quiet.

Feluda rose instantly and began running towards the back of the garden. We followed him. Lalmohan Babu had been staring at the water and humming under his breath. He, too, broke off and joined us.

We found Feluda standing by a gap in the compound wall. A portion of it had crumbled away.

He was shining his torch on the wall.

'Did you see anyone?' Jeevanlal asked.

'Yes, but not closely enough to recognize him. He slipped out through that gap.'

We spent the next thirty minutes searching the grounds. Thousands of mosquitoes kept us company, as did as many crickets who kept up an incessant chorus. What we eventually found was immensely mystifying. At the far end, under what must have been the last tree, was a big hole in the ground. It had obviously been recently dug. Jeevanlal, who appeared as surprised as us, could not offer any explanation. 'Hidden treasure!' Lalmohan Babu declared. 'Someone just removed it.' But Jeevanlal shook his head. 'No,' he said, 'Nobody in our family ever hid any treasure. I would have known if they had. I mean, there would have been stories and gossip.'

The comment Feluda made sounded just as mysterious. 'Jeevan Babu, didn't I say I was waiting for something to happen? I think it now has.'

We returned home after this. After dinner, Lalmohan Babu and I wanted an early night. He had ended up with cuts and bruises, for some of the plants in Jeevanlal's garden were thorny. After dabbing himself with Dettol, he declared he was ready for bed. So was I.

Feluda was the only one who didn't seem tired at all. He opened his notebook, applied Odomos all over his hands and feet and face, and settled down on his bed, leaning against a pillow. Tulsi Babu came in with a plate of paan. Lalmohan

Babu started to yawn, but broke off as Feluda glanced at our host to ask him a question.

'Tell me, Tulsi Babu,' he said, 'if you told a good and honest man a way of cheating others, and that man then actually put that into practice, would you still call him good and honest?'

Tulsi Babu looked flustered. 'Good heavens, Mr Mitter, I am hopeless with puzzles and riddles. But since you ask, if the man is really good, surely he wouldn't stoop so low? And if he did . . . no, I would not call him good any more.'

'Ah. I am glad to see you and I agree on this.'

I was too tired to worry about why Feluda was making cryptic remarks. So I got into bed, but could not go to sleep. My mind was still buzzing with questions: why did Shyamlal Mallik have mud on his feet? Who sent the anonymous note and that noose? Who did his mother see this evening in the garden? Who dug that hole and what did it contain? Why didn't Shyamlal want us to see the paper on which a spirit was supposed to have written?

God knows when I dropped off. When I opened my eyes, it was still dark. Then I realized I had been woken by a scream. It had probably come from Lalmohan Babu, for he was sitting up on his bed, having flung aside the mosquito net.

'What happened?' I asked.

'A dream . . . a nightmare! Oh God, it was terrible. Do you know what I saw? I was being given a reception and my own grandfather was there, putting a garland round my neck. "See, what an exciting garland I have given you!" he said. I looked and . . . and . . . saw that they weren't flowers, but tiny human heads, dripping with blood! Can you imagine it?'

'Why, Lalmohan Babu, why must you have such an awful dream at this beautiful moment when dawn is just breaking?' asked Feluda.

With a start, I realized Feluda was already up. I saw him coming in through the door that led to the terrace. He had obviously been doing his yoga.

'What am I to do, Felu Babu? It's all this talk of a reception and speaking to dead ancestors, and old Kali temples . . . all of those things got mixed up in my mind!'

There was no point in going back to bed. I rose and went out on the terrace quietly. Tulsi Babu might still be asleep. The moon was still shining, but its light had turned pale. I noticed a few stars, winking bravely, but they couldn't possibly last long. The eastern sky had just started to turn pink.

This morning I had decided to chew on a neem twig instead of using a toothbrush. It was far more healthy, Feluda had said. So I picked one from the pieces I had kept ready the previous night, and had just put it into my mouth, when someone arrived at the front door and began screaming loudly:

'Mr Mitter! Come quickly. Please, sir . . . Mr Mitter!'

We rushed down the stairs. It was Bholanath Babu. 'Last night . . .' he gasped as he saw us, 'we were attacked by burglars. They tied me up, and they tied and gagged the master. There were two of them. Everything the big chest contained . . . all the money . . . has gone. Only Jeevan Babu was spared somehow. He came and untied me, and told me to call you. Please, sir, you must come at once!'

Shyamlal Mallik was not injured, but the two hours he had had to spend with his hands and feet tied had shaken him very deeply. He was sitting on the mattress in his room, staring blankly into space. 'If they had to tie me up like that, why didn't they kill me?' I heard him mutter. I wondered if he knew all his money was gone.

Feluda searched Shyamlal's room very thoroughly. Only the big chest had been opened. Everything else had been left undisturbed. The key to the chest used to be kept under his pillow. Bholanath Babu, who also slept on the first floor, was attacked in his sleep. Naturally, he had not been able to offer any resistance at all. The bearer had slept through it all, no one had gone anywhere near his room. One of the guards was away, and the other had been struck on his head by a heavy rod, which had left him unconscious for several hours. Jeevanlal's grandmother lived in the rear portion of the house. Fortunately, she knew nothing of what had happened.

We spent fifteen minutes talking to Bholanath Babu and the servants, but there was no sign of Jeevanlal. 'Did he go off to call the police?' Feluda asked.

'I don't know, sir,' Bholanath Babu faltered, 'He sent me to your house and I saw him go out, but I haven't seen him since.'

Without a word, Feluda ran towards the stairs, with Lalmohan Babu and me behind him. We climbed down to the ground floor, crossed a courtyard and went into the garden through the back door. The sun had just risen, and there was a thin mist. The grass and the leaves were wet with the early morning dew. Crows and mynahs and some other birds I couldn't recognize had started going about their business.

We made our way through the garden, but had to stop in just a few minutes. Under a jackfruit tree lay the figure of a man. I recognized the blue shirt he was wearing, the white pyjamas and the chappals. It was Jeevanlal Mallik. Feluda strode forward quickly and looked down at him.

'My God!' he exclaimed in horror, stepping back.

'Felu Babu!' Lalmohan Babu called, pointing at an object lying a few feet away from the body.

'I know, I have seen it. Please don't touch it. That's what was used to kill Jeevanlal.'

It was a square piece of cloth, with a stone tied round one corner.

Bholanath Babu had followed us out and realized what had happened.

'I don't believe this!' he cried and looked as if he was about to faint.

'Please pull yourself together,' Feluda said to him, laying a hand on his shoulder. 'This is not the time to give way to despair. You must inform the police. If you like, Lalmohan Babu will go with you. Nobody must touch either the body or the weapon. This must have happened pretty recently. Perhaps the killer is still in the area. Go at once, but please make sure your master is not told about the murder.'

Feluda ran towards the compound wall, and stopped before the gap in it. Then we both slipped out of it and found ourselves facing the bamboo grove through which we had walked on our first night here. There were no houses within a hundred yards. We stepped into the bamboo grove. What was that structure, tucked away in a corner? Oh, it was probably the old Kali temple Tulsi Babu had mentioned.

A man was standing by the temple, looking at us. 'Why are you up so early?' he asked, coming forward. It was Tarak Kaviraj, the ayurvedic doctor.

'Haven't you heard?' Feluda asked.

'Heard what?'

'The old Mr Mallik—'

'What!'

'No, no, it's not what you think. Mr Mallik is fine, but his house was burgled last night and . . . his son has been killed. But the old man does not know that, so please don't tell him.'

Tarak Kaviraj hurried on. After a few moments, we decided to return. The culprit had clearly escaped.

We slipped back into the garden. What I saw next—or, rather, what I did *not* see—made me blink and wonder if I was dreaming. Could this really be true?

The ground under the jackfruit tree was empty. Jeevanlal's dead body had vanished, and so had the piece of cloth.

Lalmohan Babu was standing a few feet away, trembling visibly. He had to make an effort to speak: 'Bh-bholanath Babu and I went back to the house, but he s-said he'd go to the police station al-alone. I let him g-go, and then I walked this way to look for you, b-but th-then I s-saw . . .'

' . . . that the corpse had gone?'

'Y-yes.'

Feluda ran again, but in a different direction. This time, we made our way to the far end, where we had found the hole in the ground. Behind the garden, we now realized, was another large pond as well as a bigger gap in the wall. No doubt the body had been dragged out through the gap and thrown into the pond. The tree under which the hole had been dug, I noticed, was a mango tree.

We retraced our steps and went back into the house, using the staircase at the back to go up to the first floor.

'Jeevan! Jeevan!' we heard his grandmother call, 'Where's he got to, now? Didn't I just see him?'

We saw the old lady—clad in a white saree—come out of her room. Her heavily lined face looked sunken, her hair was cut very short and her eyes were hidden behind thick lenses. She must be at least eighty, I thought.

Feluda stepped forward to speak to her. 'Jeevanlal had to go out. Do you need anything? Perhaps I can get it for you?'

'Who are you?'

'I am a friend of his. My name is Pradosh.'

'I haven't seen you before, have I?'

'No. I arrived from the city only two days ago.'

'From Calcutta?'

'Yes. Can I get you anything? What did you want Jeevanlal for?'

The old lady suddenly seemed uncertain. She raised her face, looked around and said a little helplessly, 'I can't remember. What *did* I want him for? I can't remember anything any more.'

We left her mumbling to herself and made our way to Shyamlal's room. The doctor was with him, feeling his pulse. 'Where's Jeevan gone?' Shyamlal asked, his tone as helpless as his mother's. The doctor had obviously refrained from saying anything about the murder.

'Didn't you want him to go back to Calcutta?' Feluda asked.

'Back to Calcutta? You mean he left without telling me? How did he go? In a palki?'

'No. There's no way anyone can go all the way to Calcutta in a palki. You know that very well.'

'Are you mocking me?' Shyamlal sounded hurt.

'I am not the only one, Mr Mallik,' Feluda replied. 'The whole village makes fun of you. Surely you realize your present lifestyle is not doing any good to anyone, least of all yourself? If you had a guard with a gun, that would have been far more effective than one with an old and blunt spear. Tell me, isn't this kind of a shock as bad as the electric shock you received years ago? Trying to put the clock back doesn't achieve anything, Mr Mallik. You cannot bring back the times that have gone by. It's just not possible.'

I expected Shyamlal Mallik to flare up and order Feluda to get out at once. To my amazement, he didn't. In fact, he did not speak at all. All he did was sigh, and stare at the opposite wall.

SIX

'God, just look at my face!' Lalmohan Babu exclaimed, peering into his shaving mirror. Our faces looked just the same. We were all covered with mosquito bites.

'I should have warned you,' Tulsi Babu remarked, 'Mosquitoes are a big menace here. In fact, they are the only drawback of Gosaipur.'

'No,' Lalmohan Babu said, 'not the whole village, surely? I would say it's just that garden the Malliks own. That's where most of the mosquitoes breed, that's where they are the most vicious.'

We were back in our room after lunch. The police had arrived and started their investigation. Feluda had lapsed into silence once more. Perhaps Jeevanlal's murder was so totally unexpected that it had thrown all his calculations haywire. If Jeevanlal had been killed by burglars, the police were in a far better position to track them down. Feluda could hardly do anything on his own.

The inspector in charge—a man called Sudhakar Pramanik—had already talked to him. He had heard of Feluda, but did not seem to have a great deal of regard for him. He was particularly cross about the disappearance of the body.

'You amateur detectives simply do not believe in systems and methods, do you?' he said irritably. 'I know your sort, I have had to work with private detectives before. If you had to leave the body, why didn't you get someone to guard it? Now we have to dredge the pond at the back. If that doesn't work, then we have to do the same to all the other ponds and lakes here . . . and there are eleven of them. It's all your fault, Mr

Mitter. You really shouldn't have rushed off, leaving the body unattended.'

Feluda heard him in silence, without saying a word to defend himself. What he did say after a while irritated the inspector even more. 'Do you believe in ghosts?' Feluda asked. Inspector Pramanik stared at him, then shook his head and said, 'I had heard you took your work seriously. Now it's obvious that is not the case.'

'I had to ask you,' Feluda explained, 'because if you cannot catch the killer, I have to turn to Mr Bhattacharya. Perhaps he can contact Jeevanlal Mallik's spirit? Surely the spirit of the dead man will be able to reveal the truth?'

'Do you admit defeat, Mr Mitter? Are you giving up?'

'No. I cannot continue with my investigation . . . yes, I admit that . . . but if Mr Bhattacharya helps me, I can bring the culprit to justice. Of that I am certain.'

'Can you tell the difference between a dead man and a live one?'

'Mr Pramanik, I don't think I need answer all your questions, especially since I have no wish to join the police force. If I am talking of ghosts and spirits, it's only because my methods are quite different from yours.'

'Oh? Have you no reason to suspect Bholanath?'

'My only suspicion—no, my fear—is that you will arrest him immediately simply because you have heard his family history and you think he had a motive. If you do that, Inspector, you will be making a big mistake.'

The inspector laughed and stood up. 'Do you know what your problem is?' he said, clicking his tongue with annoyance, 'You see complications when there are none. This is a very simple case. Just think for a moment. Isn't it obvious whoever opened that chest knew where the key was kept? Had it been an ordinary burglar, surely he'd have broken it open? Bholanath took the money and was running away with it, when Jeevanlal caught up with him. Bholanath might not have planned to kill him, but was obliged to. Then he went off to call you, so that suspicion did not fall on him. He says he, too, was tied up, and Jeevanlal came and untied him. But can he prove it? How do we know he is not lying through his teeth?'

'Very well. But where did all that money go? What did Bholanath do with it?'

'We have to look for it, Mr Mitter. Once we find the body, we'll arrest Bholanath. He'll talk . . . oh yes, he'll tell us everything, never fear.'

I did not like to think of Bholanath Babu as the culprit, but what the inspector said made sense to me. What I could not understand was why Feluda was brushing it off. Just as the inspector began climbing down the stairs, he called after him, 'Jeevanlal's spirit will talk tonight in Mr Bhattacharya's house. You may learn a thing or two, if you come!'

Tulsi Babu was the only one who appeared more concerned with the reception the next day than with Jeevanlal's spirit. If the killer was not caught by then, the reception would have to be cancelled. Naturally, no one would be in the right mood for songs and speeches. Lalmohan Babu had accepted this, and was heard saying, 'I don't mind at all. After all, I sell murder mysteries, don't I? Here I've got a real murder, and a real mystery. If I can't have a reception, who cares?'

He said this, but couldn't get the idea of a reception out of his mind. I caught him, more than once, muttering lines from his speech and then quickly checking himself.

'Could you please tell Mr Bhattacharya that we'd be calling on him this evening?' Feluda said to Tulsi Babu. 'Tell him we cannot wait in a queue with his other clients. He must give us top priority.'

This time, Tulsi Babu realized that Feluda was absolutely serious about consulting Mr Bhattacharya. He looked very surprised.

'I have done all I could,' Feluda told him. 'Now I cannot proceed without Mr Bhattacharya's help.'

I thought again about what he had told me about keeping

an open mind. There were dozens of occurrences every day, all over the world, that could not be explained by scientists. That did not necessarily mean they were all hoaxes. Only recently, I had read about a man called Uri Geller who could stare at steel forks and spoons and bend them simply through his will-power. Well-known scientists had watched him, yet no one knew how he had done it. Perhaps Mriganka Bhattacharya was a man like Geller?

Tulsi Babu looked at his watch. 'It's half past five now,' he said. 'I think you and I should go together and make our request.'

'Very well,' Feluda said, getting to his feet. 'Why don't you two go for a walk?'

This struck me as a very good idea. Lalmohan Babu had mentioned how pleasant an October evening in Gosaipur could be, and I wanted to stretch my legs. So we left as soon as Feluda and Tulsi Babu went off to speak to Mr Bhattacharya.

SEVEN

Two days ago, the village had seemed a totally different place. Today, I felt strangely tense as we began walking away from the house. I simply could not stop thinking of the missing corpse. It could well be lying behind any of the bushes and shrubs we passed . . . no, no, I must not dwell on it, I told myself firmly.

We found the bamboo grove and turned into it. It was appreciably darker here, and the creepy feeling I was trying to overcome grew stronger. But at this moment, I saw the mime artist, Benimadhav, walking towards us. The sight of a third person helped me pull myself together. 'Hey, where are you off to?' he asked genially. 'I was going to your house. Didn't I tell you I'd come and show you my acting on Friday?'

'I know,' Lalmohan Babu replied, 'but after what happened, none of us are in the mood to watch a performance. I mean, who knew such an awful thing was going to happen? We're all worried and upset. You do understand, don't you?'

'Of course, of course. You're not going back to Calcutta immediately, are you?'

'No, we should be here for another three days.'

'Good. So where are you going now?'

'Nowhere in particular. Is there something we should see? *You* should be able to tell us!'

'Have you seen the Bat-kali temple? It was built in the seventeenth century. It's full of bats, but the outside walls still have some carvings left. Come with me, I'll show you.'

I did not tell him I had seen the temple this morning. At

that moment, of course, I had not had the time to look at wall carvings.

We reached it in three minutes. I began to get goose pimples again. It would have been far better to have come here during the day. There was a banyan tree next to the temple. Its roots had grasped the roof, making it crack and crumble.

'This is where they used to have sacrifices, sir,' Benimadhav said, pointing at a spot near the trunk of the banyan tree.

'S-sacrifice?' Lalmohan Babu asked, his voice hushed.

'Yes, sir. Human sacrifices. Haven't you heard of Nedo *dakaat*, the famous bandit of Gosaipur? He used to worship Kali and hold sacrifices here. Why, you could write a whole book on him! Would you like to go inside? Have you got a torch?'

'In-inside? No, I don't think so. Didn't you say it was full of bats? Besides, we didn't bring a torch.'

'No, the bats will have gone out now, on their evening excursion . . . heh heh. If you wish to see them you'll have to come back—'

'No! We have no wish to see them, thank you.'

'All right. Look, I've lit a match. May I smoke a beedi?'

'Yes, certainly. Smoke as many as you like.'

Benimadhav lit his beedi, then held the match near the broken door. What I saw in its flickering light made my heart skip a beat. Lalmohan Babu had seen it, too.

'J-j-jee-jee-jee-' he stammered.

It was Jeevanlal's dead body. There could be no mistake. His blue shirt and white pyjamas were peeping out from behind a pillar inside the temple. I even caught a glimpse of his left arm. He had been wearing a watch this morning. Now the watch was gone.

'Look, someone left their clothes here!' exclaimed Benimadhav, and began to stride forward to retrieve the clothes, possibly with a view to returning them to their owner.

'D-don't!' Lalmohan Babu pulled him back urgently. 'Th-that's a dead body. We sh-should tell the p-police!'

At these words, the mime artist turned totally mute. Then he showed us just how gifted he was. We saw, in a flash, the expression on his face change from amazement to horror, in one single step; then he turned around and legged it, in absolute silence. We, too, decided not to spend another moment there, and came back home immediately, walking as fast as we could.

Feluda had already returned. He glanced at me briefly and said, 'Why do you look so pale? Get ready quickly. We have to be back in Mr Bhattacharya's house in fifteen minutes.'

Lalmohan Babu, I noticed, had regained his composure on seeing Feluda.

'Felu Babu,' he announced calmly, 'we made an important discovery. Jeevanlal's body is lying inside that old Kali temple. Are you going to tell the police, or will you let them go on looking for it?'

Lalmohan Babu had taken an instant dislike to the inspector. So he seemed all in favour of not doing anything to make it easier for him.

'Did you actually go into the temple?' Feluda asked.

'No; nor did we touch the body. But there can be no doubt about what we saw.'

'OK. I met the inspector just now. He'll probably be coming to Mr Bhattacharya's house. We can tell him when we see him.'

We left in ten minutes. Tulsi Babu said he'd have to go and see Mr Chakladar, just to warn him that the function he was supposed to preside over the next day might well be cancelled.

'You carry on, I'll join you later,' he said.

On our way to Mr Bhattacharya's house, Feluda told us how eager he had seemed to get in touch with Jeevanlal's spirit. He'd offered to do this first, even though it meant making three other clients wait outside.

This evening, his room had a table instead of the divan. Five chairs had been arranged around it. On the table was an oil lamp. Mr Bhattacharya was sitting on one of the chairs. On his right was a writing pad and a pencil. Behind the table were two small stools and a bench. Nityanand was seated on the bench.

We took three chairs. The fourth remained empty for Tulsi Babu.

'Should we wait for Tulsicharan?' Mr Bhattacharya asked.

'Let's give him five minutes,' Feluda replied.

'Very well. I knew . . . you'd have to come to me,' Mr Bhattacharya's deep voice boomed out. 'I realized it that day, when I first set my eyes on you. I could tell you would not scoff at this highly specialized branch of science, for that's what it is. Only the ignorant, only those who know nothing about the different ways through which one may arrive at the truth, mock and laugh at my methods. A true believer in science—such as yourself—keeps an open mind. He does not ridicule.'

I began to feel a bit bored with all this talk of science and truth. Why didn't he start?

'You have all met Jeevanlal, and he has only just died,' he went on. 'For these two reasons, I expect today's session to be a success. His soul has not yet had the time to lose all its earthly bonds and escape into the other world. It is still lingering near us, waiting for our call. It knows it cannot refuse our invitation. I know we simply have to say the word, and it will be with us. It is immortal, and it is aware of not just the past and the present, but also the future. It will speak through me, it will reveal the truth on this sheet of paper, just as we . . .'

Feluda interrupted him. I failed to see how he could speak, for my own throat had started to feel parched, and I suspect Lalmohan Babu was feeling the same. There was a hypnotic quality in Mr Bhattacharya's voice that inspired awe.

'Everyone will want to see what you write,' Feluda said,

'but with the exception of myself, everybody is sitting opposite you. Will you mind if I read out what you write?'

'No, not at all. What do you want to ask the spirit?'

'Three things—who burgled the house, who killed Jeevanlal, and when he was killed.'

'Very well. You shall soon have the answers,' said Mr Bhattacharya.

EIGHT

Five minutes passed, but there was no sign of Tulsi Babu. Mr Bhattacharya decided to get to work.

'Please place your hands—palm downward—on the table. Your little fingers should touch those of your neighbour's.'

We placed our hands as instructed. A tapping noise started at once, caused by Lalmohan Babu's trembling fingers. He might have been playing a tabla. I saw him grit his teeth to steady his hands.

Mr Bhattacharya's eyes were closed, but his lips moved. He was reciting a Sanskrit shloka. A minute later, he stopped. There was a deathly silence in the room. The lamp flickered. Around its flame three insects hovered. Our shadows, large and trembling, fell on the walls nearly touching the ceiling. I gave Feluda a sidelong glance. His jaw was set, and he was staring steadily at Mr Bhattacharya with a totally expressionless face. Mr Bhattacharya himself was sitting still as a statue. He had picked up the pencil, which was now poised over the blank sheet of paper.

Then his lips started to tremble. Beads of perspiration broke out on his forehead. Lalmohan Babu began playing the tabla again, perfectly involuntarily. I could see why. The atmosphere in the room was decidedly eerie. My heart beat as fast as Lalmohan Babu's fingers shook.

'Jeevanlal . . . Jeevanlal . . . Jeevanlal!' Mr Bhattacharya called softly. His lips barely moved.

'Are you there? Have you come?'

This time, to our amazement, the questions were spoken

by a voice behind us. It was Nityanand. Now I realized what his role was. He spoke on behalf of his uncle. Perhaps Mr Bhattacharya found it impossible to speak at a time like this.

'Yes,' said Feluda. The word had been scribbled on the pad by Mr Bhattacharya. His eyes were still closed. I watched his hands carefully.

'Where are you?' asked Nityanand.

'Here, very close,' wrote Mr Bhattacharya. Feluda read the words out.

'We'd like to ask you a few questions. Can you answer them?'

'Yes.'

'Who stole the money from your father's chest?'

'I did.'

'Did you see your murderer?'

'Yes.'

'Did you recognize him?'

'Yes.'

'Who was it?'

'My father.'

But we didn't get to hear when the murder was committed, for Feluda stood up abruptly and said, 'That'll do.' Then he turned to me and said, 'Topshe, go and get that lantern from the passage outside. I can hardly see anything.' Considerably startled, I got up and fetched the lantern.

Feluda picked up the piece of paper Mr Bhattacharya had scribbled on, ran his eyes over the few words written and said, 'Mr Bhattacharya, your spirit may have left the earth, but it hasn't yet learnt the truth. There are discrepancies in his answers.'

Mr Bhattacharya glared at Feluda looking as if he wanted to reduce him to a handful of dust, but Feluda remained quite unmoved. 'For instance,' he continued, 'he is being asked who opened the chest and took the money. He says, "I did", meaning Jeevanlal. But that chest was empty, Mr Bhattacharya. There was no money in it.'

As if by magic, the fury faded from Mr Bhattacharya's face. He began to look rather uncertain. Feluda went on, 'I can say this with some confidence because it was not Jeevanlal Mallik who opened that chest, but Pradosh Chander Mitter. Jeevanlal helped me do it by opening the front door for me in the middle of the night and telling me where the key was kept. He also helped me to tie up his father and Bholanath Babu. Anyway, instead of any money, what we found in the chest was this.' He slipped a hand into his pocket and brought out another piece of paper.

'The old Mr Mallik had refused to show it to me. But I needed it urgently as I had serious doubts about Mriganka Bhattacharya's intentions. My suspicions were aroused the minute I met him. He pretended to have guessed my name and profession by some supernatural means. The truth is that Tulsi Babu had already told him who I was and what I did. Am I right, Tulsi Babu?'

I realized with a start that Tulsi Babu had joined us, though I had not seen him arrive. He looked profoundly embarrassed and tried to explain: 'Y-yes, I am afraid . . . you see . . . I wanted you to get a good impression, so I . . . '

Feluda raised a hand to stop him. 'I don't blame you, Tulsi Babu. *You* don't pretend to be something you are not. But this man does. Anyway, when I realized Mr Bhattacharya was simply putting on an act to impress me, I was determined to get hold of the paper that Shyamlal Mallik wanted no one to see. There were a few doubts in my mind about Shyamlal, too, which I thought this piece of paper would help clarify.'

Mr Bhattacharya was now sweating profusely. Feluda held the paper closer to the lamp and said, 'Durlabh Singh's departed soul was supposed to have answered some questions. The questions were spoken, but it isn't difficult to guess what was asked. The written answers are good indicators. I shall now read out to you all the questions and the answers given. If I get any of it wrong, I hope Bhattacharya will correct me.'

Mr Bhattacharya was breathing so fast that the flame flickered strongly. Feluda began reading, 'The first question was: "Who is my enemy?" Answer: "he is in your house. Does he want me dead?—No. Then what does he want?—Money. How can I save my money from him?—Don't keep it in your chest. Where should I kept it?—Bury it under the ground. Where?—In your garden. Where in the garden?—At the far end—under the last mango tree—by the gap in the wall."'

Feluda put the paper back into his pocket. 'The traces of mud on his feet and the mosquito bites on his face had suggested that Shyamlal Mallik had spent some time out in the garden. Now I know why he had done that. He simply followed the instructions Mr Bhattacharya gave him, except that *he* thought they were given by his dead father. Mr Bhattacharya knew about the money Shyamlal possessed and had been planning to steal it for quite some time. But he knew it was impossible as long as the old and trusted Bholanath remained with his master. At first he tried to poison Shyamlal's mind against Bholanath. Sadly, that did not work. Then, miraculously, Mr Bhattacharya found a new opportunity. Shyamlal himself called him to his house and asked him to contact a spirit. Mr Bhattacharya seized this chance to kill two birds with one stone. He got Shyamlal to believe that someone in his own house had become his enemy, and he managed to get the money removed from the chest and placed at a spot which would be accessible to him. Shyamlal raised no objection to burying his money in the garden, for this was an ancient method of keeping things safe, which was perfectly acceptable to him, as Mr Bhattacharya knew it would be. So he put everything in a separate box and buried it under the last mango tree. Yesterday—!'

A sudden noise made him stop. Nityanand had suddenly sprung to his feet and leapt out of the door. But he could not get very far. A pair of strong arms caught him neatly and pushed him back into the room. Then their owner stepped in himself. It was Inspector Pramanik.

'We found the box, Mr Mitter,' he said, 'with everything intact. He had hidden it under some clothes in an old trunk. Constable!'

A constable stepped forward and placed a fairly large steel box on the table.

'Why, the lid's been broken!' Feluda exclaimed. Then he lifted it. The box was crammed with bundles of hundred-rupee notes. Never in my life had I seen so much cash.

'But . . . but . . . what about the murder?' Mr Bhattacharya cried desperately. 'I did not kill Jeevanlal!'

'No, I know you didn't,' Feluda spoke scathingly. '*I* did. The murder was also my idea. What I did manage to kill and destroy, Mr Bhattacharya, was your greed, your deception and your cunning. Your career in fraud is over, for everyone in this village will soon learn what you achieved today. Tell me, have you ever heard of anyone speaking to the soul of the living? Come in, Jeevan Babu!'

As a collective gasp went up, Jeevanlal entered the room through the front door. A piercing scream tore through Mr Bhattacharya's lips, and he scrambled to his feet. The constable quickly put handcuffs on him.

*

Inspector Pramanik had only one complaint to make. 'Why did you make us dredge two lakes, Mr Mitter? We wasted such a lot of time!'

'No, no, please don't say that. It was necessary to pretend that Jeevanlal had really been killed, and we were looking for his body. How else could we have exposed Bhattacharya so completely?'

It turned out that Feluda had planned the whole thing to the last detail. When he and I left the 'body' and Bholanath and Lalmohan Babu went back to the house, Jeevanlal had got up and slipped into an old store room in the house. His grandmother had seen him, but Feluda managed to cover it up quickly. In the evening, he had stolen out to make his way to Mr Bhattacharya's house, so that he could hide among the bushes and come out at the right time; but, rather unfortunately, we were walking through the bamboo grove at the same time, which made him dive into the old temple and pretend to be a corpse once again.

After dinner that night, Tulsi Babu came up to Feluda and said a little ruefully, 'Are you cross with me, Mr Mitter?'

'Cross? Of course not. If anything, Tulsi Babu, I am most grateful to you. If you hadn't told that man my name, he wouldn't have dared to make up a puzzle about my initials, and I would have had no reason to wonder if his powers were genuine. You helped me a great deal.'

Jeevanlal Mallik turned up a few minutes later. 'My father is speaking to me again!' he said, beaming.

'What did he say?'

'When I went and touched his feet this evening, he spoke to me with an affection he hasn't shown for years. He even asked me how our business was doing, and seemed really interested. I could scarcely believe it!'

Lalmohan Babu was busy dealing with the head of a fish. Now he finished chewing and opened his mouth.

'The . . . er . . . tomorrow? . . .' he asked tentatively, looking at Tulsi Babu.

'Oh yes. It's definitely going ahead. Everything's ready.'

'Very good. My speech is ready, too. Felu Babu, will you please cast an eye over it?'

The Curse of the Goddess

Lalmohan Babu looked up from his book and said, 'Ram Mohan Roy's grandson owned a circus. Did you know that?'

Feluda was leaning back, his face covered with a handkerchief. He shook his head.

Our car had been standing, for the last ten minutes, behind a huge lorry which was loaded with bales of straw. Not only was it blocking our way, but was emitting such thick black smoke that we were all getting choked. Our driver had blown his horn several times, but to no avail. I was tired of being able to see nothing but the painting of a setting sun and flowers on the back of the lorry, and all that a lorry usually said: Ta Ta, Horn Please, Goodbye and Thank You. Equally bored and tired, Lalmohan Babu had started to read a book called *The Circus in Bengal*. His next book was going to be set in a circus, so he'd taken Feluda's advice and decided to do a bit of reading on the subject. As a matter of fact, we had stopped in Ranchi earlier in the day and seen posters advertising The Great Majestic Circus. It was supposed to have reached Hazaribagh which was where we were going. If we happened to be free one evening, we had decided to go and see the circus.

Winter had only just started. All of us wanted a short break. Lalmohan Babu's latest book—*The Vampire of Vancouver*—had been released last month and sold two thousand copies in three weeks, which naturally pleased him no end. Feluda had objected to the title of the book, pointing out that Vancouver was a huge modern city, the most unlikely place for vampires. For once, Lalmohan Babu had overruled Feluda's objection, saying that he had been through the atlas of the world, and Vancouver had struck him as the most appropriate name.

Feluda, too, was free for the moment. He had solved a case in Bihar last September. His client, Sarveshwar Sahai, had been so pleased with Feluda's work that he had invited us to his house in Hazaribagh. He did not live there permanently. It remained empty for most of the time. There was a chowkidar, whose wife did the cooking. We could stay there for ten days. All we would have to pay for would be the food.

The offer seemed too good to miss. We decided to go by road in Lalmohan Babu's new Ambassador. 'Let's see how it performs on a long run,' he said. We might have gone via Asansol and Dhanbad, but chose to go through Kharagpur and Ranchi instead. Feluda drove the car until we got to Kharagpur, then the driver took over. We reached Ranchi in the evening and stayed overnight at the Amber Hotel. This morning, we had left Ranchi at nine o'clock, hoping to reach Hazaribagh by a quarter past ten. But, thanks to the lorry, we were definitely going to be delayed.

After another five minutes of honking, the lorry finally moved and allowed us to pass. Much relieved, we took deep breaths as our car emerged in the open. The road was lined with tall trees, many of which had weaver birds' nests. If I looked out of the window, I could see a range of hills in the distance. Small hillocks stood by the side of the road. We passed these every now and then. Lalmohan Babu saw all this and muttered 'Beautiful! Beautiful!' a couple of times. Then he began humming a Tagore song, looking more comical than ever. He was totally tone-deaf as well, and inevitably chose songs that were quite inappropriate. For instance, on this cool November morning, he had started a song that spoke of the new joys of spring. He had once explained his problem to me. Apparently, he felt like bursting into song the minute he left Calcutta and came into closer contact with nature; however, his stock of songs being rather limited, he couldn't always think of a suitable one.

But there was one thing for which I had to thank him. In the last twenty-four hours, he had told me a lot of things about the circus in Bengal that I did not know. A hundred years ago, it was circuses owned by Bengalis that were famous all over the country. The best known among these was Professor Priyanath Bose's The Great Bengal Circus. There were American, Russian, German and French artists, in addition to Indian. Even women used to take part. An American called Gus Burns used to work with a tiger. Unfortunately, when Professor Bose died, there was no one to take charge. His circus went out of business, as did many others in Bengal.

'This Great Majestic in Hazaribagh . . . where does that come from, I wonder?' Lalmohan Babu asked.

'It has to be south India,' Feluda answered, 'They seem to have a monopoly in that line now.'

'How good is their trapeze? That's what I'd like to know!'

In this new book he was planning to write, trapeze was going to play an important role. One of the artistes was going to grab the arm of another while swinging in mid-air and give him a lethal injection. His hero, Prakhar Rudra, was going to have to learn a few tricks from trapeze artistes to be able to catch the culprit. When Lalmohan Babu revealed these details to us, Feluda remarked dryly, 'Thank goodness there is at least one thing left for your hero to learn!'

We saw the second Ambassador soon after passing a post that said '72 kms'. It was standing by the side of the road with its bonnet up. Its driver was bending over it, only partially visible from the road. Another gentleman was waving frantically at us. Lalmohan Babu's driver placed his foot on the brake.

'Er . . . are you going to Hazaribagh?' the man asked. He was probably around forty, had a clear complexion and wore glasses.

'Yes, we are,' Feluda replied.

'My car . . . the problem seems to be serious, you see. So I wonder if . . . ?'

'You may come with us, if you like.'

'So kind of you. I'll try and get a mechanic and bring him back in a taxi. Can't see what else I can do.'

'Do you have any luggage?'

'Only a small suitcase, but I can take it with me later. It shouldn't take me more than forty-five minutes to return.'

'Come on then.'

The man explained to his driver what he had decided to do, then climbed into our car and said 'So kind of you' again. Then he told us a great deal about himself, even without being asked. His name was Pritindra Chowdhury. His father, Mahesh Chowdhury, was once an advocate in Ranchi. He had retired ten years ago and moved to Hazaribagh. Everyone there knew him well.

'Do you live in Calcutta?' Feluda asked him.

'Yes. I am in electronics. Have you heard of Indovision?'

I remembered having seen advertisements for a new television by the name. Mr Chowdhury worked for its manufacturers.

'My father turns seventy tomorrow,' he went on, 'I have an elder brother. He has already reached Hazaribagh, and so have my wife and daughter. I was away in Delhi, you see, so I very nearly did not make it. But my father sent me a telegram saying "Must come", so here I am. Could you please stop the car for a minute?'

The car stopped. Mr Chowdhury took out a small cassette recorder from his shoulder bag and disappeared among the trees. He returned in a couple of minutes and said, 'I heard a flycatcher. It was still there, luckily. It is something of an obsession for me—I mean, this business of recording bird calls. So kind of you.'

The last words were meant to convey his thanks for stopping the car. Strangely, although he told us so much about himself, he didn't seem interested in us at all.

We dropped him outside Eureka Automobiles in the main part of Hazaribagh. He said, 'So kind of you' yet again and got out. Then he suddenly turned around and asked, 'Oh by the way, where will you be staying?'

Feluda had to raise his voice to make himself heard, for a lot of people were gathered nearby, talking excitedly about something. We learnt the reason for such excitement a little later.

'I can't give you directions for this is our first visit to Hazaribagh. All I can tell you is that the house belongs to a Mr Sahai, and it isn't far from the District Board Rest House.'

'Oh, then it can't be more than seven minutes from our house. Do you have a telephone?'

'Yes. 742.'

'Good.'

'My name is Mitter. P.C. Mitter.'

'I see. I didn't even ask your name. Sorry.'

We said goodbye and went on our way. 'He's probably tense about introducing a new product,' Feluda observed.

'Eccentric,' Lalmohan Babu proclaimed briefly.

The District Board Rest House was not difficult to find. Mr Sahai's house stood only a few houses away. Our car stopped and tooted outside the gate over which hung colourful branches of bougainvillaea. A short, middle-aged man emerged immediately and opened the gate. Then he stood aside and gave us a salute. We drove up a long driveway and finally stopped before a bungalow. The man who had opened the gate came running to take our luggage. It turned out that he was the chowkidar, Bulakiprasad.

I realized how quiet everything was when we got out of the car. The bungalow was surrounded by a huge compound (Lalmohan Babu took one look at it and said, 'At least three acres!'). On one side was a garden with pretty flowerbeds. On the other side stood quite a few large trees. I could recognize mango and tamarind amongst them. Beyond the compound wall, in the far distance, were the Kanari Hills, about two miles away.

The house seemed ideal for three people. Three steps led to a veranda, behind which were three rooms. The one in the middle was the living room, the other two were bedrooms. Lalmohan Babu chose the one that faced the west since he thought it would give him a good view of the sunset every evening.

We had only just begun unpacking, when Bulakiprasad came in with three cups of tea on a tray, and said something that made us drop everything and stare at him.

'When you go out, sir,' he said, 'please take great care.'

'Why? Are there pickpockets about?' Lalmohan Babu asked.

'No, sir. A tiger from the Great Majestic Circus has run away.'

What! What on earth was the man talking about?

Bulakiprasad did not hesitate to give us all the details. A huge tiger had escaped from its cage only that morning. He didn't know how that had happened, but the entire town was in a state of panic. The star attraction of the circus was this tiger. I remembered the painting of a tiger on all the posters I'd seen in Ranchi. Feluda had even noticed the name of its trainer. 'A Marathi man,' he said, 'His name is Karandikar.'

Lalmohan Babu remained silent for a few moments after hearing this news. Then he said, 'This has to be telepathy. Would you believe it, I had been wondering if I could include something like this in my book? I mean, a tiger escaping from a circus is such a thrilling event, isn't it? But you, Felu Babu, must remain totally incongito. If they realize you are a detective, they'll get you to track the animal down, mark my words!'

Feluda and I were both so taken aback by what we had just heard that neither of us bothered to point out that the word was actually 'incognito'. He need not have feared, however.

Feluda never disclosed his profession to anyone without a good reason.

Bulakiprasad also told us that, in the past, the circus used to be held in a park called Curzon Park which was in the middle of the town. But this year, for some reason, they had gone to an open area at one end of the town, beyond which stretched a forest. The tiger only had to cross the main road to go into it. There were small Adivasi villages in the forest, so it could quite easily feed on their domestic animals.

None of us had imagined we'd hear something so sensational within minutes of our arrival in Hazaribagh. But it seemed a great pity that we couldn't walk in the streets without having to watch out for a wild animal. Lalmohan Babu suggested after we had finished our tea that it might be a good idea to visit the circus in the afternoon to find out what exactly had happened.

'When you say visit the circus, do you mean going to the show?' Feluda asked.

'No, not really. I was actually thinking of meeting the owner. He'd be able to tell us everything, surely?'

'Yes. But, in order to do that, Mr Jatayu, you most definitely need the assistance of Felu Mitter.'

Bulakiprasad's wife made arahar daal and chicken curry for lunch. We did full justice to it, and then left in the car. Feluda was clearly as curious as Lalmohan Babu about the escaped tiger. He rang the local police station before we left. He had had to work with the police in Bihar on the last case, and Sarveshwar Sahai's name was well known in Hazaribagh. The inspector who answered the phone—Inspector Raut—recognized Feluda's name as soon as he had introduced himself and explained why he was calling. We did need help from the police to see the owner of the circus, under the present circumstances. 'One of our men is posted outside the main entrance,' Inspector Raut said. 'He will let you in.' Feluda told him he wanted to go there purely out of curiosity, not to start an investigation.

On our way to the circus, we saw groups of men gathered around street corners, still talking animatedly. Near a big crossing, someone was actually beating a drum and shouting words of caution. Feluda stopped at a small stall to buy a packet of cigarettes. The stallholder told him the tiger had been seen near a village called Dahiri to the north of Hazaribagh, but there were no reports of any damage.

My heart suddenly lifted at the sight of the tents as we got closer to the circus. It reminded me of all the circuses Feluda had taken me to when I was a small child. The blue and white striped tent of The Great Majestic Circus was very neat and tidy, which meant they were true professionals and knew their trade well. A yellow flag fluttered on top of the tent, and rows of bunting had been carefully arranged between the compound fence and the main entrance. Hundreds of people were jostling outside near the ticket counters. The show was going to go on even without the tiger. Various other posters showed what else the circus had to offer. The artist who had drawn them did not appear to be particularly gifted, but what he'd managed was enough to arouse both curiosity and excitement.

The constable on duty had been told about us. He gave Feluda a smart salute, and let us in immediately. 'Mr Kutti—that's the owner—has been informed, sir. He's waiting for you in his room,' the constable said.

Behind the tent was an open space. It ended where a partition made with corrugated tin sheets began. Mr Kutti's caravan stood just behind the partition. Like the tent, it was tidy and well maintained. There were rows of windows on both sides. Curtains with attractive patterns hung at these, through which the sun came in and formed patches on the furniture. Mr Kutti rose as he saw us arrive and shook our hands. Then he gestured towards a mini sofa. He seemed to be around fifty, although his hair had turned totally white. When he smiled, his teeth gleamed in the semi-darkness of the caravan. They were clearly his own, not dentures.

Feluda explained, as soon as we were seated, that he had decided to call not because he had anything to do with the police, but because he had heard a lot about the Great Majestic and wanted to see their show. 'It's such a pity we can't see your best item!' he exclaimed. Then he introduced Lalmohan Babu as a famous writer who was interested in the circus and wanted to write a book about it.

Mr Kutti nodded. 'Before I joined a circus, I spent six years in Calcutta working for a shipping company,' he told us. 'I like Bengalis. They seem to understand and appreciate the true spirit of the circus. Please don't be disappointed just because our tiger is missing. There are quite a lot of other things to be seen. We had a special show yesterday. Many well-known personalities were invited. I am inviting you now, you are welcome to any of our shows.'

'Thank you,' Lalmohan Babu spoke unexpectedly, 'How did it happen? I mean, the tiger? . . . '

'It's all very unfortunate, Mr Ganguli,' said Mr Kutti, 'the door of the cage was not fastened properly. The tiger pushed it open. Even so, it might not have got out in the open, but someone had removed a portion of the partition to make a short-cut and then forgotten to replace it. So the tiger slipped out through the gap. I have taken steps to find out who was responsible, and make sure it does not happen again.'

'Didn't a tiger once escape like this in Bombay?' Feluda asked.

'Yes, from the National Circus. It actually got out in the streets of Bombay, but the ringmaster caught it before it could get very far.'

Mr Kutti told us something else about the escaped tiger. Apparently, it had been spotted by at least fifty different people. There had been reports from various sources. A lady had seen it enter her courtyard and promptly fallen into a swoon. Why and how the tiger had left her unharmed was not known. Then there was a Nepali man who had seen the tiger cross a road. He himself happened to be driving a scooter at the time. Startled by the sight, he had driven straight into a lamp-post and was now in a hospital with three broken ribs.

'Surely you have a ringmaster?' Lalmohan Babu asked.

'Yes, Karandikar. But he hasn't been too well for sometime. He is nearly forty, you see. He gets a pain in his neck every now and then, but goes on to perform despite that. I have told him a million times to see a doctor, but he won't listen. So, about a month ago, I got another trainer, called Chandran. He's from Kerala and is very good in his work. It is he who acts as the ringmaster when Karandikar feels unwell.'

'Who performed with the tiger at the special show yesterday?' Feluda wanted to know.

'Karandikar. He seemed fine. There is one special item which only he can do. Chandran has never tried it. Karandikar puts his hands into the tiger's mouth, opens it wide, then puts his head in it. Unfortunately, something went wrong yesterday. He tried twice, but the tiger refused to open its mouth. Instead of trying again, Karandikar simply gave up and finished his show. There was some applause, but many people booed and jeered at him.'

'Didn't you do anything about it?'

'Of course. He's been with me for seventeen years, but I had to speak to him very sternly last night. Now he's saying he will leave the circus. That would be most unfortunate, both for him and for us. He can easily perform for at least another three years, I think. His work with the Great Majestic has made him quite well known.'

'Hasn't anyone from your team gone to look for the tiger?'

'Karandikar should have gone, but he flatly refused to have anything to do with a search party. So I sent Chandran with people from the Forest Department.'

'Could we see Karandikar?' Lalmohan Babu asked rather boldly.

'You could try, but there's no guarantee he'll agree to see you. He's extremely moody. I'll ask my bearer, Murugesh, to take you to his tent.'

Murugesh was standing outside. He came with us as we thanked Mr Kutti and left his caravan.

The ringmaster's tent was divided into two sections. One half of it acted as a living room. The other was clearly where he slept. Much to our surprise, he came out of this 'bedroom' as soon as he was informed of our arrival. One look at him told me why a tiger obeyed his command. I had rarely seen anyone who looked so strong physically. He was as tall as Feluda, but his body was much more muscular. A jet black moustache on a fair skin gave him an added air of strength and power. His eyes seemed distant, but sometimes they glowed with emotion as he spoke. He told us he could speak Marathi, Tamil and

Malayalam, in addition to English and Hindi. Feluda decided
to speak to him in English.

The first thing Mr Karandikar asked was whether we had
been sent by a newspaper. Perhaps the notebook and pencil in
Lalmohan Babu's hands prompted this question. Feluda had
to choose his words carefully before making a reply. 'Suppose
we *were* newspaper reporters. Would that make any
difference? I mean, would you object to talking to the Press?'
Feluda asked.

'Oh no. On the contrary. I'd be glad to talk to them. People
must be told that if the tiger escaped from his cage, it was
certainly not the fault of his old trainer. The owner of this
circus must take all responsibility. A tiger does not obey two
different trainers. It can respond to only one. Sultan had
started to get irritable soon after the other trainer arrived. I had
explained this to Mr Kutti, but he didn't pay any attention to
me. Now I hope he's happy with the result.'

'Why didn't you go to look for your tiger?'

'Why should I? Let them find him again!' he said,
sounding deeply hurt.

Lalmohan Babu whispered something into Feluda's ear.
This meant he wanted to ask Mr Karandikar something, but
was afraid to. Feluda translated quickly.

'Would you go if the others fail, or if your presence
becomes absolutely necessary for some reason?'

'Why, yes! If I hear anyone is thinking of killing my
Sultan, I'll certainly go and try to save him. I look upon him
as family—no, I think he's even closer to me than a family
member.'

I, too, wanted to ask him something. As it turned out, I
didn't have to. Feluda spoke before me.

'Did a tiger ever scratch your face?'

'Yes, but it wasn't Sultan. I used to work for The Golden
Circus before I joined the Great Majestic. It was one of their
tigers. It clawed my face; one of my cheeks and my nose were
badly injured.' He than took his shirt off. We were amazed to

see endless scars on his body. Heaven knows how many times he had been mauled.

Before we left, Feluda asked him one last question. 'Will you continue to stay here?'

'I don't know. A small tent in a circus has been my home for more than seventeen years. Now . . . I may well have to look for something different. Who knows?'

Lalmohan Babu wanted to see all the other animals. He had already spoken to Mr Kutti about it. When we left Mr Karandikar, Murugesh took us to where the animals were kept. There were two other tigers, a large bear, a hippopotamus, three elephants and six horses. Sultan's cage stood on one side. There was something rather eerie about its emptiness.

By the time we got back home, it was five o'clock. Bulakiprasad came in with the tea a little later, and told us that someone from Mr Chowdhury's house had called in our absence. He would call again later, he had said.

Pritindra Chowdhury arrived at half past six. The sun had set by this time, and the temperature had dropped appreciably. We had all slipped on our woollen pullovers.

'You didn't tell me you were a detective!' Pritin Babu said most unexpectedly, 'When I told my father about you, he said he knew you were coming. Your client, Mr Sahai, knows him, you see. He had happened to mention your visit. I am here now to invite you to our picnic tomorrow. Baba would like all of you to come.'

'A picnic?' Lalmohan Babu raised his eyebrows.

'Didn't I tell you? It's Baba's birthday tomorrow, so we are all going to Rajrappa for a picnic. We'll have lunch there. If you came to our house in your car at around nine o'clock, we could all leave together. Our house is called Kailash. It's not far from here, I'll tell you how to find it. And,' he added, 'if you came a little earlier than nine, you'd be able to see my father's collection of butterflies and rocks.'

Rajrappa was fifty miles from Hazaribagh. It had a

waterfall and an old Kali temple called the temple of Chhinnamasta. It was well known for its scenic beauty. We had heard of it before and had, in fact, planned to go there ourselves during our stay.

'But . . . ' Lalmohan Babu began doubtfully, 'haven't you heard about the tiger?'

'Yes, of course,' Pritin Babu laughed, 'but there's no cause for alarm. My brother is a crack shot. He'll be taking his gun with him. Besides, the tiger is supposed to have gone to the north. Rajrappa is to the south of Hazaribagh, near Ramgarh. You may relax.'

Feluda thanked him and said we would arrive at his house at eight-thirty. Pritin Babu gave us the necessary directions and left.

'Why is the house called Kailash, I wonder?' Lalmohan Babu asked.

'Possibly because its owner is called Mahesh,' Feluda replied, 'Mahesh is another name for Shiva, isn't it? Since Shiva lives in Mount Kailash, Mahesh Chowdhury decided to call his house by the same name.'

It was now pitch dark outside. But we did not switch the lights on since the moon had risen and we wanted to sit by its light on the veranda. For some strange reason, Lalmohan Babu was muttering the word 'Chhinnamasta' under his breath, over and over. Then he suddenly stopped at 'Chhin—' because Feluda had raised a hand.

We sat in silence for a few seconds. There was no noise outside except the steady din made by crickets. Then, from the far distance, came a different noise. It froze my blood, for I had heard it before. It was the roar of a tiger. We heard it three times.

Sultan was calling from somewhere. Only an experienced shikari could tell how far he was, and from which direction he was calling.

THREE

I had thought the news of an escaped tiger would be the highlight of our stay. But who knew something else would happen, and Feluda would get inextricably linked with it? I will not be able to forget Mahesh Chowdhury's birthday on 23 November for a long time to come. And the memory of the scenes in Rajrappa, particularly the temple of Chhinnamasta, standing against its strangely beautiful dry and rocky background, will always stay alive in my memory.

But I must go back to the previous evening. The roar of the tiger made Lalmohan Babu go rather pale. However, just as I was about to suggest he should sleep in our room, he announced that he was fine, but could he please have the big torch with five cells? The reason for this was that he had heard somewhere a tiger would retreat if a bright light shone in its eyes for more then a few seconds. 'Mind you,' he said before going to his own room, 'if the tiger roared outside my window, I'm not sure if I'd have the nerve to open it and shine the torch in its face. But Bulakiprasad tells me he has a weapon, and he's not afraid of wild animals.'

Luckily, even if the tiger did pay us a visit in the middle of the night, it decided not to roar; so all was well.

*

We reached Kailash the following morning on the dot of eight-thirty. Lalmohan Babu took one look at the house and said, 'The Shiva who lives in this Kailash must be an English one!' Feluda and I had to agree with him. It might have been built only ten years ago, but its appearance was that of a house built fifty years ago during British times.

A chowkidar opened the gate for us. We passed through and parked in one corner of the compound. There were three cars. Pritin Babu's black Ambassador, a white Fiat and an old yellow Pontiac.

'Look, Felu Babu, I have found a clue!' Lalmohan Babu exclaimed. He had found a piece of paper near the edge of the lawn. Like Mr Sahai's house, Kailash had a garden on one side.

'How can you find a clue when there's no mystery?' Feluda laughed.

'I know, but just look at what's written on it. Doesn't it seem sort of mysterious?'

It was a leaf torn from a child's exercise book. A few letters from the alphabet were written on it. There was no mystery in it at all. Whoever had written it seemed to be rather fond of the letter 'X'. It said:

XLNC
XL
XPDNC
NME
OICURMT

Feluda put it in his pocket with a smile.

A very old Muslim bearer was standing near the portico. He said 'Salaam, huzoor', and took us inside. A familiar voice had already reached our ears. We saw Pritindra Chowdhury as soon as we stepped into the drawing room. He came forward to greet us warmly: 'Oh, do come in. So kind of you to come!'

We returned his greeting, then stood still, staring at the walls. Instead of framed paintings, they were covered by framed butterflies. Each frame had eight of them, carefully pinned and beautifully displayed. There were eight such frames, which made a total of sixty-four butterflies, each with its wings spread, looking as though it was ready to take flight. The whole room seemed to glow with their bright colours.

The collector himself was seated on a sofa. He rose with a smile when he saw us enter the room. In his youth, he must have been both good looking and physically strong. He was still tall, and held himself straight. His complexion was very fair, he was cleanshaven and dressed in a fine dhoti, a silk kurta and a heavily embroidered Kashmiri shawl. On his nose were perched rimless glasses.

Pritin Babu only knew Feluda's name, so Lalmohan Babu and I had to be introduced by Feluda. Before Mahesh Chowdhury could say anything, Lalmohan Babu piped up, 'Happy birthday to you, sir!'

Mr Chowdhury laughed. 'Thank you, thank you! I don't see why an old man like me should celebrate his birthday, but this whole thing was arranged by my daughter-in-law. Look, she even made me dress up. But I am very glad you were able to come. Hope you didn't find it difficult to find our K dash eyelash?'

Lalmohan Babu and I stared dumbly at him. But Feluda raised his eyebrows only for a fleeting second before saying, 'No, sir, we found it quite easily.'

'Good. I knew you'd get my meaning. You must be used to dealing with codes and ciphers. However, your friends are still looking puzzled.'

Feluda had to take out his small notebook and pen and write the code down to explain. K—eyelash, he wrote. 'Now say the words quickly,' he said with a smile. Lalmohan Babu promptly started saying 'K eyelash, K eyelash' rapidly, breaking off suddenly to say, 'Oh, oh, I see. It does sound like Kailash, doesn't it?'

I had to laugh. Then I saw a little girl of about five, who was sitting on the floor in the middle of the room with a doll in her lap. In her hand was a pair of tweezers. She kept pinching the doll's forehead with it, possibly to pretend that she was tweezing its eyebrows.

'That's my granddaughter,' Mr Chowdhury said, 'She's a double-bee.'

'I see. You mean she is called Bibi?' Feluda asked. This time, even I could figure out double-bee could only mean BB. Feluda and I often played word games at home, so this wasn't difficult.

'Yes. I like playing with words,' Mahesh Chowdhury explained.

'Let me get my brother,' said Pritin Babu and left the room. We sat down. Mr Chowdhury was smiling a little, looking straight at Feluda. Feluda returned his look without the slightest trace of embarrassment, and smiled in return.

'Well, well, well!' Mr Chowdhury said finally. 'Sarveshwar Sahai praised you a lot. So when I heard you were here, I told Trey to call you. My life is full of mysteries, Mr Mitter. Let's see if you can solve any.'

'Trey? Do you mean your third son?'

'Right again.'

'I like word games, too.'

'Very good. My oldest son—I call him Ace—can occasionally understand my meaning when I speak in codes, but Trey is quite hopeless. Anyway, how long have you been working as a detective?'

'About eight years.'

'I see. What about Mr Ganguli? What does he do?'

'He writes murder mysteries, under the pseudonym of Jatayu.'

'Really? What a fine combination! One creates mysteries, the other destroys them.'

'I can see your collection of rocks and butterflies,' Feluda remarked, 'but is there anything else you used to collect?'

The rocks and stones were displayed in a glass case that stood in a corner. I had no idea stones could be of so many different types and colours. But what did Feluda mean? Mr Chowdhury looked quite taken aback and asked, 'Why do you ask about other collections? What else could I have collected?'

'Those tweezers young Bibi is using appear to be quite old.'

'Brilliant! Brilliant!' Mr Chowdhury exclaimed, 'What sharp eyes you've got! But you are absolutely right. I used to collect stamps, and those were my tweezers. Even now, I sometimes look at the Gibbons catalogue. Philately was my first passion in life. When I used to practise as a lawyer, one of my clients called Dorabjee gave me his own stamp album to show me how grateful he was. He must have lost his interest in stamps by then, or certainly he would not have given it away like that. It had quite a few rare and valuable stamps.'

I felt quite excited to hear this. I had started to collect stamps myself, and knew that Feluda, as a young boy, used to do the same.

'May we see that album?' Feluda asked.

'Pardon?' Mr Chowdhury said after a few moments of silence. He had suddenly grown a little preoccupied. Then he seemed to pull himself together.

'The album?' he said. 'No, I'm afraid I cannot not show it to you. It's lost.'

'Lost?'

'Yes. Didn't I just tell you my life was full of mysteries? Mysteries . . . or you may even call them tragedies. But let's not talk about it on a fine day like this . . . Come on, Ace, let me introduce you!'

Pritin Babu had returned with his brother. He was much older, but there was a marked resemblance between the two brothers. 'Ace' was a handsome man, if just a little overweight.

'Trey could probably tell you a lot about mikes,' Mr Chowdhury said. 'Ace can only talk about mica. He has a business that deals with mica. His real name is Arunendra. His office is in Calcutta, but his work often brings him to Hazaribagh.'

'Namaskar,' Feluda said, 'you are Ace and Pritin Babu is Trey. Is that Deuce?' He was looking at a photograph in a silver frame. It was a family group photo, taken at least twenty-five years ago. Mahesh Chowdhury and his wife were standing with two young boys. A third much smaller boy was in his wife's arms. The younger of the two boys standing had to be Deuce.

'Yes, you are right,' Mr Chowdhury replied, 'but you might never get the chance to meet him, for he has vanished.'

Ace—Arun Babu—explained quickly: 'He was called Biren. He left home at the age of nineteen to go to England, and did not return.'

'We don't know that for certain, do we?' Mr Chowdhury sounded doubtful.

'If he did, Baba, surely you'd have heard about it?'

'Who knows? He didn't write me a single line in the last ten years!' Mr Chowdhury's voice sounded pained.

No one spoke after this. The atmosphere suddenly seemed to have become rather serious. Perhaps Mr Chowdhury realized this. He stood up, and said cheerfully, 'Come on, let me show you around. Akhil and Shankar haven't arrived yet, have they? So we have a little time.'

'You don't have to get up, Baba,' Arun Chowdhury said, 'I can take them upstairs.'

'No, sir. This is *my* house; I planned it and I had it built. *I* will, therefore, show it to my visitors.'

We followed him upstairs. There were three bedrooms, and a lovely wide veranda that overlooked the street on the north side. The Kanari Hills were dimly visible in the distance. Mr Chowdhury's bedroom was in the middle. The other two were occupied at the moment. Arun Babu was in one, and Pritin Babu was in the other with his wife and daughter. There was a guest room on the ground floor, we were told. Mahesh Chowdhury's friend, Akhil Chakravarty, was staying in it.

I noticed more butterflies and rocks in Mr Chowdhury's bedroom. A bookshelf in a corner contained rows of notebooks, almost identical in appearance. Mr Chowdhury caught Feluda looking at these and said they were his diaries. He had kept diaries regularly over a period of forty years. On a bedside table was another small framed photograph of a man, but not of anyone from the family. Lalmohan Babu recognized him instantly.

'Ah, it's Muktananda, isn't it?'

'Yes. My friend Akhil gave it to me,' Mr Chowdhury replied. Then he turned to Feluda and added, 'He has three continents to back him up.'

'Correct!' Lalmohan Babu sounded quite excited, 'He is a famous Tantric sadhu. Asia, Europe and America—he has followers everywhere.'

'How do you know so much about him? Are you a devotee yourself?'

'Oh no. But one of my neighbours is. He told me about his guru.'

There was nothing more to see on the first floor. As we began climbing down, I heard a car arrive. The two men Mr Chowdhury was waiting for soon made an appearance. One of them was of about the same age as Mahesh Chowdhury. He was wearing an ordinary dhoti and kurta and had a plain dark brown shawl wrapped around his shoulders. It was obvious that he had never had anything to do with the complex world of the law; nor did he seem even slightly westernized in any way. The other man was much younger, probably under forty. He had a smart and intelligent air. He came forward quickly and touched Mr Chowdhury's feet as soon as he saw him. The older gentleman was carrying a box of sweets. He passed it to Pritin Babu and said, 'Look, Mahesh, please listen to me. Drop the idea of a picnic. The time's not auspicious at all, and then there's that tiger to be considered. What if he decides to visit the temple of Chhinnamasta?'

Mr Chowdhury turned to us. 'Please allow me to introduce you. This man here who cannot stop seeing danger and pitfalls everywhere is a very old friend, Akhil Bandhu Chakravarty. He used to be a schoolteacher. Now he dabbles in astrology and ayurveda. And this is Shankarlal Misra. I am exceedingly fond of this young man. You might say I look upon him as a sort of replacement for my missing son.'

We greeted one another, and then everyone began to get ready to leave. Akhil Chakravarty tried one last time: 'So nobody's going to heed my warning?'

'No, my dear,' Mr Chowdhury replied. 'I hear the tiger is called Sultan. That means he's a Muslim. He's not likely to want to visit a Hindu temple, never fear. Oh, by the way, Mr Mitter, do go and see the circus, if you can. We were invited the day before yesterday. I went with little Bibi and her mother. I had no idea that Indian circus had made such progress. The items with the tiger, particularly, were most impressive.'

'But didn't something go wrong towards the end?'

'Yes, but that wasn't the ringmaster's fault. Even animals have moods, don't they? The tiger was not in the right mood, that's all. After all, it's a living being, not a machine that will run each time you press a button.'

'Yes, but see what the animal's mood has done,' Arun Babu remarked. 'There's panic everywhere. That tiger ought to be killed. This would never have happened if it was a foreign circus.'

His father smiled dryly, 'Yes, your hands must be itching to pick up your gun. Anyone would think you were the President of the Wildlife Destruction Society!'

We met another person before leaving for Rajrappa. It was Pritin Chowdhury's wife, Neelima Devi. Like the rest of her family, she was very good looking.

FOUR

Rajrappa was 80 kilometres from Hazaribagh. We had to take a left turn when we reached Ramgarh, which took us through a place called Gola. Beyond Gola was the Bhera river. All cars had to be left here, and the river had to be crossed on foot. Rajrappa lay on the other side, only a short walk away.

Shankarlal Misra did not have a car, so he travelled with us. Two bearers had also joined the group. One of them was the old Noor Muhammad, who had been with Mr Chowdhury since he started working as a lawyer. The other was the tall and hefty Jagat Singh, who was carrying Arun Chowdhury's rifle and cartridges.

Mr Misra proved to be very friendly and easy to talk to. From what he told us about himself, it seemed there was a mystery in his life as well. His father, Deendayal Misra, used to work as Mahesh Chowdhury's chowkidar. Thirty-five years ago, when Shankar was only four, Deendayal suddenly went missing one day. Two days later, a woodcutter found his body in a forest nearly eight miles away. He had been killed by a wild animal. No one knew why he had gone to the forest. There was an old Shiva temple there, but Deendayal had never been known to visit it.

Mahesh Chowdhury took pity on Deendayal's child. He brought him to his house, and began to bring him up like his own son. In time, Shankar proved to be a very bright student. He won scholarships and finished his graduation from Ranchi University. Then he opened a bookshop called Shankar Book Store in Ranchi. Recently, he had opened a branch in Hazaribagh. He travelled frequently between the two cities.

This mention of books prompted Lalmohan Babu to ask, 'What kind of books do you keep in your shop?'

'All kinds,' Mr Misra replied, smiling, 'including crime thrillers. We have often sold your books.'

After a few moments, Feluda asked, 'Mahesh Chowdhury's second son must have been the same age as yourself. Is that right?'

'Who, Biren? He was younger than me, but only by a few months. We went to school together, and were in the same class. All three brothers went to Calcutta for higher studies, but Biren was never really interested in them. He was always restless, fond of adventures. I was not surprised when he left home at nineteen.'

'Does his father believe in Tantrics and holy men?'

'He didn't earlier. But he has changed a lot over the years. I didn't see it myself, but I've heard that he used to have an extremely violent temper. He may not actually visit holy men, but today . . . I believe the reason for going to Rajrappa is that temple of Chhinnamasta.'

'Why do you say that?'

'He doesn't talk about it, but I have gone to Rajrappa with him before, more than once. I've seen how the look on his face changes when he visits the temple.'

'Could this be linked to something in his past?'

'I don't know. I know very little about his past. Don't forget I was only his chowkidar's son, never really one of the family.'

At around ten-thirty, three cars stopped by the side of the Bhera river. Ours was the last, just behind Pritin Chowdhury's car. We saw him get out, tape recorder in hand, and disappear among the trees on our left. Mahesh Chowdhury was in the first car. He got out, and came towards us. 'Let's have a cup of coffee before going across,' he said. 'Rajrappa isn't far from here. There's no point in hurrying.'

We walked towards the river. There wasn't much water in it now, but after the monsoon it often became knee-deep, which made it difficult to cross. Even now, it was flowing with considerable force, rushing over a great many rocks of various sizes and different colours, polishing and smoothing their surface, as if it was in a great hurry to jump into the great Damodar. Rajrappa stood at the point where the Bhera met the Damodar.

Neelima Devi opened a flask and began pouring coffee into paper cups. We went and helped ourselves. Pritin Babu was the only one missing. Perhaps he had had to go deeper into the wood to record bird calls. A variety of birds were chirping in the trees.

I looked at and tried to make a study of every new character I had met since my arrival. Feluda had taught me to do this, although his own eyes caught details that I inevitably missed.

The youngest in our group had placed her doll on a flat stone and was talking to it: 'Sit quietly, or I'll throw you into the river. You wouldn't like that, would you?'

Arun Babu finished his coffee, threw the cup away, then disappeared behind a bush. The faint smoke that rose a little later told me that he didn't like to smoke in his father's presence.

Mahesh Chowdhury was standing quietly by the river, staring at its gushing water. His hands were clasped behind his back.

Feluda had picked up two small stones and was striking one against the other to see if they were flint, when Akhil Chakravarty walked up to him and said, 'Do you know what sign you were born under?'

'Yes, sir. Aquarius. Is that good or bad for a detective?'

Neelima Devi picked up a wild yellow flower and stuck it into her hair. Then she looked at Lalmohan Babu and said something which made him throw back his head and laugh. But, only a second later, he stopped abruptly, gasped and jumped aside. Neelima Devi's laughter broke out this time.

'That was only a harmless chameleon!' she said, 'Don't tell me you are afraid of them?'

I looked around for Shankarlal, but saw that he had already crossed the river and was talking to a man in saffron clothes, on the other side. A busload of visitors had crossed over a few minutes ago. The saffron-clad sadhu must have been one of them.

We finished our coffee, and Pritin Babu returned. It was now time to wade through the river. Everyone lifted their clothes by a couple of inches. Little Bibi decided to ride on Noor Muhammad's back, and I saw Lalmohan Babu stop, close his eyes and mutter something before stepping on to a stone. He nearly lost his balance at least three times before he got to the other side. Then, landing safely on the dry ground, he said, 'Hey, who knew that was going to be so easy?'

There were more trees here, though not enough to call it a wood. Nevertheless, from the way Lalmohan Babu kept casting nervous glances over his shoulder, I knew that he had not forgotten about the tiger. We turned a corner in a few minutes, and stopped. It was as if a curtain had been lifted to reveal Rajrappa. Lalmohan Babu said, 'Waah!' so loudly that two little birds flew away.

He had every reason to say that. I could see both rivers from where we stood. On our left was the smaller river, the Bhera, and to our right, down below, flowed the Damodar. There was a waterfall, not yet visible, but I could hear it. Huge rocks stood out from the water, looking like giant turtles. The forest began at a distance, beyond which stood the hills in a faint, bluish line. It was a truly charming sight.

The temple was only twenty yards away. It was obviously quite old, but parts of it had been restored recently. Only a few days ago, we were told, a buffalo had been killed here for Kali Puja. 'I bet once they used to have human sacrifices!' Lalmohan Babu muttered into my ear. He might well have been right.

None of the passengers who had come by bus seemed

interested in the scenery. All of them had gathered before the temple. Shankarlal was right about Mahesh Chowdhury. I saw him stand still at the door of the temple and stare inside. He spent nearly a minute there, although it was so dark inside that the statue was almost invisible. Then he moved away, and slowly followed the others.

The waterfall came into view in a few minutes. The two bearers began spreading a *durrie* on the sand.

'This is an unexpected bonus, isn't it?' Lalmohan Babu said. 'Who knew we'd be invited to a picnic on the second day of our visit?'

'This is only the beginning,' Feluda observed.

'Really?'

'Have you ever played chess?'

'Good God, no!'

'If you had, you'd have understood my meaning. When a game of chess comes to a close, and only a few pieces are left on the board, something like an electric current flows between the two players. Neither of them moves, but they can feel it with every nerve in their body. All the members of the Chowdhury family remind me of these pieces. What I still don't know is who is black and who is white—or who's the King, and if there's a Bishop.'

We chose a spot between the temple and the place where the main picnic was being arranged, and sat down under a peepal tree. It was not yet eleven o'clock. Everyone was relaxed and roaming around lazily. Bibi was sitting on the sand, and Akhil Chakravarty was talking to her, explaining something with different gestures. Neelima Devi was sitting on the *durrie*. I saw her take out a paperback from her bag. It was probably a detective novel. Pritin Babu was walking aimlessly; then he sat down on a small mound and began inserting a new cassette into his recorder. Arun Babu took his gun from Jagat Singh, and Mahesh Chowdhury picked up a stone from the ground, only to throw it away again.

'Shankarlal is not around,' Lalmohan Babu commented.

'Yes, he is, but at some distance. Look!'

I followed Feluda's gaze and saw that Shankarlal was standing under a tree behind the temple, still chatting with the sadhu.

'Somewhat suspicious, isn't it?' Lalmohan Babu asked. I looked at Feluda to see if he agreed, but before he could say anything, Arun Chowdhury walked over to us, gun in hand.

'Is that adequate for a tiger?' Feluda asked him.

'That tiger from the circus is not going to come here,' Arun Babu laughed. 'I have killed sambar with this gun, but usually I only kill birds. This is a twenty-two.'

'Yes, so I see.'

'Do you hunt?'

'Only criminals.'

'Do you work for an agency? Or are you private?'

Feluda handed him one of his cards with 'P. C. Mitter: Private Investigator' written on it.

'Thanks,' said Arun Chowdhury. 'I may need it one day, who knows?'

Then he moved away.

I saw Feluda clutching the same piece of paper we had found near the lawn in Kailash. This surprised me, for I hadn't seen him taking it out.

'Why this sudden interest in letters from the alphabet?' Lalmohan Babu wanted to know.

'Look carefully. These aren't just letters from the alphabet. These are words, proper words.'

'Nonsense! If they are, it must be some strange foreign language.'

'Not at all. These are ordinary English words, and you know them very well. Try reading them out.'

Lalmohan Babu leant across to read the letters.

'Eks El En See,' he read, 'Eks El. Eks Pee Dee . . . oh, I see! The first word is "excellency", isn't it? One has to read it quickly. And the second word is "excel". Then it's "expediency", and the last word is "enemy". But what's this beginning with an O?'

'OICURMT,' I read quickly, 'That's "oh I see you are empty".

'Good. How clever!' Lalmohan Babu beamed.

With a grin, Feluda turned the paper over. More words and figures were written on it:

UR
2 good
2 me
2 be
4 got
--
10
--

'Read it,' he said to Lalmohan Babu, who seemed to have got the hang of things and was enjoying it hugely.

'You are too good to me to be four-got-ten? I see, that should read "forgotten". Yes, that's right.'

'OK, now look at the other words. Topshe, try and work it out.'

I looked carefully. There were two columns, one showing words, and the other possibly their meaning:

Revolution	to love ruin
Telegraph	great help
Astronomers	no more stars
Festival	evil fast
Funeral	real fun

'Anagrams?' I asked.

'Yes. The last three are called "antigrams", for they give you the opposite meaning to the real one. I mean, "funeral" could hardly be called "real fun", yet if you rearrange the letters . . .'

' . . . where did you find that?' asked a voice. Mahesh Chowdhury was standing near us, smiling.

'It was lying near your garden,' Feluda replied.

'I was just . . . trying to find some amusement.'

'Yes, I'd guessed as much.'

All of us began rising, but Mr Chowdhury said, 'Please don't!' and sat down beside us.

'Let me show you another piece of paper,' he said. He wasn't smiling any more. He took out his wallet, then extracted an old folded card from it. It was a picture postcard, showing the city of Zurich including the lake.

'This was the last postcard sent by my second son,' he said gravely. On the other side of the postcard there was no message at all. All that was written was his name and address.

'That's what he had started to do,' Mr Chowdhury explained. 'He sent postcards just to let me know where he was. He was never much of a letter writer, anyway. His earlier postcards seldom had more than a couple of lines.'

He took the card back from Feluda and put it back in his wallet.

'Did you ever learn what kind of work your son Biren did in England?' Feluda asked.

'No. He wasn't the type to do an ordinary job. He was a rebel, totally different from most young men. And he had a hero. Another Bengali, who left home a hundred years ago and went to England, working as crew on a ship. Eventually, he ended up in Brazil . . . or was it Mexico? . . . and joined its army. He became a Colonel and greatly impressed everyone by his valour and courage.'

'Do you mean Suresh Biswas?' Feluda asked. Lalmohan Babu, too, had recognized the name. His eyes gleamed.

'Yes, yes,' he said hurriedly, 'Colonel Suresh Biswas. He died in Brazil.'

'Right,' Mahesh Chowdhury went on. 'My son Biren had read the story of his life. He wanted to be like him, and have as many adventures. I did not try to stop him, for I knew I couldn't. So, one day, he vanished. Two months later, I got his first letter from Europe. He didn't always write from England, you know. He'd seemed to travel all over Europe . . . Holland, Sweden, Germany, Austria. He never told me what he was doing. His short letters simply meant that he was alive. I was very sorry he had left me without a word; at the same time, I couldn't help feeling proud to think that he had made it entirely on his own. Then . . . after 1967, he stopped writing altogether.'

Mahesh Chowdhury stopped, looking sadly at the distant hills. 'I know he will never come back to me,' he sighed. 'I will never know any peace. I have been cursed.'

'What? Since when did you start to believe in curses?'

This was another voice, and it was speaking lightly. We turned to find we had been joined by Akhil Chakravarty.

'You only looked at my horoscope, Akhil,' Mahesh Chowdhury complained. 'You didn't bother to consider me as a man.'

'Rubbish. A man and his horoscope are linked together. Didn't I tell you in 1942 a big change would come over you? Have you forgotten that?' He turned to Feluda. 'Would you believe me, Mr Mitter, if I told you this amiable old man that you see today had once pushed his car off a cliff in a fit of rage, just because its engine had died on the way from Ranchi to Netarhat?'

Mr Chowdhury rose slowly to his feet. 'People change as they grow older. One doesn't need to be an astrologer to see that,' he said shortly and walked away, possibly to look for stones.

Akhil Chakravarty took his place. He seemed to be in the mood to tell stories. 'Mahesh is an extraordinary character,' he began. 'I used to be his neighbour. We came from two different worlds. I was only a schoolteacher, and he was a rising star in his profession. I worked for a while as his sons' private tutor and got to know him well. He didn't believe in conventional medicine. If any of his children was unwell, he used to come to me for ayurvedic herbs. Never did he let me feel that we belonged to two different social classes. He treated my son with the same affection that he treated his own. He was devoid of snobbery.'

'What does your son do?'

'Who, Adheer? He's an engineer. He went to IIT Kharagpur, and then to Dusseldorf. He spent ten years there, but he returned home and . . . '

The sound of an explosion made him stop.

'Uncle's gun!' Bibi shouted. 'Uncle's killed a partridge. We'll have it for dinner!'

'Let me go and find Mahesh,' Akhil Chakravarty said, getting up. 'At his age, he shouldn't go looking for stones. Heaven forbid, but if he slipped and fell near the water, his birthday would . . . ' he moved away.

'It doesn't feel like a picnic at all!' said Neelima Devi. She had put her book away and come over to join us. 'Why has everyone disappeared?'

'Don't worry,' Feluda reassured her. 'They'll all turn up when they're hungry and it's time to eat.'

'Probably. In the meantime, why don't we play a game?'

'Cards?' asked Lalmohan Babu. 'But all I can play is Screw.'

'No, I'm afraid I didn't bring any cards,' Neelima Devi said. 'It will have to be something we can play orally.'

'Let's try water-earth-sky. Lalmohan Babu could join us quite easily,' Feluda suggested.

'How do you play that?'

'It's very simple, really. Suppose I look at you and say "water!", or "earth!", or "sky!", and then start counting up to ten. You have to think of a creature that can be found in it, within those ten seconds.'

'Is this a very difficult game?'

'Try it,' Neelima Devi smiled, 'Let me ask you the first one.'

'OK.' Lalmohan Babu took a deep breath, and sat crosslegged, holding himself straight. Neelima Devi looked at him in silence for a few moments. The she suddenly shouted, 'Sky! One, two, three, four . . . '

'Er . . . er . . . er . . .'

' . . . five, six, seven . . . '

'Bafrosh!'

Feluda was the first to break the amazed silence that followed this perfectly weird remark.

'What, pray, is a bafrosh? A creature of the sky in a different planet, perhaps?'

'N-n-no. You see, I had thought of a balloon, a frog and a shark. But I mixed them all up!'

'A balloon? You think a balloon qualifies as a living creature?'

'Why not? Every living being needs oxygen. So does a balloon.'

'Really? Well, I must confess I did not know that. I've heard of hot air balloons, hydrogen and helium balloons, even balloons that fly with gas made from coal, but this is the first time anyone mentioned oxygen. Perhaps you'd like to . . . '

Neelima Devi raised a hand to stop further argument. As things turned out, she need not have bothered. Something happened at this moment that automatically put a stop to all arguments.

It was Pritin Babu.

A long time ago, Feluda had shown me a painting by Leonardo da Vinci, which showed a man who had both fear and sadness etched in every line on his face. Pritin Babu's face wore the same expression.

He emerged from behind a bush, took a few unsteady steps, then sat down quickly, trembling visibly. Neelima Devi got up and ran towards her husband, but Feluda had reached him already. Pritin Babu had to swallow a few times and make an effort to speak.

'B-b-b-baba,' he managed finally, pointing at the direction from which he had come.

FIVE

By the time Mahesh Chowdhury was brought home, it was half past two. He was still unconscious. Judging by the injury on his head, he had been standing when he fell. The doctor who examined him said it was a heart attack. His heart was not particularly strong, anyway. The attack might have been caused by a sudden shock. His overall condition was critical; the doctor could not hold out much hope for a recovery.

He was found lying in an area behind a large boulder. We could see the boulder from where we sat, but not what lay behind it. None of us had seen him go there. Pritin Babu, who had climbed up a slope to go into the trees on the top of a hill, found him on his way back, as he came out in the open and looked down. At first, he had thought his father had died. That was why he had rushed to us, looking deathly pale. Feluda felt Mr Chowdhury's pulse and said he was still alive. His head had struck against a stone the size of a brick. A pool of blood lay around it. Like everyone else, I felt dazed, but couldn't help noticing two pretty yellow butterflies fluttering around the unconscious man.

A minute later, we were joined first by Arun Babu, and then Akhil Chakravarty. Shankarlal was the last to arrive. He broke down immediately as he realized what had happened. There could be no doubt about his attachment and devotion to the old man.

It was clearly impossible for us to pick him up and carry him across the river. His two sons left at once to go back and get an ambulance. It took them more than two hours to return with a medical team, and another hour to move their father away in the ambulance. All of us returned to Kailash and remained there for a while. Since no one had had any lunch, Neelima Devi served the food that had been packed for the picnic: parathas, aloo-dum and kababs. Once she had got over the initial shock, she had regained her composure fully. I had to admire her.

Little Bibi was the only one who didn't understand the seriousness of the situation. She kept saying her Dadu had simply had a dizzy spell, and would soon be playing with her again. We waited in the drawing room. Arun Babu remained upstairs with his father, and Pritin Chowdhury came and joined us every now and then. Shankarlal was sitting still like a statue. He hadn't spoken a single word since we left Rajrappa. Akhil Chakravarty was saying the same thing over and over: 'I *told* him not to go out today, but he didn't listen to me!'

We left at around four o'clock. 'We'll come back tomorrow,' Feluda told Pritin Babu. 'Please do let us know if we can do anything to help.'

'Thank you.'

On reaching our own house, each of us had a quick wash before going and sitting on the front veranda. I was still feeling dazed. Feluda wasn't speaking much, which meant he was thinking hard. I knew he wouldn't like being disturbed, but there was something I felt I had to ask him. 'I heard the doctor say Mr Chowdhury's heart attack might have been caused by a sudden shock. How could he have received a shock in Rajrappa, Feluda?'

'Good question. That is what I've been thinking. Of course, we don't know that for a fact.'

'So all we need to do is wait until Mr Chowdhury gets better. Then the whole thing will become clear,' Lalmohan Babu remarked.

'Yes. But will he get better?' Feluda sounded doubtful.

He was clearly curious about Mahesh Chowdhury. While

we were waiting in the drawing room, I saw him looking closely at the books and every other object in the room. He did this very discreetly, but I knew he was making a mental note of everything he saw. The group photograph of all the Chowdhurys seemed to intrigue him the most. He spent at least five minutes looking at it closely.

Drums were beating in a distant village. It suddenly made me think of the escaped tiger. Obviously, it had not been captured, or Bulakiprasad would have told us.

It was now quite chilly outside. Lalmohan Babu pulled his cap tighter and said, 'It's significant, isn't it?' Perhaps he had expected one of us to ask him what he meant by that; but when we didn't, he expanded further, 'When Mr Chowdhury suffered this heart attack, we were with Neelima Devi and that little girl was playing with her doll. But we know nothing of the movements of the others, do we?'

'Yes, we do,' Feluda replied. 'Arun Babu was trying to kill birds, Pritin Babu was recording bird calls, Akhil Chakravarty was looking for his friend, Shankarlal was chatting with a sadhu, and the two bearers were sitting under a cotton tree, smoking beedis.'

'Yes, I saw them. But what about the others? They were all out of sight. How do we know they're telling the truth?'

'There is absolutely no reason to think they are not. I don't know them well, and I'm not prepared to start by treating them with suspicion.'

'OK, you're right, Felu Babu.'

But Lalmohan Babu had more to tell. It came a few hours later, while we were at dinner. I saw him give a sudden start, slap his forehead and say, 'Oh no, no!'

'Whatever is the matter, Lalmohan Babu?' Feluda asked.

'I forgot to tell you something—something very important. I found another clue, a terrific one this time. As we got close to the spot where the body—sorry, I mean Mr Chowdhury—was lying, I stumbled against an object. It was Pritin Chowdhury's tape recorder.'

'Have you got it with you?'

'No. I thought I'd pick it up later and give it back to him. But with all the hue and cry and everything, I totally forgot. When we were returning, however, I did remember, but by then it had gone!'

'Maybe Pritin Babu himself had picked it up?'

'No. He most definitely did not go anywhere near it. Besides, it was lying under a bush. I wouldn't have seen it myself if my foot hadn't actually struck against it.'

Feluda started to make a comment, but was stopped by the phone ringing.

It was Arun Babu. Feluda spoke briefly, put the phone down, and turned to us.

'We must go back to Kailash. Mr Chowdhury has regained consciousness, and is asking for me.'

It took us only a minute to reach their house by car. Everyone was gathered around his bed, with the exception of Bibi. Mr Chowdhury was lying in his bed with a dressing on his head, his hands folded and resting on his chest, his eyes half closed. His lips parted in a faint smile as he saw Feluda. Then he slowly raised his right hand and straightened his index finger.

'A j-j-j-' he tried to speak.

'A job for me?' Feluda asked anxiously.

Mr Chowdhury gave a slight nod. Then he raised his middle finger as well.

'We . . . we . . . ' he folded his fingers and raised his thumb, shaking it.

With an effort, he then moved his head and looked at the bedside table. Muktananda's photograph rested on it. As he tried to stretch his arm towards it, Arun Babu picked it up and offered it to him. Instead of taking it, Mr Chowdhury looked at Feluda. Arun Babu passed the photo to Feluda without a word. Mr Chowdhury sighed and raised two fingers again. He tried to speak once more, but no words came.

After a while, he gave up trying and just stared in silence.

SIX

We had returned to our room. The passport-size photograph of Muktananda was now with Feluda. I could not imagine why Mr Chowdhury had given it to him and told him he had a job. Lalmohan Babu, however, ventured to hazard a guess.

'I think he asked you to become a follower of Muktananda,' he observed.

'Then why did he raise two fingers?'

'Maybe he meant . . . as a follower of Muktananda, your skills at your job would double themselves? Mind you,' Lalmohan Babu added sadly, 'I cannot figure out why he then shook his thumb at you!'

Early in the morning, Akhil Chakravarty rang us to say that Mahesh Chowdhury had breathed his last two hours after we had left his house the previous night.

By the time the funeral was over, it was past eleven o'clock. On our way back from the cremation ground, Lalmohan Babu asked, 'Where do you want to go now, Felu Babu? To Kailash, or back home?'

'I don't think we should spend any more time in Kailash, just at this moment. They are bound to receive a lot of visitors. I won't get any work done.'

'What work do you mean?'

'Gathering information.'

After lunch, Feluda took out his blue notebook and began scribbling in it. When he finished, he let us see what he had written:

1. Mahesh Chowdhury: Born 23 November 1907; died 24 November 1977 (Natural causes? Heart attack? Shock?). Fond of riddles, stamps, butterflies, rocks. A valuable stamp album given by Dorabjee—lost (how?). Attached to second son. What about his feelings towards the other two? Deep affection towards Shankarlal. No snobbery. Violent temper in the past; drinking. A changed man in later years, amiable. Why a curse?

2. His wife: Dead. When?

3. First son: Arunendra. Born (approx) 1936. Deals with mica. Travels between Calcutta and Hazaribagh. Fond of shooting. Doesn't talk much.

4. Second son: Birendra. Born (approx) 1939. Very bright, a rebel. Left home at nineteen. Admired Col Suresh Biswas. Wrote to father until 1967. Alive? Dead? Father thought he had returned.

5. Third son: Pritindra. Younger than Arunendra by at least nine years (basis: family photo), i.e. born (approx) 1945. Electronics. Bird calls. Talks a lot, chiefly about himself. Left tape recorder in Rajrappa.

6. Pritin's wife: Neelima. Age 25/26. Intelligent, smart, collected.

7. Akhil Chakravarty: Age (approx): 70. Ex-schoolteacher. Mahesh's friend. Astrology, ayurveda.

8. Shankarlal Misra: Born (approx) 1939. Same age as Biren. Mahesh's chowkidar Deendayal's son. Deendayal died in 1943. Question: why did he go into the forest? Mahesh raised Shankarlal. Owner of bookshop. Griefstricken by Mahesh's death.

9. Noor Muhammad: Age between 70 and 80. Serving Mahesh for over 40 years.

*

Feluda was right in thinking there might be a lot of visitors. When we arrived at Kailash long after lunch, we were told the last of them had just left. Mr Chowdhury's two sons and Akhil Chakravarty were in the drawing room. Pritin Babu seemed more restless than ever. He was sitting in a corner, fidgeting and cracking his knuckles. Akhil Babu was sighing and shaking his head from time to time. Only Arun Chowdhury seemed calm and composed. Feluda addressed him directly.

'Are you going to be here for a few days?' he asked.

'Why do you ask?'

'I need your help. Your father gave me a job to do, although he was in no condition to explain the details. What I want to know is this: did any of you understand his meaning?'

Arun Babu smiled slightly. 'Few of us could understand his meaning even when Baba was alive and well. A serious man in many ways, there was a childish streak in him, which you probably saw for yourself. I don't think there is any need to pay too much attention to his last words.'

'But his last words did *not* strike me as totally without meaning.'

'No?'

'No. But obviously, I could not understand the significance of each little gesture. For instance,' he turned to Akhil Chakravarty, 'I do not know why he wanted me to have that photograph. Perhaps you can help me there? Didn't you give it to him?'

Akhil Chakravarty smiled sadly. 'Yes, I did. Muktananda once came to Ranchi, and I went to see him. He struck me as a genuine person, so I said to Mahesh: "You have never believed in sadhus and gurus, but if you keep a photo of this one with you, it cannot do any harm. He is worshipped in three continents, his influence can only do you good." But I had no idea he had kept it in his bedroom. I never went into his bedroom until yesterday.'

'Do *you* know anything about it?' Feluda asked Arun Babu, who shook his head.

'No, I'm afraid not,' he said. 'In fact, I didn't even know he had such a photograph. I saw it yesterday for the first time.'

'I don't know anything either,' Pritin Babu piped up before anyone asked him.

'Very well. But may I request you to give me two things? They would help me a great deal.'

'What are they?'

'The first thing I'd like are the letters and postcards your brother Biren sent your father.'

'Biren's letters?' Arun Babu sounded very surprised. 'What do you need those for?'

'I believe your father wanted me to give that photo to his second son.'

'How strange! What made you think that?'

'Well, your father asked you to pass the photo to me, and then raised two fingers. All of you saw that. It could be that he meant to say "deuce". Isn't that what he called Biren? I could be wrong, of course, but I must proceed—at least for the present—on that assumption.'

'But how will you find Biren?'

'Suppose Mr Chowdhury was right? Suppose he has returned?'

Arun Babu forgot himself for a moment and burst out laughing.

'Mr Mitter, do you know how many times in the last five years my father claimed to have actually seen Biren? He *wanted* to believe he had returned. If he had, wouldn't he have got in touch? Besides, how could anyone expect to recognize him after twenty years, if they saw him from a distance? Particularly an old man like my father, with failing eyesight?'

'Please don't get me wrong, Arun Babu. *I* am not saying he came back. That was a suggestion made by your father. However, even if he is living abroad, I still have to fulfil my responsibility. I must try to find out where he is and arrange to send him the photo.'

Arun Babu seemed to relent a little.

'Very well, Mr Mitter,' he said. 'I will separate Biren's letters from my father's correspondence and give them to you.'

'Thank you. The other thing I want are Mr Chowdhury's diaries. I'd like to see them, if you don't mind.'

I had expected Arun Babu to object to this, but surprisingly, he did not.

'You're welcome,' he said. 'My father's diaries are no secret. But you are going to be disappointed.'

'Why?'

'I doubt if anyone ever kept diaries that could be as dry, mundane and boring as my father's. You won't find anything except the most ordinary record of his daily life.'

'I don't mind. I am perfectly willing to risk being disappointed.'

'All right, so be it. You may take the diaries right now, if you like. I will let you have the letters tomorrow.'

We thanked him and came out a little later, all three of us carrying heavy packets wrapped with newspapers. There were seven of these, each containing Mahesh Chowdhury's diaries. Feluda would get very little sleep tonight, I thought, for the total number of diaries was forty and he had promised to return them the next day.

As we emerged out of the house and reached the driveway, we saw Bibi roaming in the garden, playing with her doll. She appeared to be looking for a flower to put in her doll's hair. She turned her head to face us, and spoke unexpectedly.

'Dadu didn't tell me!' she complained.

'What didn't he tell you?' Feluda asked her.

'What he was looking for.'

'When?'

'The day before yesterday, and the day before that, *and* the day before that.'

'Three days?'

'I saw him looking, but I asked him only one day.'

'What did you say?'

'I said: "What have you lost, Dadu?" because he was in his room, and he was moving his books and all the papers on

his table and everything else, and he wouldn't play with me
. . . so I asked.'

'What did he say?'

'He said . . . a pier, that which opens and . . . and that
·which shuts.'

'What utter nonsense!' Lalmohan Babu muttered under
his breath.

Feluda ignored him. 'Did he tell you anything else?'

'No. No, he said he'd explain later, and he'd tell me
everything . . . but he didn't. He died.'

Bibi had found a flower for her doll. She lost interest in
us, and turned to go back inside. We came away.

SEVEN

Since Feluda was now going to start reading the diaries, Lalmohan Babu and I decided to go for a drive soon after a cup of tea at four o'clock.

'If we go towards the main town, we might get to hear the latest on Sultan,' Lalmohan Babu told me. 'Your cousin may have found a mystery related to Mahesh Chowdhury's death, but I think an escaped tiger is much more interesting.'

We didn't have far to go to get news of the tiger. We had to stop for petrol at a local station, where we saw another group of men gathered round someone who was speaking very rapidly. He raised a hand and pawed the air, so there was no doubt that he was talking of the tiger. Lalmohan Babu got out of the car and went forward to make enquiries. This wasn't easy, for his Hindi was not particularly good. However, what we eventually managed to learn was this:

To the east of Hazaribagh was a forest, near the town of Vishnugarh. Sultan's new trainer, Chandran, and a shikari from the Forest Department, had found Sultan there. Apparently, it had looked for a while that the tiger was willing to be captured, but he had then changed his mind and run away again after clawing Chandran. The shikari had shot at him, but no one knew whether the tiger was hurt. Chandran was in a hospital, but his injuries were not serious.

'Do you know anything about Kandarikar?' Lalmohan Babu asked his informant. I felt obliged to correct him. 'It is Karandikar, Lalmohan Babu, not Kandarikar. He's the old trainer.'

'No, I don't know anything about him,' the man replied,

'but I do believe the circus isn't doing so well since the main show with the tiger is off.'

We were both curious to know how Mr Karandikar had reacted to the news of Sultan being shot at, so we went from the petrol station straight to the Great Majestic.

Normally, if Feluda accompanies us, Lalmohan Babu keeps to the background. Today, however, he walked up smartly to the man outside the main entrance and said, 'Put me through to Mr Kutti, please.' God knows what the man thought of this strange request, but he let us in without a word. Perhaps he had recognized us from our first visit.

We found Mr Kutti in his caravan, but what he told us sounded like another mysterious riddle. Karandikar had disappeared the previous night.

'The audience has been demanding to see the tiger,' Mr Kutti said. 'I went and personally apologized to Karandikar. I promised him I wouldn't allow anyone else to train the tiger, if it could be captured. Even so, he left without telling a soul. He used to go off occasionally, but he always came back in a few hours. This time . . . I don't think he's coming back.'

There didn't seem to be anything else to say. We thanked Mr Kutti and left the circus. Lalmohan Babu said as we came out, 'Now we'll never get to see Sultan being captured, Tapesh. We simply won't get another chance.'

I, too, felt sad and depressed. So we decided to go for a long drive instead of returning home. Debating over whether to go towards the Kanari Hills in the north, or Ramgarh to the south, we eventually tossed for it and got Ramgarh.

'There are hills there, didn't you see them that day? They're just as beautiful,' Lalmohan Babu remarked.

I agreed with him, and we set off in the direction of Ramgarh. Neither of us had any idea of what lay in store.

Things began to go wrong as we passed a milepost that said '11 kms'. To start with, Lalmohan Babu's car—which he had bought only six months ago—hiccuped three times, slowed down and then died altogether. His driver got out to investigate. He was our only hope, for Lalmohan Babu knew nothing of cars and engines. 'If I can move about without knowing how many bones and what muscles I have in my legs, where is the need to worry about how my car moves on its four wheels?' he had once said to me.

We climbed out of the car and went and sat on a culvert. The sun was about to set, and the time was 5.20 p.m. There were dark patches of clouds in the sky, behind which the sun happened to be hiding at the moment. It peeped out for just a second a little later, only to call it a day almost at once.

'I think I've fixed it, sir!' the driver called. 'I am ready when you are.'

We rose, and I looked at my watch. It said 5.33 p.m. It is important to mention the time, for it was at this precise moment that we saw Sultan.

I might have described the event in a much more dramatic fashion, but Feluda has always told me not to use cliches and other hackneyed phrases just to create an effect. 'Keep your descriptions brief and simple,' he tells me often, 'and you will see how effective that can be.' I shall therefore try to relate what happened as briefly as possible.

I had seen a tiger in the wild before, about which I have written in *The Royal Bengal Mystery*. On that occasion, we were accompanied by several other armed men, including Feluda; and Lalmohan Babu and I were sitting on a treetop, out of harm's way. Now, we were standing by the side of an open road that was lined by trees and woodland. There were bound to be wild bears in the wood, and it was quickly getting dark. Worst of all, Feluda was not with us.

The tiger came out of the trees to our right and appeared on the road, barely fifty yards away. All three of us saw it together, for each one turned into a statue. The driver had stretched an arm to open a door. He stood still with an outstretched arm. Lalmohan Babu had leant forward slightly to blow his nose. He remained in that position, clutching his handkerchief. I was in the process of dusting my jeans. My hands remained stuck to my waist.

The tiger, at first, did not see us. It began to cross the road, took four steps, then suddenly stopped and turned its head to look at us.

My legs began shaking and a hammering started in my chest. Yet, I could not move my eyes away from the tiger. Out of the corner of my eye, I could vaguely see the outline of Lalmohan Babu's body getting lower and lower, which could only mean that his legs were going numb and were unable to support the weight of his body. Then my vision began to blur. The figure of the tiger became hazy, and its stripes suddenly started to vibrate.

It is impossible to say how long Sultan stared at us. The time seemed endless. Lalmohan Babu likes to call it eight to ten minutes, but I think it was eight to ten seconds. Even so, it was a long time.

Once he had finished looking at us, Sultan simply turned his head away, crossed over to the other side and made for the wood. We saw him gradually disappear among the tall trees.

Strangely enough, we remained rooted for nearly a whole minute even after Sultan had gone (Lalmohan Babu calls it fifteen minutes). Then we uttered only three words before getting back into the car. The driver said, 'Sir!'; I said 'Coming!'; and Lalmohan Babu said 'G-go!' Fortunately, it turned out that the driver's nerves were strong and steady. He began to drive with admirable equanimity. Apparently, when he used to work in Jamshedpur before, he had once seen a tiger by the roadside.

We returned home to find Feluda still deeply engrossed in Mr Chowdhury's diaries. I knew Lalmohan Babu was dying to tell him about our experience, so I said nothing. Instead of coming straight to the point, he decided to create a preamble. First, he began humming a tune, then remarked casually, 'Tell me Tapesh, tigers have padded feet, don't they?'

'Yes, so I've heard,' I replied, hiding a smile.

'It must be true, for we didn't hear its footsteps, did we? And we were only a few feet away!'

Sadly, this great build-up to his story had no effect on Feluda. He didn't even look at us. All he did was put one diary away, pick up another and say, 'If you have seen the tiger, you should tell the Forest Department immediately about the exact spot and the time it was seen.'

'The time was 5.33 and the place was near a culvert close to the 11 kilometres milepost on the road to Ramgarh.'

'Good. There's a directory in the living room. The Forest Department's office will be closed at this hour, but you can look up the residential number of the Chief Forest Officer and inform him. I'm sure he'll appreciate it.'

Lalmohan Babu licked his lips. 'You are asking *me* to ring the officer?'

'Yes. You saw the tiger, I didn't.'

'That's true. So what should I tell him? "The tiger which escaped from the circus . . . "?'

'Yes, that's right. Go on.'

I found the number in the directory. Perhaps I should have made the phone call as well, for Lalmohan Babu picked up the phone, coughed twice and said, 'Er . . . the circus that escaped from the Great Majestic tiger . . . oh sorry!'

Luckily, Feluda had heard him from the next room. He rushed in, snatched the receiver from his hand and passed on the information himself.

EIGHT

Bulakiprasad brought us tea in our room. He had already told Feluda about the attempt made to catch Sultan, and Chandran being injured in the process. It was Feluda's belief that no one but Karandikar could catch the tiger alive.

Lalmohan Babu took a long, noisy sip from his cup and asked 'Did you find anything interesting in those diaries? Or was Arun Babu right?'

'You tell me.' Feluda opened a diary and pushed it towards Lalmohan Babu.

'Self elected President of club—meeting on 8.4.46,' he read aloud, 'Tea party at Brig Sudarshan's,' and, on a different page, 'Trial for new suit at Shakur's . . . why, Felu Babu, you think any of this stuff has any relevance?'

'Topshe, have a look and tell me what you think.'

I had been leaning over Lalmohan Babu's shoulder. Now I picked the diary up.

'Bring it closer to the light,' Feluda ordered. I went forward and put it directly under a table lamp. A shiver of excitement ran down my spine.

The diary was fairly large in size. The main entries had been made in ink, but on the top of the page, over the printed date, something had been scribbled with a hard pencil. The words were barely legible.

'Why, this seems to be a message of some kind!' I exclaimed.

'Read it out.'

'Conveyance destroyed because of two.'

'Good heavens, more puzzles?' Lalmohan Babu gave a start.

'Yes. Now look at this. This is the first diary, going back to 1938.'

On the very first page, Mr Chowdhury had written: 'Shambhu is ruled by two and five'.

'Who is Shambhu?' Lalmohan Babu asked, surprised.

'Shambhu is another name for Shiva, like Mahesh. Mr Chowdhury referred to himself in his diaries by using various names for Shiva.'

'All right, but what's this about "two and five"?'

'Do you know about the six deadly sins that Hindus believe in?'

'The six *ripus*? Yes, yes. They are . . . let me see . . . *kaam, krodh, lobh, maud, moha, matsarya*.'

'Yes, but not in that order. The correct order is *kaam, krodh, lobh, moha, maud, matsarya*. What do they mean?'

'Lust, wrath, greed, attachment, drinking, envy.'

'Right. So two and five are wrath and drinking.'

'I see, I see. That's easy, isn't it?'

'Yes. Now if you look at the message Topshe read out, you'll get his meaning.'

I had, in fact, already worked it out. "Conveyance destroyed because of two". Could that mean car destroyed because of wrath? Because of his temper?' I offered.

'Shabaash. But there's more. I have not yet been able to understand what the second message means, and that involves these same six numbers.'

Feluda had marked the pages where coded messages appeared. He opened one of these and showed it to us. '2+5=X', it said.

'X is an unknown quantity, isn't it?' Lalmohan Babu asked. 'Why don't you just ignore it? Why are you assuming every strange message has a significant meaning?'

'If a man writes a code on just twenty occasions in a whole year—and don't forget he writes in that diary three hundred and sixty-five times—then I *must* assume every code has a special meaning. I just have to work harder to find out what it is, that's all.'

'Isn't there anything else in the diary that might help?'

'No, but there's another message ten days after he wrote 2+5=X. Look!' I read the message Feluda pointed out: 'Old friend—herbal hair oil. Calms two.'

'A hair oil that might help him control his temper? This one's easy, Felu Babu. Only, I can't make out why he calls it an old friend. Maybe he'd been using it for a long time?'

'No. You didn't pay attention to the "dash" after the word "friend". It can only mean an old friend is in some way related to the oil.'

'Akhil Chakravarty! He knows about ayurvedic herbs, doesn't he? He must have given the oil to his friend!' I exclaimed.

'Very good, Topshe. Now read these other messages.'

There were two. The first said, 'Getting rid of five from today'. That meant he gave up drinking. But, only a month later, he wrote: 'Bholanath goes back to five. Five helps forget'.

'The question is, what did he want to forget so desperately?' Feluda muttered. Lalmohan Babu looked at me, I scratched my head. Now it was obvious why Mr Chowdhury had said his life was full of mysteries. Feluda opened another diary and showed us one more message. 'I am as feather today. I took charge of SM. SM will be my salvation.'

'SM is Shankarlal Misra, surely?' I said. 'But why is he as a feather?'

'I think that simply means "light as a feather",' Feluda replied. 'He was happy and possibly relieved by something. Maybe a load had been lifted from his mind. Taking charge of young Shankarlal clearly had a lot to do with it.'

Feluda rose and began pacing. I sat staring at the diaries. If Mahesh Chowdhury had lived a little longer, he and Feluda would have got on very well. Feluda was just as interested in word games and riddles. Lalmohan Babu was sitting quietly, frowning thoughtfully. After a while, he said, 'Why don't you have a chat with Akhil Chakravarty? He knew him pretty closely, didn't he? He made his horoscope, gave him ayurvedic medicines . . . surely he'll be able to tell you a lot more about the man than his diaries?'

Feluda stopped pacing and lit a Charminar. 'I was trying to get to know the man myself, through his thoughts. Those few messages written with a pencil have kept him alive.'

'Did you find anything about his sons? Did he mention any of them?'

'There isn't much in the first fifteen years. But later—'Feluda broke off. A car had arrived outside. It stopped and tooted at the gate.

We came out on the veranda to find Arun Babu getting out of his Fiat. In his hand was a small packet.

'I was on my way to see Mr Singh—he's our Forest Officer,' he explained, 'Since your house was on the way, I thought I'd stop by and give you Biren's letters. They can hardly be called letters, mind you, but you wanted to see them, so . . . ' he shrugged.

'I'm very sorry if I have caused you any trouble. You must have a lot on your plate,' Feluda said.

'No, no, it's no trouble at all. Frankly, I cannot imagine what Baba might have tried to say. See if you can figure out his meaning. I hardly knew my father, you see. My visits to Hazaribagh have always been short. I used to come here frequently in the past to go on shikar, but now big game has been banned. However, I may get a chance tomorrow. Let's see.'

'What do you mean?'

'That's the reason why I am going to see Mr Singh. I believe the tiger has been spotted near Ramgarh. One of its trainers is lying in hospital, and the other has disappeared. I've already spoken to Mr Singh. "If you must have the tiger killed," I said, "let me do the job." It's already been shot at. If it was injured, it's now a most dangerous beast.'

I opened my mouth to say the tiger hadn't appeared to be injured, but shut it at a glance from Feluda.

'I am taking my .315 with me,' Arun Babu continued. 'There's panic everywhere. I believe it attacked a herd of goats in a village. I don't think being killed in a forest is in any way worse than growing old in a cage in a circus. Anyway, you can come tomorrow, if you're interested. We'll leave early in the morning.'

'OK. Let's see how far I can get with this other job I am trying to tackle. My going with you would have to depend on that. Oh, by the way . . .'

Arun Babu had turned to go. At Feluda's words, he turned back again.

'It was you who fired the shot that day at the picnic, wasn't it?' Feluda asked.

Arun Babu laughed. 'I see what you mean. You must be wondering what happened. I fired a shot, but didn't produce a dead bird. Your detective's mind finds that suspicious, doesn't it? The truth is, Mr Mitter, I missed it. It was a partridge. Sometimes even the best of shikaris miss their targets.'

The letters sent by Biren Chowdhury told us nothing. They were all postcards, most of which had nothing but Mahesh Chowdhury's name and address on them. The few that had hastily scribbled messages had been signed 'Deuce'.

Bulakiprasad served dinner at nine o'clock. Feluda came to the dining table with some of the diaries and his notebook. There were a few more coded messages that he hadn't yet been able to solve, he told us. I saw Feluda write these down in his notebook, using his left hand as easily as he used his right. Halfway through the meal, Lalmohan Babu said, 'Look, Felu Babu, do stop writing; or you won't be able to do any justice to this terrific lamb curry.'

'I am busy with monkeys, Lalmohan Babu, so please don't disturb me by talking of lambs.'

Feluda was frowning deeply, but a smile played around his lips. I had to ask him to explain. He read out a line from a diary:

'Great generosity by the worshipper of fire. The nine jewels, according to the monkeys, value two thousand Shylock's demands.'

Lalmohan Babu swallowed quickly. 'There's a loony bin in Ranchi, isn't there?' he asked, 'I've heard the people of Ranchi are all a bit . . . you know, not quite normal!'

Feluda ignored this remark. 'Parsis worship fire,' he commented, 'but the rest of the message doesn't make any sense at all.'

'Shylock . . . isn't that from *The Merchant of Venice*?' I asked.

'Yes. That's what makes me wonder. What did Shylock demand, Topshe?'

'A pound of flesh?'

'Correct. But that doesn't help, does it?'

'Felu Babu, please give it a rest,' Lalmohan Babu pleaded, 'at least while you're eating!'

Perhaps Feluda was really tired. So he put away the diaries and his notebook, and said he'd like to go for a walk after dinner with both of us.

The moon had just risen when we set out. It still had a yellow glow. But there were patches of clouds as well, which made Lalmohan Babu say, 'I think the moonlight's going to be shortlived.' Gusts of wind came from the west, bringing with them the faint sounds of a circus band.

A right turn soon brought Kailash into view. We could see the house through a row of eucalyptus trees. A window on the first floor was open, and the light was on. Someone was moving restlessly in the room. Feluda stopped. So did we. Whose room could it be? The moving figure came and stood at the window. It was Neelima Devi. Then she moved away again and began pacing once more. Why was she so agitated?

We began walking once more. Kailash disappeared from sight. Each house we passed had a large compound. A radio was on somewhere. We could hear snatches of the local news. Lalmohan Babu cleared his throat and had begun humming another unsuitable Tagore song ('In the rice fields today, do the sun and shadows play hide-and-seek'), when my eyes fell on the figure of a man coming from the opposite direction. He was wearing a blue pullover.

I recognized him as he got closer. 'Namaskar,' said Shankarlal Misra. 'I was going to call at your house.' He seemed to have recovered somewhat, but had not yet regained his normal cheerful looks.

'Is anything the matter?' Feluda asked politely.

'I . . . I would like to make a request.'

'A request?'

'Yes. Please, Mr Mitter, stop making enquiries. Drop your investigation.'

I was quite taken aback by such a request, but Feluda spoke calmly.

'Why would you like me to do that, Mr Misra?'

'It won't do anyone any good.'

After a short pause, Feluda smiled lightly. 'Suppose I told you it would do *me* some good? I cannot rest in peace if there are doubts in my mind. I have to settle them, Mr Misra. Besides, someone spoke to me from his deathbed and asked me to do something for him. How can I leave that task undone? I am sorry, Mr Misra, but I have to continue with my investigation. As a matter of fact, I need your help. Different people may say different things about Mahesh Chowdhury, but you had very deep respect for him, didn't you?'

'Of course.' Mr Misra's reply came a few seconds later, possibly because he couldn't immediately accept what Feluda had said to him. Then he added more firmly, 'I certainly did. But . . . ' his voice changed, 'should one allow that respect, all those feelings, to be destroyed by one single blow? All that had built up over a number of years . . . should one let it go, just like that?'

'Is that what you were doing?'

'Yes. Yes, I nearly allowed that to happen. But then I realized my mistake. I will not let anything destroy my beliefs. I have decided that, and now I have found peace.'

'May I then expect you to help me?'

'Certainly. How may I help you?' Mr Misra sounded almost like his old self. He met Feluda's eyes directly.

'I would like to know how Mahesh Chowdhury felt about his other two sons. No one but you can give me an impartial assessment.'

'I can only tell you what I felt. I don't think Mr Chowdhury had any affection left for anyone except Biren. Arun and Pritin had both disappointed him.'

'Why?'

'I don't know the precise details, for I've never been very close to either of them. But Arun had started to gamble. Mr Chowdhury himself told me one day; not directly, but in his own peculiar style. He said, "I would have been pleased if Arun was good. But I worry because he's better. I believe he visits the equine communities quite often." It took me a while, but eventually I figured out that "better" meant one who lays bets and the "equine communities" simply meant horse races.'

'I see. But why should Pritin have disappointed him? Surely he's doing quite well in electronics?'

'Electronics?' Mr Misra sounded perfectly amazed, 'Is that what he told you?'

'Why? Doesn't he have anything to do with Indovision?'

Mr Misra burst out laughing. 'Good God, no! Pritin has a very ordinary job in a small private firm, which he managed to get only because his father-in-law knew the right people. Pritin is a good man, basically, but is extremely impractical and impulsive. Luckily for him, his wife is the only daughter of a wealthy father. That car you saw him using belongs to his father-in-law. He came here later than his wife and daughter because he had problems getting leave.'

It was our turn to be astounded.

'But,' Mr Misra added, 'his passion for birds and bird calls is absolutely genuine.'

'I have one more question.'

'Yes?'

'You were seen talking to a man dressed as a sadhu when we went to Rajrappa. Was that Biren?'

Mr Misra was naturally taken aback by such a question, but he recovered quickly. The reply he made sounded rather cryptic. 'You are so clever, Mr Mitter, I'm sure you'll soon unravel every mystery.'

'There is a special reason for asking this question. If indeed that man is Biren, I have got something that his father wanted him to have. I must hand it over to him. Can you arrange a meeting?'

'I will try my best to make sure Mr Chowdhury's last wish is fulfilled. I promise to try . . . but I cannot tell you anything more.'

Mr Misra turned abruptly, and went back in the same direction from which he had come.

I hadn't realized how far we'd walked. Feluda looked at his watch and said, 'Ten-thirty'. We decided to go back. When we reached Kailash, the whole house was in darkness. The sky was now overcast, the moon had disappeared and the distant band was silent. Purely out of the blue, Feluda broke the silence by shouting one word: 'Monkeys!' Lalmohan Babu automatically turned his head and asked, 'Where?'

'In that diary,' Feluda explained quickly, 'Sorry if I startled you, but I've just realized what he meant by it. What a brilliant mind that man had! I'd totally forgotten about those monkeys that produce catalogues.'

'Felu Babu, why are you doing this to me? Monkeys was bad enough, but now you want monkeys that produce *catalogues*? What catalogues?'

'Gibbons! Gibbons! Gibbons!' Feluda shouted impatiently.

Of course! Gibbons was a species of monkeys. I knew that, but could never have made the connection.

'He would have made a lot of money,' Feluda said.

'Who?'

'The thief who stole the stamp album.'

*

Lalmohan Babu remained in our room until midnight to watch Feluda solve more puzzles. He had to call Arun Babu at eleven o'clock to get the answer to one of them. On 18 October, 1951, Mr Chowdhury had written, 'He passes away.' Arun Babu told Feluda that was the day his mother had died, and she was called Heronmoyee. That explained who 'He' was.

A few entries made in 1958 said, 'Be foolish', 'Be

stubborn', 'Be determined'. These sounded like mottoes, but 'Be' in this case could only mean 'B', i.e. Biren.

One page in 1975 said, 'A is ruled by three.' He was obviously referring to the six deadly sins, and 'A' meant Arun. His father thought he was greedy.

The last entry had been made the day before he died. All it said was, 'Come-back. Hope, return.' The following pages were all blank.

By the time we finished with the diaries, it was one o'clock. I went to bed, but Feluda began reading the book on the circus in Bengal that Lalmohan Babu had lent him. It had been agreed long ago that Feluda would read it after Lalmohan Babu, and would pass it to me when he'd finished.

I heard him speaking just as my eyes began to feel heavy.

'When there's a murder, the police place a mark over the spot where the body is found. Do you know what it is?'

'X marks the spot?' I said sleepily.

'Exactly. X marks the spot.'

I fell asleep almost immediately, and had a rather awful dream. A huge figure of Kali was standing before me, her arms and legs spread like the letter 'X'. But she wasn't looking at me. She was staring at Arun Babu, and saying, 'Three rules you, three rules you, three rules you!'

Then, suddenly her face dissolved and it became Lalmohan Babu's face. He was grinning from ear to ear and saying, 'Three thousand copies sold in one month . . . Kalmohan Bengali, that's my name!'

Then I woke with a start. A noise at the door had woken me. This was followed by the sound of two men struggling with each other. It was raining outside.

I reached out automatically and pressed the switch of the bedside lamp. Nothing happened. I had forgotten Bihar, like Calcutta, had frequent power cuts.

Something fell on the floor with a thud. 'Get your torch, Topshe,' said Feluda's voice, 'I dropped mine.'

I groped in the dark and eventually found my torch, but not before I had knocked over a glass of water and broken it.

Feluda was standing near the door, his face flushed with helpless rage.

'Who was it, Feluda? He got away, didn't he?'

'Yes. I didn't see his face, but he was large and hefty. I think I know why he had been sent here.'

'Why?'

'To steal.'

'Did he take anything?'

'No, but he would have taken something very valuable, if I wasn't a light sleeper.'

'Something valuable? But we haven't got anything valuable, have we?'

Feluda did not answer me. 'One thing is now quite clear, Topshe,' he said slowly. 'I am not the only one who was been able to work out the meaning of Mahesh Chowdhury's riddles. But for this other man, it is a bit too late.'

When Lalmohan Babu heard about the thief the next day, he said, 'I told you to keep your door locked, didn't I? There have always been petty thieves in these areas!'

'You keep your door locked for fear of the tiger, Lalmohan Babu, not because of possible theft. Come on, admit it.'

'All right, but it's better to be safe than sorry, isn't it? A locked door would protect you from both a thief and a ferocious animal . . . Bulakiprasad, where's our breakfast?'

'Why are you in such a hurry this morning?'

'Why, aren't we going to watch the capture of Sultan?'

'Who's going to catch him? Karandikar has vanished, hasn't he?'

'Yes, but he's still bound to be around somewhere, and I bet he's heard of plans to kill his tiger. He won't be able to stay away, Felu Babu, mark my words. Just think what a thrilling event we might get to watch! Oh, we mustn't miss this chance. I don't understand how you can take this so calmly.'

We finished breakfast by eight o'clock and got ready to go to Kailash to return the diaries and the letters. Akhil Chakravarty turned up unexpectedly.

'One of your neighbours is a homoeopath, and a friend of mine,' he explained. 'I was going to see him, but I thought I'd just drop in to say hello, since your house was on the way.'

'Good. Please have a seat. Tell me,' Feluda said, 'did the herbal oil help in controlling your friend's temper?'

'Good heavens, did Mahesh mention that in his diary?'

'Yes, amongst other things.'

'I see. To tell you the truth, what really helped Mahesh

was his own will-power. I saw how difficult it was for him to give up drinking, but he did it. It wasn't simply because of a herbal oil or anything like that.'

'Since you mention the word "will", can you tell us if he made one?'

'I don't know the details, but I do know that Mahesh changed his first will.'

'I think his second son, Biren, was dropped from the second will.'

'What makes you say that? Did he mention this in his diary?'

'No. He told me just before he died. Do you remember his gestures? He raised two fingers, then he said "we . . . we . . . " and then he shook his thumb. He couldn't quite manage to say "will". If the two fingers indicated "Deuce", then the rest of the message could only mean that Deuce had not been left anything in his will.'

'Brilliant! And you're quite right. Biren had a share in the first will Mahesh made. But when he stopped writing, Mahesh waited for five years before changing it, cutting him out altogether. He was deeply hurt by Biren's silence.'

'If Biren came back, do you think Mahesh Chowdhury would have changed his will a second time?'

'Undoubtedly. I am sure of it.'

Feluda paused for a second before asking his next question.

'Did you ever think Biren might have become a sadhu?'

'Look, it was I who drew up Biren's horoscope. I knew he would leave home quite early in life. So the possibility of his renouncing the whole world and becoming a sadhu cannot be ruled out.'

'One last question. That day, in Rajrappa, you said you were going to look for your friend. But you arrived on the scene long after we had found Mr Chowdhury. Did you get lost? It's not a very large or complex area, is it?'

'I knew you'd ask me that,' Akhil Chakravarty smiled.

'You're right, of course. It's not a complex area, but you must have noticed how the main path parts in two directions. I would have found Mahesh easily enough if I'd turned left. But I turned right instead. Do you know why? It was only because my childhood memories suddenly came back. Fifty-five years ago, I had visited the same spot and carved my initials and the date on a rock. I remembered that and felt an irresistible urge to go and see if it was still there. And it was, as were the figures I had carved: A B C, 15.5.23. If you don't believe me, you can go and see it for yourself.'

*

We reached Kailash to discover that Arun Babu had already left. Old Noor Muhammad told us Pritin Babu was at home, and went off to inform him. He came down to see us in a few moments.

We handed him the packets of diaries and the letters and were about to leave, when someone else entered the drawing room, it was Neelima Devi. I noticed her husband going pale as she came in.

'There is something you ought to know, Mr Mitter,' she said. 'My husband should tell you himself, but he doesn't want to.'

Pritin Babu looked at her appealingly, but Neelima Devi didn't even glance at him. 'When he found my father-in-law that day,' she went on, 'my husband dropped his tape recorder. I found it and put it in my bag. I think you'll find it useful. Here it is.'

Pritin Babu tried once more to stop his wife, but failed.

'Thank you,' Feluda said and took the small, flat recorder from Neelima Devi. Then he put it in his pocket.

Pritin Babu looked as if he was about to break down.

*

I had a feeling Feluda was as interested in watching the capture of the tiger as Lalmohan Babu and myself. The instructions he gave our driver upon leaving Kailash proved that I was right.

Lalmohan Babu's enthusiasm, however, now seemed to be mixed with a degree of anxiety.

'Arun Chowdhury has a number of guns. Why didn't you ask for one, Felu Babu?' he said after a while. 'What good will your Colt 32 do if we see the tiger?'

'Well, if a fly came and sat on the tiger, my revolver would be quite adequate to destroy it, Lalmohan Babu, I assure you.'

Then Feluda lapsed into silence, holding the recorder close to his ear and listening intently. He did not tell us what he heard, and we knew better than to ask him.

Last night's rain had left the earth wet and muddy in many places. As we got closer to a crossing, it became clear that a car and other vehicles had turned left from here, for there were fresh tyre marks going towards the forest. We made a left turn, too, and followed these marks. A mile later, we saw three different vehicles standing next to a banyan tree: a jeep from the Forest Department, Arun Babu's Fiat and a huge truck from the circus that had the tiger's cage in it. Five or six men were sitting under the tree. They told us a team had already gone into the forest to look for the tiger, and pointed us in the right direction. I recognized one of the men, having seen him at the circus before. Feluda asked him if Sultan's trainer had gone with the others. He said the new trainer, Chandran, was with them, but there was still no sign of Karandikar.

We got out of the car and began walking. I had no idea what lay in store, but knew that Arun Babu had a gun, and the shikari from the Forest Department was undoubtedly similarly armed. There was therefore little fear of the tiger being allowed to attack anyone. Lalmohan Babu looked a little disappointed, presumably because Chandran was there instead of Karandikar.

Faint footprints on the damp ground guided us. There were not many trees in this part of the forest, so movement was fairly easy. A peacock cried out a couple of times, which could well be a warning to other animals that a tiger was in the vicinity.

Ten minutes later, we heard a different noise. It was decidedly the tiger, but it wasn't actually roaring. It sounded more like a growl, as though the tiger was irritated by something.

We walked on and, only a few minutes later, through the gap between two trees, our eyes fell on a strange sight. I call it strange because I never thought I'd see something like this outside the arena in a circus.

Three men stood in a row a few feet away from where we had stopped. Two of them had guns. The one in Arun Chowdhury's hands was raised and pointed at some object in front of him.

What they were facing was an open area, a bit like a circus ring. A man was standing in the middle of this ring, a long whip in his right hand and a torn branch in his left. Judging by the dressed wound on his left shoulder, he was the new trainer, Chandran.

Chandran had his back to us. He was moving forward slowly and with extreme caution, cracking his whip every now and then. The animal he was approaching was one we had met already. It was Sultan, last seen on the road to Ramgarh.

Four other men were standing at a little distance. Two of them were holding a heavy chain, which would no doubt be put around Sultan's neck, if he allowed himself to be captured. What was most amazing was Sultan's behaviour. He clearly did not wish to be caught, but—at the same time—was making no attempts to run away. His eyes seemed to convey not anger or ferocity, but annoyance and a great deal of contempt. The low growl he kept up indicated the same thing.

Chandran was getting closer every minute, but he did not seem too sure of himself. Perhaps he could not forget that the same animal had attacked him already. I cast a quick look at Arun Babu. From the way he was holding his gun, I had no doubt that he would fire at once if Sultan showed the slightest sign of aggression. Feluda was standing before me, a little to the left; and Lalmohan Babu was by my side. His mouth was hanging so wide open that he didn't look as if he'd ever be able to close it. He told me afterwards that the memory of everything he had seen in circuses before had been totally wiped out by the show we witnessed in the forest.

When Chandran came within five yards, Sultan suddenly stiffened and began to crouch. At the same instant, Feluda leapt and reached Arun Babu, stretching a hand to change the position of his gun. Its point now faced the ground.

'Sultan!'

A deep voice boomed out. We had been joined by another man. Feluda had obviously seen him arrive and decided to act before it was too late.

'Sultan! Sultan!'

The voice became softer, and the tone much more gentle. The man stepped forward and entered the stage. It was Karandikar. In his hand was another whip, but he was not cracking it. He moved closer, calling Sultan softly in a low voice, as if he was a pet dog or a cat.

Chandran looked absolutely amazed, and stepped back. Arun Babu lowered his hands. The officer from the Forest Department gaped, very much like Lalmohan Babu. There were eleven men present in the forest to witness what followed in the next few minutes. With incredible tenderness and dexterity, Sultan's old trainer calmed him down, put the chain around his neck and then walked him over to where the truck stood with his cage. The men waiting outside quickly opened its door and placed a high stool before it. Mr Karandikar cracked his whip just once and said, 'Up!' Without further ado, Sultan ran, jumped on the stool and into the cage. The men locked the door instantly.

We had followed Mr Karandikar and were standing at a

distance. He turned to face us as soon as the tiger was safely back in his cage. Then he gave us a salute, and made his way to a taxi waiting near the other cars. Without a word or a glance at anyone else, he got into it and drove off.

'Brilliant!' exclaimed Arun Chowdhury. Turning to Feluda, he added, 'Thanks.'

All of us returned to Kailash. With Arun Babu's permission, Feluda rang someone, though I couldn't tell who it was. Then he joined us in the drawing room. Neelima Devi sent us tea. Pritin Babu was taking her and Bibi back to Calcutta the very next day, we were told. On hearing about Sultan's capture, Akhil Chakravarty said, 'Oh, I wish I'd gone with you!'

'I think tomorrow I'll go back, too,' said Arun Babu, 'unless you need me here for your investigation.'

'No, that won't be necessary. I've finished my investigation and even arranged to fulfil your father's last wish.'

Arun Babu gave Feluda a startled look over the rim of his cup.

'You mean you know where Biren is?' he asked, very surprised.

'Yes. Your father was right.'

'Meaning?'

'Biren is here.'

'In Hazaribagh?'

'In Hazaribagh.'

'I find that . . . amazing!' Arun Babu said, his tone implying that he also found it impossible to believe.

'Yes, that's understandable,' Feluda said. 'But isn't that something you yourself had started to believe?'

Arun Babu put his cup down on the table and stared directly at Feluda.

'Not only that,' Feluda went on calmly, 'you were afraid

that your father might make a new will and leave you out of it, giving your share to Biren.'

No one spoke for a few seconds. The atmosphere in the room suddenly became charged. Lalmohan Babu, who was sitting next to me, grabbed a cushion and clutched it tightly. Pritin Babu sat in a chair, supporting his head with one hand. Arun Chowdhury slowly rose to his feet. His eyes had turned red and a vein throbbed at his temple.

'Listen, Mr Mitter,' he roared, 'you may be a famous detective, but I am not going to let you sit there and throw totally baseless accusations at me. Jagat Singh!'

His bearer slipped into the room through an open door.

'Stop! If you take another step, I will shoot you,' Feluda threatened coldly, holding his revolver. 'Jagat Singh, it was you who stole into our room, wasn't it? I managed to take off a fair amount of your hair. And I know who sent you there, with what purpose.'

Jagat Singh froze. Arun Babu sat down again, his whole body shaking with rage.

'Wh-what are you trying to say?' he demanded.

'Listen very carefully. You knew your father was thinking of changing his will. You didn't want him to find and destroy the old one. So you hid his key. Bibi saw him looking for it, and he even told her what he was looking for: "a pier . . . that which opens and that which shuts". By a "pier" he meant a "quay". Bearing in mind that he liked to play with the sound of words, I realized that the "quay" was really a "key", something which could be used to open and shut an object. Presumably, the will was kept in a locked drawer. But even after stealing the key, you weren't satisfied, were you? So, that day in Rajrappa, you seized your chance and played your trump card. You knew it would come as an enormous shock to your father, which might well be enough to kill him. If that happened, you would no longer have anything to worry about.'

'You are mad. You're just raving. You don't know what you're saying, Mr Mitter.'

'I do, I can assure you; and I can produce witnesses. There are three of them, although none of them might wish to admit what they have seen and heard. Your own brother, Akhil Chakravarty and Shankarlal . . . they all know.'

'Well then, Mr Mitter, if your witnesses won't talk, I think you are wasting your time, don't you? How are you going to prove your case?'

'Very simply. There is a fourth witness who will not hesitate at all in revealing the truth.'

Suddenly, the room was filled with strange noises. Where were they coming from? There were birds calling from somewhere, and a waterfall gushed in the background.

Feluda quietly placed a small black object on a table. It was Pritin Chowdhury's tape recorder.

'What your brother accidentally saw and heard that day made him drop his recorder near a bush. His wife saw it and picked it up. There is much more on that tape besides the chirping of birds.'

Arun Babu swallowed. His heightened colour had started to recede. In just a few minutes, he turned quite pale. Feluda kept his revolver raised and pointed at him. The tape recorder continued to run. Now there were voices, rising over the sound of the water.

'Baba, what makes you think Biren has come back?' asked Arun Babu's voice.

'If an old man likes to believe his missing son has returned, why should that bother you?' Mahesh Chowdhury asked.

'You must forget Biren. He will never come back. I know that. It simply isn't possible.'

'How can you say that? Who are you to tell me what to believe? You have no right—'

'I have every right. I don't want you to do something wrong and unfair, just because of your stupid belief.'

'What is wrong and unfair?'

'I will not let you deprive me of what is rightfully mine!'

'What are you taking about?'

'You know very well. You changed your will once, thinking Biren was not going to come back. Now you're planning to . . . '

'What I am planning is my business. I was going to change my will, in any case,' Mahesh Chowdhury had raised his voice, sounding angry, as though his old violent temper was about to burst through. 'How can you expect to be mentioned in my will at all?' he went on. 'You are dishonest, you are a gambler, you are a thief! You took Dorabjee's stamp album from my safe—'

Arun Babu's voice cut him short, 'And what about you? If I am a thief, what are you? You think I don't know about Deendayal? Your screaming and shouting woke me that night. I saw everything through a chink in the curtain. I've kept my mouth shut for thirty-five years, but I know exactly what happened. You hit Deendayal on the head with a heavy brass statue of Buddha. Can you deny that? Deendayal died. Then you got Noor Muhammad and your driver to take his body . . . '

He broke off. Something heavy fell with a thud, and then there was nothing except the birds and the waterfall. Feluda switched the recorder off and returned it to Pritin Babu.

There was absolute silence in the room. Everyone was looking tense, with the only exception of Feluda. He put his revolver back in his pocket. 'What your father did was utterly wrong,' he said. 'There can be no doubt about that. But he realized it, and for thirty-five years he suffered in silence, trying to make amends in whatever way he could. Still he didn't find any peace. From the day Deendayal died, Mahesh Chowdhury began to think he was cursed and one day he would be punished for his sins. What he did not know was that the final blow would come from his own son.'

Arun Babu sat very still staring at the floor. When he

spoke his voice sounded faint, as though he was speaking from a long way away.

'There was a dog,' he said slowly. 'An Irish setter. Baba was very fond of it. For some reason, the dog did not like Deendayal. One day, it tried to bite him, so Deendayal got very cross and hit it with a heavy stick. The dog was injured. That night, Baba returned quite late from a party and found that his dog was not waiting for him in his room, as it did every day. Noor Mohammad had to tell him what had happened. Baba called Deendayal, and in a fit of rage . . . when he lost his temper, you see, Baba used to become a different man altogether.'

*

We rose with Feluda to take our leave. Akhil Chakravarty also got to his feet.

'Could you come with us for a minute?' Feluda asked him. 'There's something I'd like you to do. It won't take long.'

'Very well,' Akhil Chakravarty replied. 'With Mahesh gone, there's nothing left for me to do here, anyway. I have all the time in the world.'

TWELVE

Akhil Chakravarty began talking to us in the car. 'I did go off in a different direction,' he said, 'but I didn't go far. In fact, I could hear every word from where I stood near the rock with my initials on it. I used to ask Mahesh why he grew preoccupied at times and sank into silence. He used to laugh and tell me to look at his horoscope to find out. It is amazing isn't it, that such an important event in his life remained a secret, even from me? Perhaps it's my own fault, I failed to study his stars properly.'

As our car drew up outside our gate, I realized who Feluda had called from Kailash. Shankarlal Misra was waiting for us.

'Mission successful?' Feluda asked him, getting out of the car.

'Yes,' Mr Misra replied. 'Biren has come to meet you.'

We walked into the living room to find the same sadhu from Rajrappa sitting on a sofa. He rose as he saw us and said, 'Namaskar.' Clad in long saffron robes, he was tall and well-built, his thick matted hair almost reaching his waist. An equally thick beard covered most of his face.

'He agreed to come only when I told him about his father's last wish,' Mr Misra said. 'He has got nothing against his father.'

'No,' agreed Biren, 'But then, I don't feel any love or attachment for him, either. Shankar tried very hard to bring me back. He thought if I saw my father and other members of my family, even from a distance, I might wish to come back. That is the reason why I was in Rajrappa that day. But I

realized after seeing my family that that was not going to make
any difference at all. I had ceased to care for them. My father
was a complex man, but he was the only one who seemed to
have understood me. So, in the beginning, I used to write to
him. But later . . .'

'But those letters were not sent from abroad, were they? I
don't think you ever left the country!' Feluda said coolly.

We gasped, but Biren Chowdhury simply stared at
Feluda with an expressionless face. Then, unexpectedly, he
smiled. 'Shankar had told me how clever you were. I was only
testing you,' he laughed.

'Very well. Now you may take off your disguise,' Feluda
suggested. 'It may be enough to fool the whole town of
Hazaribagh, but you don't fool me.'

Biren Chowdhury continued to laugh as he took off his
wig and his false beard. I gave another gasp as his face was
revealed. Lalmohan Babu clutched at my sleeve and
whispered, 'Kan-kan-kan—'. He had got the name wrong
again, but I was too astounded to correct him. Mr Karandikar
looked at us and nodded.

Akhil Chakravarty broke the silence. 'What do you mean,
Mr Mitter? Biren never went abroad? Well then, his letters—?'

'It is possible to send letters from abroad, Mr
Chakravarty, if one has a friend like your son.'

'*My* son? What's he got to do with anything?'

'Mr Mitter's right,' Biren Chowdhury—or should I call
him Mr Karandikar?—replied, 'Adheer was in Dusseldorf,
wasn't he? I wrote to him and got him to send me several
European postcards. Then I used to write Baba's name and
address on them, sometimes adding a line or two, put them in
envelopes and send them back to Adheer. He would then
arrange to have them posted from various parts of Europe. He
travelled a lot himself. But when he returned to India,
naturally I had to stop.'

'How extraordinary! Why did you have to be so
secretive?'

'There was a reason,' Feluda said. 'I would like Mr Karandikar to confirm if my guess is correct.'

'Yes?'

'You were much impressed and inspired by the life of Colonel Suresh Biswas, and you wanted to be like him. I knew Colonel Biswas had left home as a young man and made his way to England and Brazil, but what I didn't know was that he was the first Bengali who had learnt to train tigers to perform in a circus. I read about this last night in a book called The Circus in Bengal. One of the items for which he became famous was parting the tiger's mouth and placing his head in it.'

Lalmohan Babu opened his mouth to speak once more.

'Sh-sh-sh-sh-' he began.

'What is it, Lalmohan Babu? Would you like us to be quiet?'

'N-n-no. Sh-shame on me, Felu Babu, shame on me! I read that book before you, and yet I failed to pick that up. I must be crazy, I must be blind, I must be . . . '

'All right, all right, you can blame yourself later. Now please let me finish.'

Lalmohan Babu simmered down. Feluda went on, 'Biren Chowdhury wanted to work with wild animals, like his hero. But an educated young man from a well-known family is not expected to join a circus as a trainer of tigers, is he? Mahesh Chowdhury might have been different from most men, but even he would not have approved. Biren knew that, and so he decided to indulge in a little deception. Am I right?'

'Absolutely,' Biren Chowdhury replied.

'What is most astonishing is that Mahesh Chowdhury could recognize his son even after so many years when he went to the circus on the first day. Arun Babu failed to do that, although he saw you from only a few feet away. You had to have plastic surgery done on your nose, didn't you, when you were attacked by a tiger? That's why you even look different from the old photo in your father's house.'

'Ah, that explains it!' Akhil Chakravarty exclaimed. 'I did wonder why everyone was calling him Biren, and yet I could not recognize him at all.'

'Anyway,' Feluda said, 'I must now tell you why I really wanted you to come here.'

He took out the photo of Muktananda from his pocket. Then he turned to Biren Chowdhury again. 'You are probably unaware that your father made a new will when he became convinced that you would never return. He left your name out of it. However, he didn't want you to be deprived altogether. So he left you this photograph.'

Feluda turned the photo over and took it out of its frame. A small folded cellophane envelope slipped out. There were a few tiny square, colourful pieces of paper in it.

'There are nine rare and valuable stamps here, which come from three different continents,' Feluda explained. 'Mr Chowdhury was afraid his album might be stolen, so he removed the most precious stamps and hid them here. According to the prices mentioned in the Gibbons catalogue twenty-five years ago, the total value of these was two thousand pounds.'

'How do you know that?'

'There was a message in your father's diary. He referred to these nine stamps as the "nine jewels", and Gibbons as "monkeys". Then he said they were worth "two thousand Shylock's demands". Tapesh reminded me that Shylock had demanded a *pound* of flesh. That's how I got the word "pounds". But now, I think, these jewels would fetch a lot more.'

Biren Chowdhury took the envelope from Feluda and stared at it. Then he said, 'I am only a ringmaster, Mr Mitter. I spend my life like a nomad, travelling all the time. What shall I do with something like this? Where shall I keep it? It will be such a liability! Mr Mitter, what am I going to do?'

'I can understand your problem,' Feluda replied. 'Tell you what, why don't you leave them with me? I know a few stamp dealers in Calcutta. I will speak to them and see that you get the best possible price. Then I will send you the money. Is that all right? Could you trust me, do you think?'

'Oh, absolutely.'

'Very well. But I shall need to have your address.'

'The Great Majestic Circus,' Biren Chowdhury replied. 'Kutti has realized he cannot do without me. I am going to be with them for some time. In fact, Sultan and I will be performing tonight. Please do come and watch us, all of you.'

*

We went to find Biren Karandikar after the show that evening to thank him and to say goodbye. He and his tiger had enthralled the audience by working together with perfect understanding and coordination. The idea of seeing him backstage was Lalmohan Babu's. It soon became clear why he was so keen.

'I am going to write a new novel,' he told him. 'The main action will take place in a circus and the ringmaster will have a very important role. May I please use the name "Karandikar" in my novel? I quite like it.'

'Of course,' Biren Chowdhury laughed. 'It is not my real name, so you may use it wherever you want!'

We thanked him and came away.

'So you changed your mind about the injection?' Feluda asked Lalmohan Babu as we emerged out of the big tent.

'Certainly not. The tiger will now be given an injection. Its second trainer is going to be the villain. He'll give the injection to make the tiger drowsy, so it doesn't perform well and the ringmaster gets the blame.'

'I see. What about the trapeze?'

'The trapeze?' Lalmohan Babu gave a derisive snort, 'The trapeze is nothing. Who wants it now?'

READ MORE IN PENGUIN

In every corner of the world, on every subject under the sun, Penguin represents quality and variety—the very best in publishing today.

For complete information about books available from Penguin—including Puffins, Penguin Classics and Arkana—and how to order them, write to us at the appropriate address below. Please note that for copyright reasons the selection of books varies from country to country.

In India: Please write to *Penguin Books India Pvt. Ltd. 210 Chiranjiv Tower, Nehru Place, New Delhi, 110019*

In the United Kingdom: Please write to *Dept JC, Penguin Books Ltd. Bath Road, Harmondsworth, West Drayton, Middlesex, UB7 ODA. UK*

In the United States: Please write to *Penguin USA Inc., 375 Hudson Street, New York, NY 10014*

In Canada: Please write to *Penguin Books Canada Ltd. 10 Alcorn Avenue, Suite 300, Toronto, Ontario M4V 3B2*

In Australia: Please write to *Penguin Books Australia Ltd. 487, Maroondah Highway, Ring Wood, Victoria 3134*

In New Zealand: Please write to *Penguin Books (NZ) Ltd. Private Bag, Takapuna, Auckland 9*

In the Netherlands: Please write to *Penguin Books Netherlands B.V., Keizersgracht 231 NL-1016 DV Amsterdom*

In Germany : Please write to *Penguin Books Deutschland GmbH, Metzlerstrasse 26, 60595 Frankfurt am Main, Germany*

In Spain: Please write to *Penguin Books S.A., Bravo Murillo, 19-1'B, E-28015 Madrid, Spain*

In Italy: Please write to *Penguin Italia s.r.l., Via Felice Casati 20, I-20104 Milano*

In France: Please write to *Penguin France S.A., 17 rue Lejeune, F-31000 Toulouse*

In Japan: Please write to *Penguin Books Japan. Ishikiribashi Building, 2-5-4, Suido, Tokyo 112*

In Greece: Please write to *Penguin Hellas Ltd, dimocritou 3, GR-106 71 Athens*

In South Africa: Please write to *Longman Penguin Books Southern Africa (Pty) Ltd, Private Bag X08, Bertsham 2013*

TWENTY STORIES
Satyajit Ray
Translated by Gopa Majumdar

This new selection of stories by Satyajit Ray, which appears in English for the first time, concerns itself, in the main, with tales of the supernatural, a genre the author has always excelled in...In 'Bhuto' a ventriloquist's dummy slowly but surely turns malign and more human than its master; in 'The Pterodactyl's Egg' we meet a man who claims to have devised a way to travel, economy-class, into the fourth dimension; in 'Anath Babu's Terror' a ghost-hunter finds himself stalked by his terrifying quarry—these and the seventeen other stories in the book will send shivers down your spine, ensure you keep the lights on when you go to bed at night and occasionally, allow you the luxury of nervous laughter.

...(Satyajit Ray) communicates with zest and an 'ebulient exuberance.'

—*The Hindustan Times*